More praise for
SEASON OF THE MONSOON

"Sansi's passion becomes him, along with the genre he serves so brilliantly."
—*The New York Times Book Review*

"Harrowing and memorable . . . This first-rate crime novel employs the classic elements of the noir thriller."
—*Publishers Weekly*

"A thoroughly absorbing thriller in the 'relentless pursuit' tradition, reminiscent of *The Day of the Jackal.*"
—*Australian Book Review*

Also by Paul Mann:

PRIME OBJECTIVE
THE TRAITOR'S CONTRACT

SEASON OF THE MONSOON

Paul Mann

IVY BOOKS • NEW YORK

Ivy Books
Published by Ballantine Books
Copyright © 1992 by Paul Mann

All rights reserved under International and Pan-American Copyright Conventions. Published in the United States by Ballantine Books, a division of Random House, Inc., New York, and distributed in Canada by Random House of Canada Limited, Toronto. Originally published in somewhat different form in Australia in 1992 by Pan Macmillan Publishers Australia, a division of Pan Macmillan Australia Pty Limited, Sydney.

Library of Congress Catalog Card Number: 92-54998

ISBN 0-8041-1259-2

Manufactured in the United States of America

First American Hardcover Edition: June 1993
First Mass Market Edition: February 1995

10 9 8 7 6 5 4 3 2 1

ACKNOWLEDGMENTS

I HAVE OFTEN been touched by the kindness of friends and the spontaneous generosity of strangers whenever I have sought their help in researching a book. The gathering of material for this novel was greatly assisted by generous contributions of time and information from many kind people in India, England and Australia. I would like to express special thanks to the following people. In India, Dr. Pritam Phatnani, Deputy Coroner, Bombay; Dr. Vyankatesh Chincholkar, Deputy Director, Forensic Science Laboratory, Bombay; Arvind S. Inamdar, Joint Commissioner, Crime Branch, Bombay Police; Dr. R. K. Bhatnagar, Department of Science and Technology, New Delhi; the Maharashtra Film, Stage and Cultural Development Corporation; the staff and members of the David Sassoon Library; the management of The Willingdon Club; also Krishna Murthy, Mario Rodrigues, Niloufer Bilimoria and Aloo Daruwalla. In England I owe thanks to the History Society of Oxford University, various students and tutorial fellows of Worcester College and Magdalen College and especially to the modest and anonymous groundsman at Iffley Road athletics track in Oxford who gave me a jar of ash from the finishing line of the track where Sir Roger Bannister broke the four-minute mile in 1954. In Australia, my thanks go to photographer and adventurer Michael Coyne, journalist Nigel Hopkins and PR person Suzie Morris, all of whom gave unstintingly of their own knowledge and experiences of India.

For things we never mention,
For art misunderstood—
For excellent intention
That did not turn to good
From ancient tales renewing
From clouds we would not clear—
Beyond the Law's pursuing,
We fled, and settled here.

"The Broken Men"
RUDYARD KIPLING

48 Hours in the Life of India

FIVE KILLED OVER A "ROTI"

Ranchi, April 30. A demand for a roti led to a shoot-out by CRPF militia, claiming five lives at Nagar Utari in Palamu district on Friday night.

At around 8:20 P.M. the CRPF personnel posted at the camp adjacent to the Bansidhar temple were having dinner in their mess. Jawan Baldeo Singh demanded from the mess-in-charge, Ram Suresh Singh, a roti but the latter allegedly refused and abused Baldeo Singh. An altercation followed and later Baldeo Singh fetched his rifle and shot him dead.

Meanwhile, other CRPF personnel picked up their rifles and gave chase to Baldeo Singh. There was an exchange of fire. Baldeo's indiscriminate shots hit three bystanders who were killed instantaneously. The exchange came to an end when Baldeo, finding himself cornered, shot himself dead. Apart from the five dead, four CRPF personnel were injured.

The Times of India

16 KILLED IN PUNJAB BOMB BLASTS

Chandigarh, April 30. Sixteen people, including four security personnel, were killed while 22 people were injured in two bomb blasts in Punjab today.

In other incidents, five terrorists and two intruders

from Pakistan were killed in the state. The terrorists
were killed in intergang rivalry.

The Hindustan Times

TWO KILLED IN HOLDUP

Aurangabad, May 1. Two persons, a conductor and a
passenger, were killed and eight others injured when a
gang of dacoits armed with swords looted the Aurangabad Asiad bus near Imam Ghat yesterday.

Indian Express

8 TERRORISTS KILLED, 100 HELD IN KASHMIR

Jammu, May 1. Eight terrorists were among 12 people killed in different incidents in the Kashmir Valley
since last night as the security forces nabbed nearly
100 subversives in stepped-up raids.

The subversives were carrying one rocket grenade, a
light machine gun, five AK-47 rifles, 17 antipersonnel
mines, an antitank missile and huge quantities of ammunition and explosives.

The Times of India

17 KILLED IN PUNJAB

Chandigarh, May 2. Seven members of a family and
a CPI(ML) leader were among 17 people killed in un-
abated violence while police rescued two of the four
persons kidnapped by extremists in Punjab since last
night.

The Times of India

3 HELD FOR IA LOADERS MURDER

Bombay, May 2. The crime branch (DCB, CID) yesterday arrested three alleged agents of a Dubai-based smuggler who were responsible for the killings of two Indian Airlines loaders last month.

The Daily, Bombay

MOVE AGAINST CHILD PROSTITUTION URGED

New Delhi, May 2. The Supreme Court yesterday took a serious view of child prostitution and asked law-enforcing agencies to come down heavily on pimps, brokers and brothelkeepers.

Saying that prostitution always remains a "running sore on the body of civilization," the two-judge bench asked courts to punish the offenders and directed state governments to fulfill their obligation to safeguard the interests of children.

The Times of India

1

MOLLAJI AWOKE FROM a deep sleep and looked into the eyes of the dead whore lying next to him. He had forgotten about her until the moment of waking and her blank, death-puddled eyes gave him a start. The pupils were rolled back beneath wide-open lids, leaving visible most of the whites, now yellow and congealed like egg yolk. Her lips had begun to curl back from her purplish gums to form a mocking leer. Mollaji thought she had surprisingly good teeth for a whore. But she was young; nineteen or twenty, he guessed. There was hardly a mark on her apart from a single comma of crusted blood on her right nostril where someone had torn a ring loose before Mollaji had rescued her. There would have been other trinkets too: rings from her fingers, plastic bracelets, a few chains around her neck, a purse, perhaps, and sandals. They had all gone, looted from her corpse by the human jackals who lived off the streets of Bombay.

It was only her karma. Her fate.

There was no room for a luxury like pity among the street tribes of India. If she died badly it was because of her sins. Now that she was dead, the living had more need of her things. All she had left was the gaudy red and gold sari that covered her body. She would have been stripped of that too if Mrs. Patel hadn't seen what was going on from her husband's shop on the other side of Dimtimkar Road. Mrs. Patel had called out to Mollaji, the *kuli*, a little after midnight. She had noticed a pack of children squabbling with each other and picking at what looked like a bundle of

4

rags—until they were illuminated by the headlights of a passing taxi and Mrs. Patel saw that the rags had a human face. She had rushed out into the street, haranguing the scavengers in her high, shrill voice. Then, because her husband was away visiting his parents in Pune, she had screamed for Mollaji, who was asleep in his shanty in the alleyway alongside the Patels' shop.

Mollaji had come quickly, wearing only a pair of dirty khaki shorts and brandishing an army bayonet he kept near his bedmat for protection. At first he thought Mrs. Patel's shop had been robbed. When he realized that she had only seen a body he relaxed. He waved his bayonet at the children and sent them scurrying back into the darkness followed by a string of curses.

Mollaji had been an infantryman in the army and had fought on the northwest frontier during the 1973 war against Pakistan. He could take care of himself in the streets of Bombay. And he was familiar with death. His whole life had been spent in its service. For in addition to the cartons of mangoes, the stacks of sugar cane and the bolts of cloth that he carried on his long-handled cart, the little *kuli* also carried unclaimed corpses for the Bombay police.

The police were too busy to attend promptly to every corpse that turned up daily in a city of twelve million. Half a dozen people died each day merely by falling from the grotesquely overloaded passenger trains that shunted in and out of Bombay Central Station. Scores more died from sickness, neglect, drug abuse, poisoned liquor, traffic accidents, petty crime, gang wars, personal feuds and every other permutation of human malice that thrived in the Indian metropolis. Many bodies were never claimed—they were left to the city authorities to dispose of, like garbage. Only the most extreme or unusual fatalities attracted attention: an exceptionally gruesome murder, or the death of a foreigner or a VIP. Often, when there was no need for a detailed investigation at the scene, it was quicker and easier to use someone like Mollaji. He would carry the corpse to the mortuary on the back of his cart for twenty rupees: less than a dollar.

When he had driven off the corpse robbers, Mollaji had casually sheathed his bayonet, hefted the dead woman across his bare shoulders and carried her back to his shanty. There he had wrapped her in the frayed blue plastic sheet he kept in the back of his cart, tied it tightly with twine and laid her on the coconut-matting floor. She would be safe there until morning. Mrs. Patel watched his ministrations with a shudder, then left, preferring to know no more.

In the morning Mollaji would take the body to the police substation a mile away at Jacob Circle and they would decide what to do with her. It never occurred to him that moving the corpse might be wrong. Mrs. Patel had said she was a prostitute, a *randi*. Men paid twenty or thirty rupees a time for her. She had spent her short life on the lowest rung of the ladder of human commerce. Nobody seemed to know her name, only that she had been working one of the local brothels for a few months.

All Mollaji knew was that she was Shudra, like him. Or Harijans, a child of God: the name given the Untouchables by Mahatma Gandhi in a bid to give them dignity. Others still called them Shudra—untouchable. The lowest caste in India. Even in death, her treatment would depend on how much, or how little, she was worth, whether she had family or friends who would come forward to pay for a respectable cremation. But if the brothelkeeper had been involved in her death and if there was a valuable client to protect, a few thousand rupees in baksheesh would be distributed among the police and there would be no postmortem examination. A death certificate would be issued and destined only for the filing system of the police bureaucracy with appropriate copies to the city health department. Then the body would be sent to the city crematorium for burning. There would be no fragrant sandalwood cremation for her, just another dirty scribble of smoke in the despoiled skies of Bombay for an epitaph.

Looking at her in the slats of early-morning light that filtered through the matted palm fronds of his shanty it was impossible for Mollaji to see how she had died. Poison? Suffocation? Strangulation? Heart attack? He could see no obvious marks: no bruises, wounds or signs of a struggle. The previous night she had not looked dead at all. Her skin had felt cold to the touch but her limbs had been loose and floppy like a rag doll and the expression on her face was relaxed, as though she had been sleeping. He understood enough about death to know that she couldn't have been dead for long when he had picked her up—an hour, perhaps, no more. Now, six hours later, rigor mortis was well advanced. Her face was gray and set in a frozen grimace and her limbs were as stiff as tree branches. There were tiny white bubbles in the crevices of her mouth and, for a moment, Mollaji thought they were grains of rice. Then he realized that flies had already laid their eggs and the maggots had begun to hatch. Others would start hatching soon, beneath her eyelids and in her nostrils. It was time he got rid of her.

She stirred slightly and smiled at him. Mollaji recoiled, staring back at her in shock. He glanced quickly around, searching for a rational explanation. Then he saw them. A huddle of furry black shapes feeding on her exposed calf. Mollaji swore and swatted at them with a bony hand. They scattered through the open doorway into the alley, mewing and squeaking in protest. One came back, willing to fight for his meal. Mollaji got up, kicked it squarely with a leathery foot and watched it skitter across the filthy pavement into the gutter, only to squirm nimbly back to its feet and scuttle off after its mates in search of easier pickings among the other shanties lining the alley. Mollaji bent down and rearranged the plastic sheet to cover the exposed face and legs again. Then he lifted her off the ground with a grunt, carried her outside and laid her on the back of the cart parked beside his shanty, safe from the rats—for the moment.

His neighbors were already awake: thin, wrinkled women, old before their time, dressed in worn and dirty saris and crouched in the open doorways of their hovels, priming small kerosene stoves, frying rice, banana and curried potato for the breakfasts of husbands, sons and daughters—all those lucky enough to have jobs in the factories and sweatshops of India's richest city. Mollaji looked out along Dimtimkar Road at the once graceful Victorian terrace houses, now cannibalized for shops, offices and squalid apartments, their mildewed, pockmarked faces plastered with advertising signs and daubed with political slogans. Whole walls were blotted out by garish posters of plump, pouting movie stars and thickets of lurid, painted billboards in comic opera English offering "Patel's shirtings, suitings and trouserings," "Sanla Brothers—electric stationery," "Bedlam saris," and "Stanrose—Bedsheets You Can Build Your Life Around."

Mollaji lifted his eyes briefly above the enveloping squalor and looked at a pristine blue sky. He put the time somewhere between six-thirty and seven. It was early April and the cool, soothing rains of the monsoon were still a few weeks away. Reluctantly he lowered his eyes from the perfection of heaven and looked around him again. It was already suffocatingly hot in the city streets and the air was thick with flies and dust. All along Dimtimkar Road the street poor tiredly rolled up their bedmats, squatted in the gutters to relieve themselves, then lined up to wash at the nearest water pipe. Naked children squealed and frolicked innocently amid piles of filth and human ordure.

The first paper sellers arrived from the railway station and fanned out their newspapers and magazines on the pavement for the inspection of passersby. After a few minutes the shopkeepers and food stall operators began opening up to catch the commuter trade. The traffic grew in noise and volume and quickly clogged the street with chaos: cars, trucks, buses, bicycles, motorbikes, black and yellow Premier taxis—their drivers jostling, honking and cursing each other as they fought for space amid the bedlam. Solemn-faced *kulis*, eyes dulled by years of economic enslavement, committed their lives to the gods and manhandled their long-handled barrows into the maelstrom, each carrying a more preposterous load than the last. Mountains of watermelon, piles of bricks, teetering skyscrapers of shiny new cooking pots. Mollaji's sympathetic eye was drawn to a single laborer, a scrawny, bowlegged man wearing only a dirty grey *dhoti*. On his turbaned head the man balanced a metal tray that held a dozen one-gallon cans of engine oil. The veins on his neck bulged like electric cables and his face was stoic with suffering. Mollaji imagined he could hear the knuckles of the man's vertebrae creaking under the strain and blessed himself again for having the good fortune to own a cart.

The tumult grew with every passing minute. Freshly scrubbed factory workers and office clerks teemed out of tenements and shanties to join the escalating clamor, their glossy black hair still damp and neatly furrowed by the comb. Somehow they wrested the mantle of human dignity anew each day from the engulfing tide of despair and carried it proudly, wearing their clean faces and spotless clothes like victory medals.

The smell of cooking tugged at Mollaji's nostrils and his stomach growled. He might not get a chance to eat again until nightfall and he wouldn't pull his cart far on an empty stomach. He ducked back inside his shanty, picked up the sweat-stained khaki army shirt he used for a pillow and patted a thin wad of rupee notes folded carefully around a few paise coins inside the breast pocket. He would make time for breakfast at Mrs. Kakaria's shanty a few yards farther down the alley. A cup of *chai*, a *chapatti* with a ball of sticky, saffron-flavored rice for ten paise. And this morning, perhaps, another two paise for a cigarette. Somebody had died. He could afford to indulge himself.

Mrs. Kakaria, her husband, Avtar, and their eight children were Bangladeshi refugees who had joined the wretched millions driven from their disaster-prone homeland by flood, drought and famine to the cities of India in search of a new life. For them it was a matter of survival— and most often that was all they got. Like Mollaji, the

Kakarias had found a niche for themselves on the pavement of Bombay. And, like Mollaji, they paid for their few square feet of pavement with a weekly contribution of *hafta* to the gangsters who controlled the streets. *Hafta* was Bombay's version of the protection racket and was paid by everybody who did business on the streets of Bombay: shopkeepers, tradesmen, hawkers, stall owners and slum dwellers. The amount of *hafta* you paid was calculated precisely according to the amount of pavement you occupied. Mollaji's miserable shanty occupied sixteen square feet and cost him eight rupees a week; the Kakarias occupied forty square feet and paid twenty rupees a week.

The city could sweep them all from the alley on one of its occasional slum-clearance binges without a moment's notice—and all the thousands of rupees the slum dwellers had paid in protection would count for nothing. But still they had to pay, or they would be beaten and burned out of their hovels by the hoodlums who controlled their district. And the police and politicians would stand idly by because they had taken their *hafta* too—from the gangs.

Mrs. Kakaria's husband was lucky. He had found a job as a dhobi wallah, washing laundry for a small tourist hotel at the dhobi ghats for 120 rupees a month. It was barely enough to meet their *hafta* payments and feed the family. But Mrs. Kakaria supplemented their income by selling meals cooked with food that had been stolen or scavenged by her eldest boys. Her nine-year-old daughter, Meena, was also an accomplished beggar and with her two-year-old brother, Salman, in her arms she had been known to extract as much as fifty rupees in a single day from tourists on Marine Drive.

Bombay was the richest city in India. So rich it contributed a third of India's tax revenue. So rich it had become a beggar's paradise. The most successful beggars, those with the most ghastly mutilations whom the tourists would guiltily bribe to go away, could make a hundred rupees a day. Most of them had been deliberately mutilated to make them more effective beggars. Mrs. Kakaria didn't like

Meena begging. If she was too successful she could be kidnapped and forced into a lifetime of servitude by one of the gang lords.

The Kakarias had lived in the alley for three years. Mollaji had been there for eleven years. He expected to die there. One of thirteen children, he had left his village in Uttar Pradesh to join the army and had never seen his family again. On leaving the army he had used most of his discharge pay to buy the long-handled cart that now gave him his living. It never seemed to be enough. By the time he had paid his *hafta* he was lucky to have twenty or thirty rupees left for himself each week. He was glad he had made friends with the Kakarias. He often brought them bananas, mangoes, the occasional pineapple and papaya he pilfered from his market deliveries. In return, when he had no money, they made sure he didn't starve.

Mollaji always seemed to have just enough for a couple of meals a day, a cigarette or two and the one nightly indulgence that he never missed—a leafy wad of *paan*. When times were tough Mollaji would rather forsake a meal in favor of his ration of *paan*, the mildly narcotic mixture of betel nut, lime paste, tobacco and a sprinkle of opium powder, all wrapped tightly in a glossy betel leaf. Each night, when his day's work was done and he had finished his meal with the Kakarias, Mollaji would amble down to the paan-wallah's stall half a block away. There he would spend the rest of the evening, hunkered down at the side of the road in the dim yellow glow of the naked, low-wattage light bulbs that illuminated the *paan*-maker's stall, and he would pass the time chatting idly with other *kulis*, stretching out the pleasures of his daily fix, spitting the occasional dark red jet of betel juice into the road. After a while the warm balm of the opium would creep deliciously through his body, gently fogging his mind and easing away the muscular aches and pains that tormented his thin body more and more with each passing year.

Mollaji knew that the time was fast approaching when he would no longer be able to pull his cart through the streets of Bombay. Somehow, before his health collapsed, he would have to find enough money for a down payment on a three-wheeler auto-rickshaw and then he would be able to make his money riding around town in comfort, ferrying passengers to and from Sahar International Airport. Of course, he would never own the rickshaw: it would always be the property of the moneylender. But that didn't matter . . . as long as he had enough money to buy food and his daily allowance of *paan*. Like all men, however modest, Mollaji had his dreams and his plans. And most evenings, as the opium lulled him into warm drowsiness, the little *kuli* could almost convince himself that life was not really so bad, that perhaps everything in the world was in its proper place after all.

Karma was only the philosophy. Opium made it work.

2

"HEY, MOLLAJI ... *MADARCHOD*. We've been looking for you. The boys up at Vihar have a nice dirty job for you."

Sergeant Chabria strolled down the police station steps at Jacob Circle and greeted Mollaji in a coarse blend of Hindi and Marathi, the language of Maharashtra State. A half-dozen policemen grouped around the gates and armed with antique .303 rifles sniggered at the seargeant's casual use of *"madarchod,"* the Hindi word for motherfucker. It was a favorite insult among the Bombay police, but it was rarely used so casually.

Chabria had stepped outside in response to Mollaji's message, which had been relayed to him by one of the khaki-uniformed police constables who stopped all visitors at the gates. There was a great deal of violence and unrest in Punjab and Kashmir. Sikh and Kashmiri terrorists had been active in both Delhi and Bombay. A slab of plastique had been found inside a thermos left on a platform at Bombay's Churchgate railway station four days earlier, timed to go off during the morning rush. That bomb had been disarmed before it could explode, but only two weeks earlier a woman had been killed and eleven people injured when a hand grenade had been lobbed into a city bus by a terrorist who fled on the back of a scooter. Now every government building and police station in Bombay was guarded by armed police. The station at Jacob Circle looked as though it was under siege. It was impossible for a man like Mollaji to get inside.

13

"Who's in the cart, Mollaji?" the sergeant asked, smiling slyly as he stepped through the half-opened iron gates.

"Your mother," answered Mollaji. "A dead *randi*."

The smile disappeared from Chabria's face and he glanced around at the watching constables to make sure they were no longer sniggering. Chabria scowled at Mollaji and slapped his *lathi*—the bamboo club used by the police to beat rioting crowds into submission—restlessly in the palm of his left hand. Bombay police were notoriously casual in its application.

"Don't push your luck with me, *madarchod*."

This time the insult was meant.

Mollaji stood his ground and stared dumbly into the sergeant's face. They were about the same height, though Chabria looked more threatening than the *kuli*. The sergeant was sleek, heavyset and paunchy with mean black eyes set in a puffy, pockmarked face. Twin rolls of fat spilled like suet over the waistband of his trousers and glistening threads of sweat trickled from the deep crevices of his jowls and ran down his neck. There were damp patches under both arms and on his gut, where Mollaji could see thick black hairs pressed wetly against the sergeant's transparent khaki shirt. Mollaji looked puny by comparison. His skin was blue-black, his gray hair cropped almost to the skull, and he still wore the military-style mustache he had grown while he was in the army. He hadn't trimmed it for a while and it drooped thickly now around the corners of his mouth, giving his face a melancholy look. It made him seem vulnerable.

But appearances were deceptive. Mollaji might have been older and lighter than Chabria but he was street-hard with a sinewy toughness reinforced by years of hauling heavy loads around the city. The sergeant was soft and spoiled by the good life that came with years of taking *hafta* at one of the most corrupt police precincts in Bombay. If it came to a fair fight, Mollaji would win. But he knew that there was no such thing as a fair fight against a police officer in front of a police station. If Mollaji fought back he would be wrestled inside, thrown into the cells and beaten half to death. If he *did* die of his injuries, no one would know or care. If he survived, he would be charged with assaulting a police officer, and spend years rotting in jail waiting for his case to come to trial. Mollaji knew that if Chabria decided to slash him across the face with the *lathi* he would have to take it. Then he would do what all the other nobodies did to extort their revenge from the police. He would spy on Chabria for days, weeks, and months if necessary. He would wait for the sergeant to appear at one of the city's frequent street disturbances and then he would maim the fat, crooked cop with a rock thrown from the sanctuary of the crowd. For the moment, Mollaji waited and stared silently back at the sergeant. The British Army had a name for it: dumb insolence. It had been a punishable offense in the Indian Army too. Chabria appeared not to notice. After a while he seemed satisfied that he had cowed the little *kuli* into submission and the tension eased from his sweating body.

"Who's in the cart?" Chabria asked again.

Mollaji shrugged. "A dead woman. I found her last night on the street . . . on Dimtimkar Road, where I live."

Chabria strolled around to the back of the cart, pulled back the folds of blue plastic and looked at the dead woman. Her face was now almost black and her lips had curled back into a snarl. Chabria remained impassive.

"How do you know she's a *randi?*"

"Mrs. Patel, the shirtmaker's wife, knows her. Not to talk to, but she used to see her every day. Mrs. Patel is a respectable woman. She says the woman is a *randi*. Women know these things."

Chabria nodded and his smile returned. He dropped the *lathi* to his side and tapped it absently against his boot.

"Any marks on her?"

Mollaji shook his head. "I didn't see any. She's been robbed but she wasn't stabbed or beaten. She wasn't too bad at all."

"Is that so . . . ?" Chabria said, a sly smile forming on

his thick lips. "You sure you didn't fuck her last night while she was still warm, eh?"

He laughed loudly and the watching policemen knew it was safe to start smirking again.

"How long has it been since you had a woman, eh, how long?" Chabria was enjoying himself. "Ever had a woman suck your dick, Mollaji?" The sergeant chuckled to himself. "Wouldn't that be something? I doubt there is a *randi* in all Bombay who would sink that low."

Mollaji looked at Chabria and thought they could sink much lower, but he kept it to himself.

Chabria stuck two fingers into a breast pocket and poked around in a small, greasy paper bag he kept there, which contained a mixture of tobacco and lime called *khaini*. He pulled out a twist of white, powdered tobacco, flattened it into a pellet between his thumb and forefinger then pushed it into the space between his jaw and his bottom lip where it made a small bulge. The sergeant worked his jaw slowly to extract the first tangy surge of tobacco and lime and his mouth filled with saliva. He swirled it across his palate until he had extracted every last atom of taste, then spat a thin stream of dark brown liquid at Mollaji. The *kuli* tried to step back but he wasn't quick enough. The juice spattered across his thigh and trickled slowly down his leg, leaving a shiny trail that looked as though a snail had crawled across his skin. Mollaji wiped the stain away with his hand and fought to suppress the anger that rose in him. He could wait until the opportunity came to pay Chabria back. Indians were good at waiting.

"I should make you take her down to the coroner's mortuary yourself," Chabria went on, chewing as though nothing had happened. "But . . . the boys up at Vihar need you."

The smile returned as he remembered what he had wanted to tell Mollaji. "They've got a floater in the lake up there. Somebody found it this morning. Been in the water a while, they tell me. A real stinker. The boys don't want to touch it; they got on the radio and asked if we could send somebody up. Naturally, I thought of you. You can swim, can't you?"

Mollaji nodded. Like many poor Indians he had learned to swim as a boy in the murky lakes and creeks near his village when he had been forced to catch water rats, snakes and turtles for food.

He knew Chabria had to be talking about Lake Vihar, the largest of the three northern lakes that supplied much of Bombay's drinking water. Considering the usual quality of Bombay water, the *kuli* doubted that a decomposing corpse could make much difference. The job itself didn't worry him. He had done messier body retrievals for the police. And it was another twenty rupees. That meant forty rupees in two days—enough to keep him in rice, cigarettes and *paan* for a week.

"This is your lucky day, isn't it, Mollaji?" The sergeant read the *kuli*'s thoughts. "They want someone up there quick, so you'll have to come up in the car with me."

Mollaji allowed himself one small smile. He knew how it must irk a man like Chabria to be put in a position where he had to provide a police escort across town to an Untouchable. They must need a corpse-collector pretty urgently up at Vihar, the little *kuli* realized. Still, there was business to take care of.

"What about my money for this?" Mollaji nodded at the bundle in his cart.

Chabria sniffed at the Shudra's presumption.

"Put in a chit tomorrow," he growled. "You know the drill. There's still paperwork to be done, even for a whore."

The sergeant turned to a couple of the watching constables and told them to pull the cart inside the compound. "Call the mortuary and tell them we want that thing out of here before the end of the day," he ordered. Then he beckoned toward a row of cars parked a few yards away inside the police station compound. A boxy black late-model Premier crawled uncertainly toward them.

Chabria opened the front passenger door and sat down with a grunt beside the police driver. "Get in the back," he told the waiting *kuli*. "And try not to stink up the car too much."

Mollaji did as he was told while the constables opened the gates to let the car out and bring the corpse-carrier's cart inside. The driver nosed the little Premier cautiously into the milling traffic with Mollaji perched self-consciously on the backseat. It was a novel experience for him; he had not been inside any kind of government vehicle since he had left the army.

"You know what's out there, don't you?" Sergeant Chabria asked vaguely, without turning to look at his passenger.

Mollaji had no idea what the sergeant was talking about. He waited, feeling stupid.

"Hollywood," Chabria announced, his voice thick with sarcasm. "We're taking you to Hollywood, Mollaji. Maybe you're going to be a star, eh? The girls won't be able to keep their hands off you." Mollaji stared uncomprehendingly at the back of Chabria's head, hating him more than he had ever hated anyone. Chabria chuckled and spat a long black spurt of tobacco juice through the open window.

No one spoke as they battled northward for almost an hour through traffic that clogged the Western Expressway. The police driver leaned on the horn most of the way, swearing and gesturing at other drivers, flicking on and off the blue emergency light on the roof. All to no avail. There were no concessions to police cars in the Bombay traffic. Cars, trucks, buses, rickshaws, motorbikes and gnat-sized scooters thronged all three traffic lanes, swerving, braking, honking, fighting for a piece of the pavement—all of them oblivious to the concept of road rules. Every couple of miles or so they had to negotiate another traffic circle where a lone policeman pretended to orchestrate the anarchy. Even Mollaji caught his breath when he saw a Vespa scooter dart between a truck and one of the big red Tata double-decker buses. There was a man, a woman, a small child and a baby on the scooter. The woman held the baby loosely in one arm; its head flopped wildly back and forth and Mollaji swore that it missed the side of the bus by an inch.

The chaos continued without respite all the way up the island peninsula of Bombay until at last they struggled into the northern suburb of Nagpada. The driver took the right fork and drove inland on Goregaon Road through a dilapidated landscape of industrial estates, factories, shops, food stalls and ramshackle housing developments that looked like ruins the day they were built because the cement had been mixed with so much sand. And everywhere there were the slums: filthy, tumbledown slums that filled every nook and cranny and spilled out onto the pavements like a ubiquitous cheap putty that held the city together.

After a couple of miles the traffic thinned out and the few remaining cars and rickshaws were quickly outnumbered by the throng of people walking along the road. Most of them were shrivelled, sunken-eyed women with bad teeth and tea-colored skin that was stretched thin as cellophane across jutting cheekbones. Their saris were dirty and ragged, they carried gallon tins of water on their heads and they were accompanied by mobs of scrawny, yapping dogs and naked children whose faces were webbed with yellow mucus. Mollaji watched them flash past the open windows of the car in eddies of dumb despair and recognized the familiar, fixed grimace of suffering on every woman's face.

The road started to climb up from the coastal flatlands, gradually at first and then more noticeably—until suddenly the crowds seemed to evaporate and the slums stopped as sharply as if a line had been drawn across the landscape. Mollaji stared in bewilderment as the tide of shanties washed up against some kind of invisible barrier and yielded to open, rolling countryside. One moment there was only the anonymous brown murk of the slums and the shrouded zombies of the poor shuffling through a pall of dust and flies. The next, there was open country and rolling green hills as far as the eye could see.

Then he saw why. A chain mesh fence crowned with untidy coils of barbed wire halted the march of the slums. The fence slashed across the countryside like the blade of a knife, lifting momentarily for the passage of the narrow highway. Glittering steel mesh flashed by on both sides of the crumbling blacktop, telling the occupants of the police car they had crossed one of the many frontiers that kept India divided. Every one of them knew that India was not only a mosaic of cultures. It was a mosaic of economies. Behind them lay the province of poverty. In front of them lay the province of privilege.

They had gone about half a mile when the fence on the right-hand side of the road metamorphosed into a high brick wall, coated with flaking white plaster and topped with barbed wire. The road followed the wall in a long, gentle curve for a few hundred yards until they came upon an open driveway flanked by square white columns. The driver took his foot off the gas pedal and the police car coasted slowly past the open gate, all three passengers craning for a glimpse of what was inside. The pink gravel drive was sheltered by an avenue of ashoka trees and lanced neatly through an expanse of open lawn to a distant cluster of buildings. Just inside the entrance was a white wooden gatehouse. Two uniformed security guards lolled on metal stools that had been set up in the shade of the hut. The guards looked up briefly at the sound of the police car then went back to their conversation. Chabria, his driver and Mollaji stared down the pink gravel drive to what looked like an abandoned factory, a featureless building with a low, arched roof and a two-story office block.

"Film City," Chabria grunted for Mollaji's benefit.

Mollaji was even more confused. Like everyone else in Bombay, he knew something about the movies. Even though he could not afford to go to any of the big cinemas in town he saw the occasional street movie projected onto a sheet hung from the side of a building. He saw the posters. He saw all the fan magazines sold on street corners. He knew that movie stars were paid fabulous sums of money and lived like gods. He enjoyed the stories, the scandal and the gossip that surrounded them. Chabria had been right when he had tormented Mollaji earlier. Like Hollywood, Bombay was a movie town—except Bombay was bigger. The Indian movie capital turned out six hundred movies a year, more than twice the number of movies produced in the American movie capital. All of them were Hindu epics, made for an insatiable domestic audience of 850 million. But like most poor people in Bombay, Mollaji had never expected to see Film City. For him it had always existed only as a distant mirage. A kind of fantasy land that just happened to be real. Now he realized he had not known what to expect. A city of palaces, perhaps. A rajah's shining citadel. A movie mogul's shrine. But not this, not something . . . drab and ordinary. Mollaji stared in silence, his jaw slack. Film City looked like just any other industrial estate—except this one had the luxury of landscaped gardens.

"What's wrong?" Chabria turned to Mollaji, his voice revealing his own disappointment. "Did you expect to find Dimple Kapadia waiting here to flash her tits just for you?"

Mollaji glanced briefly at Chabria's scornful face. Dimple Kapadia was one of the Indian movie industry's most famous sex sirens. There wasn't a man in India who did not want her. Yet just like the stars of the Western cinema, she was so beautiful, so elusive, so ethereally lovely she might as well have been a real goddess. Mollaji ignored the jibe and stared back at the distant film studios as they slid slowly out of view behind the high brick wall. For a moment each man was lost in his own thoughts. Film City might not look like much on the surface but they all knew what delicious secrets must lie guarded behind those drab walls, hidden from the eyes of jealous mortals. And they all understood that this was the closest any of them would ever get to a real nirvana.

The driver slipped his foot back onto the gas pedal, the car lurched forward and the three men drove on in sullen silence. The wall continued for another few hundred yards, then the chain mesh fence returned and whatever lay beyond was hidden by thick undergrowth. The road narrowed to a single lane and continued to climb and wind between a series of squat, scrubby hills. After another mile the fence veered off sharply to the right and marched up the side of a hill, defining the eastern limits of Film City. The road pursued its own tortuous path across the belly of the hill until a moment later they rounded a tight bend and came upon the spectacle of Lake Vihar.

Despite the long, dry days of summer, the lake looked full and beautiful—a startling blue against the dusty brown and green backdrop of the surrounding hills. The surface of the lake shimmered in the sunshine like crushed diamonds, and the driver squinted and swore as he began the slow, difficult drive down to the lakeshore. Mollaji leaned forward on his seat. He saw a cluster of vehicles and a small knot of people far below at the water's edge. As the car drew closer to the lake, Mollaji noticed a cloud of seagulls about fifty yards out from the shore, swooping and diving at something floating in the water.

Chabria grinned. "Now we'll see you earn your pay, *kuli*," he said.

The driver added the Premier to the crescent of parked cars at the top of the grassy bank which led down to the lake. There was another black Premier and a battered green Mahindra jeep with a canvas canopy, both police vehicles from Zone Eight, the police district which encompassed the northeastern suburb of Goregaon and Lake Vihar. There was an old gray pickup truck from the Bombay City engineers' department and a white Mercedes Benz. Chabria climbed out of the car and looked over the Mercedes. A car like that meant civilians—rich, influential civilians. The sergeant knew he had been wise to bring the corpse-collector himself. There was something unusual about this particular body and he wanted to know what it was.

Chabria hitched his trousers up beneath his fat gut. They soon slid back down to where they usually sat, the crotch hanging in loose folds almost to his knees. He surveyed the men gathered at the bottom of the slope. There were four uniformed policemen, two men in work clothes from the

engineers' department and four men wearing civilian
clothes. A couple of constables prowled the waterline, hunt-
ing out stones amid the dried cakes of mud and throwing
them at the seagulls hovering above the shape in the water.
Far above the gulls a half-dozen bigger birds, vultures,
wheeled around the flawless blue sky, biding their time. A
dozen more of the scrawny-necked carrion-eaters perched
in a stand of athel pines nearby.

Chabria focused on the civilians. He recognized two of
them as police officers. One was an inspector called Sansi.
George Sansi. A half-caste bastard who thought he was too
good to take *hafta* like everybody else. The other was
Sansi's sergeant, a man called Chowdhary who, like his
boss, had been spoiled early in life by a disruptive streak of
principle. Chabria spat the last of his *khaini* onto the grass
beneath his feet and frowned. Police life was not the easy
meal ticket it once had been. There were too many bastards
like Sansi and Chowdhary rising to the top in the Bombay
police force: new men who had peculiar ideas about elim-
inating all the time-honored methods of padding out a policeman's meager pay. Chabria scorned them as much as
they scorned him.

He turned his attention to the other two men. He had no
idea who they could be. One was strikingly tall, though he
carried himself with the scholarly stoop of a man who had
never been comfortable with his height. He wore glasses
with elegant tortoiseshell frames and his long gray hair
curled thickly over the collar of a rumpled white safari
jacket. He looked like some kind of intellectual, Chabria
thought. All intellectuals were weak and troublesome. Certainly he seemed to be the most uncomfortable with what
was taking place, as he walked restlessly back and forth
along the shore of the lake, his hands moving constantly in
and out of his trouser pockets. The tall man's companion
hurried alongside like a pet terrier trying to keep up with its
master. Chabria recognized the type immediately. A small-
time pimp. The flamboyant multicolored shirt, the jewelry
that flashed on his fingers and around his neck, the long

black hair combed vainly to disguise a bald spot . . . they were all trademarks of the species.

The men at the water's edge had all noticed Chabria's arrival and the two police officers now stared expectantly in his direction.

"Acha," Chabria muttered to himself, using the Hindi word for okay. He signaled to Mollaji to follow and started down the slope toward the water.

"Sahib." Chabria gave Inspector Sansi a lazy salute when they met at the water's edge.

Sansi nodded his acknowledgment and eyed the sergeant with wry mistrust. "Sergeant . . . Chabria, isn't it?" he asked in Hindi. "Aren't you stationed at Jacob Circle now?"

"Yes, sahib," Chabria answered. The bastard, he thought. Sansi remembered everything about everybody.

"Long way from home, aren't you?"

"We picked up a general call on the radio for assistance," Chabria answered officiously. "This man was available so I brought him immediately."

"How kind." Sansi spoke softly, without a trace of sarcasm. The inspector knew Chabria was one of the most corrupt policemen in the city. He understood perfectly that Chabria had come nosing around for some scrap of information that might be useful to the gang bosses who were his biggest paymasters.

"So," Sansi turned his attention to the *kuli* waiting patiently nearby, "this is the man who is going to do our dirty work for us today?"

Mollaji stepped forward, gaped at Sansi in undisguised amazement, then collected himself, raised both hands in front of his chest, pressed his palms together and bobbed his head in a gesture of respect.

"Sahib," he murmured and waited.

Mollaji had never seen an Indian with blue eyes before. And this police officer had the most startling sea-blue eyes set in a distinctly Indian face. It was difficult for Mollaji not to stare. There was so much about this man that seemed different: the soft, civilized way he spoke; the way he carried himself; the way he looked at people with those vivid blue eyes. He was not like a policeman at all. Mollaji thought Sansi looked like a good man. He had a handsome face, his hair was swept straight back from his forehead and his coloring was lighter than most Indians'. Obviously he had mixed blood or he came from a far superior caste to other police officers. Inspector Sansi was an oddity. An oddity in a country of oddities. And there was the faintest trace of a smile permanently attached to his lips. He knew the *kuli* was reading him.

"You really are quite honored to have an important man like Sergeant Chabria bring you down here personally," Sansi remarked gently, ignoring the *kuli*'s discomfiture.

"Yes, sahib. Thank you, sahib." Mollaji bobbed his head again and waited. If he noticed the irony in Sansi's voice, it didn't show in his face.

"I gave him the picture on the way down," Chabria offered helpfully. "I told him what the job involves."

"Yes, sahib," Mollaji added. "Sergeant Chabria is a very clever man. He has told me much of his cleverness."

"Really?" Sansi drawled, his right eyebrow lifting a fraction. "That couldn't have taken more than a minute."

Chabria's face darkened but he held his tongue. It was his turn to fume silently.

Mollaji smiled fleetingly, revealing the lurid red stains of the betel nut on his teeth and gums. He caught an answering smile in Sansi's eyes. The *kuli* felt partially avenged against the loutish Chabria. For once in his life the power in another man's hands had worked in Mollaji's favor.

There was a sudden chorus of excitement behind them as one of the constables scored a direct hit on a seagull. They turned to look as the gull faltered and splashed into the water in a flurry of feathers. It struggled desperately to get airborne again but was crippled by a broken wing trailing from its right side. The other gulls pounced. The stricken bird fought briefly, then disappeared beneath a blizzard of yellow, jabbing beaks.

"That's it." Sansi nodded in the direction of a blue-gray lump lying motionless in the water. "Can you bring it into shore? We can't get a boat here till tomorrow and my men say they can't swim. I would try it myself but ... I'm afraid I don't swim very well at all."

Mollaji did not believe that none of the other policemen could swim. But he believed Sansi. He shrugged. "It is easy, sahib. For me there will be no problem."

Without another word he kicked off his sandals, pulled off his shirt and, wearing only his shorts, padded across the hard baked mud to the water's edge.

All the men on the foreshore moved in closer to watch what happened. The seagulls on the lake finished dining on their fallen comrade and went back to their games with the corpse. A mood of morbid expectancy settled over the placid lake.

The water felt cold. From the hilltop the lake had looked blue, picturesque and inviting. Up close it looked dull, gray and sinister. Mollaji suppressed a shiver. The mud felt slick beneath his feet and fell away steeply into deep water. He waded in to midthigh, then braced himself, took a deep breath and plunged in head first. The moment his head broke the surface he started swimming in a quick, choppy crawl toward the floating corpse. From a distance it could have been a floating garbage bag, a shapeless lump of jet-sam with a smudge of black at one end. A couple of times Mollaji lost sight of the corpse and looked as though he was about to veer off at a tangent. Then, just as the men on shore were about to call out to him, he would stop, tread water for a few seconds, get the corpse in view and start swimming again.

As he swam closer Mollaji realized that the black smudge was long hair spread out on the surface of the wa-ter like a fan, and he decided the corpse must be that of a woman. It looked to him as though it was naked, though it seemed oddly truncated, as though the legs were missing. As he came within a few yards of the corpse Mollaji real-ized that the legs weren't missing at all. It was floating facedown in the water with both legs trussed tightly to the arms at the back. Just like a pig for slaughter, he thought. Or a torture victim.

A warm gust of wind ruffled the surface of the lake and the cloying stench of bad meat filled Mollaji's nose and throat. Once again he shut down all his human senses. Disgust was not a luxury he had ever been able to afford. Chabria was right, he thought. This one was a stinker. It must have been in the water for a long time before it had floated to the surface. He would have to be careful how he touched it; he didn't want it to break apart in his hands. Everyone would get angry at him and he would not get paid.

Something tugged at his right foot and tried to pull him under. Mollaji kicked but it bit harder and locked around his ankle. An eel? Panic surged inside him and filled his throat like bile. He forgot about the body and fought the reflex to cry for help. No one could help him. He was on his own—as always. He forced himself to breathe deeply and stay calm. It wasn't easy: whatever had attacked him was trying to drag him down. He took a deep, desperate breath, steeled himself and ducked beneath the surface of the water. The men watching from the shore saw him disappear and there was a grumble of concern.

"Oh, *Bhagwan*," Inspector Sansi muttered to himself. It was Hindi for "Oh my god." "Something's gone wrong."

Mollaji dived low and opened his eyes, but saw nothing except a gray murk filled with tendrils of weed and fragments of floating vegetation. He reached down with both hands and felt frantically around his right ankle.

Wire. A twisted length of steel wire floating beneath the surface had snagged around his leg. He tried to yank his foot free but the wire only pulled tighter, like a noose. Fear ran through him like an electric current. He could already feel his breath and his strength ebbing inside. The fear was burning up the oxygen in his lungs and in his blood. A sharp pain lanced his left eardrum: water pressure. He was sinking deeper. He used his left hand to pinch his nose and equalize the crushing pressure on his eardrums. The murk intensified into a cold and terrifying darkness.

The wire must be attached to something, a wooden fence post or an oil drum ... it could be part of a huge floating coil, a tangled nest of steel mesh drifting sluggishly through the depths, waiting to ensnare anything unfortunate enough to get in its way. He struggled against the pain and the rising sense of hopelessness and bent double again to reach his foot. Slowly, desperately, he wormed two fingers under the wire around his ankle. At the same time he felt himself spin slowly in the water. His whole body filled with nausea and he wanted to vomit. His heart began to race, his eardrums creaked as though ready to burst. He felt the wire bite deep into his fingers, but ignored the pain and pulled with all his might. He gave an involuntary grunt and a long stream of bubbles escaped his lips, robbing him of precious air. The wire yielded a fraction. He pulled harder and at the same time twisted and dragged his foot free, the skin scraping painfully against the cutting edge of the wire.

Mollaji knew he was almost finished. His eardrums screamed and his chest felt as though it were about to explode. He stroked frantically for the surface. Every animal instinct urged him to open his mouth too soon and to drink in great drowning gulps of water. Suddenly the darkness lightened and he saw the glittering surface of the lake rushing rapidly toward him. And then he saw the grotesque, staring face of the cadaver grinning malevolently down through the water, welcoming him into its world. Mollaji gave a last feeble kick and broke the surface with a shout that was an agonized harmonic of fear and triumph. The world spun crazily around him and again he thought he might vomit. He sucked at the tainted air as though it were perfumed with marigolds. Then he floated weakly on his back and stared at the sky, his whole body trembling while he breathed in hungry, life-giving mouthfuls of air. The dizziness faded and his heart began to calm.

Mollaji allowed himself a feeble smile and a prayer of gratitude. Not yet, he thought to himself; his karma was not ready to consign him to the next life quite so soon. For one brief moment he felt ashamed. It was not that he was faithless. The little *kuli* believed in reincarnation—or rather, he wanted to believe in it. He just wasn't yet prepared to undergo the necessary pain of transition.

Mollaji floated for a few minutes more until his strength returned then signalled to the men on the shore that he was all right. The sight of Inspector Sansi shaking his head in disbelief made Mollaji smile. Something inside made him want to please the inspector. Mollaji felt strangely exhilarated and strong again, strong enough to finish the job. He looked around and saw the body rotating slowly in the water a few yards away. He breaststroked across to it and laid his hand lightly against the torso. It felt cold and spongy. There was blood in the water and Mollaji noticed that the flesh on the two fingers of his right hand had been shredded almost to the bone, though they were numb now and he felt no pain. Carefully he positioned himself behind the corpse and then, as gently as he could, he began maneuvering it slowly ahead of him toward the shore.

It took Mollaji almost half an hour to steer the corpse to the water's edge. The waiting constables had laid out a gray plastic body bag on the mud bank. They were all strangely silent. Each one of them had forgotten the drama of Mollaji's near-drowning and was steeling himself for the full awfulness of the corpse that was about to be revealed. When he was within a few yards of the shore Mollaji probed tentatively for the muddy bottom with his toes. It took him a moment to find a good foothold and then he planted his feet solidly in the mud with the corpse just in front of him. Before anyone could protest, he took another deep breath, ducked beneath the surface and got into a crouch under the body. Carefully he eased the corpse across his shoulders. The body was much heavier than he expected and every fiber in his body quivered with the strain. They had all enjoyed the show, he thought. Now he would find out just how strong their stomachs really were.

Slowly, like a monster emerging from the deep, the

corpse seemed to levitate itself out of the water, its swollen head lolling sickeningly to one side. There was a sharp intake of breath from the men standing on the shore and Mollaji heard someone give a soft moan of revulsion. He smiled inwardly. Then, in short, awkward steps he walked unsteadily up the mud bank, water streaming in torrents from the bloated corpse slumped across his shoulders. Suddenly he faltered, wavered for a moment, then regained his balance. He took the last two short steps, kneeled down slowly beside the open body bag and carefully lowered the corpse onto the plastic.

"There is your body, sahib." His voice seemed directed to no one in particular. Then he stood up, walked over to his clothes and began to dry himself with the shirt, leaving a circle of silence behind him. The smell of putrefaction soiled the air.

Inspector Sansi was the first to step forward and take a long, careful look at the corpse. It was impossible to tell what sex it was. It lay facedown, thick black hair plastered to the skull, obscuring the features. Whoever it was had been given no dignity in death. The arms and legs were trussed brutally behind the back with a length of chain. The skin was a mottled blue-gray and badly blistered, the soles of both feet a stark, shriveled white by comparison. In the heel of one foot was a hole made by parasitic water borers. Despite the obvious effects of decomposition on the skin, Sansi could see there was a fretwork of deep welts across the buttocks.

A large shadow flitted over the scene and the men looked up to see that a vulture had moved in closer to settle on the uppermost branch of a nearby tree. The bird shuffled from one foot to the other and stared brazenly back with soulless black eyes.

The tall man with the glasses looked ready to faint. He held a clean white handkerchief tightly to his nose and mouth.

It was Inspector Sansi who spoke first. "Turn it on its side," he ordered.

No one moved.

Sansi shook his head and stepped forward. "Sergeant," he said, looking at his assisting officer, the thin, mournful-looking Chowdhary. "Take the legs . . . help me roll it over."

Sansi bent down and used one hand to support the cadaver's head and the other to hold a shoulder. The flesh on the shoulder yielded beneath the policeman's touch like wet tissue paper. The muscles beneath the skin felt loose and formless like water-sodden rags. Sergeant Chowdhary reluctantly did as he was told and took hold of the legs.

"Careful," Sansi said. "When I say the word . . ."

He waited until they were both in position. The midday sun beat down and the flies swarmed in, settling on the corpse, picking out choice nooks and crannies to lay their filthy eggs. There was no breeze to disperse the stench and a couple of men lit cigarettes. Sergeant Chabria pulled another twist of *khaini* from his shirt pocket.

"Now," Sansi said. And they rolled the corpse slowly onto its side.

The sight that met their eyes would stay with them for the rest of their days.

Even Chabria had to struggle to suppress the writhing in his guts. The man with the glasses gagged and wheeled away. He only managed a few stumbling steps before he was racked by a convulsion and began retching onto the ground. The pimp hurried after him.

"Oh, *Bhagwan*," Sansi mumbled once more. He spoke for all of them.

It was still impossible to tell whether the corpse was male or female because the head and torso had been ravaged beyond recognition. The face could no longer be defined as human. The eyes, nose and lips had been consumed by parasites and a gelatinous gray ball of silt worms could be seen squirming in the socket where the left eye had been. Much of the facial tissue had rotted away, exposing raw patches of skull and insanely grinning teeth.

But the worst mutilations had been performed by a human hand.

Where the breasts should have been there were two concave wounds, dreadful in their precision. But that was not all. The most grotesque mutilation had been inflicted on the genitalia. The whole genital region had been cut away, leaving a horrific wound that exposed the pelvic bone. There was nothing left to indicate whether the corpse was male or female.

Inspector Sansi fought back the sour taste that rose in his throat and gladly took his eyes off the thing on the ground to look at the appalled face of his sergeant.

"It will be a complete waste of time getting them to try and identify this. . . ." His words trailed away, though he managed a nod in the direction of the man in the glasses and his companion. "We'll have to leave it to Forensic."

He stood up and looked at the two Zone Eight constables who had driven out in the jeep after the call from the engineers who first saw the corpse floating in the reservoir. "Take it to the mortuary," he said softly. "I'll warn the coroner's office it's coming."

Sansi wiped his hands on his trousers and turned his back on the mutilated corpse to speak to Sergeant Chowdhary. "Rohan will have to examine it right away." Dr. Rohan was the deputy coroner of Bombay. "He won't thank me for this one," Sansi added needlessly.

He paused for a moment to regain his composure then walked over to the two men from Film City to tell them that they would not be needed after all. The man in the glasses nodded weakly and looked relieved. The two constables pulled the plastic flaps of the body bag shut and hid the obscenity on the ground from the innocent gaze of the sun. Then they carried it gingerly up the grassy slope and put it carefully in the back of the police jeep. Chabria watched, his face a grimace of disgust. He didn't envy them that drive back into Bombay on a hot afternoon.

Everyone seemed to have forgotten Mollaji, the corpse-collector. It didn't bother him. He was used to going unnoticed. Sometimes it worked to his advantage: he heard things that he wasn't supposed to hear—like today. Mollaji kept his face solemn while he buttoned his shirt and strained to overhear the conversation between Inspector Sansi and the two civilians a few yards away. It wasn't much, but enough to tell Mollaji that the two civilians were bigwigs from Film City. Somehow the body he had just retrieved from the lake had something to do with them.

Sansi finished his conversation and the two men walked shakily back up the slope toward the white Mercedes, the pimp guiding the taller man by the elbow. The others had started back toward their vehicles too and Mollaji slipped on his sandals and hurried after them. He was about to follow Chabria when he heard someone calling him.

"Hey, *kuli*," Sansi called from his car. "Come over here."

Mollaji looked at Chabria, shrugged and did as he was told.

"Here," the inspector said and casually handed Mollaji two ten-rupee notes.

Mollaji stared at the money in disbelief then pushed it quickly into his shirt pocket before anyone else saw. The inspector was a strange man, he decided, unlike any other policeman he had known. Perhaps, Mollaji decided, he was rich, had more money than sense. Or perhaps he simply had a kind heart, which was a rarity on the streets of Bombay and rarer still in the police department.

"You earned double pay today," Sansi said. "Despite that little bit of theater when you brought it out of the water."

Mollaji maintained his expression of obliging dimness. "Thank you, sahib." He pressed the palms of his hands together again, bobbed and hurried back to Chabria's car. He climbed into the backseat, barely able to believe his good fortune. First there had been the dead whore, then his own brush with death and now another completely unexpected reward. And he still had his pay to come for retrieving this corpse.

Chabria waited until all the other vehicles had left before

twisting around in his seat to glare at Mollaji. "How much did he give you?"

Mollaji looked crestfallen. He knew it was pointless to argue. Chabria beckoned with the fingers of his pudgy right hand. Mollaji reluctantly pulled the two notes from his shirt pocket and handed them over.

The sergeant stared at them suspiciously. "Is that it?" he demanded roughly.

"Yes, sahib," Mollaji answered, devastated.

"It's piss all," Chabria huffed. "*Acha.* Ten rupees commission for giving you the job. Ten rupees for the car." He tucked the money into his own pocket, turned back in his seat and nodded to his driver. The engine started and the car began its slow, bumpy climb back up the hill and away from Lake Vihar.

In the backseat Mollaji stared ahead through the windshield in resentful silence. But his anger was more feigned than real. He didn't like losing twenty rupees to a *salah*—a bum—like Chabria. But he had acquired some information that might yet prove more valuable. The body was someone important. Someone from Film City. Someone who had been missing for a while. Maybe a big movie star—that would explain the presence of the bigwigs from Film City. Information like that had to be worth money to the newspapers, Mollaji knew. Especially in a city where every scrap of scandal about the movie business was seized upon eagerly by millions of insatiable movie fans. The *kuli* allowed himself one small smile. He might yet have the last laugh on that buffoon Chabria. Bombay truly was a city of hope. A city where movie stars could be worth more dead than alive.

3

_____

"I KNOW IT's not fashionable to say so, but the British were the best thing that ever happened to India . . . and I don't care who hears me say it."

Aloo Madhubala set her cup down so hard she thought she had cracked the glass on top of the large bamboo coffee table. She flashed an apologetic smile at her hostess, the imperturbable Pramila Sansi. Pramila smiled back reassuringly. Aloo was one of the most timid women Pramila Sansi had ever known. The repressed and mousy wife of a successful Bombay lawyer, she was always apologizing for having a point of view, especially to her husband.

"I mean it." Aloo resumed her little speech, encouraged by Pramila's beneficence. "Ever since independence it has been fashionable to behave as though the only way to be a good Indian is by having something bad to say about the British first. Well, that's all _bakwas_. . . ." She faltered slightly. "If you'll pardon the expression."

Pramila blinked. _Bakwas_ was Hindi for bullshit. She had never heard Aloo Madhubala use such a strong word. Secretly, she was pleased. She had hoped to draw Aloo out of her shell by inviting her to these informal, women-only tea parties where they could all speak their minds, free from the censorship of male disapproval. Apparently it had worked.

"India was managed much better by the British," Aloo went on in the comic, singsong accent that afflicted all Indians, however cultivated, when they spoke English. "Quite frankly, I wish they were still running the place. At least the

35

streets would be safe and clean. I can remember when I was a little girl, the water carts would come around every morning before dawn and sprinkle water on the streets to keep down the dust. And when there was trouble it would take only one British officer to appear on the street and poof!" She waved a thin hand dismissively in the air. "The crowds would just melt away. And . . ."

Pramila watched apprehensively. Aloo seemed trapped by her own momentum.

"If the British were still in charge we wouldn't have anywhere near the amount of corruption in government that we have today—"

She was interrupted by a sudden skeptical laugh from the youngest woman at the table, a newcomer to Miss Sansi's tea parties. A pretty, light-skinned woman with short, coppery hair and sharp eyes who wore a sari like the others, though she was not Indian.

"I'm sorry," the newcomer said in a confident, unmistakably American manner. "I was willing to listen to all that stuff about how great things were under the British—if you were part of the ruling class. But I can't buy that business about less corruption. Everything I've heard since I've been here says that, if anything, the British were worse. I mean, they really raped this place . . . raped and plundered it. And anybody who got in the way got shot or put in jail. At least with your own government you can vote the bastards out when you get sick of the corruption.

"Sure . . ." She was the only woman smoking and she paused to take a deep pull on her cigarette. "It gets messy from time to time. But that's democracy. Keep swapping them around, y'know? They'll get the message eventually. The British did whatever the hell they liked here for two hundred years and nobody was allowed to vote them out."

"Bravo!" said Mrs. Kumar, the other woman at the table. Dozens of gold and silver bracelets on her wrists jingled prettily as she gave the American a brief round of applause. Janata Kumar was a plain, plumpish woman in her late forties. Like Mrs. Madhubala she had the red-paste thikka

mark of a married woman in the middle of her forehead.
She wore her graying hair braided into a long thick rope
that lightly brushed the floor when she was sitting. She was
also the director of the women's bureau at the Maharashtra
Ministry of Social Welfare, a career bureaucrat who could
be expected to support any statement made in favor of Indianization.

"We should have done the same as the Americans," she
said smugly, "and kicked the British out much earlier in our
history."

"Oh, we tried," Pramila interrupted. "It was called the
Indian Mutiny, remember?"

Mrs. Kumar made a face, as though Pramila had just
scored a cheap point. But Aloo Madhubala seemed content. At least she had contributed to the afternoon's conversation, even if it was only to reveal herself as a closet
imperialist. She usually allowed herself to be over-
whelmed by the bright and abrasive career women with
whom Pramila seemed to surround herself at these occasions. It had not yet occurred to Aloo that Pramila was
more concerned with building her friend's confidence
than with what she had to say.

At sixty-seven, Pramila Sansi was one of Bombay's most
celebrated women. A feminist from the dark days of the
1950s, when it was not possible to be a feminist in India,
she was now a successful author and a lecturer in Feminist
Studies at the University of Bombay. Her friends ranged
from the most influential power brokers in the city to the
poorest of her students. No one could be sure whom they
might meet when invited to tea on the terrace of Pramila's
spacious apartment on Malabar Hill. Famous faces mixed
with the unknown and the aspiring on guest lists that included students, feminists, authors, poets, journalists, publishers, filmmakers, academics, bureaucrats and politicians.
There Aloo had been introduced to Maneka Gandhi, the
controversial Minister for the Environment and widow of
Sanjay Gandhi, the doomed first son of the assassinated Indian Prime Minister, Indira Gandhi. Sometimes famous

people from Europe or America dropped in unexpectedly for tea or to stay for a few days with their friend Pramila Sansi, the equally famous Indian feminist. Aloo had met Germaine Greer at Pramila's apartment the year before.

The glass door leading from the apartment onto the terrace slid open and Pramila's son appeared, looking sheepish and disheveled. George Sansi's trousers were badly creased and soiled with grime.

"Ah," Pramila announced. "An inspector calls."

"I'm sorry," Sansi apologized in English, taking his cue from his mother. "I didn't know. . . ."

"It's all right, darling." Pramila glanced at her wristwatch and saw that it was a little after six o'clock, though the sun still blazed fiercely overhead. "We've been talking for nearly four hours. I daresay we could tolerate a little male company, especially as you live here."

Pramila got up from her cane chair in the shade of a tall potted palm, crossed the terrace to her son and kissed him on the cheek. The other women noticed how Pramila moved with the grace and fluidity of a much younger woman. Despite her age and the gray hair which she wore short and defiantly untinted, there was still a dynamism in Pramila that showed in her eyes, her speech, her movements and her handsome, animated face.

"You look awful," she said. "Come and sit down. Say hello to the others. I'll ask Mrs. Khanna to make a fresh pot of *chai*." Mrs. Khanna was the Sansis' *bai*.

"I'd rather have a whiskey," Sansi answered, allowing his mother to coax him toward an empty chair.

The women at the table smiled. George Sansi was the only man any of them had ever seen Pramila fuss over.

"That sounds good to me too," the young American woman chimed in.

Sansi looked at her curiously. She was about thirty and exceptionally pretty, and she looked back at him with an uncompromising curiosity.

"Miss Ginnaro is from California," Pramila said as

though no further explanation was necessary. "You know Mrs. Kumar and Mrs. Madhubala."

"Annie," the American gave her first name and held out her hand.

Sansi gave Annie Ginnaro's hand a polite shake then nodded politely to his mother's friends and sat down. According to the protocols of Indian society it was all right to shake hands with a Western woman but still inappropriate for a man to touch an Indian woman who was not a member of his family.

"Would anyone else like something stronger than *chai*?" Pramila asked.

Both Aloo and Mrs. Kumar declined and Pramila disappeared into the apartment to find the *bai*.

"My god," Annie Ginnaro exclaimed as George Sansi settled into his chair. "You've got Paul Newman's eyes."

"He can have them back after the things they've seen today," Sansi answered wearily.

"No, you know what I mean," Annie went on. "Blue eyes . . . you've got blue eyes. I suppose they're for real—I mean, they're not contacts, are they?"

Aloo and Mrs. Kumar exchanged disapproving looks. Both of them had decided that Annie Ginnaro's manners were deplorable, even for an American feminist.

"Actually, they're my father's eyes," Sansi explained patiently. "My father was English."

"Incredible." Annie shook her head. "The odds against you getting your father's eyes must be . . . incredible."

"Yes," Sansi agreed pleasantly. "I suppose the golliwog in me would be expected to drown out all that pure Anglo-Saxon blood."

There was a sudden, heavy silence at the table. Aloo and Mrs. Kumar both looked uncomfortable and stared vaguely out over the ocean. Annie Ginnaro was on her own.

"All right . . ." She gave a soft outward breath of regret. "I apologize. I didn't mean to come on quite so strong. It's just that, well, I believe the best way to be with people is to be direct, you know? Then we all know where we stand.

And if some people can't deal with it, that's okay too. But you're right, I didn't mean to be quite so insensitive. And I'm sorry."

"Apology accepted," Sansi said with a strangely solemn smile. "I'm afraid I've had rather an unpleasant day and I'm not quite ready for . . . light conversation."

Aloo and Mrs. Kumar took the hint immediately and began making noises about going.

"No, please, not on my behalf," Sansi protested. He appeared sincerely concerned that he might seem rude and inhospitable. "Don't let my bad mood drive you away. Pramila will be furious with me."

Mrs. Kumar shook her head. "It is after six o'clock and I still have work to do at my office before I can go home," she said graciously. Aloo Madhubala insisted that she had to be home in time to prepare her husband's supper. The instant Pramila returned they both got up and began their good-byes and she had to turn around and walk them back through the apartment to the front door, leaving George and Annie alone on the terrace together. A moment later the *bai*, Mrs. Khanna, arrived with two glasses of Scotch and a small plastic ice bucket on a tray. They waited in silence while Mrs. Khanna set down their drinks and cleared away the tea things. When she had gone, George politely wielded the ice tongs and dropped a couple of ice cubes into each glass. They picked up their drinks, took an exploratory sip of the whiskey then set their glasses down on the table with a light clink, almost in perfect unison.

Annie Ginnaro laughed softly. "Just like the Rockettes," she said.

"I'm sorry?"

"The Radio City . . . oh, never mind."

Sansi smiled. There was an awkwardness between them that he didn't quite understand. He found it surprising. "So, are you visiting Bombay?" he asked, trying to reel the conversation back in to a comfortable level.

"No." Annie shook her head gently. "Working. I'm a reporter for the *Times of India*."

"A reporter?" A shadow of concern flitted across his eyes.

"Look." She smiled. "I know you're a cop. But Pramila is a friend and there's on the record and there's off the record. Right now, everything is off the record. If anything comes up that I'd like to use sometime, I'll ask you first if it's okay. We're not as bad as people make us out to be, you know."

Sansi gave her a polite smile but looked unconvinced. He knew many of his mother's friends in the media. She entertained them at home and he saw them at social gatherings. He liked to keep them on friendly terms but he was careful never to tell them anything he didn't want them to know. It was all part of a game whose rules were well understood by both sides.

"How did you get the job?" he asked. "I thought it was very difficult for foreigners to get positions in the Indian press."

"It is," she said. "But I'm persistent. And I had friends at the embassy speak to a few people on my behalf. It's purely temporary. I only plan to work here for two years. And I sure couldn't live off the salary they're paying me. If it wasn't for my own money I couldn't do it at all."

"Do you speak Hindi or Marathi?"

"I speak a little," she said in awful Hindi. She smiled self-consciously and switched back to English. "I go to classes two mornings a week. I have friends who help me at work. I figure I ought to be able to get by for a couple of years on English and Hindi. It's amazing how many people here speak English—even street people."

Sansi nodded. "We were well colonized."

"You think of yourself as Indian and not half English?"

"I am more Indian than English," he said. "Black blood does make a difference."

Annie nodded but preferred not to touch on the subject of race again with Sansi so soon after his earlier rebuke. She took a long sip of her whiskey and ice water and let the silence grow.

"Were you a reporter in California?" he asked, mildly irritated that he was forced to make conversation in his own home.

Annie knew she should follow the example of the others and leave but she was determined to spend just a few more minutes with George Sansi, even at the risk of alienating him. She wanted to get something going—whether it would be personal or professional, she wasn't quite sure, but something told her that Sansi was a man worth cultivating.

"With the *LA Times*," she answered. "Nearly ten years. I went there as soon as I graduated from USC. But I was ready for a change and I wanted to do something different, something radical."

"Radical?" Sansi nodded thoughtfully. "I don't know about radical . . . but India can be very difficult for Westerners."

"The difficulty was part of the attraction," she answered quickly. She opened her mouth to say more but hesitated, and for a moment he glimpsed the uncertainties beneath the tough veneer of American self-assurance. She tried again.

"I, ah, the real reason why I wanted such a big change is because I got divorced last year. My husband—my exhusband—was the paper's night editor. It got so I couldn't stand to work next to him. But he had been at the paper twenty years and he wasn't going to quit, so it had to be me. Then, when I started to think about where I should go, I realized that what I really wanted to do was get off the goddamn planet, not just leave the paper. It wasn't just the divorce. It was him, it was the paper, it was the city, it was southern California, it was my friends, it was my mother . . . thank God I didn't have any children. I was just so sick of it all. And sick of myself. Yeah, if I'm honest, that too. So I decided that the closest I could get to living on another planet would be India. I figured it would be different enough and weird enough that maybe it would teach me a thing or two about myself. I thought if I could handle India, if I could deal with all that's going on here, living in the States would have to be a cinch afterward."

Sansi smiled. "It sounds to me as though you are going to an awful lot of trouble just to learn to live with yourself."

"Oh," she shook her head, "it isn't just me. Something huge is going on in the States right now and there are millions of people over there, and I mean millions, who just can't figure it out. Can't figure it out at all. America is changing . . . mutating might be a better word. The good old U.S. of A. is incubating a Third World country in its midst and there are a lot of people over there who don't know how to deal with that—they just cannot cope at all. Because they look over here, you know, and they see the real thing and it absolutely scares the shit out of them. They know that this is what the States is going to be like in another, oh, twenty years or so. And to them it's . . . the end of civilization, the end of the world. America has been living on the edge for a long time." She gave a deliberately melodramatic emphasis to "the edge" and Sansi smiled.

"Now," she went on, "it's about to fall over. In the meantime, all the people I know are locking themselves up in Gucci ghettos with guards and dogs and Star Wars security systems . . . because that way they don't have to deal with reality. Because they don't know how. They've never had to. And I'm looking at all of this, watching these people trying to make sense out of their lives and failing, and I look at India and I think to myself, why not just welcome it? Why not learn to live with the inevitable? I mean, this is the ultimate doom culture. Civilization ended for you guys more than a thousand years ago and it's been downhill ever since. And yet you're still here, still playing the game in the shithouse at the end of the universe. The ultimate survivalists. You've had it all: famine, disease, overpopulation, conquest, poverty, corruption and injustice on a massive scale . . . and yet here you all are, getting up every day at seven and going to work like everything is normal. And meanwhile, there are people starving on the sidewalk. You'll be in a taxi going to lunch, and you'll see people out there with fucking leprosy, with pieces falling off them.

There are men and women and babies drowning in their own shit in the gutter outside every door . . . but life goes on. You guys live through the end of the world every day and I want to know how you do it. You see, that's the big mistake all Americans make about India. They look at India and they think of it as the past. It isn't. India is the future. That's what's really so scary. India is the way the world is going to be. I want to look it in the face now and avoid the rush."

"Oh," Sansi said wryly. "Just another jaded American divorcée come to India in search of the meaning of life."

"You got it, pal." Her laugh was loud and relaxed and she slapped her thigh in a way that he found masculine and unattractive. He wondered why it bothered him.

"How long have you been in Bombay?" Sansi asked, keeping his voice conversational.

"Four months."

"And what have you found so far?"

"Well . . ." She gave him an arch look. "One thing you can say about India: It never disappoints you. It's always worse than you expect."

Sansi chuckled softly. He decided on a change of subject and nodded at the expensive, richly patterned sari she wore. "I see you have already embraced the Indian way of dressing."

"If you're a woman," she said, "you only have to try it once to know that it is absolutely the right way to dress for the climate. This is the coolest and most comfortable clothing I have ever worn. If I can get away with wearing these things at home when I go back, I will."

Sansi suddenly seemed to have run out of conversation. He looked tired and Annie knew she would have to go—in just another moment or two.

"You're a detective in Crime Branch, aren't you?" she asked suddenly.

He nodded.

"That's supposed to be the best, isn't it? I mean, like our FBI or something?"

"We're part of the state," Sansi answered. "We're not federal. We model ourselves after Scotland Yard in London."

She nodded. "What have you been doing today that's so awful?" Her voice was softer and more earnest. "I know I'm being nosy ... but I'm interested. I want to know. What's all that gunk on your pants?"

"Oh ..." Sansi glanced absently down at the gray smears on his trousers. "That is from someone's body."

Her face froze into an uneasy half-smile.

"You ... really ... ?"

"Yes." Sansi nodded. "All that misery you were talking about earlier? Sometimes it spills out of the gutter and comes in your front door ... and it leaves marks."

"Jesus Christ," Annie exclaimed softly. She stared at the polished ocher floor tiles for a moment, then shook her head. "On the level?"

Sansi shrugged. "We found a body today. There will be an investigation."

"Was it anybody import—?"

"Are we on the record or off the record?"

A smile passed briefly across her lips but she said nothing.

"India may look like the end of the world," Sansi added quietly. "But as long as we have the law, we have civilization. To a Westerner like you it may look like anarchy ... but there is order underneath. I know my job is important and I do it as well as I can. And there are many others out there like me. Because of us, the city still works. Sometimes we even manage to temper the corruption and the chaos with a little justice. Sometimes we lock away a major criminal. Sometimes we even lock away a corrupt politician, a judge or a policeman. So there are still rules. And to survive in Bombay you have to know those rules."

This time the message was unmistakable. Annie stared at Sansi for a long time in silence, her face expressionless, her eyes aglow with secret calculations. Now she knew why she had stayed. She wondered how long it would be before she could get him into bed.

4

Bombay, 1971

"I'VE MADE UP my mind," George Sansi announced suddenly to his mother. "I've applied to join the police service. I take the examination next week. If my marks are high enough, they will have no excuses for keeping me out."

Pramila looked up from the book she had been studying and stared at her son with a calm she did not feel. Inside, her heart ached for him.

"A law degree from Oxford," she sighed, "and you want to be a policeman."

It was late Sunday morning and they were on the terrace of the apartment on Malabar Hill. Pramila was in the second year of a degree program in social studies at the University of Bombay. At the same time she had begun campaigning on behalf of migrant women workers in the harshly exploitative textile industry and was trying to organize the women into a cooperative that would be recognized by the Maharashtra Ministry of Social Welfare. Pramila Sansi was rapidly becoming a political celebrity in Bombay. The press called her a firebrand feminist. The state government called her a nuisance. Younger women students at the university admired her and listened to her. Her name had begun to appear in newspapers and magazines and on television. The previous weekend there had been a picture of her on the front page of the *Indian Express*, leading a march of women textile workers in protest

47

against the acquittal of a powerful factory owner charged with the sexual assault of his female employees.

After years of sacrifice on behalf of her son, Pramila had built a new life of her own and found it exhilarating. She also knew that she had been neglecting him lately. When the initial rush of excitement had subsided following his return from England, she had plunged back into her work and seen him only in passing in the weeks that followed. She knew he had been having difficulty finding work but she had not been surprised. The government's dogmatic application of the policy of Indianization made it almost impossible for an Anglo-Indian like George to find a good job. The public prosecutor's office treated him like an outcast and many of the big legal firms saw him as more trouble than he was worth. He might have come home with a law degree from the most prestigious university in the world but in the stultifyingly parochial atmosphere of Indian politics, it did not rate as highly as a degree from a second-rate Indian university. His attempts to find employment had been rebuffed everywhere. It looked very much as though Sansi was to be denied the opportunity to play his part in the building of the new India—for that most ironic of reasons in a country which prided itself on the Gandhian principle of equality for all. Sansi was the wrong color in the wrong place at the wrong time. Pramila knew that her son had been brooding and she had intended to speak to him soon, except that she had never seemed able to find the time.

"I don't want to be a policeman," George answered his mother calmly, "but it looks very much to me as though it is the only way I am going to get any kind of job in Bombay."

"I don't understand," Pramila said, putting her book down among a litter of notes and papers on the table. "Why this sudden rush into employment? You've worked hard for three years and you've done very well. You should enjoy having a year off. Most graduates do take a year off for a bit of fun, you know, before committing themselves to a career."

"It's been almost a year," Sansi answered, his voice somber with sarcasm.

"Nonsense." Pramila looked genuinely shocked. "It's been, what, three, four months at—"

"I came back just before last Christmas," he interrupted. "It is now July. In three days it will be August. That's eight months by whatever calendar you happen to be using."

She ignored the petulance in his voice and looked long and hard at her twenty-four-year-old son.

"I still don't see the need to rush things," she said, struggling to keep all undercurrents of maternalism out of her voice. "We've never been desperate for money. You're very fortunate in that respect, you know. You can take another year to find a position if you want. It makes no difference to me."

"It makes a difference to me," he answered flatly.

Pramila frowned. It had been so much easier when he had been a boy. Now that he was a man she had to tread so carefully. She had never been married and living with an adult son was as close to it as she ever wanted to come. Accommodating a burgeoning male ego was not something she was particularly good at.

"Hasn't the bar association been any help?"

Sansi looked at her scornfully.

"I can be accepted to the bar without any problem," he said. "But that doesn't mean anybody will give me a job. I'm still the wrong kind of Indian with the wrong kind of degree. The only way I'll get to practice law in Bombay is if I go into business for myself. But how I'd get clients and how I'd get legal experience is a mystery that still needs to be solved."

"What about Mr. Billimoria? He's a partner with one of the bigger legal firms, isn't he?"

"That slimy fat shit?" Sansi hung his leg over the side of the chair and began to rock his foot briskly back and forth.

"Darling." She gave him a mildly admonishing look.

"He suggested that I might like to pay him for taking me on for the first three years," Sansi said. "It was bad enough going begging to him in the first place. Everyone in Bombay knows how corrupt he is . . . and he expects me to pay for the pleasure of having my name tainted along with his just so I can get into the old boys' network."

"I don't know a legal firm in Bombay that isn't corrupt," Pramila rejoined.

Sansi sniffed and gave his mother an impatient look. She resisted the temptation to smile.

"That's why I don't see any point in waiting," he said after a long pause. "The situation isn't going to get any better. I've been considering the alternatives. If I get high marks in the police service examination they have to take me. It doesn't matter if I am a half-caste English bastard. They have no choice."

"You'll be the most highly educated constable in the Bombay police department," Pramila remarked gently.

"It would be something. It would be somewhere to start."

"You think the legal profession is corrupt and the police service isn't?" She dreaded the idea of his wasting his talents and his hard-earned qualifications on the Bombay police force. She was sure that if he went ahead with his idea he would drop out after a year. Perhaps, an inner voice told her, he needed the experience, painful though it might be. The moment the thought occurred to her she felt a stab of pain in her heart, as though she were betraying her son.

Sansi saw none of this. He felt as though he was exercising great patience to explain himself to someone who clearly didn't understand.

"I know it's corrupt," he said. "But I don't have to be part of it. I can be different from the others. And it would be a beginning. It's still the law. I can do something worthwhile by bringing the right kind of cases forward for prosecution."

"If they let you."

"They'll let me," he mumbled.

Pramila smiled. She got out of her chair, padded across to her son on bare feet and knelt down beside him. He looked at her sullenly through the eyes of a young man who knew that he was about to be subverted by unfair means. Pramila looked lovingly at her son then pulled him gently to her breast, pressed her face against his hair and kissed the top of his head, inhaling the long-distant perfume of the child in him.

"It is your life," she said softly. "I love you ... and I will support you in whatever you decide to do."

Sansi passed the police service examination with the first perfect score in the post-independence history of the service. He was sworn in the following month and sent to the police academy at Nasik for two years' training. When he graduated he was not given a city posting. Even though Sansi was by far the wealthiest man in his graduating class he refused to join the traditional bidding game between graduates for postings to the best police stations in Bombay—those stations which harvested the most bribes.

His reward was a posting to a town called Tamori, the administrative capital of a remote and blighted desert region in the northeastern corner of Maharashtra State. Tamori was a miserable and decaying backwater that had been stricken by drought for eleven years. Its meager agricultural economy was close to collapse. Gangs of heavily armed dacoits infested the countryside and were responsible for an increasing number of violent attacks on trucks, buses, cars and trains.

To add to the local police commander's woes, a group of Naxalites had moved into the area and launched a campaign of terror and subversion in the villages around Tamori. Naxalites were hard-core Marxists, also known as the People's War Group, and had acquired a fearful reputation for cruelty. Their name came from the village of Naxalbari in West Bengal where their ideology of power through terror was born in 1967. It was their practice to infiltrate isolated rural areas and take over towns and villages, one at a time, until they controlled an entire region. When they had become entrenched they would consolidate their strength and increase their numbers until the only way to dislodge them was to send in the army. Once they had been driven out they would simply go underground for a few months and then surface somewhere else and begin all over again. Despite twenty-five years of counterterrorist campaigns by the government in Delhi, Naxalites were still active in half a dozen states. In the year before Sansi was posted to Tamori, they had murdered eight policemen. The distant desert town had acquired a reputation as a graveyard for unwanted police officers. If Sansi's superiors wanted to get rid of him quickly, they could scarcely have sent him to a better place.

Sansi arrived in Tamori at six o'clock in the morning after a three-day train journey from Bombay, most of which had been spent sitting upright in a compartment shared with eight others. By nine o'clock he had washed, shaved and changed into a clean uniform and was ready to report to Inspector Vissanji, the commanding officer of Tamori police barracks. Vissanji was too hung over to see him. Instead, Sansi was directed to Sergeant Singh, a large, friendly and heavily bearded Sikh who was responsible for most of the day-to-day running of Tamori barracks. It was Singh who took Sansi into the operations room and showed him a wall map of the Tamori area. The map had been divided into twelve separate patrol zones and was impressively studded with red, blue and green plastic-topped pins that signified police operations in progress. They were all fake, Singh explained matter-of-factly, but acted as an important morale booster. There were only forty men to police an area of twenty-two hundred square miles with a scattered and largely rural population of around five hundred thousand. Most of the patrol zones hadn't seen a policeman in more than a month.

Sansi was assigned to Zone Five, an area which involved a round-trip of two hundred miles and included half a dozen villages strung out along the west bank of the parched Tamori River. In theory, he would conduct two patrols a month and would have to provide detailed reports on every patrol. In practice, there were only a few patrol vehicles available and all were subject to frequent breakdown, which cut projected patrol targets by at least half. His primary task, he was told, would be to elicit information from village headmen about the Naxalites to enable the police to counter their activities in the area. It was also Sansi's responsibility to deter crime by demonstrating a high police presence, Sergeant Singh added, without any suggestion of irony.

That afternoon Sansi was issued with a .303 rifle, a Webley revolver, a few boxes of ammunition and a worn, plastic-coated map. His first patrol would commence the following day, he was told. It was expected to take him three days. If he had not returned or radioed in after five days, Singh reassured him, they would try to send someone out to find him. Subject, of course, to available manpower. Sansi's last stop of the day was the police garage, where he was shown the vehicle he would drive on patrol, a battered Mahindra jeep with badly chipped green paint. The clutch slipped, the four-wheel drive didn't work, the radio was dead and there were five bullet holes in the back fender.

Sansi survived his first six months at Tamori by turning fear and desperation into a talent for deception. He knew that if he drove openly through the countryside, proclaiming his presence, sooner or later he would be ambushed and killed. Or worse. He would be captured and tortured and his head severed from his body and used as a plaything by the Naxalites before they exhibited it on a stake in some village square to show their contempt for the law.

Instead of slipping into a predictable patrol pattern, he improvised. He hid out amid the ravines and gullies of the desert during the daytime, screening his jeep with the branches of trees, sitting in the shade and sipping water from his canteen. At odd hours he would venture out cautiously, calling on villages at random—sometimes at dusk, sometimes at dawn—staying only for a few minutes to speak to the headman and to replenish his water. He refused all invitations to eat or stay overnight and always lied about his future movements. Sansi was Indian enough to know that his life depended mostly on his karma. But he was English enough to try and weigh the odds of survival a little more in his favor by sheer rat cunning. Most of the intelligence he gathered was useless and he knew that his patrols were ineffective. But he learned how to play the game and how to pad his reports, like everyone else did, and he stayed alive. And for a young and inexperienced constable in a place like Tamori, that was a triumph in itself.

It was in his seventh month that Sansi's karma changed in the most dramatic and unexpected way—and altered the course of his life. It happened on the last night of patrol about sixty miles from Tamori. He had found a perfect hideaway in the bank of a dry creek bed and after a cold supper of *chapatti*, rice, banana and chutney had settled down for an uncomfortable night's sleep, without the telltale company of a campfire to keep him warm.

Sansi had been asleep for several hours when he heard voices. At first he thought they were part of a dream but then some primitive warning instinct jangled his nerves and he was awake, alert and fearful. He lay still inside his quilted sleeping bag and listened. They were men's voices—two or three of them. Close.

Sansi looked at the luminous green dots on his watch. It was almost three-thirty in the morning. He lay motionless in the back of his jeep for another hour before the voices faded and he dared to make a move. Slowly he eased his body out of the sleeping bag, afraid to make the slightest sound. It could have been local herdsmen or travelers or even pilgrims on their way to distant Benares. But it probably wasn't. Innocent people did not prowl through the desert night. It was almost certainly dacoits or Naxalites.

Sansi was wearing only a T-shirt and shorts. The chill night air felt clammy against his bare skin and his breath fogged in the cold. He pulled on his socks and trousers but left off his boots so that his stockinged feet would not make any noise among the dry twigs and branches that littered the ground. He fastened the Webley securely in its holster, then picked up the .303 and made sure there was a round in the breech ready to fire. Then he started to shiver. His heart thudded painfully and he seemed unable to get enough breath. Fear, he realized. Sansi had heard that some men were energized by fear, their bodies coursing with adrenaline as they prepared to confront danger. His legs felt weak and watery. There was no hint of adrenaline. For a long time he stood there in the dark beside his jeep, immobile and afraid, his ears straining to pick up the slightest sound. But the desert only taunted him with its stillness. Nothing stirred; there was not even the whisper of a breeze. A half-moon and a brilliant slash of stars shed a cold light on a bleak and pitiless landscape. Sansi realized he would never be ready. He forced himself to move.

He began picking out a wide, circular path which he hoped would bring him around to the source of the voices. He held his body in a tense crouch, his footsteps were small and painfully slow. It took him half an hour to cover fifty yards. The ground was latticed with moon shadows that only reinforced in him the sensation of stark unreality. Sansi saw his own crippled shadow on the sand. It looked sinister and threatening. He didn't feel threatening.

Then he saw the flames of a small campfire, about eighty yards away to his left. He hunkered down to the ground and watched. He could see no one. Nothing moved. Whoever it was had not bothered to post a lookout. Sansi forced himself to creep in for a closer look. He came within thirty yards of the camp and stopped. He could see four people in sleeping bags around the campfire. There was no vehicle. If they were Naxalites it meant their main camp had to be within easy walking distance, perhaps only five or six hours away. There were a few tin plates around the fire and a couple of small cheap backpacks. Then he saw the gun: the unmistakable profile of an AK-47 assault rifle glowing red in the firelight. They were Naxalites.

Sansi retreated into the shadows and looked at his watch. It was almost four-thirty. He had to do something. Their camp was barely a hundred yards from his jeep. He had three choices. He could hide and hope. He could run. Or he could attack. But he had to decide soon because the sun would be up in ninety minutes and the choice might be taken out of his hands.

By the time he had made it back to the jeep, Sansi knew what he had to do. He had to try to be a policeman.

With painstaking caution, he prized a jerry can out of its rack on the back of the jeep, his nerves jarring every time metal scraped agonizingly against metal. Then, with the can in one hand and his rifle in the other, he set off back in the direction of the terrorist camp. This time it took him longer because the jerry can was heavy and it was harder for him to move quietly.

It was almost five o'clock before he was once again within striking distance of the camp. There were still four people asleep on the ground. No one appeared to have moved, although the campfire was dying down. Sansi set the jerry can down on the sand and began prizing the tension lever back off the cap. He was sweating, despite the cold, and his hands were trembling. The lever came free with a sudden bang, followed by the gasp of escaping gasoline fumes. He looked up. One of the figures around the campfire stirred. Sansi grabbed the can and sprinted forward, fear frozen into a hard lump in his chest. He tipped the jerry can upside down and splashed gasoline in a wide, messy ribbon across each of the four sleeping bags on the ground. The man who had begun to stir jolted upright with a warning shout and lunged for the AK-47. Sansi dropped the jerry can, took one step forward and kicked the assault rifle into the darkness. Gasoline pulsed from the can and spread in a dark, widening stain toward the campfire. The other three guerillas woke up and began to struggle out of their sleeping bags.

It was going wrong, Sansi realized. He fumbled the .303 from his shoulder, pointed it to the sky and pulled the trigger. The crack it made was deafening in the stillness of the desert and echoed eerily across the open flats. Everyone froze.

"Lie still," Sansi shouted. "Or I'll burn you alive." His voice sounded thin and unconvincing, even to him.

But the stench of gas fumes filled the camp and the guerillas hesitated, equally unsure of what might happen next. One of them dabbed at the wet fabric of his sleeping bag and swore. Sansi yanked the bolt back on the .303, ejected the spent shell casing and slid a fresh round into the breech. He scanned the campsite for other weapons but saw none. There seemed to have been only one AK-47. He glanced quickly from face to face. There were three men and a girl, all dressed the same in ragged shirts and pants.

The girl could not have been more than eighteen or nineteen. She stared sullenly at Sansi and said something in a dialect he didn't recognize. He thought it might have been Urdu or Bengali but the words weren't meant for him. They were directed to the man who had gone for the AK-47, a man with dirt-matted hair and a stringy beard, who appeared to be their leader. He spoke rapidly back to the girl, his eyes still fixed on Sansi.

Sansi didn't like it. They were planning something right in front of him in a language he didn't understand. "Police," Sansi said in Hindi. "Put your hands on your heads."

The four guerillas stared dumbly back at him but did not move. For a moment Sansi wondered if they understood him. The girl shrugged, then looked at her leader and said something in that strange, alien dialect again. A sly smile spread slowly across the man's face and he motioned with one crooked finger to the others. They weren't at all intimidated by him, Sansi realized. They had decided to rush him.

They all moved at once.

Sansi bent quickly toward the fire and plucked a smoldering branch from the embers with his free hand and gestured toward the leader. The smile vanished from the man's face and he stopped . . . but the girl was already on her knees and still moving. Sansi felt a surge of pure terror. He was about to get himself killed.

"Don't—" The word sounded hollow and strangely distant.

Her right hand moved quickly and Sansi saw a shiny sliver of metal. The next few seconds blurred into a kaleidoscope of horrific, frenzied images filled with screams and panic and death. Sansi reacted instinctively. He threw the smoldering branch at the Naxalites' leader, swung the rifle around at the girl and fired point-blank. The bullet hit her in the chest, lifted her off her feet and flung her backward into the dirt where she spasmed briefly, making ugly choking sounds. Sansi had no time to worry about what he had done. At the same instant he pulled the trigger, the branch he had thrown at the man on the ground exploded in a shower of sparks and the whole camp erupted in flame.

Sansi hurled himself sideways out of the inferno and leapt for the safety of the creek bed a few yards away. Behind him he heard only screams and felt a searing blast of heat across his back. Then the flames reached the fuel left in the jerry can and there was a loud, whooshing explosion followed by a fireball that lit up the desert landscape with a ghastly yellow light. Sansi dived headlong into the dry creek and buried himself gratefully in a cold, sheltering sandbank.

The blaze and the clamor of destruction died as abruptly as they had begun and were replaced by the muted crackling of a dozen spot fires amid the desert brush and in the branches of a few withered trees. Sansi hauled himself along the creek bed and approached the devastated camp from a new direction, his rifle poised. It was an unnecessary precaution.

The girl was dead, though untouched by the fire, and there were two bodies burning in the midst of a wide, charred circle of earth where the camp had been only a few moments before. The sickly stench of burning flesh caught in Sansi's nose and throat and he turned away, fighting the urge to gag. He forced himself to look for the AK-47 and found it lying where he had kicked it. He picked up the rifle, slung it across his shoulder, then looked around numbly for the remaining terrorist. Sansi found him curled up on the ground twenty yards away. His hair had been burned away and almost all his clothes had been scorched from his body. He lay in the fetal position, fists clasped to his chest, rocking back and forth and moaning softly to himself. The man may have escaped the inferno but he had been caught by the heat and the blast of the explosion.

Sansi remembered the first-aid kit in his jeep and set off back toward his own camp. He had taken only two steps when he was stopped by an unbearable jolt of pain like a hot needle penetrating deep into his lower left side. It was then that he noticed the blood. It started at his waist, soaked the whole left leg of his trousers and trickled from his foot onto the sand. Sansi stared at the blood and his ripped and tattered clothes as though they belonged to somebody else. Then, slowly and apprehensively, he peeled his shirt away from his body. The handle of a small knife hung loosely from the flesh on his side. He remembered the glimmer of metal he had seen in the girl's hand. Amid the panic and the violence he had not felt it strike him. Now it had begun to work itself loose.

Sansi could see it was only a flesh wound—but blood poured from it in a steady and frightening stream. He was surprised that it did not hurt more. Perhaps, he thought, that was the effect of the adrenaline, after all. Hesitantly, he took the knife handle between the finger and thumb of his left hand, braced himself, then quickly pulled it free. The nerves in the cut flesh screamed. Sansi gave an involuntary sob of pain. His head swam and for a moment he thought he might faint. The knife was a single, thin length of sharpened steel with a short, wide blade—a throwing knife. Sansi was lucky it had not struck him somewhere vital. He used it to cut a length of material from his shirt, then tucked it beneath his belt. He bunched the material in his hand and held it tenderly to the wound. Within moments it was black with blood. Sansi knew he was in more trouble than he had at first realized.

The moment he reached the jeep he retrieved the first-aid

box, placed a thick gauze pad against the wound and covered it with surgical tape. Within minutes a fine trickle of blood had worked its way under the gauze and was trickling down his side, now stained beet red. Sansi knew he needed to lie down and rest for a few hours and give the blood a chance to coagulate in the wound. But he didn't have the time. He had to get to Tamori soon. He took a deep breath. He could do it in three hours if he hurried, though it was a rough road. He wondered how much blood he could afford to lose before he blacked out at the wheel.

Sansi looked around. The sky had begun to lighten. In a few minutes it would be sunrise. He started the jeep and drove back across the flats to where the injured terrorist still lay moaning in the sand. The man's eyes were glazed and he had begun to shiver from head to foot with the shock of his burns. The thought occurred to Sansi that neither of them might make it to Tamori. It took several long minutes of painful struggle by both of them to get the injured man off the ground and into the back of the jeep. His burns looked worse in the growing dawn light. Sansi covered him with a blanket, propped his head up and held a water canteen to his lips. The man drank thirstily, his eyes closed. Sansi saw that his lips were blistered, his eyebrows and eyelashes had been scorched away and his scalp was a grisly patchwork of burned and peeling skin. After a moment he stopped drinking and Sansi saw his eyelids twitch, as though he were having difficulty opening his eyes. It took him a long time but then they fluttered open and the man stared blankly up into Sansi's face. Sansi waited while the terrorist struggled to focus his gaze. Then he saw the slow light of recognition creep into the man's eyes. The terrorist opened his lips to speak but no sound came out. He swallowed painfully and tried again. This time he was able to croak two words in Hindi. Sansi looked at him, puzzled.

"Blue eyes," the man had said. That was all. Then he lay back down on the floor of the jeep and looked away. Sansi watched him for a moment, then took out his handcuffs and cuffed the man's left wrist to the back rail of the jeep. In-

jured though he was, something about the man told Sansi
not to take any chances.

It took Sansi almost four hours to drive the sixty miles
back to the police barracks at Tamori; afterward, he could
recall nothing of the journey except that it was undertaken
through a constant blaze of pain. By the time he drove
through the barracks gates he was so weak he was unable
to bring the jeep to a complete stop. He merely fumbled the
key from the ignition and let it roll to a halt in the middle
of the barracks square. His arms felt like deadweights and
much of his body felt numb. The only sensation left was
the prickling torment of pins and needles in both his legs.
He heard the man in the back of the jeep utter a low,
wretched moan. Sansi smiled bleakly. At least his prisoner
was alive. Gratefully, he closed his eyes against the sinister
red mist that threatened to drown him and let his head loll
forward onto his chest.

Somewhere Sansi heard distant shouts and the sound of
running footsteps. The last words he heard before he lapsed
into unconsciousness were from Sergeant Singh.

They were "*Are Bapre*." Hindi for "My god."

"There are easier ways of getting back to Bombay, you
know."

It was Sergeant Singh again. Sansi opened his eyes and
looked up from his bed in the police infirmary to see the
burly, turbaned Sikh looking down at him.

"You did not have to become a dead hero," Singh added,
his voice mock serious.

Sansi smiled faintly. It was a week since he had driven
back to the Tamori police barracks, half dead from loss of
blood, with a burned and cowed terrorist handcuffed in the
back of his jeep, and three more dead in the desert behind
him. Nearly twenty pints of blood and plasma had to be
pumped through Sansi before he stabilized. He had spent
the rest of the time convalescing. His prisoner had not been
so fortunate. The police had little pity for Naxalites. Because of his burns and his weakened condition the man had

broken down quickly under torture. Sansi did not want to know the details. The terrorist had given the strength and the exact location of the Naxalites' main camp. Sergeant Singh had left that same day with forty armed men. The attack he led on the terrorist camp at dawn the following day represented the most successful police action against terrorists in the history of Maharashtra. Five Naxalites had been killed and eleven taken prisoner. The police were still reaping the intelligence benefits and expected to be able to launch more sweeps against Naxalites' cells in other areas. And it was all due to Sansi.

"I'm serious," Singh went on. "I sobered Vissanji up long enough to sign your recommendation for a commendation. You're a hero . . . and you are going back to Bombay as soon as you are well enough to travel. I hear the governor and the commissioner are fighting to see who should pin the medal on you."

Sansi shook his head slowly in disbelief. He still felt weak and the stitches in his left side tugged painfully if he moved too quickly.

"You don't belong in Tamori," Singh added. It was said kindly but the sergeant's big bearded face was solemn. He pulled up a chair and sat down beside the bed. "You were lucky to last as long as you did. You didn't know what you were doing. Sending you out there was like tying a lamb to a stake in the jungle to draw out the tiger. I didn't think you would last one month. You were lucky you found the Naxalites before they found you—and you were even luckier that they did not kill you first. Your karma must be very strong. It is time you went back to Bombay . . . quickly."

Sansi looked at Singh for a moment. "You mean . . . you sent me out there deliberately, to lure the Naxalites out of hiding?"

Singh looked sheepish. "They send us raw recruits all the time. We have to do what we can. Everyone learns on the job out here. Some survive, some don't. You have done your share. You have been lucky. Your karma says you must go now."

Sansi smiled despite himself. "What about you?" he asked. "Is there no reward for the man who led the ambush?"

"Oh, yes," Singh nodded, his eyes newly bright with irony. "I will probably get Vissanji's job."

Sansi had to struggle not to laugh.

Singh shrugged. "I do not want to go to Bombay," he said. "I do not belong there. Sikhs are not well treated in Bombay. I was in the army before I joined the police service. I know this kind of country. I can live out here. Someone like you . . ." He left the rest unsaid.

"Bombay." Sansi repeated the name slowly, as though he had never been there before. It was hard to believe that he had a life there before the police service, before Tamori. His mother still did not know he had been wounded and that he would be coming home soon, a hero.

"I don't know what you did wrong or whom you offended to be sent out here," said Singh, "but it is over now. It is behind you. You're getting a chance to start afresh: a hero, a man with a fearsome reputation. Three terrorists killed—single-handed." He paused and then his voice took on a new seriousness. "The police service has to take care of its heroes," he said. "Everybody will be very nice to you in Bombay now, you will see. You will be taken to see the commissioner; he will probably make you a detective. You are a clever man, Sansi, an educated man. You belong in a city like Bombay. It is your home; you will do well there. I know these things. You are going to be a great and famous detective, Sansi. It is your karma."

Now, twenty years later, Sergeant Singh's words came back to haunt George Sansi, sitting on the terrace of his mother's apartment on Malabar Hill. He often wondered what had happened to the burly Sikh, whether he had been made inspector and given command of the hellhole that was Tamori.

Sansi was tired but unable to unwind. The American woman, the inquisitive Annie Ginnaro, had left an hour

ago. His mother had gone inside to escape the worst of the
mosquitoes, leaving him alone on the terrace. It was after
eight o'clock and the sun was just setting over the Arabian
Sea. He sat with a glass of Scotch in his hand and one leg
raised on the parapet that bordered the terrace of the apartment Sansi's father had bought Pramila for a pittance back
in 1947, the year of India's independence. The year Sansi
had been born.

It was one of the oldest apartment buildings on Malabar
Hill, a four-story Victorian wedding cake with a flaking
pink and white stucco exterior. Despite the corrosive effects
of salt and pollution on the exterior, the interior was spacious and retained a dilapidated charm. The terrace was
crowded so thickly with potted palms and boxes of flowers
that it looked and smelled like a tropical garden. There
were even a couple of lime trees, a papaya tree and a banana palm that bore fruit every year. Sansi loved the apartment. It was home—where he had grown up. A rock in a
shifting sea.

From where he sat, Sansi could look due east, right
across Back Bay, to the glittering arc of Marine Drive and
the jumbled city skyline beyond. To the left he could see
the golden wedge of sand that was Chowpatty Beach.
When he was a boy he had run the length of the hill, along
Walkeshar Road, every weekday morning, to the lookout at
Kamla Nehru Park and then down the rickety wooden staircase to the beach where he would chase seagulls until the
bus came to take him to Campion School at Colaba.
Chowpatty Beach had been cleaner then. Now it was unsafe
to put your feet in the water. Everything had been cleaner
then. The whole world had seemed brighter, shinier, more
innocent. Or perhaps it was just the eyes of a child that
made it seem that way, Sansi mused. He had noticed how
slum children never seemed to see the squalor in which
they lived, how they made boats out of palm leaves to sail
down the open sewers.

Once upon a time, Bombay had been the most glamorous
city in the British Empire. A triumph of colonial civiliza-

tion where British merchants and Indian princes had prospered and played polo, then forged deals and drunk *stengahs* together in the palaces that were their private clubs. Now it was a monument to Indian failure; because so many wanted a share of the good life, there was no longer a good life left. In the decades since independence the population of Bombay had exploded from two million to twelve million. They filled the streets and alleys, begging, fighting, cheating, stealing—clamoring for a share of the elusive wealth that would never be enough to sustain them all.

Now when he looked at Bombay, Sansi saw only corruption and chaos, decay and decline. Annie Ginnaro had disturbed him because she had been closer to the truth than he liked to admit. The richest, most powerful city in all India was dying. The city that provided one-third of all India's tax revenues was dying because too many people demanded a piece of the action. Bombay was suffocating beneath a tidal wave of human greed.

From his perch on Malabar Hill Sansi saw that Bombay could still masquerade as a city of charm. The dying rays of the sun gilded the film of scum that coated the greasy gray waters of Back Bay and added a brassy luster to the white ramparts of the apartment buildings along Marine Drive. But it was only an illusion. The glamour dissolved under scrutiny. Most of the buildings were shoddy, crumbling, streaked with dirt and mold. Landlords did not repair them. Owners did not paint them. Greedy developers bribed corrupt politicians to blot out the city's few remaining green spaces with more shoddy building complexes. The moment they were finished, slum shanties flooded in and lapped at their foundations like a tainted sea. It alarmed Sansi to see how few trees there were left in Bombay. When he was a boy the city had seemed like one vast gold and green park. Now, beyond that bright and shining facade there was only concrete . . . and the desperate millions who struggled to make a living from every form of human commerce. Heroin, opium, ganja, guns, gold, fake passports,

American green cards, policemen, politicians, judges, magistrates, men, women, little girls, little boys—they were all for sale. And the price was always dirt cheap.

For the first time in his life, Sansi could sit on his terrace with a drink in his hand and look out at the counterfeit beauty of Bombay and feel no hope. That was why Sergeant Singh's words had come back to haunt him. Sansi had returned to Bombay a hero. He had become a detective. He had even become an inspector with Crime Branch, the most elite crime-fighting unit in the police service. And still he felt it had all been for nothing. Nothing had improved. Anarchy was winning. The forces of evil were greater than the forces of good.

And just when he thought he had seen every evil the human mind could conceive, the city had shown him something more—something worse. Something he couldn't even begin to understand. He shifted his seat on the terrace wall. The first cool breeze wafted in from the sea and even though it was not cold it made him shiver.

Sansi drained his glass and let his eyes wander restlessly back and forth across the city skyline until the sun had gone down and the city had assumed the mask of darkness. He thought about the body they had found in the lake that morning. He thought about it still floating in the cold water, facedown, grinning insanely into eternity. And he wondered about the others he knew must still be out there.

5

"Is IT SOMEBODY famous . . . or a nobody?"

Narendra Jamal, Joint Commissioner of Crime Branch, leaned back in his chair and waited for Sansi to answer. It was late Friday morning and they were seated in Jamal's office on the second floor of the Crime Branch building at Bombay police headquarters.

Sansi shrugged. He was used to his boss. What Jamal really wanted to know was if this was a case important enough for him to worry about or whether it was politically safe to let Sansi take care of it all. After thirty years in the police service, Jamal never did anything without considering the political implications first.

"We don't even know *what* it is," Sansi answered. "The body had been in the water a while. It was badly bloated and partially decomposed . . . and there was extensive sexual mutilation."

"What do you mean, 'sexual mutilation'?"

"Somebody cut off the breasts and all the sexual organs. There was nothing left. We'll have to wait till the postmortem to see whether it's male or female."

"Couldn't you tell by looking at the face? Couldn't you make a guess?"

"Most of the face had been eaten away by worms," Sansi answered coolly. It was never possible to win with Jamal. Whenever things didn't go smoothly he liked to make you feel as though you, personally, were to blame.

"It had long hair, like a woman," Sansi added. "But from the musculature of the arms and legs I'd guess it was male.

Who can ever be sure . . . ?" He let the sentence hang unfinished. It was up to the coroner's office to issue the definitive report. Jamal would just have to wait.

The joint commissioner appeared dissatisfied. "What's your opinion?" he pressed. "What do your instincts tell you about it?" It was a typical Jamal question. The joint commissioner placed as much reliance on a policeman's intuition as he did on his powers of deduction.

"I think we are looking for a madman," Sansi said quietly. "The kind of violence used in this killing was bizarre, perverse. Even if it was somebody trying to disguise a conventional motive, like revenge or money, to throw us off the scent. But I don't think so. This is the work of a psychopath. It has to be. This was obscene—it was done by somebody who enjoys killing."

The joint commissioner grimaced. A plumpish, somber-faced man in his late forties with thick, oily hair and wary eyes, Jamal wore expensive gray slacks and a plain, open-necked white shirt. A Rolex the size of an ingot glittered on his left wrist. Jamal was the only policeman Sansi knew who wore a solid-gold Rolex. Most senior officers spurned such obvious displays of wealth because they wanted to avoid even the appearance of corruption. But somehow Jamal seemed to float above it all, his reputation unblemished by all rumor and innuendo. He was his own man: vain, calculating, manipulative and ambitious—but he was not corrupt. Not in any conventional sense. He traded in power and influence, not money. In Bombay that made him an honest man.

In many ways Jamal was the most powerful policeman in Maharashtra. He was the only man to share the rank of commissioner. But unlike the police commissioner himself, Jamal had real power. The commissioner spent most of his time enmeshed in administrative and ceremonial chores and relied on a coterie of deputy commissioners to manage the city's twenty-three thousand officers and men on a day-to-day basis. Jamal, however, enjoyed direct command of an elite unit of four hundred officers and men with the authority and the resources to conduct investigations anywhere in India or overseas. Jamal could use his unit almost as he wished. He could pursue and break anyone, from the most vicious hoodlum to the mightiest politician. Jamal was a man who enjoyed power for its own sake. And it was widely believed that his ambitions led higher still, that he intended to be Chief Minister of Maharashtra one day.

"What kind of cooperation have you had from Film City?" Jamal asked abruptly.

"Full cooperation and none of it any help at all."

"Yes," Jamal smiled. "They're very good at that."

"I don't think it was Kilachand's fault," Sansi qualified. Noshir Kilachand was the managing director of Film City. "He was there at the scene. He looked at the body—but there was nothing left to recognize. I sent him home. I told him we'd want to go through their cast lists to see who is missing. But that will take time—there are thousands of names. Obviously it isn't anybody ... important. They know where all their big names are on a day-to-day basis. From looking at the body I would say this person must have been missing for at least ten days. It's got to be somebody small-time."

"*Acha,*" Jamal nodded. "Some of these people will do anything to get their name in the newspapers." Jamal smiled alone at his little joke. "Kilachand couldn't offer any ideas at all?" he continued.

Sansi shook his head.

"Interesting," Jamal murmured softly. "It was Kilachand who called me and asked me to look into this, you know. He told me they might have a problem. One of their people was missing and he was worried about it. He thought something was wrong—but he wanted to keep it out of the newspapers. Film City attracts enough scandal without adding to it unnecessarily. That's why I sent you up to Vihar when we got the call about the body. Otherwise I wouldn't have worried about it. If it was just another missing person, I'd have let the boys at Zone Eight take care of it."

Jamal hesitated, then expressed his thoughts aloud to

Sansi. "I was willing to take Kilachand at his word . . . but I got the distinct impression that he had some idea who this body might be. I think Kilachand knows a little more about this than he has told either of us."

Sansi recalled the tall, scholarly, bespectacled man stooped with nausea at the lakeside, wiping the spittle from his chin after seeing the body. "He may have been too shocked to talk about it at the time," Sansi offered. "I think his shock was genuine. It wasn't one of the most pleasant sights I've seen in a while."

Jamal looked skeptical. "You will be talking to him again soon, won't you?"

"Yes."

"Good." Jamal nodded. "Don't be too soft on him. Don't be taken in by his English gentleman act. If he's hiding something, I want to know."

Sansi nodded but wondered privately whether it was the police side of the investigation that interested his boss or whether it was the chance of getting a little dirt on Kilachand, which might be used later to Jamal's political advantage. As managing director of the state-owned film industry, Noshir Kilachand was one of the most influential public figures in Maharashtra, a man with many important contacts who could prove useful to someone with ministerial ambitions.

"What else have you got on your plate at the moment?" Jamal asked.

Sansi had to pause for a moment and run through the mental notes of his current caseload. There was only one that stood out in his mind.

"According to my informants, Paul Kapoor is planning another visit from Dubai soon."

Jamal looked interested. Until recently, Paul Kapoor had been the undisputed gang lord of Bombay: a charismatic former slum kid who schemed, fought and murdered his way to the top until he had become the rajah of the rackets. Kapoor was thought to have a hand in more than half the protection, prostitution, liquor and drug rackets in the city.

But his most lucrative sideline had been gold smuggling. In the past five years, Kapoor had smuggled so much cheap Arab gold into India that he had become a threat to the federal gold reserve. New Delhi had finally leaned on the Chief Minister of Maharashtra to do something. Despite the millions he paid in bribes, Kapoor's protection was pulled overnight and Jamal had been given the job of smashing him. As always, Kapoor's extensive network of informers inside and outside the police service had kept him one step ahead. The night before Crime Branch was due to swoop, Kapoor had fled Bombay for the tiny Arab state of Dubai in the Persian Gulf, where he used his millions to buy sanctuary at a heavily guarded bungalow on the beachfront.

That had been six months ago. At the time, Jamal had tried to present it as a kind of victory. But Kapoor had astounded the police, the government and the press by maintaining his hold on his criminal empire from exile, through the brutal hand of his loyal lieutenant and enforcer, Jackie Patro. Kapoor's rackets still flourished; Kapoor still smuggled gold into India and Patro still murdered anyone who got in Kapoor's way. But even Paul Kapoor couldn't stay away indefinitely. He had smuggled himself back into Bombay at least once to remind everyone of his power. Now, according to one of Sansi's informants, Kapoor was planning another visit. Along with another load of illegal bullion.

Jamal nodded. "Any dates?" he asked.

Sansi shook his head. "Kapoor is too cunning to tell anyone when he will come. He doesn't even tell Patro until the last minute. The first we'll hear is when he's actually in the city . . . and then we'll have to move fast. Faster than we did last time."

Jamal's brow furrowed at his recollection of the last bungled raid. "I would prefer to stop playing games with Mr. Kapoor," he said softly. "He is not the kind of man who is easily discouraged. I think he is the kind of man who will have to be shot while resisting arrest. And, as that is the case, I would be happier if he resisted arrest on the beach."

Jamal leaned forward over his desk. The meeting was coming to a close. "Stay with it, Sansi. You have time enough to take on this Film City business as well. But the moment you get another whisper on Kapoor, I want to know, understand? Everything takes second place to Kapoor."

Sansi nodded. No one wanted Kapoor more than he did.

"Don't forget to keep me informed about Kilachand," Jamal added finally. "That is a curious business. I want to know if the crafty old bugger has something to hide."

Sansi took his cue and got up to leave.

"One more thing." Jamal fixed him with a warning stare. "No leaks. Kilachand is right about the press. They will go mad if they get any hint of this. I don't want to see anything in the newspapers until I say it's all right. Do you understand?"

"*Acha,*" Sansi responded. "I will do my best, sir."

Mollaji had been waiting in the lobby of the *Times of India* building all afternoon and still no one had come to see him. Dozens of visitors had arrived, completed their business and left while he had waited patiently on a hard wooden bench near the elevators, ignored and unattended. Just another *salah* off the street. He looked up at the ornate Victorian wall clock for the thousandth time. It was almost six-thirty. Once again, under the watchful eye of four uniformed security guards, he approached the young woman at the reception desk. Like most young women in Bombay she dressed in the modern style: a short red dress that contrasted dramatically with her black, shoulder-length hair. She was very pretty, Mollaji thought. Her whole manner radiated the arrogant nonchalance of youth and beauty.

"Excuse me, memsahib?"

The girl glanced at him, then went back to the magazine she was reading. "Yes?" Her voice sounded contrived and bored.

"I am very sorry to bother you, memsahib, but please, does anybody know I am waiting?"

"I do," she said.

Mollaji hesitated. "Yes, memsahib, but what I mean is . . . I have some very important information."

"I told you." She licked her fingers and turned a page of the magazine. Mollaji noticed that the tip of her tongue was an exquisite bright pink. "I spoke to the news editor's secretary. She said someone will come down when they are free."

"Yes, memsahib," Mollaji persevered. "But it has been a very long time. All afternoon I have—"

"If you are tired of waiting, you should go home." She looked at him with enormous dark eyes that brimmed with indifference. "We'll be locking the doors soon anyway. Come back tomorrow if you like."

"Please, memsahib . . ." He leaned forward on the front of the reception desk. One of the security guards at the door sauntered over in his direction. Mollaji realized he was about to be thrown out. He tried his most beseeching look but it was directed futilely at the top of the girl's head. She was completely absorbed in the magazine. Then he realized—it was a movie magazine.

"Come on, *kuli.*" The security guard took Mollaji's arm in a firm grip. "Time you were going home."

"Please . . ." Mollaji said. "I have information about a movie star . . . somebody famous . . . a big movie star."

The girl glanced up at him, a derisive smile on her lips. "What would you know about movie stars?" she asked. "What do you do? Take out their garbage?"

The security guard grinned and began pulling Mollaji toward the door.

"Sometimes I do jobs for the police, memsahib," Mollaji protested. "I picked up a body for them yesterday morning . . . out at Lake Vihar . . . near Film City. All very hush-hush. But it was somebody important, I know. It was a movie star."

The girl was interested despite herself. Mollaji's hunch had been right. She was a movie fan. She couldn't resist the idea that she might be the first to hear a bit of scandal about the goings-on at Film City. The guard noticed the change in the girl's expression and relaxed his grip on Mollaji's arm.

"Are you telling me the truth?" she asked, her skepticism replaced by curiosity.

"Yes, memsahib, I swear I am telling you the truth." Mollaji suddenly saw doors opening to him that had been barred all afternoon. If only he had thought of it sooner. He cursed himself inwardly. Bribery, deceit and manipulation—they were the only ways to get anything done.

She hesitated a moment longer, then made up her mind. She was going to play it safe.

"Sit down," she told him. The guard let him go and Mollaji took his seat near the elevators again. The girl picked up the phone and spoke softly but rapidly to someone upstairs. She shrugged a couple of times and shot him the occasional worried glance. Then she hung up and called across to him.

"Somebody is coming down now," she said. "And I hope you are telling me the truth or we will both be in trouble."

"Yes, memsahib," Mollaji reassured her. "I swear to you, I am telling the truth."

To his right the antique elevator grunted, clanged and sighed as someone pushed a button on the editorial floor four stories above his head. Perhaps, Mollaji thought, he would get a few rupees for his patience after all.

A moment later Annie Ginnaro stepped out of the elevator.

6

"Good morning, Inspector." Dr. Vyankatesh Rohan, deputy coroner of Bombay, greeted Sansi in the postmortem examination room in the basement of the city mortuary. "I think you may need this."

Rohan handed Sansi a red plastic clothes peg. Sansi was used to Rohan's black humor. It was a game two could play. Unsmilingly he accepted the peg and clipped it to his nose. It pinched more than he expected but he put up with it. Over the twelve years he had known Rohan the two had become close friends.

The deputy coroner was a short, stocky man in his midfifties with a head as bald as a betel nut except for a narrow crescent of gray hair and a neat goatee. The perpetual sparkle in Rohan's eyes belied the hardships of his childhood. Sindi by birth, his family had lost everything when they fled Karachi during the bloody mass migrations that preceded Partition in 1947. Rohan had recalled his earliest childhood memories for Sansi over a shared bottle of whiskey one evening. The deputy coroner had been six years old when he stood with his parents and brothers and sisters on the balcony of their home and tipped pots of boiling water onto the heads of the rioting Muslims below who wanted to slaughter them all. Like many exiles, Rohan had worked hard in his adopted city. He had earned medical and scientific degrees at Bombay University, gone on to become Professor of Forensic Medicine at Bombay Medical College and had written for half a dozen scientific publications. In his role as deputy coroner he had conducted more than six thousand postmortems and had helped send eleven murderers to the gallows on the basis of his forensic evidence.

Rohan's dark eyes betrayed a glimmer of amusement as he watched Sansi clip the clothes peg onto his nose, but he said nothing. Instead, he turned and led the way to the naked corpse lying faceup on a white porcelain slab. The slab had a lip to prevent spillage. There were taps and an array of hoses at one end and there was a sluice under the body to carry blood and other wastes into the sewer.

The postmortem room was old and, despite the clothes peg on Sansi's nose, it stank of phenol and putrefaction. There were two fluorescent lights in the ceiling and they filled the room with a milky glare that leeched the color out of Sansi's face. The floor and walls were covered with white tiles, many of them yellowed and splintered with age. The room felt cold and damp and there were streaks of rust on the walls that reminded Sansi of dried blood. Next to the postmortem slab there was a table filled with the ghastly steel tools of Rohan's trade: knives, scalpels, forceps, tweezers, clamps, dishes, a large pair of shears to cleave open the rib cage, and the circular blade of an electric handsaw to slice open the skull. On the floor was a bucket for intestines and other large organs.

Sansi took his first good look at the murdered movie star. The long black hair had been swept back from the forehead to reveal a ruined, cretaceous face. The worms and parasites had died and congealed into gray mucus in the cavities of the eyes, nose, mouth and throat. The jaw was still locked open in a lunatic grin, as if mocking all those who dared look at it. Sansi put all his emotions into deep freeze, as he had done so many times before. He stared at the teeth for a long time. They were in excellent condition, he thought. Picked clean. Sansi guessed that they were the teeth of a young male.

"Got a matinee idol's smile, hasn't he?" Rohan observed blandly as he pulled on his rubber gloves.

"A real heartthrob," Sansi agreed with feigned insouciance. He had seen dozens of autopsies performed over the years but, unlike Rohan, he had never grown used to them.

"If he's anybody special, my daughters will know all about him," Rohan commented. "Think I should take a picture home so they can see how he looks without makeup?"

Sansi shook his head disbelievingly. No one could trump Rohan for gallows humor. It was a trademark of the career pathologist.

"Is it male or female?" Sansi asked, trying to steer Rohan onto the business at hand.

"Male," Rohan answered briskly. "Couldn't you tell that much? It's quite obvious if you look at the shape of the jaw and the size of the teeth, especially the molars."

"I thought . . . never mind. What do you make of the wounds?"

"Well," Rohan looked at the wounds on the corpse as though seeing them for the first time. "There is so much discoloration it's very hard to establish postmortem lividity just by looking at him.

"There are no obvious signs of entomological activity; no traces of maggots in the wounds and orifices. So I don't think he was in the open air for long before he was dumped in the lake. Some tissue damage appears to have been done by small fish and water parasites, of course, but even that is not substantial. Despite the appearance, overall decomposition is not too far advanced at all. I would say he was dumped in the lake pretty soon after he was killed. As to what would have caused such clean, precise wounds, well, obviously a very sharp blade applied with some force. Any decent butcher's knife would do it."

Sansi nodded. "Cause of death?"

"Oh . . ." Rohan looked surprised that Sansi should even have to ask. "He almost certainly had his throat cut."

"How can you be so sure?"

"Well," Rohan shrugged, "if you look past the tissue damage caused by the fish and the worms, you can see that there are still clearly defined edges on both sides of the throat injuries. They are clearly visible beneath the lobes of each ear, or what's left of his ears. That's a pretty clear indication that this fellow was cut, quite literally, from ear to ear."

Sansi suppressed a small shiver. The postmortem room always felt too cold.

"But," Rohan went on cheerfully, "I'll have to take a look inside him before telling you anything more. What do you say, shall we go exploring?"

Rohan plucked two oval surgical masks from his worktable and handed one to Sansi. "I think you'll be better off with this," he said. "God knows what creepy-crawlies we'll find inside when I open him up."

Sansi gratefully took off the clothes peg.

Rohan glanced at the welt on Sansi's nose and smiled but said nothing. He put on his own mask then picked up a small, thin-bladed scalpel. "Ready?"

Sansi nodded.

Rohan pressed the "record" button on an old-fashioned tape recorder, then stepped up beside the corpse, the scalpel poised in his right hand.

"The deceased is a young, adult Indian male," he began, his voice strong and clear for the benefit of the typist who would later transcribe his report from the slowly rotating spools. "The body is at an intermediate state of decomposition and shows evidence of severe external trauma."

Rohan held the scalpel to the throat of the young man on the slab, inserted the gleaming tip of the blade and firmly and quickly drew a line down the length of the torso to the gaping wound where the crotch had been. The bloated gut deflated like a punctured balloon and the skin peeled back like the flaps of a diver's wetsuit, revealing the foul black stew inside. A vile, choking odor filled the room. Sansi could smell it through the filter of his face mask. Hydrogen sulphide: rotten-egg gas.

Immune to all the disgusting sights and smells of the decomposing human shell, Rohan put down his scalpel and used his fingers to prize away some of the skin that clung stubbornly to the rib cage.

"We must have lunch together soon," the deputy coroner mumbled absently. "I've found a nice cheap restaurant near the market that does a wonderful *biryani*."

Sansi looked away. Rohan had done it to him again.

The deputy coroner labored over the body for three long hours. When it was over Sansi knew almost everything there was to know about the murdered movie star's medical history, his sex life and his death. Everything but who he was and who had killed him. But the most intriguing information came toward the end, when Rohan thought he had finished.

The deputy coroner had taken samples of the dead man's heart, liver, kidney, stomach and brain for further forensic analysis to determine the presence of drugs, alcohol or other lethal chemicals. He had also set aside a small steel kidney dish which contained what looked like ten separate flakes of tissue paper floating in formalin. Except that they weren't paper. They were pieces of skin, epidermal skin taken from the dead movie star's fingertips. Complete with grooves, whorls and lines, they would provide a perfect and enduring set of fingerprints. Along with the plaster casts that Rohan had taken of the dead man's teeth, they would help Sansi confirm the victim's identity beyond doubt.

Rohan was about to close the incision on the torso when Sansi stopped him.

"I want you to check something else," he said.

Rohan looked up, eyes arched above the surgical mask, which was now spattered with gray mucus. "Any particular reason?"

Sansi realized that Rohan thought he was trying to play a joke. "I'm serious," said Sansi.

He had thought of little else but the body since it had been dragged from the waters of Lake Vihar twenty-four hours earlier. It had been impossible to get the sight of that butchered corpse out of his mind. It haunted his every waking moment. In twenty years of police work in a city where people seemed to be capable of any crime, Sansi had never seen anything like those mutilations. There had to be a reason for them, he knew; a kind of crazed calculation as well as an incomprehensible cruelty. Somehow he had to force himself to comprehend the incomprehensible. He had to penetrate the mind of a psychopath. He had to find a motive in the madness. If he could determine a motive for the cruelty, he could determine a motive for the crime. He might know where to look first.

"Our friend was young and he was in the movie business," Sansi explained. "Perhaps he was a ladies' man, perhaps he wasn't. Perhaps he was a good guy—but perhaps he fell in with the wrong kind of people. I know some people in the movie business. So does my mother. I've heard a lot of stories about Film City over the years: about the drugs, the money, the sex and the craziness. They're not all just magazine headlines. And the worst stories never make the newspapers. There are a lot of strange little cliques in the movie business. It's an industry that attracts strange people and encourages strange behavior." Sansi paused and struggled to focus his thoughts into some kind of theory, some kind of hunch that might make sense to Rohan. To himself.

"My first thought was that the mutilations had to be a kind of message," he continued. "It had to be a gang killing or some kind of ritual murder. But I've never seen the gangs kill like this. I've seen crimes of passion, I've seen dismemberment, decapitation and sexual mutilation before. But not like this. Not with this kind of . . . willful savagery. The more I think about these mutilations—the complete removal of the breasts, the penis, the testicles—the more I know this wasn't an attempt to disguise the victim's identity. This was sexual obliteration. This was done by someone who hates men. All men.

"But . . ." He raised a finger as though to punctuate his thoughts, one by one, "I don't think the murderer was a woman. There's a symbolism here that does not suggest a woman to me. When a woman kills . . . it is personal. She doesn't do it to send a message to the world. A woman might want to castrate an unfaithful lover, but she doesn't do it for pleasure. She does it for spite. It wouldn't occur to her to mutilate the breasts as well. A woman attaches no special significance to male breasts—they mean nothing to her. That's why the sexual signals are so confused here.

"I think this is a different kind of crime from any other we have ever seen. Crimes of passion can take many different forms, Rohan, we both know that. I think this may have been done by a *man* who hates all men. Perhaps by a man who hates himself. Because of the clear sexual nature of the mutilations I think we have to consider a man who is pathologically obsessed . . . by male sexuality. A man who is attracted and repelled by other men, a man who is fascinated and repelled by his own sexual desires.

"I want you to look for signs of homosexual activity, doctor. Can you do that? If you find nothing it will rule out a whole area of investigation for me. But if you find something . . ." His words tapered off into a cold and eerie silence.

Sansi realized that Rohan was staring at him, the usual glimmer of mischief in his eyes replaced by something else, something wary and curious.

"All right," the deputy coroner answered quietly. "I'll look. I might be able to tell you something."

Rohan leaned forward and peered intently into what remained of the gutted abdominal cavity. Much of the small intestine had been removed but there was still a thickly coiled section of large bowel. He poked around in his stainless-steel armory for a moment then selected a long, slender pair of forceps and a scalpel and deftly cut away fifteen inches of the large bowel that reached from the rectal opening to the cecum, the small pouch that marks the beginning of the colon. It only took him a minute and when he had finished he pulled the large intestine out of the corpse and held it up in the light as though it were a dead eel he had fished from a pond. It was a pale yellowish gray and looked like a deflated section of inner tube from a bicycle.

"We'll turn it inside out," Rohan said, "swab the whole thing and see what we can find. But," he paused, "I can tell you something now."

Sansi waited.

"See that distension at the end of the colon, just above the forceps?"

Sansi stared but saw nothing.

"There's quite obvious dilation there," Rohan said. "And a degree of trauma that is quite exceptional for a healthy young man . . . unless there had been recent and quite consistent anal penetration.

"So . . ." He turned and dropped the severed organ into a large kidney dish, where it lay in the clear formalin like a dead reptile. "Your . . . theory may be right, Inspector. This movie star might have been a gay boy."

An hour later Sansi sat in Rohan's office with his feet on the desk and a glass of whiskey in his hand. Rohan was sitting on the other side of the desk wearing an open-necked striped shirt and blue suit trousers, pouring from a half-gallon flagon of Johnnie Walker Red Label. Both men had ditched their protective clothing and scrubbed their hands and faces in strong hospital soap but Sansi still couldn't get rid of the stink of putrefaction that hung like poison gas in the little nooks and crannies at the back of his throat. He took a series of long sips at the whiskey, washed it around the inside of his mouth, then tipped his head back and gargled. It burned like hell and the vapors seared his nasal cavities. He let it run down the back of his throat in a long, scorching stream. It helped, but only a little.

"I want a bath," Sansi grumbled. "I want to get drunk. I think I'll go home and get drunk in the bath."

Rohan offered the mammoth bottle of duty-free Scotch with a droll smile. "Take it all if you want."

Sansi shook his head. "This one frightens me, Doctor. It really frightens me."

"Why?" Rohan looked amused. "Afraid you might have to lock up some of your friends?"

Rohan finally succeeded in making Sansi smile. The deputy coroner knew how much Sansi disliked the society label he sometimes attracted through his mother's social contacts.

"I'm afraid that this is only the start of something," Sansi said.

"It's the start of another investigation, that's all. You'll get your man. You usually do."

"Yes." Sansi nodded. "And some judge usually lets him go."

Rohan shrugged. "You won't have any trouble making this one stick. I'll bet my professional reputation on it. . . . This one is definitely murder."

"You should be sitting on the bench." Sansi smiled again. Either the whiskey or Rohan's relentless irreverence was having an effect.

"You really think there's something so different about this one?"

"Yes," Sansi sighed, "I do. It's not like any other murder I've ever seen. It doesn't fit any kind of pattern. I don't know how to place it. You saw what was done to that man. It wasn't done in a frenzy. It wasn't the thrill of torture. Some of the mutilations were performed after death. It was something more than sadism. It was an act of cold, calculated madness. How do you explain the psychology behind something like that?"

Rohan suddenly swung the conversation off at a tangent. "Did I ever tell you about the body we pulled out of the marsh near Santa Cruz? That bully boy who had been murdered by his drinking cronies? They strangled him, threw acid on him, chopped him up with an axe and threw the pieces in different parts of the marsh. None of that made sense until we found out that it was a bunch of morons who couldn't agree on the best way to get rid of the corpse. So they all had a go at it. Murder by committee. Every one is different. Every one is the same. But it is all . . . murder."

Sansi finished his whiskey, eyed the big bottle for a moment then decided against it. *"Acha,"* he decided. "You're right. There is no point in making this harder than it needs to be. I am letting the psychology of the murderer get to me. That's what he wants. To fill me with such disgust that I won't be able to think straight. Let's get down to business."

Sansi swung his feet off the desk and pulled a small notebook and pen from the breast pocket of his shirt. "Can you give me a time of death yet?"

Rohan pursed his lips. They were shiny with whiskey. "Well," he began, "I can tell you that death occurred ten to fourteen days ago. I will be able to give you something more specific when we have finished our tissue analysis and examined the contents of the stomach. There's just enough in there, rotten as it is, to tell us what he ate and how long before his death he ate it. We will also know if he consumed drugs or alcohol in the period just before his death. Then we can get down to the business of plotting his movements in the hours that led up to his death."

"You're sure he was dumped in the lake soon after he was murdered?"

"Oh yes." Rohan nodded emphatically. "I have no doubts about that. Flies lay their eggs on a body between two and four hours after death has occurred. Maggots hatch and begin feeding on the tissue within twenty-four hours. There was no sign of eggs or maggots anywhere on the body. That suggests he was dumped in the lake within one or two hours of the murder taking place."

"So the murder had to have been committed fairly close to Lake Vihar? Or within an hour or two's drive ... Or," Sansi mused, "somewhere inside Film City."

"Actually," Rohan added confidently, "I would say that is the most likely scenario."

Sansi looked up from his notebook. "Why?"

"Whoever murdered that young man was not worried about spilling a lot of blood," Rohan explained. "Assuming that the murder was premeditated, the murderer would know that cutting a man's throat is a rather messy business. An adult human male holds approximately nine pints of blood. As we both know, that is a lot of blood to be splashed around a single room. This murder was also attended by extensive mutilation of the torso. Indeed, so much blood has been lost from this body that it would seem the mutilations occurred only seconds before the throat was cut and the blood was still circulating. It is almost as though the murderer wanted to drain the body of all its blood in as short a time as possible—as though he took pleasure in the sight of blood and suffering. That suggests to me a number of possibilities, but most importantly that the murder had to have taken place out of doors, where a large spillage of blood could be easily washed away or buried with dirt. I also do not think that anyone would be foolish enough to try and transport a body very far in this condition."

"Why not?"

"Well," Rohan paused, "again, the bloodstains would be enormous; very difficult to hide. The risks of someone noticing something would be too great. Whoever murdered this young man may be insane ... but I don't think he is stupid. There was some method here, some premeditation."

"*Acha,*" Sansi said. "I gave you my theory about the murderer. Now it's your turn."

Rohan smiled faintly.

"I agree with you on a couple of points. I don't think this was a crime of passion or opportunity either. I think it was very coldly planned. I think there was a conspiracy by more than one person to commit this crime. This was a healthy young man, a man at the peak of his physical powers. If he knew he was threatened with death, his strength to resist would have been enormous. I have examined stabbing victims who endured terrible wounds while fighting for their lives: deep and massive cuts, fingers and thumbs cut off ... There is no sign on the body that this man put up any kind of a struggle until after he was restrained. That suggests to me that he was either drugged ... or he was duped into going willingly with his killers, that he did not know what they had in store for him. Then he struggled, as the abra-

sions to his wrists and ankles show, where he was restrained. But by then it was too late."

Sansi valued Rohan's opinion. He listened carefully to
every word.

"You must also remember the multiple lesions in the area
of the buttocks," Rohan continued. "They indicate that the
victim was whipped quite severely before he died. That
makes it almost certain that he was restrained by one person or more before the whipping could take place. *Acha,*
now I will tell you where I digress from your theory. I do
not think you are looking for some kind of mysterious homosexual psychopath here. Most murders are committed for
quite ordinary reasons ... and often by people who are
rather stupid. Murder is the most unnecessary of crimes;
murder is committed by people who cannot solve their
problems by more intelligent means. It is not sophisticated,
Sansi, it is the trademark of the brute. And then, of
course ..." he paused to take a sip of whiskey, "there are
those unfortunate people who are murdered by accident.
How many times in your career have you heard some fool
say 'But I didn't mean to do it'?"

Sansi stifled a small smile. "Something tells me this was
not an accident."

"Well, just hear me out," Rohan gently admonished his
younger colleague. "I think there was some kind of ritual
involved here—and the mutilations were an attempt to
cover it up when it went wrong. This is India. A country
filled with exotic cults and religious sects. We tolerate them
all. We are even a little proud of them. They're part of the
fabric of the place; civilization and barbarism side by side
in living color. We live with them and we get so used to
them we don't even notice them after a while. But the truth
is that many of them have rituals that are primitive,
disgusting ... and quite illegal. You've heard of the Hijdas,
haven't you?"

"Hijdas? The eunuch society?"

"Yes."

A small current rippled through the hairs on the back of

Sansi's neck. Rohan was right. Sansi saw the Hijdas almost every day in the streets of Bombay. So obvious and so . . . invisible. Eunuchs who dressed as women: transsexuals so effeminate, so convincing in their gorgeous saris and jewelry as they skipped between the ranks of cars waiting at traffic lights, clapping their hands, soliciting money, showering good fortune on those who gave and curses on those who didn't. Sansi tried to recall what he had read about the sect's activities.

The Hijdas were one of the most bizarre sects in all of India. A sect so large and so pervasive it had 400,000 followers and was sometimes called the eunuch empire. The empire was divided into 450 districts called *sthans*, with each *sthan* under the control of a guru who exercised the power of life and death over his followers. There were supposed to be about 35,000 Hijdas in Maharashtra alone. Somehow they had endured where other sects had failed. Sects like the Thugs, who worshiped the goddess Kali and preyed on travelers, were wiped out by the British by the middle of the eighteenth century. Yet the Hijdas, who were every bit as brutal as the Thugs, had continued to thrive and prosper and could still be seen on the streets of every big city in India. Their greatest weapons were fear and blackmail. It was their practice to appear uninvited at weddings and christenings and to demand payment for their blessing. No one ever refused—to do so was to invite an unspeakable revenge. Sometime in the future the Hijdas would return to the offending household in the dead of night and steal one of the family's sons. Sansi had seen one report which said as many as forty thousand young males were kidnapped throughout India each year, subjected to ritual castration then forced into beggar servitude by the Hijdas.

Rohan interrupted Sansi's thoughts. "Let me tell you a story." He pulled the flagon of whiskey out from under his desk, topped up their glasses then leaned back in his chair.

"It was many years ago, when I was doing my internship at the hospital in Allahabad. One night a boy of fifteen or sixteen was brought in by his brothers. They told me they

had rescued him from the Hijdas. He had been sexually
mutilated and had lost a lot of blood . . . I had never seen
anything so bad. We were able to save his life but . . . I am
not so sure we did him a favor. He had to learn how to
walk again. I spent a lot of time with that boy in the following weeks. He told me what happens when the Hijdas
get their hands on you.

"He came from a small village outside Allahabad and
they had been waiting for him at the side of the road. They
must have had their eye on him for some time. He was a
very handsome boy, very pretty, I suppose you would say.
They took him to a little hut somewhere in the countryside
and for three or four days they fed him only milk spiked
with opium. He knew what it was: it was so strong he
could taste the opium in the milk. But it was either drink
it or starve. So he was in a stupor much of the time, which
is just as well, when you consider what happened to him.

"One night they carried him out into a clearing where
there was a fire and the guru and the surgeon and all the
other Hijdas in the clan. About four or five of them held
him down while someone tied a leather cord around his testicles and pulled it tight. I suppose that was to stop the flow
of blood to the genitals so the victim didn't bleed to
death—and it also acts as a kind of crude anesthetic.

"Then," Rohan leaned forward, "the Hijdas surgeon produced a large knife and he took hold of the boy's penis and
testicles and he sliced them off in one stroke . . . just like
that." Rohan made a rapid slicing motion with his right
hand and at the same time he let out a sharp hiss of air between his teeth.

Sansi flinched. His scrotum contracted and he felt a sudden queasiness deep in his gut.

"You know what happened then?" Rohan asked.

Sansi wasn't sure he needed to know any more but some
dreadful, morbid compulsion kept him quiet.

"The severed penis tried to get hard."

Sansi felt sick.

"The Hijdas surgeon held it up where everyone could see

it . . . including the boy. And it was twitching and trying to get stiff even though the veins and nerves were all severed and there was no blood to fill it up. Can you imagine that, Sansi? The amputated penis attempts to become erect?"

"Bhagwan," Sansi muttered. "Enough."

"I have talked to my colleagues about it since," Rohan added, his voice clinical and detached. "It is quite a phenomenon, is it not?"

Sansi looked into his glass. The whiskey seemed to have congealed in his stomach.

"They buried the severed genitals in the dirt," Rohan went on. "But it wasn't over for the boy. The eunuch then pushed the small branch of a pipda tree into the wound to make sure that it wouldn't heal shut, so it would form an artificial vagina. The pain is impossible to imagine. Who knows how many boys die from the shock? Then they poured hot oil onto the wound and smeared on some *kathha*, which works as a kind of antiseptic. After that the boy was taken back to his hut while the rest of the Hijdas threw a party and a big feast to celebrate the birth of a new baby—a female.

"I have since learned that there is one more ceremony for those boys who survive. Two months after the initiation the newly castrated novice has to squat, with his rectum spread wide, on the handle of a grinding stone. Two of the Hijdas then keep pushing him down on the handle until blood pours from his anus. According to Hijdas lore this represents the novice's first menstrual period and he, or she, or it, is finally a full member of the sect."

Sansi took a deep breath and shook his head in an effort to clear away the dreadful images.

"Colorful little group, aren't they?" Rohan commented drily. "Just the kind of thing for the tourists."

Sansi nodded, still not really thinking. "You think that's what happened here?" he asked after a while. "A bungled Hijdas ceremony?"

Rohan shrugged. "I can't think of anything else that would fit the pattern of mutilation so closely. How many boys disappear in Bombay each year? Hundreds? Thousands? How many of them are taken by the Hijdas? There is no way of knowing, is there?"

The deputy coroner took another sip of whiskey. "My guess is that this was a botched initiation. This young man was intended to be a Hijdas novice but something went wrong. He didn't survive the initiation and they had to get rid of the body."

"What about the marks on his buttocks?" Sansi asked. "Where do they fit in?"

"I don't know," Rohan answered candidly. "There is an explanation, obviously. It may not make any sense to us but then it doesn't have to. It only has to make sense to the killers."

Sansi looked doubtful. "How would the Hijdas get access to Lake Vihar or Film City?"

"Bribery," Rohan answered glibly. "They must have plenty of money. All it takes is a few thousand rupees for some security guard to look the other way and the Hijdas could walk in there one evening and do what they liked. Film City is a big place, I believe. I know Vihar is still open country. There are hundreds of acres out there where they could hide."

"Why did they dump the body in the lake?"

"That is what adds extra weight to my theory," Rohan smiled. "The torture and mutilation obviously involved some time and preparation, which would support my idea about a ritual. Yet the disposal of the body was very badly thought out—quite amateurish. Disposing of the body is often the most difficult part of the murder. Human bodies are very awkward things to get rid of. That is why the murderer who has given the matter any thought at all knows that the best way to get rid of a body is to obliterate it: burn it, dismember it, boil it, dissolve it, feed it to animals, do anything but leave it lying around where it can be found. When you cannot find the body, all you really have is a missing person. A good lawyer can get you off very easily. As you know yourself, the police won't even bother to lay charges unless there is a body, because all the evidence is purely circumstantial. That is why I am sure that this was a murder committed by fools. Malicious amateurs. Exactly the type of people who belong to the more peculiar sects. Because the best way to make sure that a body will come back to haunt you is to throw it in a lake."

Sansi listened, glad to be back on familiar territory.

"It doesn't matter what you use to weigh a body down," Rohan continued, "if you throw it into water, sooner or later it is going to pop up again and point a finger at you."

"How can you be so sure?"

"Simple physics," Rohan explained. "When a body starts to decompose, it generates internal gases. Hydrogen sulphide, principally. You smelled it downstairs. The amount of gas an adult corpse can generate during decomposition is much greater than most people realize. Human intestines are quite large. Two cubic feet of hydrogen sulphide gas is quite enough to float 187 pounds of dead weight to the surface."

"Why 187 pounds?"

"That is what our movie star weighed. I told you, he was a big strong boy."

"And two cubic feet of gas would float that weight to the surface?"

"It did, didn't it?"

"How much did the chain weigh?"

"Only another twenty pounds. It is a very common type of steel-link industrial chain, by the way. The kind used in hoists and cranes. I would imagine there is a lot of it at Film City to move scenery and equipment."

"So whoever dumped the body in the lake intended it to stay down for a while."

"Forever, I imagine."

"Good." Sansi nodded. "That means he might tell us a little more yet about who killed him."

"Talk to the guards at Film City," Rohan said. "I'm sure they're all on the take. One of them will crack if you apply enough pressure."

Sansi didn't mention what his boss, Jamal, had told him about Noshir Kilachand and what directions his own instincts might take him. He didn't like to remind Rohan who was the detective. Sometimes the deputy coroner's ideas were right.

"But not—"

"I'm sorry?"

"Oh, just thinking out loud," Sansi said. He looked into his empty glass. He had drunk two large glasses of Scotch and he felt nothing. No warm, comforting fire in his belly, no welcome blurring of the senses. All he felt was cold and numb.

"There is no other country on earth where a conversation like this could even take place," he added. "Here, when a policeman has to investigate a murder, he not only has to look at all the usual motives like greed and jealousy and revenge and madness—he has to take into very serious consideration the possibility that it could have been committed by agents of . . . an illegal eunuch empire. It's crazy. It defies all logic. Yet the logical mind has to come to grips with it. Because this is India. And anything—absolutely anything—can happen in India."

7

MOLLAJI THE *KULI* was going to be rich.

He could tell from the look in the American lady's eyes. At last he had found somebody who believed him.

Annie Ginnaro had spent more than two hours grilling the little corpse-collector in a farcical blend of Hindi and pidgin English about the body he had pulled from Lake Vihar. She had gone over the story with him half a dozen times and he had never strayed from the central facts. The body had been so badly mutilated it was impossible to tell whether it was male or female. Whoever it was had to be important because there were many bigwigs at the scene, bigwigs from the police and from Film City. She had smiled at his easy use of such a peculiar word as bigwig. It was an archaic English word only Indians used to describe anyone in authority and it appeared often in the country's leading newspapers. But what really convinced her that he was telling the truth was when he mentioned that the most important police officer at the scene had blue eyes.

So that was where Sansi had been the day before. That was the body he had been talking about. If the mutilations were even half as bad as the *kuli* had described it was no wonder Sansi had been so subdued. And she had prattled on about his Paul Newman eyes, which was something she had never done with any man. Her cheeks flushed with embarrassment at the recollection. He had probably already written her off as a bimbo. In the short term it didn't matter. She would make him change his opinion of her.

She focused her mind back on Mollaji's descriptions of the other high officials who were at the lakeside. The tall long-haired man with the glasses was almost certainly Noshir Kilachand, the managing director of the Maharashtra Film, Stage and Cultural Development Corporation, which managed Film City. Mollaji was right. It was all rather unusual. Obviously it wasn't just anybody he had fished out of the lake.

At first she had resented the fact that it was she who had been sent down to talk to some *kuli* in the lobby who insisted he had a story. That was the kind of stuff reserved for juniors. But she had swallowed her pride and treated it as part of the dues-paying process that a foreigner had to go through. Now she was glad. She had a story. This guy could have his fifteen bucks. Or his two hundred rupees, which was probably a month's wages to him. An honest-to-goodness, old-fashioned exclusive would demolish the popular newsroom perception of her as some influential American dilettante, but she knew she would have to move fast to beat leaks from other sources. If the *kuli* was here in the *Times* building selling his hot tip, there were probably half a dozen bent cops with the same information trying to do exactly the same thing at exactly the same moment elsewhere in the city.

"What about my money, memsahib?" Mollaji asked plaintively. He was now at his most vulnerable. He had told her everything he knew and, if she wanted, she could have him thrown out without paying a penny and he would have to try his luck somewhere else. But she had promised him. If the information was good, she said, she would see that he got paid. And he had seen the look in her eyes. The look that said she was onto something. All they had to do now was agree on the price.

Annie grinned openly at his exaggerated discomfiture. She loved bargaining with these guys. It was one of the best free shows in India.

"All right," she said. "Fifty rupees—on condition that you don't take this to any other newspaper or TV station, anywhere. Twenty now, the rest tomorrow when the paper comes out and I don't see the story anywhere else."

"*Are Bapre!* You tell me you pay top price," he wheedled in dreadful English. "You pay top dollar. This is not top dollar. Five hundred rupees best money. All now."

"What?" Annie looked shocked. "You must be dreaming. Nobody pays five hundred rupees for anything in this city. What do you think you're selling—state secrets?"

Mollaji didn't understand, but he got her meaning. He rolled his eyes to the ceiling and tilted his head to one side. His lips writhed like worms across his betel-stained teeth and he contorted his whole face into an anguished mask of betrayal.

"You try to cheat me," he moaned. "You are rich lady. I am poor man. I have nothing. I work hard. Now you try to cheat me. Four hundred rupee. Give me four hundred rupee. Last price."

Annie looked offended. She shook her head, enjoying herself.

"No way, Jos ... ah, never mind. No four hundred rupees. One hundred rupees. Absolutely my last price. Fifty now, fifty tomorrow—if you keep your word. There's nothing to stop you going around to the *Express* right now and selling the same story twice."

Mollaji looked wounded, as though the thought had never crossed his mind. "Oh no, memsahib," he protested. "I am honest man, memsahib. You pay me, I give my word to you, I go straight home. No more sell tonight."

Annie looked bored.

"Please, memsahib ..."

She looked through the window of the cubicle at the busy newsroom on the other side of the glass and tried to stifle a smile. This guy was a better actor than Bobby De Niro. And twice as much fun. Forget Lee Strasberg. There was nothing quite like begging for survival to instill a real feeling for the Method. Nobody could do Abject Misery or Despair quite like a Bombay *kuli*.

"Three hundred rupees, memsahib. Two hundred tonight.

One hundred tomorrow. I am a poor man, I have wife and eleven children. Four baby. We have no food since yesterday. No food . . . baby die soon, memsahib. Please, memsahib. You no want my babies to die?"

His eyes grew bigger and even more beseeching as he pleaded with her. Annie had often wondered how they did that. If she could learn how to do it she would save a fortune in eyeliner.

She decided it was time to relent. She couldn't live with herself as a child murderer. "All right," she said. "I'll go to two hundred. That's as high as the paper will go: for you, for anybody. One hundred tonight. One hundred tomorrow. You don't like it, you walk out of here right now."

Mollaji stared at her as though she had just personally cut the throats of all eleven of his nonexistent children. "Ahh, *Bhagwan*," he grumbled and gave the resigned shrug of a man who had been beaten by a merciless opponent. He looked wretched. Inside, he wanted to dance. Two hundred rupees! With the few hundred he had saved and the money he would get from the sale of his cart it should be enough for a down payment on a motor rickshaw. Perhaps he would get a soft job ferrying passengers to and from Sahar Airport after all.

"Acha," Annie said. "Wait here." She opened the door of the tiny glass cubicle and left Mollaji alone.

He watched her as she walked across the busy newspaper office. She wore a pale blouse and cream colored slacks and she had a provocative way of swinging her hips as she threaded between the busy desks. Mollaji had found it difficult to speak to her at first. She was so lovely and fair and she smelled of a perfume that made his head feel light. He had never been so close to such a beautiful woman for so long before, especially not an American woman. Her hair was the color of polished copper and he had been fascinated by the light sprinkling of freckles on her face and arms. Western women were different, as he had heard. It wasn't just the color of the skin and the fact that they were higher born than any Indian. It was the way they carried themselves. This woman, who said her name was An-nee, had a confidence and a directness he had never seen in any Indian woman. And yet she looked so delicate on the outside. What a strange, wonderful place the West must be if it was full of women like her, Mollaji thought.

He lost sight of her momentarily in the bustle of bodies then found her again, almost on the other side of the room, talking to a fat middle-aged man wearing a white shirt. He was sitting at a desk and looked important. The man glanced over at Mollaji, exchanged a few words with Annie, frowned and then nodded. Then Annie vanished. She reappeared suddenly at the door of the cubicle a few minutes later and handed Mollaji five twenty-rupee notes.

"The rest tomorrow—if the story doesn't appear anywhere else," she warned. "Okay?"

Mollaji took the money and nodded. She waited while he checked it, an amused look on her face. Indians were fussy about their money. If a note was torn or spoiled they would reject it as though they had been personally insulted. Annie had once had a ten-rupee note, worth about seventy cents American, thrown back at her by a legless man because it was dirty and had a corner missing.

"*Acha.*" Mollaji got up, folded the notes into a tight wad and tucked them into the only pocket on his shirt that still had a button. "I will be back in the morning, memsahib," he promised. "You will see. I am an honest man. If there is any other information . . . ?"

"If your information is good you can come back and see me," she interrupted him. "If it's all lies, you had better not show your face around here ever again. Understand?"

It sounded harsh, even to Annie, but she had learned that sharpness was the only way to cut through all the bullshit in India. Either you went through it or you went under, trampled underfoot by the ravening hordes who saw every Westerner as a purse on legs. She led the little *kuli* out of the newsroom, back to the elevators, and left him in the care of three Sikh security guards. Then she walked back to her desk, a smile of anticipation on her face.

Sylvester Naryan, the night editor, had not been pleased when Annie told him how much she wanted to pay the *kuli* but he had relented when she promised to pay it back herself if the tip was no good. Two hundred rupees was a lot of money to a *kuli*, she knew, but it was still only fifteen bucks to her. And it was worth ten times that if it got her a byline on a front-page story that would be picked up throughout India. Annie Ginnaro figured her self-esteem was worth at least fifteen dollars. And it would give her a good excuse to call George Sansi without going through his mother.

When she had first heard that Pramila had a single, grown-up son still living with her, Annie had assumed he was either gay or some kind of sissy. Now that she had met him she had concluded that he was neither. He was by far the most interesting man she had met so far in Bombay. And she was determined to know more about him.

Downstairs, Mollaji slipped out of the *Times* building and into the sultry Bombay night. The sidewalks were still packed with people—buying, selling, haggling, begging, looking, stealing. He set off in the direction of Dimtimkar Road and after a few yards he finally relaxed and let a slow, satisfied smile creep across his angular black face. A hundred rupees in his pocket and another hundred to come in the morning. Death had been kind to him these past few days.

His mind turned to the beautiful American lady reporter and he found himself wondering how she would look without clothes. He thought of the fairness of her skin and what her breasts must look like and he thought of her red hair and wondered if her pubic hair was just as red. And gradually, the warm coals of desire that she had rekindled in his loins began to smolder anew. He knew what he would do. It would only cost three or four rupees—and he deserved a little celebration. He would stop at one of the brothels on the way home and buy himself an hour with a *randi*. He wondered if he could find one who dyed her hair red. The smile on his face broadened and he quickened his pace. A few passersby stared at him, wondering how such a scrawny, ragged beggar could look so happy. Mollaji didn't mind. In Bombay the dreams of even the poorest man could come true.

In the *Times* newsroom, Annie sat down at her desk, plucked a cigarette from a packet of Kents and began searching through the directory for Noshir Kilachand's home telephone number. After a few rings a woman answered the phone. Annie swore silently to herself. She had hoped Kilachand would answer the phone personally. She didn't want to be put off by some overprotective wife, daughter or *bai*.

"This is Annie Ginnaro from the *Times of India*," she began. "May I speak with Mr. Kilachand, please?"

"I am sorry. . . ." the woman answered. Annie's heart sank. "Mr. Kilachand isn't here at the moment. Would you like to leave a message?"

It was the easy way to avoid an unwanted call from a snoopy reporter. Annie looked at the clock on the wall. It was nearly nine-thirty. Deadline for the first edition was ten-thirty.

"Who am I speaking to, please?" Annie asked. She needed to pitch her next line just right to have the best chance of forcing Kilachand to get back to her. If it was a member of Kilachand's family and he was home he might at least get the message intact and there was a chance that his anxieties would manipulate him into returning the call. If it was the *bai* she might attempt to protect her employer by not passing on the message at all this late in the evening.

Annie waited.

"This is Mrs. Kilachand speaking." She sounded wary.

Annie was careful to compose her next few words to contain just the right mixture of threat and politesse. "I wonder, Mrs. Kilachand, if you could ask your husband to call me back, please. It is most urgent that I speak to him this evening. It concerns a matter of great . . . political importance. To your husband and the film corporation."

There was another pause at the other end. "Yes," the woman said at last. "I'll tell him."

"Thank you Mrs. Kilachand, I appreciate your help." Annie gave the number for her direct line and hung up. She plucked her cigarette out of the ashtray, inhaled, toyed with it for a moment, then put it down and began picking at the keyboard of her word processor. The first few words of her story filed across the screen in glowing green letters: *The mutilated body of a famous movie star has been recovered from the waters of Lake Vihar, north of Bombay . . .*

Annie read it and frowned. It didn't look right. She moved the cursor back and struck out *famous*. Suddenly it no longer seemed so important.

"Shit," she swore. If only she had more information.

The phone at her elbow rang. She picked it up.

"Miss Ginnaro?" a voice asked in slightly accented English.

"Yes?"

"This is Noshir Kilachand. I understand you have something important you need to discuss with me."

He had been there all the time. Probably expecting a call all night, she realized. Ego, curiosity, the need to try and exercise some damage control, maybe just wanting to find out how much she knew—whatever it was, it was enough to make him call her. She smiled. He had probably gone over his spiel a dozen times tonight already.

Annie tried her most disarming tone. "Thank you for getting back to me so quickly, sir." She plugged her tape recorder into the phone and switched it on. "We are running a report in tomorrow's paper about a body that was recovered from Lake Vihar yesterday. We have information confirming that it is one of your employees at Film City."

She wanted to hit Kilachand as hard as she could, to blend just the right amount of fact and rumor. The more he thought she knew, the better. At the same time she was letting him know that a newspaper report was now inevitable and it might be in his best interests to make an early statement. She waited for what seemed like a long time.

"Are you still there, Mr. Kilachand?"

"Yes," he answered.

She thought he sounded scared. Good. She waited.

"Are you an American, Miss Ginnaro?"

Annie sighed. He was going to try and snow her. Maybe threaten to go over her head.

"Yes I am," she answered brightly.

"And where are you from in the United States?" he asked.

"California," she said. "L.A."

"Yes," he drawled. "I know it well. I have been there many times, visiting some of the big studios there, you understand. I have many close friends in Hollywood."

Go ahead, Annie thought to herself. Try and impress me. "Yes," she answered. "So I believe." She would let him worry about what that meant.

"Forgive me for asking, Miss Ginnaro. I did not know there were any Americans working for the *Times of India*."

"The newspaper has employees of several different nationalities, sir." Make him feel like a bigot, she thought. That might shake him.

"Miss Ginnaro . . ." He tried a new approach. "I would not wish to influence you in the presentation of your report, but I can't help wondering how familiar you are with the history of the corporation. . . ."

"I'm a news reporter, sir. I've been a news reporter for ten years . . . and I've been working in Bombay for one year." She was only stretching the truth by about nine months. "This is a straightforward news report. All I need is confirmation that this is one of your people."

That ought to do it, she thought. Force the bastard to be unreasonable, if that was what he wanted. That alone would tell her something.

There was another long pause.

"This is a matter of some sensitivity, Miss Ginnaro. You must understand. The police are involved. I would not like to prejudice an investigation. We do not have the same freewheeling attitude to police investigations that you have in California."

"Oh, I'm well aware of all government restrictions on the media here," she answered breezily. "And my report will be within media guidelines, Mr. Kilachand, I can assure you."

"Yes," he answered, unconvinced.

At least he ought to know now that she wasn't afraid of him. If he thought he could pressure her into backing off, he had been wrong. She decided it was time to increase the pressure on him. He was the one who had the most to lose—not her.

"When a public figure is murdered, Mr. Kilachand, it is a matter of public interest. I can appreciate your concerns, but I am sure you understand that for the film corporation—for any government department—to try and cover up . . ."

"There is no question of anyone trying to cover up anything," Kilachand interrupted.

She thought he sounded testy. Good. She was getting to him. "Then you wouldn't mind confirming that the body pulled from Lake Vihar was someone from Film City?"

"I'm sorry," he said, "I cannot confirm that."

"Do you deny that the body was someone from Film City?"

"No, no, of course not," Kilachand blustered. "I cannot confirm or deny anything. There are a great many employees at Film City, Miss Ginnaro. Permanent and casual. You must know that. Most of them are under contract to independent film companies. We provide many services to the companies, at a cost, but our only permanent employees are those who are actually responsible for the management and maintenance of the complex. If this was someone who has worked at Film City on a regular basis, then we would be very upset. We are simply waiting for the police to provide positive identification. Naturally, we shall cooperate fully with the police and we will not do anything without their approval in case it should interfere with their investigation or cause distress to the relatives of the deceased. You ought to bear that in mind when you write your report, Miss Ginnaro. There are reasons for our laws governing the media in this country, reasons of taste and discretion."

You pompous ass, Annie thought. She had decided that Kilachand was the kind of smug bureaucrat who loved to manipulate the media when it suited him but scurried for the refuge of the high moral ground when the spotlight became a little too hot.

"Sir, you cannot deny that someone from Film City has been murdered, can you?"

Kilachand sighed. He knew what she was doing. It was what was sometimes called "The Fairy Argument." If you cannot prove that fairies do not exist then you have to admit to the possibility that they might exist. And that was enough for some newspapers to run with. Kilachand wished he had not called back.

"Miss Ginnaro, I think you are going to write a sensational report whatever I say."

"The body of a famous movie star is found in—"

"I do not think it is anyone famous, Miss Ginnaro."

"How do you know it is no one famous when you don't know the identity of the corpse?" she asked.

"We have already established that none of our major players is missing," Kilachand answered wearily. "It could be anyone. A workman, a cameraman, an extra—anyone. It doesn't have to be a . . . a big star."

She played her trump card. "Do you know why the body was so badly mutilated, Mr. Kilachand?"

She heard a sharp intake of breath on the other end of the line.

"Please, Miss Ginnaro, think of the victim's family. I do not wish to go over your head but if you—"

"We won't be describing the nature of the mutilations," Annie reassured him. She had to give him something. "But we will be sticking to the broad facts. When someone from Film City is murdered, whoever it may be, that's news. It will come out sooner or later. You must understand that."

She was only partially bluffing. Bombay thrived on gossip. Kilachand would have to know that a secret such as this could not remain a secret for long.

"All right," he conceded. "But please do one thing for me. I would ask that you include in your report that the management of Film City is cooperating fully with the police investigation ... and that our sympathies go to the family of the victim."

"Whoever it may be?" Annie added. She had him and he knew it. Kilachand either knew the identity of the victim or he had a damn good idea and he had to have a powerful reason for keeping it a secret. It might well be that the police had asked him to keep quiet ... or it might be because he had something to hide. Annie could feel it. She was scratching at the surface of something big. Something big enough to rattle a state-appointed movie mogul like Noshir Kilachand. Kilachand might come from a high caste and he might be a real power in the safe, bureaucratic world of memos and committees and lobbies and procedural guidelines, which he could manipulate to his advantage—but murder was something else. Murder was messy. Blood had been shed and some of it had splashed on his shoes. There was scandal here, she knew. A genuine whiff of scandal and corruption that could keep her byline on the front page for months if she played it properly.

"Good night, Miss Ginnaro," Kilachand said. There was a note of defeat in his voice.

The guy had to be under immense pressure, she realized. And from the pictures she had seen of him he looked like such a gentle, trustworthy, fatherly type. Then why didn't she feel sorry for him? she wondered.

The phone went dead in her ear. She switched off the tape recorder and walked over to Sylvester Naryan, night editor of the *Times*.

"I've got it from Kilachand," she said. "Confirmed."

Naryan's eyebrows shot up. "Name?"

"No name."

Naryan gave her a look of amused scorn.

"Nobody knows who it is yet," she protested. "The body was badly cut up. Boobs gone, crotch gone. Real Jack the Ripper stuff. And the face was half eaten away. The *kuli* says it was a mess."

"What does Kilachand say?"

"He says it isn't one of their big names—that in itself tells me something."

"You can't put an implication in your story."

"He knows who it is, I'm sure of it. It's somebody from Film City. Otherwise, why was he down there? We can place him at the scene. I can make a good case that this is somebody important, otherwise guys like Kilachand wouldn't be worried. Somebody like him wouldn't even be involved unless he was worried."

"He's got a lot to be worried about," Naryan agreed. Kilachand's name had hardly been out of the newspapers in the previous year. He seemed to be always involved in some dispute, some power play between government departments or between the corporation and some film company. And yet he always presented the image of the imperturbable gentleman, the gentle intellectual who was only trying to do what was right for the arts in Maharashtra.

"Write it," Naryan decided. "I'll take a look at it. Make it as strong as you can. The front page doesn't go until eleven-thirty."

Annie hurried back to her desk.

Naryan turned and called for a copyboy. "Get me the picture file on Noshir Kilachand," he ordered.

Annie sat down at her word processor, lit a fresh cigarette and typed out a new introduction to her story: *Mystery surrounds the discovery of a mutilated body believed to be that of a major personality in the Bombay film world.*

She read it back and smiled to herself. That was better. That would cause a stir when it hit the streets in the morning.

8

"*BAHENCHOD!*" IT MEANT sister fucker and it was the filthiest curse in the police vocabulary.

Inspector Sansi's driver had just crashed into a chariot. A chariot made of gold. And the chariot had come off much worse than the police car: it lay drunkenly on its side in the parking lot, one wheel broken, the other spinning uselessly in the air. A chunk of gold had broken off and lay on the ground, revealing a few papier-mâché fronds. Sansi was grateful that no one had been driving the chariot at the time of the collision. His driver, a small, thin man called Khalia, got out of the car, muttering wickedly under his breath. Sansi followed him. They had only just arrived at Film City and things had got off to a bad start.

It was another jarringly sunny morning. The relief of the monsoon was still nowhere in sight. The security guards had waved the police car through at the main gate and they had driven along an avenue of spiky-leaved ashoka trees to the administration block.

In many ways, Film City was a perfect metaphor for Bombay. From a distance it looked exquisite: a bright, shining oasis in a sea of burned browns. The carefully tended lawns, the coconut palms, the flame-red blossoms of the gulmorh trees and the yellow and white flowers of the frangipani bushes gave an impression of lushness and beauty. Up close it looked like a park in Beirut. Bald, patchy lawns, rubbish strewn among the flowers and buildings that looked like ruins. In the midst of one threadbare lawn some lunatic landscape artist had created a blaze of surrealism in the form of a rockpile painted blue. The road curled left into a parking lot facing a studio the size and shape of an airplane hangar. It was here that Khalia, disoriented by his surroundings, had crashed into a . . . a what? A phalanx of chariots? There were three of them in a row, arranged neatly between the yellow lines.

Sansi bent down and picked up a piece of gold. It felt like balsa and some of the gold rubbed off on his fingers. A prop, he realized. He had just demolished one of their props.

"Don't worry, Inspector. It is nothing. They shouldn't have been left out here. I will speak to whoever is responsible."

Sansi looked up to see Pratap Coyarjee, the studio manager of Film City, hurrying toward him from the administration building on the far side of the parking lot. Coyarjee was the man who had accompanied Kilachand to Lake Vihar when they had retrieved the body. Sansi found himself staring. The studio manager was wearing a purple paisley shirt outside a pair of canary-yellow trousers and looked like he had just been beamed in by time warp from a 1970s disco party. What was left of his hair was worn long and arranged like a meringue on top of his head, where it was held in place by half a quart of gel. As usual he was armor plated with cheap jewelry and when the sun caught him at the right angle it was like being dazzled by a mirror.

Sansi squinted painfully at him and nodded.

"Mr. Kilachand is running late," Coyarjee explained, "but he telephoned to say he will be here soon."

Sansi was not entirely surprised. He had seen that morning's edition of the *Times of India* and the front-page story by Annie Ginnaro. So much for keeping a lid on the investigation. He had decided to call Miss Ginnaro later.

Coyarjee led Sansi and his driver down a slight slope toward the administration building. The glass doors parted automatically and they stepped into a large, airy vestibule with a reception desk on the right manned by three more

security guards. Sansi left Khalia to exchange insights with
the guards and followed Coyarjee to a door marked "Production Controller." They went inside without knocking and
were met by the sight of a man in a pale blue polyester safari suit sitting behind an empty desk with a telephone in
his left hand and most of his right hand up his nose.
Coyarjee glared but the man appeared not to notice. He
went on picking his nose and grunting into the phone.

Coyarjee put on a brave face and gestured to one of two
chairs in front of the desk.

"Would you like some *chai*?" he asked.

Sansi eyed the man picking his nose and shook his head.
Coyarjee looked uncomfortable. He sat down on the edge
of the empty chair and leaned forward with one arm on the
desk in an attempt to screen the nose picker from Sansi's
view. It didn't work.

Sansi glanced around the office. It was bare except for
the desk, chairs and telephone. There wasn't even a calendar on the cement walls. Sansi's eyes drifted back to the
production controller. He was the only entertainment in the
room. The more Sansi watched, the more his fascination
deepened. Like all policemen, Sansi was a student of the
morbid in human nature, even the mildly morbid. And he
had never seen a man with such an unabashed interest in
the archeology of his own nose. He was bereft of all self-
consciousness.

The usual reaction for someone caught picking his
nose would be to desist immediately to slink away looking sheepish and resentful, as though he had been caught
masturbating. Not this man. He appeared utterly unaware
that what he was doing was both offensive and disgusting. Either that or he didn't care. Sansi concluded that
the production controller at Film City was an exceptionally well-adjusted nose picker. As far as he was concerned, his two guests might as well have been invisible.

The minutes ticked by with excrutiating slowness. Sansi
glanced at Coyarjee. The studio manager shrugged and

looked helpless. At last there was a knock at the door. Coyarjee leapt from his seat.

"Mr. Kilachand is coming now, sahib," a security guard said.

"Please?" Coyarjee gestured to Sansi that he might like to leave. Sansi got to his feet.

The production controller appeared to notice him for the first time. "Excuse me, please," he said to the person on the other end of the phone; then he stood up and offered Sansi his tainted hand. "Welcome to Film City. We are happy to have you as our guest today."

Sansi looked at the man for a moment, then put his hands in his trouser pockets, turned and walked outside.

The production controller watched him go, appalled at such rudeness. He glanced at Coyarjee, shrugged, then sat down and went back to grunting and picking.

There was a black Contessa at the front of the building and, either because of his height or because of the car's poor design, Noshir Kilachand was having difficulty uncoiling himself from the back seat. Sansi smiled at the burdens of high office. The luxury sedan, made by the Hindustan motor company, was notorious for its discomfort.

"Hello again, Inspector," Kilachand said. He was carrying a battered Samsonite briefcase and he looked tired.

They shook hands and walked back inside the building.

"Have you got somewhere quiet where we can talk?" the Film City mogul asked Coyarjee.

"I think we should use my office," Coyarjee volunteered.

Kilachand nodded. "Is Mehrotra in today?" he asked.

"Yes," Coyarjee answered. "He knows we are here."

Sansi assumed Mehrotra was the production controller.

"Have you met our Mr. Mehrotra yet?" Kilachand asked, making conversation.

Sansi nodded.

"Did he . . . ?" Kilachand vaguely gestured in the direction of his nose with his right forefinger.

"He never stopped," Coyarjee interrupted.

Kilachand shook his head. "Disgusting man," he murmured softly. Then he looked at Sansi. "I agree in principle with the policy of promoting the lower castes but there are times when I wish they would watch their manners a little more closely before they are put into positions of responsibility. Perhaps what we need is a Shudra finishing school, eh, Inspector? What do you think of that as another efficient way of wasting the taxpayer's money?"

Sansi smiled. It would be easy to be charmed by Kilachand. Film City's chief executive had a reputation as a superb manipulator.

"Well," Kilachand added with the sigh of a man resigned to yet another onerous chore. "We'd better be getting on with it, I suppose."

Coyarjee led them almost to the opposite end of the building to an office marked "Studio Manager." Sansi followed Kilachand inside and glanced around. The office was small and grim although Coyarjee had attempted to brighten it up. There was a mauve shag rug on the floor, brightly colored cushions on the ugly metal chairs, a vase filled with chrysanthemums on the desk, and a couple of flow charts on the walls which showed various projects at different stages of production. What held Sansi's eye was the wall behind Coyarjee's desk. It was covered with photographs of Pratap Coyarjee with the biggest stars from the last three decades of the Indian cinema. Some of the pictures had been taken on movie sets, some at parties and awards ceremonies. There were no photographs of Coyarjee with women.

The studio manager fussed around for a moment until his guests were seated, then left to arrange for some tea, whether Sansi wanted it or not. Sansi wondered if Coyarjee was always this restless or was unusually nervous about the meeting.

"Have you been able to identify the victim yet, Inspector?" Kilachand seemed determined to take the initiative.

Sansi shook his head. "The victim is a young adult male," he said. "That's about all we can tell for the moment. We have more work to do." Sansi intended to conserve what little information he had until he could use it to the best advantage. "We still need to go through your lists to see who is missing."

Kilachand nodded and opened his briefcase. The lid sprang open and the mound of papers inside seemed to expand slowly upward with relief. Kilachand plucked two sheets of paper from the top of the pile and handed one to Sansi. There were two columns of type on each page. The column down the left-hand side of the paper was a list of names. Sansi counted them quickly. There were twenty-eight. The column on the right was shorter. It appeared to be a list of film titles and production companies. They both fell silent. Coyarjee returned, sat down behind his desk and crossed his legs in a way that seemed particularly effeminate.

"The names on the left are actors and other former employees from the past six months whose whereabouts are not immediately known," Kilachand said.

"And the names on the right?" Sansi asked.

"They are the films either currently in production, or recently completed, and the names of companies which have bought studio time at Film City during the past six months. Almost all of them are in the post-production stage and the actors have moved on. It isn't too difficult to find out where they are. Most of them go straight from one picture to another, as you would be aware. But it will take a little time."

"How long?"

"A few days," Kilachand answered, eyeing Sansi congenially through his tortoiseshell glasses. "Only one production has been going on longer than six months," Kilachand went on. "And that is *Chanakya*, a major new drama series for television, which is to follow on the success of *Mahabharata*."

Sansi nodded. The epic poem of the *Mahabharata*, the story of two ancient feuding families, had been turned into a popular TV soap opera that consumed fifty-two hours of airtime, and ran in weekly episodes for a year.

"*Chanakya* has been in production for seven months," Kilachand continued. "Shooting is expected to continue for another month and a half, I think. When it is finished it will have fifty-two hour-long episodes, just like *Mahabharata*. And like *Mahabharata* it has a very large cast."

Sansi nodded. "Is that all?"

"Everything but the commercials."

"Commercials?"

"Anybody can buy studio time at Film City, Inspector. If you wished, you could use our sets, our film-editing equipment, our sound-recording, mixing and post-production facilities and our staff to help you shoot your home movies. It only costs two thousand rupees a day. It isn't very much at all compared to studio time in France, Britain, Italy or the U.S.A., I can assure you. The advertising agencies use us all the time to shoot commercials. They are one of our greatest sources of income."

"I'll also need a list of which commercials have been shot here in the past six months," Sansi said.

"*Are Bapre,*" Coyarjee huffed.

"And if we have to we'll go back a year or more," Sansi added.

"Coyarjee will be happy to make up a list for you," Kilachand said.

Sansi didn't think Coyarjee looked at all happy.

"There must have been twenty or thirty commercials shot here in the past month," the studio manager protested. "Sometimes we get two or three a day. They book at very short notice too, often only a few days in advance. We have 360 acres of sets, Inspector, so we can usually fit them in somewhere. I could get you a list, I suppose, but I couldn't tell you who they had on their sets. They invite all sorts of people, you know, agency people, all their friends and hangers-on. They can be quite a nuisance."

"I'm sure," Sansi answered unsympathetically.

Coyarjee frowned and patted the gelled helmet on his head. "All right," he sulked like a resentful child. "I'll see what I can do."

"Before the end of the week," Sansi added helpfully.

Coyarjee scowled but said nothing.

There was a knock at the door and the *chai* arrived. Sansi accepted a small white china cup and swallowed half the sweet milky mixture in a single sip. Kilachand ignored his tea while Coyarjee sipped delicately and avoided eye contact with either of them.

"This column of names on the left," Sansi resumed. "Are these people who have left Bombay or have you no idea where they are at all?"

"Both," Kilachand said. "We'll find out more in time but it's the best we have been able to do at such short notice. I was hoping you might be able to tell us something, Inspector. Fingerprints or something?"

Sansi gave him a bleak smile. "You saw the body."

Kilachand gave an involuntary shiver.

"Fingerprints will only help us if the victim had a police record," Sansi added. "With dental records we should be able to make a positive identification. But it would help us now if we had some idea who it is most likely to be. To do that we have to consider everyone who has worked here for the past six months. Simple police work, gentlemen. Very routine. Very boring."

"Don't you have any . . . ideas?" Coyarjee asked.

"A few," Sansi answered. "But I am not inclined to discuss them openly because secrets have a way of getting out. . . ."

He let the sentence hang and Kilachand looked uncomfortable. He knew Sansi must have seen the morning paper.

"It was a mistake to speak to the press—" he began.

"I wouldn't make a habit of it." Sansi cut him off. "It isn't only because the press will make a nuisance of themselves. We have to expect that. But I don't want to assist the murderer by letting him know which direction the investigation will take. Nor do I want to jeopardize our chances of securing a conviction when the case goes to trial."

Kilachand nodded and looked miserable.

"You think it will go to trial?" Coyarjee asked.

"Why shouldn't it?" Sansi looked squarely into the studio manager's eyes.

Coyarjee shifted uncomfortably in his chair. "I . . . it seems you . . . we have so little to go on," he blustered.

"This is only the beginning, Mr. Coyarjee."

The studio manager fell silent and looked away.

"I hope I didn't do anything wrong by talking to that woman from the *Times of India*," Kilachand said, trying to regain control of the conversation. "She called me at my home last night. She already seemed to know so much."

Sansi switched his gaze back to Kilachand. Nice try, he thought. The Film City boss seemed genuinely anxious that he might have transgressed. Murder investigations had a way of inspiring paranoia in anyone who thought he might be a suspect, innocent or guilty. But Sansi remembered what his boss Jamal had said. Kilachand was very fond of playing politics backstage while presenting a face of bemused innocence to the rest of the world. He was hiding something. It might not be murder. But it might be something crucial that could point to the real murderer. Sansi wasn't in any hurry. He would let the pressure build gradually over time—and then he would be in a better position to start sweating people like Kilachand and Coyarjee to find out how much they really knew. In the meantime, they might just let a few more tidbits slip.

"I think it's time I had a look around the grounds," Sansi announced.

"Which . . . where?" Coyarjee looked startled.

"The studios, the sets, the grounds, all 360 acres," Sansi said. "And I would appreciate it greatly if both of you came with me."

Sansi got up to go. From the corner of his eye he thought he saw Kilachand and Coyarjee exchange unhappy glances.

Kilachand drove and he did it very badly. They headed back toward the main gate, then, just before they would have left the grounds of Film City, they took a right fork onto a dirt road that led up into the scrubby brown hills overlooking the studio complex. They climbed for several minutes, then rounded the brow of a fat, domed hill . . . and they were in the vale of Kashmir. The brown scrub was replaced by steep, rocky cliffs that flanked a winding gorge with a dry creek bed at the bottom. The grass along the sides of the creek was green, giving the gorge a cool, fertile look. They followed the road down to the creek, where Sansi could see a couple of trucks, some film equipment and half a dozen British redcoats.

"They are making a film that tells the story of the Raj from the Indian point of view," Kilachand explained. "A good idea, don't you think?"

Sansi agreed and made a mental note to mention it to his father when next they met. The road divided again to run along both sides of the small valley. This time they took the left fork, crossed an arched stone bridge and began climbing again. They crested the bluff at the head of the valley and found themselves gazing down on Lake Vihar, in the middle distance, which would easily pass for a lake in Kashmir through the lens of a camera. The road dipped down the other side of the hill and cut through a narrow gully. The lake and the sunlight disappeared and they found themselves in shadow in a still and menacing ravine.

"The Khyber Pass," said Kilachand.

They passed quickly through the ravine and followed the road across the belly of a low hill toward a small cluster of buildings set amid fresh green lawns and neatly tended rose gardens. Kilachand stopped the car and they all got out in front of a large bungalow with the windows open and pretty floral curtains lifting gently in the breeze. The front veranda was set with a comfortable array of cane tables and chairs, all of them empty and expectant. It was a hill station in Simla. There was something haunted and forlorn about the scene. Sansi felt a small tingle, a disturbing frisson of nostalgia for a British India that he had never seen. At any moment he expected to see the fair-skinned wife of a plantation owner step out onto the veranda and shade her eyes as she peered at the horizon, searching for her husband at the end of the day.

"It's the real thing," Kilachand explained. "We had it brought here and reassembled. Everything works. You could live in it."

As though on cue, the lawn sprinklers switched on, filling the air with pretty jeweled ribbons. The three of them scurried out of the way and followed a pink gravel footpath that led to the outbuildings. In the distance Sansi saw a couple of *kulis* working in the gardens, tending flower beds that could have been transplanted intact from a cottage in England. There were geraniums, chrysanthemums, dahlias, daffodils, cania . . . even roses. Fat, gorgeous roses in varying stages of bloom.

"We stagger the plantings throughout the year to make sure that there are roses in bloom all year 'round," Kilachand said.

Sansi followed the path farther into the gardens and another perspective on Lake Vihar. Something caught his eye. He turned and found himself staring at a blue tree. Next to it was a pink tree, then a silver tree, then a golden tree. The branches of all the trees were hung with fairy lights. The trees were real, Sansi realized, but the colors were false. Pieces of gaudily painted bark littered the lawn.

"They were painted for a fantasy sequence," Coyarjee explained. "Sometimes the paint kills them. We have to plant new trees all the time."

Sansi nodded. It seemed there was not a living thing in India that could not be used, killed and then easily replaced. There were always plenty of others lining up to take the place of the dead. He looked around but saw nothing to excite his suspicion. The set was too neat, too well tended . . . too English. The murder hadn't taken place here.

They climbed back into the car and Kilachand drove out the way they had come in. They drove back through the Khyber Pass, across the stone bridge, past the redcoats of the Raj and took another dirt road that wound between a series of low, scrubby hills toward a volcano. As they drew closer to the rim of the volcano, Sansi realized it was just another hill with the top cut off. Thousands of tons of earth had been bulldozed away to create a bare, windswept plateau the size of a football field. They looped around the plateau and Sansi saw that it was empty except for a helipad and a small cemetery.

"The cemetery is a fake," Kilachand explained. "We shoot a lot of action sequences up here, helicopters coming and going, helicopters chasing cars, cars going over cliffs, that sort of thing."

"We do it all the time," Sansi said.

Kilachand took a different road back down the hill and after a few minutes the scenery changed yet again. This time Sansi found himself driving through a small, neat forest. The trees formed a leafy avenue for about fifty yards and then, suddenly, they were in a large clearing, dominated by a white, shining Hindu temple, with Lake Vihar as the backdrop again. The temple sat on a high slab of cement and consisted of an open, colonnaded courtyard and an inner chamber topped by three high-pointed domes, escalating in importance like bishops' miters.

Sansi was immediately curious. Despite the backdrop, the temple was in a quiet, secluded place, screened by trees and accessible by only one road. He asked Kilachand to stop the car again and got out. Kilachand and Coyarjee stayed behind this time. Perhaps they were tired, Sansi thought. Or perhaps they wanted to talk for a few minutes with him out of the way.

Sansi walked around to the rear of the temple where the trees parted to reveal the view of the distant lake. The temple was perched on the side of a large hill and the ground fell steeply away on three sides to dissolve into a maze of gullies and ravines clogged with thick brush. It would be hard going down there, Sansi noted, and almost impossible for anyone to approach the temple from this side without being seen well in advance.

Sansi walked around to the front of the temple and found a short flight of concrete steps that led up to the small

courtyard. Unlike Hollywood, Sansi realized, the sets at
Film City were not all plywood and balsa. They were real.
This temple was solid: built of cement and stone, coated
with plaster and painted white. The floor was polished
stone, the courtyard pillars were hard and unyielding, the
temple walls were at least a foot thick and cool to the
touch. Once inside the courtyard there was an arched doorway that led to an inner enclave. It was cool and shadowy
inside and it smelled musty. It took Sansi a second or two
for his eyes to adjust. Someone was watching him from the
rear of the temple, he realized. Someone hidden in a tall,
shadowy recess in the temple walls. He took a step forward, straining to make sense of the still, dark shape. Then,
he realized it wasn't human.

It was Kali, goddess of death and destruction. She was
almost seven feet tall. Her hair was wild and matted, her
face a contorted leer of bulging eyes, lewdly parted lips and
protruding tongue. She was naked to the waist; her torso
and breasts were painted blue and her nipples a brazen red.
All four of her arms were covered with amulets made from
serpents and there was a garland of human skulls around
her waist.

Sansi approached the statue cautiously, embarrassed at
his own small fright when he had first seen it. He wondered
if he was getting old, to be startled so easily by statues of
gods and goblins. In front of the goddess was a low stone
altar which would have been covered with candles and
flowers, incense, money and other offerings if this had been
a real temple of Kali. There was something on the altar.
Sansi bent down and looked closer. A small posy of dead,
dried flowers. Somebody had decided that even a film-
world effigy of Kali deserved a token of respect. It wasn't
enough, Sansi knew. Kali's followers practiced human sacrifice and cannibalism. Homage to the mistress of Siva had
to be paid in human blood.

Sansi bent down and examined the altar more closely.
His eyes had adjusted to the gloom but he still wished he
had brought a small flashlight. He ran his fingers over the

altar's polished surface, smooth but for a few small cracks and grooves. He got down on all fours, like a supplicant to the goddess, and slowly felt across the floor, his fingers probing for cracks and seams. After a minute he fished his key chain out of a trouser pocket and opened a small pen-knife. From his other pocket he took out a clean white handkerchief. It was only a hunch, but hunches had been known to produce the occasional breakthrough, and Sansi never discounted them. Carefully he dug the tip of the knife into a seam in the floor and scraped out a long, crooked curlicue of dirt. He shook it into his handkerchief, then repeated the process in half a dozen other small notches and cracks.

Then he decided it was time to clean Kali's toenails. Her large, painted feet rested on a square stone pedestal. He peered into the murk, then dug the tip of the knife into the groove beneath the flat scarlet nail of the big toe of the left foot, and scraped out a few dark crumbs of dirt. He dropped them carefully into his handkerchief with the other samples, and went to the next toe. Slowly, painstakingly, one toe at a time, Sansi gave the goddess of death a pedicure. Finally Kali decided she had had enough. She reached down and touched Sansi on the shoulder.

His breath froze in his lungs. Sansi slowly lifted his head and looked into the unbecoming face of Pratap Coyarjee.

The studio manager looked anxious. "You were such a long time. . . ." he said.

Sansi ignored him and went back to the pedicure. A moment later he got up with a grunt, carefully folded the handkerchief and tucked it in his shirt pocket.

Coyarjee watched him. "Did you find something?"

"Perhaps," Sansi answered. "We'll know in a day or two." He preferred to keep Coyarjee and Kilachand in suspense. To give them even more to worry about.

He walked out of the darkened temple into the brilliant sunshine with Coyarjee close behind. The studio manager was sweating. An oily trickle of sweat eluded his phony hairline and ran down into one eye. Coyarjee blinked and wiped his face with a sleeve.

Sansi looked at him for a moment. The car was air conditioned. Why was he sweating so much?

The drive back to the studio took ten minutes. Sansi realized that the temple was farther away from the studio complex than any other set. They pulled up in the parking lot beside the police car and the chariots and all three of them got out. The doors to the airplane hangar were open and Sansi could see workmen inside, moving cameras and lighting equipment, hoisting scenery on chain pulleys. There was a small knot of men gathered outside idling and smoking cigarettes. Actors, Sansi realized. All of them looked the same: young, handsome, long black hair, bare chested, wearing long red and white robes from the waist down.

"Courtiers," Kilachand said. "From the court of Chandragupta Maurya, the warrior king who founded the Mauryan dynasty in—correct me if I'm wrong, Coyarjee— 350 B.C.?"

"Yes, sahib," Coyarjee agreed.

Sansi corrected them both. "321 B.C."

Kilachand looked at him. "You're familiar with the story of Chanakya?"

"The Hindu Machiavelli," Sansi answered, "adviser to Chandragupta, the only leader of the ancient world to defeat the armies of Alexander the Great. Chanakya was the power behind the throne."

"Yes." Kilachand nodded, impressed. "They're shooting an interior for *Chanakya* today. Would you like to see?"

Sansi nodded. He had never seen a movie being made. He had never been on a movie set before. But they were not the reasons for his curiosity. Sansi followed Kilachand across the parking lot, through the studio doors and into the throne room of King Chandragupta. The set was long, narrow and dazzling. Its walls were covered with sheets of fine gold and each sheet was ornately decorated with patterns of precious stones. Twin rows of pink-veined marble columns marched down the center of the room toward a throne of solid gold with a back shaped like a peacock's tail. The eyes in the peacock's tail were gorgeous clusters of rubies, sapphires, emeralds, diamonds and pearls. Electric cables snaked across the floor. Carpenters, electricians, makeup artists, grips, gaffers and gofers swarmed around the set in a scene of utter confusion. The noise level bordered on the alarming. More actors dressed as priests, warriors and noblemen wandered aimlessly around the studio waiting for the call to action which could come in five minutes or in five hours.

Kilachand excused himself and went in search of the director. Sansi looked around. Coyarjee seemed to have disappeared into the crowd, glad to be lost again in his familiar, comforting, phony world. Everyone seemed to know each other, although no one acknowledged Sansi. He was a stranger on the set, an outsider. It didn't matter that he had enough power to put the managing director of Film City behind bars, if he wanted to. He wasn't one of Them—in which case, he had to be Nobody. Sansi decided to snoop around on his own for a while anyway.

He skirted the inside of the throne room and examined the rhinestones and the gold paint. He tapped one of the marble columns and it wobbled alarmingly. Someone swore at him. Sansi looked around and a carpenter gestured to him to keep his hands to himself. Sansi smiled apologetically and wandered between a pair of maroon velvet drapes and off the set into the rest of the studio. He noticed three men nearby impressively costumed as warriors, drinking tea from paper cups.

He approached them and nodded amiably. "Nice work, if you can get it."

The three young actors smirked at each other but none of them cared to encourage him with an answer. Sansi was clearly outside the freemasonry of the film business.

"Are most of you here today . . . extras?"

The word sounded strange coming from him and only emphasized his status as an outsider.

One of the trio, a tall man with a magnificently waxed mustache, deigned to respond. "Who are you?" he asked, his voice tinged with indifference.

"Oh." Sansi looked apologetic. "I'm sorry. My name is Sansi, Inspector Sansi. From Crime Branch."

The three of them stiffened.

"I'm just curious to know how many of the actors here today are extras and how many are . . . full-time?"

Suddenly they no longer seemed so sure of themselves.

"Most of us are extras," the man with the mustache answered, the indifference replaced by a new and wary respect for Sansi's authority.

Sansi nodded. "Much turnover in extras?"

"I'm sorry?"

"Do you see the same people here every day, or do they change around all the time?"

"Most of us are regulars," answered the man who had made himself the unwilling spokesman. "But new people come and go all the time. This is not a big scene. Some days there are hundreds here."

Sansi seemed to ponder that for a moment. "And who takes care of the bookings?" he asked. "Who calls you up to tell you when you are wanted for work?"

The actor shrugged. "Sometimes the production office. Sometimes the studio manager's office."

"The studio manager? Mr. Coyarjee's office?"

"Yes. Film City has the biggest cast list in Bombay. If the production office needs more people it's usually Coyarjee who takes care of it."

"So Pratap Coyarjee decides who gets work and who doesn't, most of the time?"

Mustache glanced nervously at his colleagues. "Yes," he answered.

"Good." Sansi smiled. "Thank you."

He turned as if about to leave. "Oh, just one more thing. . . . Those of you with long hair, is it real or do you wear wigs?"

The actor looked puzzled. "Most wear wigs. Some of us have our own hair."

"Inspector . . . !"

Kilachand's call came from behind Sansi. He turned to see the managing director hurrying toward him with a smaller, familiar-looking man in tow.

"Let me introduce you to Inamdar Baran, our most famous film director," Kilachand gushed.

Sansi shook hands with Baran and found himself being expertly steered in a new direction. He thought Kilachand seemed a little too anxious to get him away from the three young actors.

"You can ask Mr. Baran anything you want," Kilachand said.

Sansi stopped and smiled. "I don't think I need to take up any of Mr. Baran's time," he said.

Both Kilachand and Baran looked perplexed.

"I have everything I need to know," Sansi explained as he stared guilelessly into Kilachand's eyes.

For a moment Sansi was certain he had seen it. There had been real fear in Noshir Kilachand's eyes.

9

"I THINK THIS is him coming now."

Sergeant Chabria trained his binoculars on a bobbing black smudge amid the phosphorescent waves. A moment later the men waiting in the sand dunes heard the low buzz of an outboard motor.

Chabria passed the binoculars to the man standing next to him, a short, bulky man in a Yamaha windbreaker with a shaven skull and a pockmarked face. Jackie Patro took the binoculars and quickly found the launch bringing in his boss. Somewhere out there, four or five miles offshore, was a Greek freighter en route from Cairo to Karachi. The ship had made only one stop along the way, at Dubai in the United Arab Emirates, where it had picked up one passenger. That passenger was now about to land on the beach without the knowledge or consent of the Indian immigration service.

Patro found the black smudge and watched it intently as it butted its way toward the shore. He could make out the silhouettes of two figures standing at the front of the boat. Patro suppressed a shiver. He hated the ocean. He could kill a man in cold blood with his bare hands, but he would never dream of crossing four miles of open water in a small boat. He tossed the binoculars back to Chabria and signaled to the half-dozen men clustered nearby around three Toyota sedans.

They flicked their cigarettes into the sand and hurried down through the dunes toward the water's edge. Two of the men were carrying AK-47 Soviet assault rifles, acquired at great expense from Mujahadeen guerillas in Afghanistan and smuggled south through Pakistan. Two men, also armed with AK-47s, were left with the cars, and there were two more hidden nearby, watching the road. Chabria was impressed. Bombay's gangsters were better armed than the police. Early in life, the sergeant had reached the conclusion that there was little point in fighting them. He had been taking money from Patro for ten years.

It was four o'clock in the morning. There was a blustery inshore breeze and the sea looked sloppy, but the night air was warm and fresh. They had been there all night. The hardest part for Chabria had been staying awake. But once he had scouted out the area for Patro's goons, he had been told he would have to stay until business had been concluded. Now he trudged dutifully down through the dunes after the others.

By the time he arrived at the water's edge the boat was only a few yards from shore. The man at the wheel cut the motor, tilted the outboard up over the stern and let the boat run in on the breakers until it hit the beach and slid high up onto the sand with a soft, grating screech. A couple of men rushed forward and held it steady. The passenger was wearing a hooded olive-green army parka, slick with spray. He stepped up onto the portside gunwale, ignored the outstretched hands and jumped down onto the beach.

Paul Kapoor, the most wanted hoodlum in Bombay, slumlord of Dharavai, gold smuggler and exile, was back on Indian soil. He pulled back the hood of his parka and took a moment to smooth and straighten his hair. Then he went to Patro, the man who held his empire together in his absence. They embraced each other and Kapoor affectionately slapped the smaller man on the back the way an elder brother would, even though Patro was ten years his senior.

"Everything cool, man?"

From anyone else it would have sounded absurd. Affected American slang with a heavy Indian accent. But no one seemed to notice. Kapoor had always modeled himself on American hoodlums he had seen in gangster movies from the forties and fifties. It was his style. In the early days there were people who laughed. But nobody had laughed at Paul Kapoor in a long time. Kapoor went to each of his men individually, patting them, squeezing their hands, using their first names, sharing a few words. Chabria realized that this was what made Kapoor different. A natural motivator, he used fear and charm to inspire loyalty. He knew his men; he knew the names of their wives and their children. He gave them money for anniversaries, birthdays and holidays. He paid for medical operations and holidays. He was generous with cash and favors and he always rewarded loyalty and sacrifice. But when anyone crossed him he was merciless. Informers had their eyes and their tongues cut out.

Kapoor was also said to have more than two thousand policemen, magistrates, judges, prison officers and bureaucrats on his payroll. He ran brothels, escort agencies, protection rackets and liquor dens. He smuggled heroin, sandalwood and gold. He had half a dozen legitimate businesses, including garages and video stores. And he controlled them all through an intricate corporate network that included offices in Athens, Amsterdam and London and bank accounts in Zurich and the Cayman Islands. When he was in Bombay he ran it all from Dharavai, the slum city that had created him and which he still proudly called home. When he wanted to socialize he rented whole hotel floors and gave parties that were attended by movie stars and government ministers.

Whenever some overzealous policeman tried to threaten him, Kapoor would usually respond with an envelope full of money. If that didn't work, someone in the policeman's family often met with a fatal accident. It was a brutal but effective strategy which had long made him seem invincible. But even Kapoor could not be allowed to undermine the authority of the state forever. And when Jamal had finally been ordered to use his "Untouchables" against Kapoor there were many prominent people who wanted to avoid the embarrassment of the gangster living long enough to go to trial. In the end, it was Kapoor's pervasive network of corruption that had saved him. Someone had made a call—someone among the half-dozen senior policemen and politicians who knew that Crime Branch was about to swoop. Kapoor received the tip-off twenty-four hours before he was due to be arrested. It was enough time to make Jackie Patro the acting crime boss and then take a chartered jet to Dubai, where refuge was always waiting.

Kapoor finished greeting his men. Without waiting for further orders, they began to unload crate after crate from the boat onto the sand. Chabria watched from a respectful distance. He was sweating after walking only a hundred yards over the sand and he didn't feel like any more exercise. The crates looked heavy and he knew what they contained. He tried to make a rough estimate based on current prices but quickly lost count. It had to be worth millions, perhaps tens of millions of U.S. dollars. More gold than he had ever seen in his life. Chabria's mind reeled at the very thought of the raw power contained in those few wooden crates. The power to topple governments. The power to buy an entire police department.

"Hey, Chabria." Kapoor finally noticed him. "I hear you been watching my back pretty good."

Chabria waggled his head in the Hindu way to signify agreement.

Kapoor approached him and gave him a friendly pat on the shoulder. "Jackie says you did okay. When times are tough, it helps to know who your friends are. You know what I mean?"

"Oh yes, sahib." Chabria's greasy jowls quivered.

"I'll see you get something extra for this."

"Thank you, sahib."

"What are they saying about me in town?"

Chabria looked uncomfortable. In truth, no one mentioned Kapoor much anymore. The *hafta* came regularly. The machinery of corruption ran smoothly without him. Patro was a crude though capable administrator. Kapoor had been quirky and unpredictable. No one missed him. But he wouldn't like to hear that.

"Everyone wonders when you will come back," Chabria lied. "They say you will not stay away too long. They say you belong here."

Kapoor's face stayed sullen. "You don't mention my name to anybody for the next few days," he said softly. "They'll all know soon enough. Okay?"

"Of course, sahib."

Kapoor seemed satisfied. He was twenty years younger than Chabria and half his size but anyone who studied their body language from a distance would know who was in charge.

Kapoor smiled in that peculiar, lopsided way of his that was half smile, half sneer. It was known as his Elvis smile—and there was more than a passing resemblance between the gangster and the late American rock idol. Kapoor had the same sullen good looks, the same brooding gaze, and he liked to style his hair just like the young Elvis. Kapoor had the looks to be a movie star if he had not chosen a life of crime instead. But in the elastic morality of Bombay there was no real shame attached to crime. It was just another form of survival.

Despite their occasional acts of barbarism, many of Bombay's gangsters became celebrities—heroes to the impressionable young. And there was never any shortage of recruits. No one who worked for the gangs ever went hungry. There was always plenty of dope, liquor and women to compensate for the risks. Any ambitious youngster with a quick mind and a strong stomach could make it to the top in the underworld much faster than he would in any honest enterprise. Kapoor was a prime example of the breed. Young, tough and smart, he had been on top for almost a decade. And he could buy all the movie stars he wanted. His sexual appetite was legendary and it was rumored that he had slept with every reigning beauty in the Indian cinema.

Kapoor's men carried the last crate of gold up the beach

to the waiting cars. Patro passed the boatman an envelope. The man nodded his thanks, then he and Patro shoved the boat back down the beach into the surf. A moment later the outboard started up and in a couple of minutes the boat was lost amid the waves.

The three of them turned and walked back up to the dunes in silence. The gold had been tucked away and the cars all sat lower in the sand. Chabria waited. His own car was hidden nearby. He would follow Kapoor at a discreet distance and make sure that Bombay's most notorious hoodlum wasn't inconvenienced by any nosy police patrols during the drive back into the city. Patro took another envelope out of the backseat of the car and tossed it disdainfully to Chabria. The sergeant fumbled and bent over with a grunt to pluck it out of the sand. Kapoor and Patro climbed into the back of their car without another word to him. The engine started and Chabria stepped back. His next movement was pure reflex. He saluted Kapoor's car as it passed.

A moment later the car bounced off the hard-packed sand and back onto the highway that led one hundred miles southward to Bombay. They sat in silence for a few minutes while Kapoor adjusted to his new surroundings. Dawn was two hours away and they seemed to be racing through a black void, except for the slender columns of coconut palms that passed them in the car lights.

"Kirian waiting for me?" Kapoor asked.

Patro nodded. Kirian Gazul was Kapoor's current girlfriend. A demure twenty-two-year-old movie starlet worshiped by millions for her innocent charm.

"*Acha,*" Kapoor sniffed. "Nobody gives head like Kirian."

Kapoor lay back and closed his eyes and after a minute Patro thought his boss had drifted off to sleep. Then, his eyes still closed, Kapoor said, "Bring me up to date."

Patro grunted. He knew exactly what his boss wanted to know. Kapoor hadn't returned because he was homesick. He had come back to settle a score. Kapoor's biggest rival in Bombay was the Bengali gangster, Jashwal Bikaner. Until Kapoor had been forced into exile they had maintained an uneasy truce. They didn't trust each other. They didn't like each other. But nobody profited from gang wars.

Now, with Kapoor out of the way, Bikaner seemed to think the way was clear to expand his territory. He had begun selling his own liquor in Dharavai. Patro had caught Bikaner's peddlers and sent them back with a few broken bones. Bikaner had responded by ambushing two of Kapoor's collectors and stealing their *hafta*. Patro had wanted to respond by killing Bikaner—not something he would do without Kapoor's permission. Kapoor had told his enforcer to wait until he got back. In the meantime, things had deteriorated swiftly. Bikaner had begun collecting *hafta* in two of Kapoor's old districts. Patro had also heard that Bikaner had been acquiring automatic weapons for his men. Patro knew he had to be the target. With Kapoor and his enforcer both out of the way, Kapoor's criminal empire would disintegrate and Bikaner would be free to take over all the rackets in Bombay. The situation was sliding rapidly toward open warfare. And Patro was impatient to get on with it. He wanted to strike first.

Kapoor listened to all of this impassively, his eyes closed, his face relaxed. When Patro had finished Kapoor looked at him and flashed his Elvis smile.

"Be cool," Kapoor reassured his loyal lieutenant, "I've got plans for Jashwal. Another week, and you and me, we're going to be out of this. For good."

10

SANSI WAS IN his office on the ground floor of the Crime Branch building at police headquarters when the phone rang. It was Annie Ginnaro.

"You've seen my stories?" she asked.

"Yes."

"Well . . . I think we should meet." Her tone was friendly but insistent. "There are a few things I'd like to discuss, if that's all right with you. How about lunch one day this week?"

Sansi smiled. He had intended calling her himself. He wanted to find out just how much she knew about this murder investigation. But he had hesitated. Despite her crassness at their first meeting he had been favorably impressed. She was not the archetypal insensitive American. On the contrary, he thought, she had merely been trying too hard. Trying to compensate for an innate sensitivity, perhaps? He saw her as a woman who had been hurt by her own enthusiasms for life and who now sought to protect herself with the armor of over-confidence. He liked the way she had chosen to wear a sari. On some Western women it looked ridiculous and affected. On her, he found it charming. She was tall and long-legged and it suited her. Annie Ginnaro was attractive and intriguing. Sansi would have to be careful: she was still a reporter. There would have to be business before there could be any pleasure. If she wanted to cultivate him for information, he could always cultivate her to spread disinformation.

"I don't eat lunch," Sansi answered. It was the truth but he was stalling too.

131

"Well . . . tea? I just think we should have an hour—"

"Dinner would be better," he interrupted. "That would give us time to talk properly."

"Oh . . ." She sounded surprised but not unhappy. "Well, that's fine. Okay, where would you like to meet? I'm still finding my way around town but I know—"

"How about your apartment?"

"Excuse me?" He had caught her off balance.

"It would be much better if we talked in private," he explained. "It would not be a good idea for me to be seen in public with a newspaper reporter when I'm in the middle of a murder investigation. And I never know who my mother will have at home. So if it's all right with you, we could eat, or have tea, at your apartment."

"It's kind of a dump," she said lamely. "Especially compared to yours."

"Nobody cares about that sort of thing," he said reassuringly. It was clear that she didn't want him to come to see her at home but because she had initiated the invitation it was hard for her to say no. And Sansi had his reasons for pressing her. Annie Ginnaro had been to his home and had confronted him at a vulnerable moment. It had given her a personal perspective on his life that he would not ordinarily choose to give to a woman he had just met. It was one of the penalties of living with his mother and it was something she did to him all the time. He wanted to get to know Annie Ginnaro personally but he had to know how to manage her professionally too. He wanted to get at least the same handle on her life as she had on his.

"Unless you don't feel safe . . ."

"Don't be ridiculous," she cut in a little too quickly. "It's just . . . I can't cook, that's all."

"I'll pick up something on the way. I know a few good places. What do you like to eat?"

"Oh . . ." He had robbed her of her momentum and she faltered again. "Anything . . . Indian. I like Indian. I don't mind if it's hot. I grew up on Tex-Mex in LA."

"Tex-Mex?"

"Never mind. All right, eight o'clock on Friday okay?"

"Fine."

"You pick something up on the way and I'll provide the wine. I know how to pick good wine."

Annie gave him the address of her apartment at Nariman Point. As she hung up the phone at her office desk she realized that her face was burning.

"Shit," she breathed softly. It hadn't gone exactly the way she had intended. She had assumed she would be able to handle a guy like Sansi easily. She caught herself. What kind of a guy had she thought he was? The kind who was used to compliant Indian women? The kind who might be a big shot in Bombay but who didn't have the sophistication to deal with a woman like her? Despite his Western education she had assumed she would be something new to him. Something challenging and unknown—and that would give her the edge. But he hadn't been intimidated at all. Instead he had taken control of the situation and now he was coming to her apartment and the thought of it made her nervous. She should have known better. Pramila Sansi wasn't a typical Indian woman. She was tough, independent, resourceful and successful on her own terms. And that was the kind of woman George Sansi had grown up with. Annie found herself wondering if she was really as perceptive as she thought or if she was in control of her life as much as she wanted to be. It wasn't the first time she had asked herself that question. Obviously, she sighed, some things hadn't changed.

Sansi hung up and smiled. He had hoped she would call him before he called her—and he had been ready. He would look forward to Friday night. It would be interesting to see who would get the most from their meeting. Sansi's boss, Jamal, had not been happy with her story in the *Times*. Every newspaper in Bombay had followed it up and made it the hottest story in the city. Every movie fan, every *kuli*, factory worker, street hawker, *paan-walla* and office worker speculated about who the murdered movie star could be.

Film City had put up the shutters and Noshir Kilachand, burned once, was no longer taking calls from anyone in the media. Sansi had refused to make a statement to confirm or deny anything. Now, after forty-eight hours of silence, a torrent of gossip had filled the vacuum. Some of the biggest names in the movie industry had been mentioned and their publicity agents had scrambled to reassure the public and the press that their clients were alive and well and still working. Those inside the industry knew that the murder victim had to be small-time but, like everyone else, they were waiting for Crime Branch to reveal the victim's name. Almost everyone believed that the police knew who the victim was and were keeping it a secret. In the meantime, Sansi had no intention of revealing to anyone how little he really knew. Fingerprint checks had revealed that the victim had no police record. That was all.

Both he and Sergeant Chowdhary had spent hours scouring the files of the Modus Operandi Branch to see if there were other unsolved murders with a similar pattern of mutilation. They had found nothing. That only meant there had been no similar murders in Maharashtra ... or no other bodies had yet been found.

The Indian police service was still not computerized and was far too fragmented to give him easy access to modus operandi files in other states. An official request would have to be made to the independent bureaucracies of the police services in all remaining thirteen states to ask them to search their own modus operandi files, many of which would be woefully incomplete. It was a process that could take months. Sansi felt certain he could engineer his own breakthrough, long before then, in Bombay. He now had four constables helping Sergeant Chowdhary work through the list of names Kilachand had provided. The key to the murderer was somewhere in that list, he knew. And he was within days, perhaps hours, of finding it.

Sansi glanced at his wall clock. It was almost two o'clock. He pushed all thoughts of Annie Ginnaro from his mind and dialed the number for Vyankatesh Rohan, the deputy coroner of Bombay.

"Good afternoon, Inspector." Rohan sounded cheerful.

Sansi hoped it was a good omen.

"I suppose you are impatient to know about those few specks of dirt you dropped off yesterday?"

Sansi had stopped by Rohan's office on the way back from Film City the previous day and left his handkerchief containing the scrapings from Kali's toenails.

"Most of it was dust," Rohan said. "But you will be pleased to know that we found several microscopic particles of blood. Human blood."

Sansi felt a small thrill of anticipation. The goddess at Film City had seen human sacrifice after all.

"Did you get a type?"

"Group O."

"Anything else?"

"We found a few microscopic chemical particles as well. We have identified ammonia and alkyl sulphonate. From the combination I would say they come from a mixture of household and industrial detergents. Where did you say you got this sample?"

Sansi reminded him.

"Well," Rohan mused. "It was such a small amount of blood, it could have come from a cut. They must have people working out there all the time. It is not inconceivable that a workman, a carpenter, perhaps, might have cut himself. And they would have to wash the place down every now and again."

"Perhaps," Sansi said. "But this was an unusual place for blood to stick . . . unless a lot of it was splashed around. Somebody could have tried to wash it away soon after the murder. That would explain the combination of blood and detergent. It depends on how fastidious they are at Film City. I don't think they wash down the outdoor sets that often. Have you pinpointed the time of death yet?"

"Ten to fourteen days ago. That's as specific as I can be. We found partially digested rice kernels in his stomach. That suggests he ate a meal three to four hours before he was killed. I am also quite certain now that he was dumped in the lake within an hour of his death. From what you have told me, it is quite possible that he was murdered at the temple then dumped in the lake very soon afterward."

"So," Sansi interjected, "if Film City's cleaners have not carried out a routine wash-down of the temple within the last two weeks then it was probably a deliberate attempt by someone who works there to remove evidence from the murder scene."

"*Acha,*" Rohan agreed.

"Do you have a blood group for the victim?"

"It was also group O."

Sansi paused. "We're getting somewhere, aren't we?"

"The fact that the victim had the same blood group as the blood sample you brought from the murder scene is promising," Rohan cautioned. "But group O is the most common blood group in India, you know. Forty percent of the population has blood group O. A good defense lawyer would give you a hard time. . . ."

"If it was all we had," Sansi interrupted. "Can you run any tests that will tell me conclusively that the sample I gave you comes from the murder victim?"

Rohan hesitated. "There isn't very much and it is very dirty, you know." Like all scientists, Rohan liked to remind people how difficult his work was before he did it well. "I would have to clean it up for an enzyme test. I might be able to tell you something in a day or two."

"Tomorrow."

"Tomorrow?"

"And something else," Sansi pressed on before Rohan could protest.

"Yes?"

"Was he gay?"

"Oh yes," Rohan answered. "No doubt about it. When we opened the colon and took a good look at it, the distension was unmistakable. There was also considerable scarring. This boy had been taking it up the bottom for a long time, I think. We swabbed the colon thoroughly and took extensive mucus and tissue samples. I should be able to tell you quite soon if we find anything interesting."

Sansi was silent. The press would go berserk if they heard some of this. It was no longer just a movieland murder scandal. It was a gay movieland murder scandal. It would be better still if the victim was a closet gay.

A terrifying thought occurred to Sansi. "Any signs of AIDS?"

"No evidence of HIV," Rohan answered reassuringly. "Just as well you took off the clothes peg and put on the mask, eh, Sansi? Besides, all the information we have indicates that the AIDS virus dies within hours of the death of the host organism. We would know from other cell damage if he'd had AIDS but it was one of the first things I looked for when I knew he was gay. It wouldn't do to have an AIDS victim floating around in the city's water supply for too long, eh?" Rohan chuckled, then added, "As far as we can tell he was not suffering from any other sexually transmitted diseases at the time of his death, although it is difficult to be absolutely certain."

"Why?"

"No genitals, remember? No genital scarring to examine. We've had to do most of our detective work through molecular analysis."

"Acha," Sansi acknowledged. He felt a pang of queasiness in his stomach. But Rohan had given him enough to decide on his next step. He would bring Coyarjee in first to question him on the gay connection. And then, perhaps, Kilachand.

"I'll call you tomorrow," Sansi promised and hung up. He pushed his chair back from his desk and walked to the open door of his office. Like most Indians he rarely closed his door. He was used to working in the midst of permanent bedlam. Sansi's office was a modest cubicle about five yards square with high ceilings and flaking walls painted white at the top and yellow at the bottom. There was a ceiling fan, a couple of filing cabinets, an ancient wooden desk with two trays piled high with paperwork and a couple of uncomfortable wooden chairs on the visitor's side of the desk. If Sansi had become the lawyer he was trained to be he would have had a bigger office than the joint commissioner by now. But

Sansi disdained ostentatious surroundings. He was comfortable with the office of an ordinary police inspector. It appeased the frugal, English side of his character.

Hanging behind the door was a cellophane bag containing his khaki police uniform with an inspector's pips on the epaulettes. Sansi couldn't remember the last time he had worn it. Almost certainly it had been for some ceremonial occasion on the parade ground outside, which was now packed with police vehicles. It seemed a lifetime ago since he had stood out there and received his commendation from the commissioner for his work in destroying the Naxalites of Tamori.

Sansi glanced up at the sky. Every day it was the same flawless blue, scoured clean by the sun. Another few days and it would be May. And there was still no sign of the cool, cleansing rains of the monsoon. Like everyone else he was sick of summer and longed for the relief the monsoon would bring. Everything would be different then. The air would be fresher, lighter. Everyone would feel better, refreshed by the rain. Then, after a few days, they would start complaining again. Complaining that they couldn't do any work because of the rain and the floods.

Indians always had excuses for not working. In the summer it was too hot. In the winter it was too wet. In the north it was too cold. In the south it was too dry. It used to drive Sansi mad. It must have been the Englishman in him. He had since learned to embrace Hindu fatalism and become more relaxed about the daily aggravations of life in India. The power failures, the phones that wouldn't work, the appointments that were never kept, the clerks who lost files or who simply forgot what they were supposed to be doing, the paperwork, the mind-numbing pedantry of the bureaucracy.

His antique black telephone clanged loudly behind him. Sansi shook off the threat of torpor and went back to his desk.

"This is Paul Kapoor," the voice said.

Sansi stiffened. He said nothing.

"You been wanting to meet me for some time, Sansi." It was a statement, not a question. "Come to Dharavai this afternoon. Four o'clock. On your own. Don't tell anybody. Be cool. You'll be okay. I've got a proposition. Wait outside the Congress Party office. Somebody will meet you."

The line went dead before Sansi could speak. He stared at the phone for almost a minute before he hung up. It was a bizarre hoax ... or Kapoor was really back in town and Sansi's informer had heard nothing. Sansi had never spoken directly to Kapoor before, so he had no idea what his voice sounded like. He had only seen pictures of Bombay's most wanted man. He had built up a profile based on police files, newspaper reports and informers' tips. But he had also built up his own personal composite of Kapoor and something told him that this call was real. Kapoor would know as much about Sansi as Sansi knew about him. And it was Kapoor's style to call personally. Nobody had ever accused him of lacking nerve.

What did he mean by a proposition? Was he planning to offer Sansi a bribe? To put him on the payroll? Or was it something more sinister? Sansi sat down limply in his chair. Every synapse, every neuron of logic in his mind, every instinctive electrical impulse told him he could not trust Kapoor. That it would be an act of willful insanity to walk unprotected into the heart of Kapoor's empire without telling anyone where he was going. But he also knew that if the gangster wanted him dead, it wasn't necessary to go to this much trouble. A simple pipe bomb under Sansi's car or a spray of bullets from a passing motorbike was all that was needed. Killing a policeman was no more difficult than killing anyone else, once you had made up your mind. There was no need to invite Sansi into an ambush.

If Kapoor wanted to see him it was because he probably did have something he wanted to discuss. And Sansi knew he couldn't afford to turn it down. The familiar bile of fear curdled in his stomach. He glanced at the clock. It was a few minutes after two. That made sense. It was a two-hour drive to Dharavai. Kapoor didn't want him to have too much time to think about it or to organize a security tail.

The gangster knew the Bombay police department didn't work that quickly.

Sansi plucked his jacket from the back of his chair, stuck his head next door to tell Chowdhary he was going out and to wait till he got back, however late that might be. The lean, mournful-faced Chowdhary accepted Sansi's order unquestioningly. It was the only concession Sansi would make to security. He walked out of Crime Branch, past the knot of armed policemen gathered around the nearest gate, and hurried toward busy Lokmanya Street. The traffic lights changed and a phalanx of black and yellow taxis hurtled toward him. Sansi rashly stepped onto the road and was almost run down in the rush for his fare. He climbed into the back of the first taxi and slammed the door.

"Dharavai Station," he said.

Sansi had been to the slum city on the northern outskirts of Bombay many times in the past but had usually been accompanied by six truckloads of armed policemen. This was the first time he had ventured into Dharavai alone. He needed to prepare himself. Dharma—the Hindu concept of duty—was all very well. But the Englishman in Sansi wouldn't stop telling him what a fool he was. He told the driver to pull over for a moment. The taxi cut across two lanes of traffic and stopped abruptly at the curb. There were wide footpaths on both sides of the bridge spanning the railway tracks that sealed the easternmost boundary of Dharavai. Both footpaths seethed with people.

The moment Sansi stepped out of the taxi, he heard the rumble of a distant ocean: a sinister, unnerving sound that vibrated dully in the air and made its presence known even through the raucous din of Bombay's traffic. The rumble intensified to a low, threatening growl as he shouldered his way through the crowds toward the parapet. Sansi had to stand on the tips of his toes and steady himself with his fingertips to look over the wall.

The growl instantly became a roar. A roar that crashed against the walls and columns of the bridge like breakers whipped by a distant storm. There was an ocean beneath the bridge: an ocean of murky waves formed by the roofs of the biggest slum in Southeast Asia. And like an ocean it was bounded only by the horizon—a squalid spectacle of sagging tarpaulin sheets and thatched palm leaves scorched by the sun. The waves of the ocean blurred and danced in the heat; their peaks plumed with spray as sudden gusts of wind plucked randomly at the rooftops and flicked spurts of dust into the air. Somewhere beneath those waves, Sansi knew, one million people were drowning. The sound that hammered at his ears was the sound of human desperation.

But not everyone in Dharavai was desperate. Even here there was money. There was always money. Tens of thousands of workers left here by train every day to toil in the factories of Bombay. Beneath these cowed shanties there were liquor dens and opium houses. People made a living from each others' needs. They sold sex and food and drink and drugs. Dharavai might look like the dung heap of the universe—but nothing could quench the fire of human enterprise. Its symbols could be seen jutting improbably out of the waves like shiny steel claws. TV antennas. There were people in Dharavai with television sets, Japanese color televisions powered by portable Japanese generators that also powered lights, refrigerators, VCRs and stereos.

No matter how many times he confronted it, there was nothing in Sansi's experience that helped him make sense of Dharavai. Dharavai existed beyond the realm of human reason. No one wanted it. No one knew how it got there. It simply appeared one day and grew in momentum until it acquired a force and a power of its own. Like a black hole in space, Dharavai defied comprehension. It could only be accepted, never understood. And now Sansi was on his way to meet the hoodlum sultan of Dharavai. A man who had been born here, who had thrived here and who had turned it into the cornerstone of a criminal empire that now controlled the rest of the city. How could a place like Dharavai do anything else but produce a man as bizarre as Paul Kapoor?

Sansi pushed his way back to the waiting taxi. He

wouldn't dare walk alone into Dharavai, even though Kapoor's men were probably already watching him. Some lone junkie needing money for a fix might be inclined to cut his throat and take his money before Kapoor's men could intervene. The taxi barged back into the traffic, turned off the bridge and into the teeming streets of the slum metropolis. The driver had to nudge his way carefully through the crowds of people and rickshaws and the packs of naked children who competed with goats and pigs and rats to forage through the piles of stinking refuse that clogged the narrow lanes. A permanent pall of dust cloaked every thoroughfare, giving Dharavai a grim, medieval look.

People stared sullenly at Sansi as the taxi passed. A beggar with an arm missing appeared at Sansi's open window. The man had lost his right arm at the shoulder and a few inches of yellowed bone protruded from the stump. Hordes of noisy children closed in on the taxi. A cart packed with sacks of flour blocked the way forward. The driver looked nervous. He began thumping on the car horn and yelling curses at the crowd. A thicket of hands reached through the windows and tugged at Sansi's clothing. He wanted to roll up the window but the car had no air-conditioning and would turn into an oven within minutes.

The one-armed beggar beseeched Sansi. "Money, sahib, give me money. Not eat for two days, sahib, give me money."

Sansi tried to look away but wherever he looked there were wretched faces filled with need or resentment at his presence.

"Please, sahib," the man begged, his voice a pitiable whine. "You are rich man, I am poor man." He thrust the stump of his arm into the car until the bone was only a few inches from Sansi's face. Sansi recoiled. Dharavai wasn't like anywhere else in Bombay. You ventured in here, you couldn't turn your backs on the beggars quite so easily. In here they could strip you and leave you naked.

"Too much troubles, sahib. Give me money, sahib, anything . . . anything."

Sansi rolled up his window.

"Please, sahib." The one-armed man pulled back, his voice escalating to a heartrending sob. "Too much troubles, sahib. Give me anything. . . ."

The window closed and the man's voice merged into the background noise. The taxi lurched forward but the man wouldn't give up. He jammed his stump against the window, the car moved forward and the bone screeched across the glass. Sansi shuddered and looked away. Everything that was compassionate in him urged him to empty his wallet into the street. But he couldn't. That would be an invitation to riot, a riot he might not survive.

The flour cart moved and the taxi driver stamped on the gas pedal. The car jerked forward, scattering children and beggars in a cloud of curses. The next half-hour was like a nightmare as Sansi's driver edged the taxi deeper and deeper into the heart of Dharavai.

"Where, sahib? Where?" the driver kept asking.

"I told you . . . the Congress Party office," Sansi repeated for the hundredth time.

"But where is it, sahib? Where is it?"

The driver was lost and afraid. Sansi looked around, hopelessly searching out the green and white flag or the upraised hand that were the symbols of the Congress Party.

"Get out," a man's voice commanded through the driver's window.

Sansi turned and recognized Jackie Patro instantly.

"You are going around in circles," Patro said contemptuously. "Get out."

Sansi swallowed his fear, handed the driver a hundred-rupee note and climbed out. The taxi lurched away and was instantly consumed by the crowds, leaving Sansi alone with the most hardened killer in all of Bombay.

"Come with me," Patro ordered.

Sansi followed Patro's dark, shaven skull across the street. Patro had two men with him, one of whom was almost bald and whose face and neck were mottled with pink scars. Sansi assumed the man had been trapped in a fire at some point in his life and badly burned. The man seemed to be equally interested in Sansi. He stared at the policeman for a long time, eyes shining with undisguised hostility, then he looked away.

Sansi also noticed that the crowds were behaving differently. They were no longer closing in, jostling and threatening him. Instead they parted respectfully, like a river yielding before the bows of a ship. Nobody would get in Sansi's way while he was with Patro.

They paused in front of a two-story shack built from corrugated iron. Patro pushed open a ramshackle wooden door set in the iron facade and stepped through. Sansi followed and was immediately plunged into blackness. His foot caught on something and he stumbled into Patro, who growled impatiently at him. A few ragged rays of light filtered through cracks in the iron, enough to show Sansi that he was in a long, meandering corridor paved unevenly with planks of wood. The heat in the corrugated iron corridor was suffocating and the air smelled foul. He heard rats scuttering around him in the gloom. He kept his eyes on Patro's stocky frame as it bobbed ahead of him as easily as if they were walking down Marine Drive.

The corridor turned at a right angle and ended with two rickety wooden doors. Patro took the door to the left and they entered a dirt-floored corridor lined with tarpaulin sheets. The temperature eased a fraction, though the stench grew worse and blowflies swarmed everywhere. The corridor was flanked by shanty homes, some dimly lit with naked bulbs strung from frayed electrical cord, some in darkness. Cooking smells came from some of the hovels and Sansi saw that they were packed with people. All around him Sansi coul hear the yammering chorus of people shouting and arguing and of babies crying. He sensed, rather than felt, the crushing weight of humanity all around him in the gloom.

In the middle of the path was a narrow trench that overflowed with human ordure. Sansi pulled a handkerchief from his jacket pocket and held it across his nose and mouth to stop himself from gagging. He stumbled again and his foot slid into something slick. The corridor came to a junction. They turned right. More rooms, more people, more filth. They passed a room filled with men and he caught the sharp, bitter tang of methanol. A moment later they passed another shanty and Sansi smelled ganja. Whenever they encountered someone coming the other way, Patro barged silently ahead and everyone else stepped aside.

They came to another intersection and turned right again. Or was it left? Sansi struggled to keep track of his surroundings but knew already that he was lost in the slum labyrinth. Which was why they hadn't bothered to blindfold him, he realized. There was no need. He would never find the way out on his own; nor could he ever find his way in again. The location of Kapoor's secret lair would remain a mystery to Sansi. Still it wasn't enough for Patro. They kept on walking. Twisting, turning, coming onto new junctions, stepping through new doors.

"*Acha,*" Patro announced. It was just another door: a flimsy, orange-painted wooden door. Except this time Patro knocked. Twice. Then he opened the door and Sansi found himself in another corrugated iron corridor with wooden floorboards, though slightly better lit than its counterparts. And there were two men standing at the opposite end of the corridor holding AK-47s.

Once they were all inside, the last man shut the door and Patro turned to face Sansi. "Did you bring a gun?"

Sansi shook his head but Patro searched him anyway. It was rough but thorough. Patro grunted. The two armed men stepped aside and Patro opened the second door. This door was attached to the corrugated iron walls by new steel hinges, Sansi noticed. When it opened, he saw that it consisted of several layers of wood reinforced on the inside with a solid sheet of steel. Bulletproof. The inside walls were layered with sheets of raw plywood and Sansi assumed there were more metal plates beneath the plywood. Somewhere nearby he heard a powerful generator thumping.

He followed Patro into a large, lavishly furnished room and stopped in amazement. The shock of transition was so profound Sansi forgot to take his next breath. One moment he had been in a filthy, stinking, sweltering, rat-infested maze. The next, he was in a Las Vegas hotel suite—or what he imagined a Las Vegas hotel suite would be like. And when he did take a breath it was cool, clean and delicious. Cool air flowed over him and his clothes began to feel clammy against his skin. Kapoor's Dharavai hideaway had better air-conditioning than Sansi's apartment.

Sansi looked around, unable to keep the astonishment from his face. He knew Bombay's gangsters liked to live in a certain lurid style—but he could not have imagined anything as grotesque as this if he had lived another thousand years. The plywood walls had been painted silver. The ceiling was painted gold and the floor was covered in a red nylon shag the color of ketchup. Lighting was provided by two acrylic chandeliers fitted with electric light bulbs. One corner of the room had been turned into a bar with mirrors and bottles of liquor. Behind the bar was an array of black-and-white snapshots that Sansi couldn't quite define. In front of the bar were a half-dozen high chairs with red vinyl cushions. In an opposite corner was a TV set with a screen the size of a Ping-Pong table. The middle of the room was occupied by a low, Formica-topped coffee table, whose multicolored specks twinkled like fairy lights beneath the chandeliers. The table was flanked by three black leather sofas cluttered with red shag scatter cushions. Finally Sansi's eyes were drawn to a couple of lurid silk tapestries hanging from the silver walls. The first showed Lakshmi, the goddess of wealth. The second was about the size of a large bedspread and portrayed a different deity: Elvis Presley wearing a white fringed rhinestone-encrusted jumpsuit.

Sansi stared. There was something odd about the portrait, something strange. Then he realized what it was. This Elvis was black. And he bore a strong resemblance to Paul Kapoor.

Sansi shook his head. The entire room looked as though Kapoor had hired an interior decorator and said, "Go ahead, make a fool of me. I won't mind."

"Take your shoes off." Jackie Patro interrupted his thoughts.

"What?"

"You've got shit on your shoes," Patro said. "You'll get it on the carpet."

Sansi looked at the red nylon shag. Without comment he bent down and delicately prized off his shoes. There was a long smear of human excrement down one side of his right shoe. Patro took them both, tossed them outside and shut the door.

"Hey, Sansi," someone called in a friendly, familiar way. Sansi looked back across the room to see Paul Kapoor emerging from another room. Before the door closed Sansi got a glimpse of a bed covered in red silk and a wall consisting entirely of mirrors. There was a girl in there too, he noticed, lying in bed with her back to the door.

Kapoor was dressed all in black: black trousers, black shirt, black shoes. The only touch of color was a gold belt buckle. Black suited him, Sansi thought. Kapoor was better looking than his photographs in a cheap, sullen way.

"Glad you made it," Kapoor continued, as if they had known each other for years. Which, in a way, they had. "Like a drink?"

"Thank you," Sansi said. He craved something cold and clean to take away the foul, sticky taste in his mouth.

"Come over here." Kapoor stepped behind the bar and beckoned Sansi to join him. "You drink whiskey, right?"

Sansi was impressed. He knew that Kapoor's favorite drink was bourbon and his favorite brand was Jack Daniel's.

Sansi declined the offer. His head was already reeling under the impact of all that was happening to him.

"Any soft drink would be fine."

"Cola . . . you want a cola?"

"Fine."

"Ice?"

"Yes, thank you."

They could have been two business acquaintances meeting at the Oberoi to discuss a new investment.

Kapoor nodded to Patro and Patro nodded to the man with the scars. The scar man disappeared through yet another door. Sansi chose one of the high chairs in front of the bar and sat down. A moment later the scar man reappeared with a plastic ice bucket filled with ice cubes. He set the bucket down on the bar and continued to stare at Sansi. Sansi stared back. The man was thin and would have been unmemorable were it not for the ugly, mottled scars on his neck and face and the backs of his hands. Sansi wondered how far the scars extended over the rest of his body. He put the scar man somewhere in his late thirties, though the scars made him look older.

"You don't recognize Ajit, do you?" Kapoor said, a hint of amusement in his voice.

Sansi continued to stare back at the scarred man and shook his head. "No," he said. Something felt wrong. All Sansi's warning circuits had started to tingle.

Kapoor gave a barely perceptible nod and the scar man drifted away across the room to wait in silence near Patro.

"He knows you . . . and I don't think he likes you very much." Kapoor smirked but added nothing more. He plucked a bottle of Campa Cola from a small fridge under the bar, flicked the cap into a corner and pushed it across the bar. Sansi helped himself to some ice, filled the glass with Campa Cola and took a long swallow. It tasted like carbonated cough syrup but it was better than the sourness that had filled his mouth and throat. He put the glass down and looked at Kapoor.

"Now what?" Sansi asked with a calmness he didn't feel.

Kapoor's face broke into a charming, lopsided grin. His Elvis grin. Sansi couldn't help but be impressed. At a certain angle and in a certain light, the resemblance was uncanny. It was a pity about the accent. American slang and an Indian accent didn't work.

"You've got a lot of class for a cop," Kapoor said. "Is it true that the reason you don't take money is because you're rich? You and your old lady, that feminist broad, you've both got your own money?"

Sansi shrugged. "Police work is only a hobby," he said. "That's why you've gotten away with so much. I haven't really been trying." Sansi surprised himself. He was being seduced by Kapoor, by the absurdity of the situation.

Kapoor liked that, Sansi could tell. The gangster chuckled softly to himself. Then he produced another tall glass, dropped in a few cubes of ice, added a splash of bourbon and a thick, viscous curl of crème de menthe.

"Mint julep," he explained and took a long sip. When he put the glass down there was a milky green film on his lips.

"Let's see. . . ." Kapoor looked around at the photographs on the wall behind the bar. "Let's see who you know here. Him?" He nodded toward a picture of a smiling young man with a greasy pompadour. "You know who that is? You recognize him?"

Sansi gazed at the black-and-white snapshots for a minute. They were all portraits, head-and-shoulders shots of singing idols from the 1950s with slick hair and Colgate smiles. Sansi studied the picture Kapoor had singled out then shook his head.

"Bobby Darin," the gangster said triumphantly. " 'Mack the Knife.' You don't remember 'Mack the Knife'?"

Sansi remembered.

"Dad da dah dah, da da dah dah, da da dah dah, dyaahh dee dah . . ." Kapoor glided through the opening bars. Flecks of crème de menthe spattered finely across his black shirt. "He was a cool guy," Kapoor pronounced.

Sansi nodded. There was something dreamy, something surreal about all of this. He had miscalculated. He was in greater danger than he had realized. He was trapped in the heart of Dharavai with a deranged gang boss who happened to be an Elvis impersonator with a fifties fetish.

"Know her?"

Sansi followed Kapoor's gaze to a picture of a wholesome-looking blonde with a manic smile. He shook his head.

"Rosemary Clooney," Kapoor said. "Some hot bitch, huh? Man, I'd like to fuck her. I'd like to go to the States and tell her how much I like her and her music and then I'd like to fuck her and fuck her good."

Sansi had an image of an aging peroxide blonde answering the door of her home in Beverly Hills to be confronted by a crazed Indian gangster and Elvis look-alike dressed in black who had an offer she couldn't refuse. Sansi was afraid to mention that all the people whose pictures were on the wall were either dead or in retirement homes. He wondered if Kapoor knew or if he was so caught up in his style warp that he didn't care.

Kapoor shot Sansi a self-conscious glance as though he had read the policeman's mind. He put down his empty glass and stepped out from behind the bar.

"Come over here." He beckoned Sansi across to one of the big leather sofas. "Sit down. It's time to talk business."

Sansi followed, relieved and hopeful that Kapoor might be about to inject a note of reality into their meeting. Something Sansi could hang on to.

"I want you to take a message to Jashwal Bikaner," Kapoor said without preamble.

It was only one more shock in an avalanche of shocks. Sansi took a moment to register his surprise. He had begun to feel numb.

"Bikaner has been getting a little greedy since I, uh, left town." Kapoor went on. "He's been pushing for territory, trying to move in on Dharavai—and I won't let that happen. If he keeps pushing there's going to be a war, Sansi. Nobody wants a war but I'll fight for what's mine. Bikaner's stupid if he thinks he can get away with it just because Jamal has had to show off what a tough cop he is and give me a hard time. But we both know Bikaner is stupid. That's why I want you to take a message to him. Tell him to stay out of

Dharavai. Tell your boss it would be better if we stopped playing games with each other. Jamal's tough-guy act hasn't changed anything. Jackie can take care of Bikaner if I want him to. And I can get in and out of Bombay any time I want."

He paused, as if daring Sansi to challenge the obvious, but Sansi stayed silent.

"Besides," Kapoor went on. "I've got something to sweeten the deal for Jamal too. I'm pulling out of Bombay. All I want is another two years."

This time Sansi couldn't keep the shock off his face.

Kapoor seemed satisfied by Sansi's reaction. "Worth your time coming out here, huh?"

Sansi had to agree. What Kapoor was suggesting was sensational—if it was true. The government and the police service did make deals with gangsters when it suited their purpose. If Kapoor really was offering to get out of Bombay within two years in exchange for a police-sanctioned truce it was a deal Jamal might find too good to ignore. Especially if the alternative was a bloody gang war that could leave the streets of Bombay strewn with the bodies of innocent dead. It took Sansi a moment to digest all that Kapoor had suggested in a few brief sentences. But his initial surprise was quickly tempered by fresh skepticism.

"I don't know," he said slowly. "Why would Bikaner listen to me? As for Jamal, I can take this back to him but I don't know how he'll react. I can't give you any guarantees here and now."

Kapoor nodded. "I understand that. But you have to understand that I haven't got a lot of time to wait around while you guys make up your minds. Bikaner either agrees to behave himself for two years—and he can have it all without a fight—or I turn Jackie loose. That should make sense to him. He's stupid—but not that stupid."

"Why would he believe me?" Sansi hedged. "He will assume I am in your pay, that I am just your messenger boy."

"You're the most honest cop in Bombay," Kapoor

smirked. "Correction ... the *only* honest cop in Bombay. You will have to make him believe you."

Sansi breathed deeply. "I'll discuss it with Jamal," he said. "That's all I can do."

Kapoor nodded but from his expression Sansi could tell he wasn't happy.

"You've got forty-eight hours."

"What?"

"I can't give you any longer." the gangster shrugged. "Bikaner probably knows I'm back by now—the whole city will know by tonight. He thinks I'm weak. He's hurt five of my people already. He's going to take a shot at me while he has the chance. I can't just sit around here and let him while Jamal thinks about it. If Bikaner and Jamal will give me two years to take care of business and get out, I'll be back in Dubai before the weekend. That's the deal. I like the view better there anyway ... even if the chicks are no good."

"Why should they believe you?" Sansi asked. "Why would you just fold and leave? Jamal may decide he doesn't have to make a deal. You're playing for time and in two years you'll change your mind."

"Look." Kapoor gestured toward the Elvis wall rug. "You know who that is?"

"Yes."

"Good. Elvis was the king, right? The king of rock 'n' roll. He came up from nothing, like me. And he didn't take shit from nobody. He could have had anything he wanted, any woman he wanted. The only problem with Elvis was ... he didn't know when to quit. He hung around too long, got fat and lazy—he made a fool of himself. He should have stepped down before it was too late. That picture up there? That's how I want to remember him. That's how the king should be remembered. Elvis should have retired when he was young and good looking ... like me. Get out when you're at the top, Sansi. That's what I want to do. I've made my money. I want to get out when I'm still at the top."

Sansi sat and listened in stoic silence. It was pure, undiluted craziness. He was drowning with a madman in a gaudy gold, silver and black sea of craziness. But it was real. And Kapoor was crazy enough to be telling the truth. It made a kind of sense.

"You promise me you won't do anything for forty-eight hours?" Sansi asked.

"Hey." Kapoor looked affronted. "I give you my word, man. You tell Bikaner he can have it all without a fight—if he waits two years. But I have my pride. I want to leave with dignity. If he tries to push me out now, I'll fight and he'll lose it all. And if Jamal lets a war start right under his nose, he can kiss the chief minister's job good-bye."

Sansi gave a wan smile. Kapoor might be under siege but he still had the ability to ruin the lives of some of Bombay's most powerful men. They would have to listen to what he had to say.

"If Jamal says it's okay to put this to Bikaner, you give me your word you won't make a move for forty-eight hours?" Sansi repeated.

"That's the deal, man. Forty-eight hours from midnight tonight."

"Acha." Sansi stood up. "Then I had better be getting back to town."

Kapoor got up, stepped around the slab of glinting Formica and shook Sansi's hand. "I like you, Sansi. We could do business together."

Sansi ignored the hint. "If I pull this off," he added, almost as an afterthought, "you'll owe me a big enough favor."

"Hey." Kapoor flashed his Elvis grin. "All you have to do is ask."

Patro and scar man escorted Sansi back out to the fetid, stifling corridor and waited while Sansi pulled on his soiled shoes. When he stood up he found himself staring directly into the scar man's eyes.

"I used to have hair," the man said. "Long hair."

Sansi looked around. The two armed guards idled a few feet away. Patro watched with a strange smile on his ugly, pockmarked face. Sansi realized there was no one here who would help him. A serpent of cold fear wriggled through his bowels.

"I'm sorry. . . ." Sansi began, but the words trailed away.

"You gave me these scars," the man said.

Sansi shook his head in bewilderment. Another madman. He wondered if he would ever leave Kapoor's stinking maze alive.

"At Tamori, a long time ago, remember? You and your friends at the Tamori garrison. Remember, blue eyes?"

It came back in a rush. Tamori . . . Naxalites . . . his fire-trap in the desert . . . the burned and injured guerilla lying on the sand looking up at him through a curtain of pain . . . blue eyes.

Sansi caught his breath. "I remember," he said. "I saved your life."

The man smiled and the web of scar tissue around his neck and jaw crinkled in a way that made him look even more grotesque. "Do you know what your friends did to me to get me to talk?"

"This won't change—"

"That bastard Singh was in a hurry," scar man interrupted, "so . . . they rubbed ground chili peppers into my open wounds."

Sansi flinched. He had never been told exactly how they had made the guerilla talk so quickly.

"They rubbed ground chili into every burn on my body," scar man went on. "Do you know . . . The pain was . . ." His voice faltered as the memory came back. His eyes blurred with the agony of recall.

"One day," the man said, his voice a malign whisper, "I will teach you what that kind of pain is like." Then he stepped back into the darkness and was gone.

11

"Sᴀʜɪʙ, I ᴛʜɪɴᴋ we may have the identity of the murder victim."

Sansi put his head in his hands and moaned softly to himself. Sergeant Chowdhary blinked. It was not the reaction he had expected.

"But sahib . . ."

"*Acha.*" Sansi saw his assistant's crestfallen face. "It isn't your fault, Sergeant. It's just that I have . . . an emergency on my hands at the moment."

Emergency was an understatement. Sansi had to reach Jamal to tell him that Bombay faced the prospect of a gang war in two days, unless Crime Branch was willing to broker a deal on behalf of the most wanted man in the city. Sansi could not predict Jamal's reaction with any certainty but he felt sure his boss would be anxious to avoid a war. Bombay's gangsters were not discreet in their use of violence. The last gang war, in the mid-1970s, had cost the lives of two hundred people, many of them innocent bystanders or valuable police informers. As Kapoor had pointed out, a repeat of something of that magnitude would not help Jamal's political aspirations.

It was almost eight o'clock. Dusk had fallen and Sansi had only been back in his office a few minutes. Enough time to make two phone calls. The first to Jamal's office, upstairs, only to discover that his boss had left for the day. The second had been to Jamal's home, where the *bai* told him that Mr. and Mrs. Jamal were having dinner at the President Hotel with friends and were expected to be out all evening. And now Sergeant Chowdhary had the break-through in the Film City murder investigation that Sansi had been pushing so hard for.

"Are Bapre," Sansi muttered. As the English said: It never rained but it poured. This felt like the monsoon. "Sit down. Show me what you've got."

Sansi would reach Jamal this evening. He would search every restaurant in the President Hotel if necessary. If that failed he would sit outside the joint commissioner's home all night. Sansi could spare his sergeant a few precious minutes.

Chowdhary folded his lean, angular body into a chair, pen in one hand and a list of names in the other. They were the names Kilachand had given Sansi the day before. All but three had been crossed out. These had been circled and one in particular had been underlined. Chowdhary and his constables had been busy, Sansi realized. Despite the fear and apprehension that had consumed him ever since he had received Kapoor's call that afternoon, Sansi felt a new thrill of anticipation.

"We had it down to these three by four o'clock," Chowdhary explained and ticked off the circled names. "This one left for London in February. He's still there, looking for work. We spoke to him a couple of hours ago. Got him out of bed. This one is on his honeymoon in the Maldives. His mother said he wanted to keep the wedding a secret. This one . . ." Chowdhary paused and slapped the underlined name with the pen. "This one is our man, I think. His name is Sanjay Nayak. He lives up at Juhu, in a small apartment building."

Sansi nodded. Juhu Beach was Bombay's Malibu. An exclusive beach enclave thirty miles north of the city occupied mostly by movie stars, actors, producers and directors and all those who thought the first step to fame was to live in the right neighborhood.

"I spoke to the building superintendent and he told me that Nayak hasn't paid this month's rent," Chowdhary continued. "He said he hasn't seen Nayak for two weeks but all his things are still in his apartment. He hasn't moved out. The superintendent thinks something is wrong. He used to see Nayak nearly every day. He confirms that Nayak was an actor and went for long periods of time without work but that he had been happy recently because he had a regular job at Film City. But—and you will be pleased to know this, sahib—the superintendent says Nayak made most of his money doing other things."

"What other things?"

"The superintendent thinks Nayak worked for an escort service."

Sansi leaned back in his chair.

"A male prostitute?"

"The superintendent did not say that Nayak was homosexual, sahib."

"No . . ." Sansi shook his head. "He wouldn't necessarily know—if Nayak didn't want him to."

Sansi knew what he should do. He ought to leave for Juhu first thing in the morning and step up the momentum of the investigation. He swore softly to himself. Damn Kapoor. Damn Jamal. Damn all the gangsters and the corrupt, manipulative politicians whose petty ambitions got in the way of real police business.

"Anything else?" he asked.

"Yes, sahib. I called Film City. Nayak's last job was on a new TV series they are making up there. Something called *Chanakya*. He was playing the role of a temple eunuch."

"A what . . . ?"

"A eunuch, sahib. A temple—"

"*Acha.* I heard." Sansi rubbed his tired face. Perhaps it was only a coincidence. Perhaps it was irony. "Who did you speak to at Film City?" he asked.

"A man called Pratap Coyarjee. He is the—"

"Studio manager," Sansi interrupted again. "He looks after the cast lists. He must have known this boy Nayak."

Chowdhary waited. Sansi had slipped deep into thought. At last he revived himself and looked across his desk into

Chowdhary's thin, solemn face. Sansi felt a momentary pang of guilt. "You've done well, Sergeant," he said kindly.

Chowdhary nodded, got up to go and saluted.

Sansi made up his mind. "Have a car ready for me at eight o'clock tomorrow morning," he said. "We're going up to Juhu."

Sansi would stay up all night if he had to. But he was not going to let anything get in the way of his investigation. Not even a gang war.

"He said *what*?" For a moment Joint Commissioner Jamal looked as though he were about to choke.

Sansi had found Jamal at Gulzar's restaurant in the President Hotel. The joint commissioner hadn't been too happy to be summoned from his dinner with the deputy chief minister and his wife. They had stepped out into the hotel lobby and closed the door on the live sitar music that filled the restaurant.

Jamal took Sansi by the elbow and they began a slow circuit of the large, half-empty lobby, just like any other hotel guests enjoying an after-dinner promenade.

Sansi summarized his meeting with Kapoor and when he had finished they both looked at the lobby clock. It was a few minutes after ten.

"I'm going to have to rely on your impression," Jamal said after a moment, shifting the responsibility for his decision back onto Sansi. "Do you think he was bluffing or is he serious?"

"I think we have to treat it as serious, sir. If we ignore it, he's liable to do something just to make a point. It's a matter of pride with him. Machismo. And we know that some of what he told me is true. There have been skirmishes between Patro and Bikaner's men. Nobody has been killed yet but it's probably only a matter of time. Kapoor seems to me to be a desperate man. He told me that all he wants is time to pull out gracefully. I don't know if we can trust him, but . . ." He dangled the unspoken threat between them.

"That little shit," Jamal swore. "What about your informer? We were supposed to know when Kapoor was coming back. I wanted to stop him getting into the city."

Sansi shook his head. "I haven't heard anything, sir. Perhaps my informer did not hear anything. Perhaps he is afraid to call me. Perhaps he's dead. If Patro suspected he was passing on information . . ."

Jamal grunted. "If he contacts you in the next few days, bring him in so I can cut his balls off personally."

"Yes, sir."

They walked in silence for a while.

"We can't take the risk," Jamal conceded reluctantly. "You'll have to see Bikaner."

"Official seal of approval?"

Jamal shot Sansi a withering glance. "We can't be seen to be lending our approval to . . . an arrangement such as this."

"So Kapoor gets his two years?"

"Tell him the only deal he'll get from me is that if he gets out of Bombay and stays out, we won't move against him. That's the most I can offer. If he breaks his word, if he keeps coming back to Bombay, he's going to wind up dead or in jail. If Bikaner goes along with that, that's his business. We won't make any deals with Bikaner. I can live with myself by going easy on Kapoor if he's really ready to pull out. At least that way we get something. And we have room to move against Bikaner later."

"So Kapoor can't lose?"

Jamal stopped and faced Sansi, hands in his suit pockets, expensive tie, snowy white shirt, thick glossy hair brushed back from his forehead, every inch the chief executive.

"We can't stop them slaughtering each other in the streets if that's what they want to do," he said. "It's all a matter of timing. I don't want them doing it now, that's all. Kapoor knows damn well what he's doing to me. State cabinet will be meeting next week for the annual police review. My tenure is up for revision. I want at least two more years as JC, Sansi. Kapoor must know that."

Sansi sighed. Someone high in the state government must have called Kapoor in Dubai.

"I understand, sir," he said. There was nothing left to debate. It was the system. And like Jamal, Sansi was trapped within the system; he had no choice but to work with it. He too had to play the political game, whether he wanted to or not.

Jamal gave Sansi's shoulder a friendly squeeze. Two men who understood each other. Sansi realized he had probably just assured himself of further promotion.

"You look tired," the joint commissioner said. "Go home, get some sleep—you've got some time. See Bikaner tomorrow. Kapoor promised not to move for forty-eight hours, didn't he?"

Sansi nodded. "If we can believe him."

Jamal shrugged and walked back down the lobby to the restaurant, his wife and his influential friends.

Sansi turned toward the hotel exit and saw his reflection in the sliding glass doors. He looked tired. He felt dirty.

Like its glamorous Californian counterpart at Malibu, the Indian movie star colony of Juhu Beach was carefully segregated according to money, power and celebrity. Like Malibu, those who wanted to protect themselves from fans, neighbors and burglars employed extensive security measures. The only difference was the style of the security. In Malibu, movie stars paid a fortune for electronic security systems monitored by private paramilitary organizations. In Juhu the stars' homes were usually guarded around the clock by a dozen armed men in uniforms. Not because there was any greater danger, but because manpower in India was much cheaper than burglar alarms in California.

Khalia drove Sansi and Sergeant Chowdhary to Juhu Beach the next morning. It was like driving into Beirut during a lull in the civil war. On one side of the road was the beach, blighted by thickets of ramshackle stalls selling noxious treats like sugarcane, puffed rice and deep-fried balls of batter and chutney called *bani puri*. On the other side of the road were the villas of the movie stars surrounded by their private armed militias. Sansi wondered if there was an unspoken competition between the stars to see who could support the biggest militia.

Khalia turned inland and the character of the town altered dramatically. For a depth of two blocks along the beachfront there were nothing but luxury hotels, private villas, expensive apartments, shops and boutiques. Four blocks in and they might well have been in another squalid suburb of Bombay.

They stopped in front of a nondescript gray apartment block near the corner of Mehta Marg, four blocks back from the Holiday Inn. Sansi and Chowdhary climbed out and looked at the building. Four stories of cheap cement boxes with handkerchief-sized balconies. Sansi knew the rents would be exorbitant simply because the building was in Juhu and within easy walking distance of the beach.

Chowdhary led the way into a small, square lobby. There were three doors, a staircase but no elevator. There was also a potted palm in one corner, and the floor was littered with dead cockroaches. Chowdhary knocked on the superintendent's door and waited.

The superintendent was a small man with uncombed, thinning gray hair. He wore dirty khaki shorts and a white T-shirt and looked as though he had just climbed out of bed. "I am Surinder Dubey," he answered in response to Chowdhary. "Superintendent of this building."

Dubey plucked a bracelet of master keys off his kitchen table, then led Sansi and Chowdhary up three floors to Nayak's apartment.

"He was a strange boy," the superintendent volunteered as he opened the door. "A good-looking boy but a little strange . . . and secretive. I would have expected a boy like that to have a lot of friends but he didn't. Most of the people who came to see him were about my age. Too old to be real friends, I thought. I would see him around the building all the time. At first I didn't think he had a job—but he always paid the rent on time. He told me he was an actor. He said he had influential friends." The superintendent shrugged. "I know where he made most of his money."

Sansi and Chowdhary waited silently on the landing in front of the open door.

"He sold himself," Dubey said. "The men who came here were all customers."

"How do you know?" Sansi asked.

"Magazines," the superintendent explained. "You'll find them in there. *Bombay Tonite*, that kind of magazine. He used to cut out the advertisements for escort agencies and leave them on the kitchen counter."

"You used to go in here when he was out, go through his things?" Sansi asked.

An expression of alarm crossed the superintendent's face. "I have to know what my tenants are doing," he said defensively.

Sansi frowned. "Have you been in here since he disappeared?"

"Yes, of course," Dubey added. "That's how I knew he hadn't been back for a while. Some of the food had started to go bad. I threw it out."

"Did you touch anything else?" Sansi couldn't keep the annoyance out of his voice.

"Well, a few things, I suppose . . ."

"Are Bapre," Sansi muttered.

"Why, I haven't . . . ?"

"Do you realize that this is a murder investigation and now your fingerprints are all over that apartment?" Sansi added.

"I—" the superintendent protested.

"Wait downstairs," Sansi interrupted. "Either myself or my sergeant will talk to you in a while. If you're lucky you won't be charged with interfering with evidence in the course of a criminal investigation."

The superintendent looked stricken. His eyes flitted back and forth from one policeman to the other, then he turned and scuttled back down the stairs without another word.

"*Bakwas,*" Sansi swore. "Fools and incompetents and meddlers. Don't they ever stop to . . ."

Sansi's words died with a sigh of exasperation. He looked at Chowdhary and then smiled at his own frustration. The impossibility of conducting an efficient murder inquiry in Bombay was getting to him again. It was the Englishman in him, he knew.

Sansi turned and stepped into the dead man's apartment.

It didn't take long to search. There was a living room with an adjoining kitchen and a bedroom with an adjoining bathroom. That was all. A sliding glass door led onto a balcony where two would have been a crowd.

The apartment was sparsely furnished and had a musty smell that already spoke of its emptiness. Sansi went first to the bedroom. It was a box, barely big enough for the queen-size bed that dominated it. There was a window overlooking the street on one side of the bed and on the other, the whole wall had been turned into a wardrobe. The doors of the wardrobe were covered with floor-to-ceiling mirrors that doubled the size of the room. Inside, Nayak's clothes were arranged in neat rows. The bed was unmade. There was a table lamp in the shape of a male nude. Under the bed Sansi found a pile of magazines. A few copies of *Bombay Tonite,* as the superintendent had said, a few movie magazines and a few American gay magazines. In the bathroom Sansi found a few male nudes cut from magazines and stuck to the mirror. He stepped back into the bedroom, leaned over the bed and studied the bedsheets closely. Then he pulled them off the bed, bundled them and stuffed them into a plastic garbage bag held by Chowdhary.

In the living room there was a small sofa, a matching chair and a couple of small tables, all made from cheap cane. On one of the tables were two framed color photographs. The first showed a handsome youth of sixteen or seventeen with a middle-aged woman and two girls, both younger than he. Nayak with his mother and sisters, Sansi guessed. No sign of a father. The second picture was more recent and showed Nayak in a swimsuit on Juhu Beach.

There was a gold chain around his neck and he looked as though he was trying very hard to seduce the camera. Sansi saw only pathos. Carefully he removed the photograph from its frame and slipped it into a large brown envelope.

Sansi found more items of interest on the kitchen counter: an address book, a few advertisements for escort agencies snipped from *Bombay Tonite* and a half-finished letter.

The letter began: "My dearest mother, I am sorry you have not heard from me for so long but I have good news. I have been working. . . ." It continued with the all-too-familiar lies of a son's letter to his family, boasting of his success and of the fame and fortune he knew was just around the corner.

Sansi opened the address book. There were perhaps twenty entries, a mixture of names and initials with phone numbers alongside. There was only one name that Sansi recognized and it hardly came as a surprise at all: Pratap Coyarjee, studio manager of Film City. There were two numbers next to his name. The number for Film City and what Sansi was sure would turn out to be Coyarjee's home number. The number for Film City could be easily explained—but a private number?

Chowdhary emerged from the kitchen and shook his head. "No drugs, nothing," he said.

Sansi nodded and slid the address book into the envelope with the photograph. Later he would have Rohan go over Nayak's apartment for fingerprints.

The superintendent was waiting for them in the lobby. "What do I do about his furniture?" he asked.

Sansi looked at him. "You stick your nose in that apartment again, before I say it's all right, and I'll put you in jail myself. Do you understand?"

"When will I be able to rent out the apartment?" Dubey asked, a note of petulance in his voice.

"When I say so," Sansi added softly. "Sometimes business has to stop for murder."

12

WHEN SANSI GOT back to his office there was a message waiting on his desk from Dr. Rohan. Sansi dialed the number, his body tense with expectancy.

"I have some interesting news for you, Inspector," Rohan began.

Sansi waited.

"Despite the poor quality of the blood sample you gave us, we have been able to establish an enzymatic pattern."

"And . . . ?"

"The sample you took from the temple at Film City has the same enzymatic pattern as the blood of the victim. The chances of two separate individuals sharing the same blood enzyme pattern are one in ten million. So the balance of probability would indicate . . ."

"That our Mr. Nayak was murdered in the temple at Film City." Sansi finished the sentence for him.

"I'm sorry?"

"Our Mr. Nayak."

"You have a name?"

"We think we've established the identity of the victim, yes." Sansi sounded apologetic. "His name was Sanjay Nayak. I just got back from his apartment at Juhu Beach. I brought back the sheets from his bed. There are some stains on them that I'd like you to examine. They might be sweat, they might be urine . . . or they might be semen. His or somebody else's. You can get a blood group from semen stains, can't you?"

"If the sample is good enough," Rohan cautioned.

"I want you to send your people up there to dust for fingerprints too," Sansi added. He gave Rohan the address.

"We're getting somewhere, Doctor. Nayak was a small-time actor, full-time male prostitute. I have his address book. I want to know who visited his apartment. I want to be able to prove they were there. No circumstantial bullshit: I want provable sexual relationships. Then we can start looking at a motive. Jealousy, argument, betrayal, whatever . . ."

"Well, I might be able to help you there too," Rohan said.

Sansi paused.

"We swabbed that colonic section I took from the victim and took tissue and fluid samples."

"Yes?"

"We found microscopic traces of semen."

"You're sure?"

"There is no doubting it, Inspector. Our victim engaged in homosexual intercourse shortly before his death. The semen traces we found could well be from the murderer. I have something else for you too. As far as I am concerned it is the most important forensic evidence so far."

"Yes?" Sansi held his breath.

"We found a fragment of pubic hair inside the colon."

Sansi waited, sensing Rohan was holding something back.

"*Blond* pubic hair."

"*Blond?*" Sansi's voice rose in disbelief.

"That's right, Inspector. Shortly before he died, our victim engaged in anal intercourse with a person of European extraction. Not Indian."

Sansi slumped back in his chair, absorbing the impact of Rohan's findings. They cast a whole new light on the investigation. If it was someone of European background it could be a visitor, a foreign resident, an American, a businessman, a diplomat . . .

"I must admit," Rohan added, "I was quite disappointed."

"Disappointed?" Sansi echoed.

"Absolutely. It destroys completely my theory about the Hijdas. But I have to admit, it does support your theory rather well. You may be right, after all, Inspector. You may be looking for a lone psychopath. Someone who likes to engage in homoerotic mutilation. Someone of European extraction. If that is the case then it is going to make your job a lot harder. Killers who fit that profile usually operate alone."

"Rohan?" While the deputy coroner had been talking, Sansi had been thinking. "Can you get an enzyme pattern from the pubic hair and the semen?"

"Of course. As long as the root of the pubic hair is intact, and I think it is. The shaft of the hair is no good but the root will give us a pattern that we can match with the enzyme patterns in blood and semen."

"So." Sansi thought aloud. "We ought to be able to establish whether the semen and the pubic hair you found in the colon came from the same man. And if you can do that . . . then all we have to do is get a blood sample from the chief suspect and if it matches the enzyme patterns in the semen and the pubic hair . . . we've got him."

"Beyond all reasonable doubt," Rohan confirmed. "Have you got a suspect?"

"Not yet," Sansi conceded. "But I think I know where to look."

"I'd like to speak to Bikaner."

There was silence on the other end of the line.

"This is Inspector Sansi calling from Crime Branch. I want to speak to Jashwal Bikaner."

The line went dead.

"Damn," Sansi swore. He put the phone down and called for Chowdhary in the office next door. Sansi had no alternative. He would have to meet another hoodlum on his own terms.

Twenty minutes later, Sansi's driver, Khalia, parked outside an impressive new apartment building on Marine Drive. Sansi got out with Chowdhary and gestured toward the top floor of the twelve-story building.

"That's Bikaner's penthouse," Sansi said. "Give me half an hour, then ring. If I don't come down within five minutes, get a tactical group here immediately. Understand?"

"Yes, sahib," Chowdhary didn't look happy. But then, Chowdhary never looked happy.

Sansi took a deep breath and walked alone into the building. The guards in the lobby let him pass when he produced his police warrant card. He stepped into the elevator and punched the button for the twelfth floor.

They were waiting for him when the elevator doors opened, two huge men barring his way out.

"My name is Sansi. I'm from Crime Branch," he said and waved his ID in their faces.

Both looked unimpressed.

"I have a message for Jashwal Bikaner. It's important. Now let me past."

The elevator doors began to close and Sansi put his finger on the "hold" button. The doors stopped and slid back.

"I know this is Bikaner's apartment. . . ." Sansi tried again.

One of the men leaned into the elevator, knocked Sansi's hand away from the "hold" button and the doors began to close again. Sansi hit the button again. The doors shimmied back and forth, then opened again, but this time the alarm bell began to clang.

"I have a proposition for Jashwal Bikaner," Sansi shouted above the racket. Neither man moved. Sansi lost his temper and took his hand off the button. "All right," he yelled as the doors began to close for the last time. "You tell Bikaner, if he doesn't listen to me, in forty-eight hours he's a dead man."

At the last moment one of the men jammed a beefy paw between the doors and pushed them apart. Sansi saw Jashwal Bikaner standing in the doorway of his penthouse. One of the bodyguards crooked a finger at Sansi and he stepped out of the elevator. The doors slammed shut, the elevator disappeared with a grateful sigh and the loud clanging of the alarm bell stopped.

"What do you want?" Bikaner asked. He was a big, balding man who had run to fat and his voice had a hoarse, gravelly sound as though he was talking through a bad cold. Bikaner wore a silk bathrobe, even though it was mid-afternoon, and the stub of a cigar glowed between the fingers of his right hand.

"I've got something of a deal for you," Sansi repeated. He tried to put it in terms Bikaner would understand. "I think you'll find it's in your best interests to listen."

Bikaner studied him for a moment. Visits from Crime Branch inspectors weren't that common. He didn't like it. He didn't like any surprise visits from policemen unless they were on his payroll. And Sansi wasn't.

"Come in," he decided.

Sansi stepped forward and was halted by a paw in his chest. The bodyguard patted him down, then motioned him to follow. Sansi shook his head. Kapoor was right. These people were dangerously stupid.

He stepped into Bikaner's penthouse and was confronted by another monstrous wall hanging. Bikaner's taste ran to a lifesize silk portrait of a lurid leaping tiger on a background of black velvet. As he followed Bikaner down the hallway Sansi found himself staring into the yellow eyes of another tiger, snarling at him from the back of Bikaner's dressing gown.

Bikaner was Bengali, Sansi recalled. Bengalis thought themselves a cut above most other Indians. Bikaner not only thought himself superior, he apparently believed he was the soul incarnate of a Bengali tiger.

Unlike Kapoor, Jashwal Bikaner lived with a certain borrowed flair. His penthouse was not the home of a street punk with a fifties fetish. It was the home of an ostentatiously wealthy man. Clearly Bikaner had superior taste in interior decorators. The walls were lined with creamy shot silk, the couches were cream-colored leather. There was a table that seemed to have been sculpted from a piece of solid black marble. The walls were decorated with portraits of Hindu gods: Hanuman, the monkey god and protector of wrestlers; Lord Ganesh, the elephant god who bestowed good fortune; and Siva, the creator and the destroyer. One whole wall consisted of glass shelves filled with vases and precious urns inscribed with Sanskrit that should have been in a museum. Sansi was sure Bikaner knew how much they all cost—but he would have no idea what they were worth.

"Sit down." Bikaner gestured toward an armchair near the terrace windows. The terrace was the size of a tennis court and had been carpeted with AstroTurf. Bikaner sat alone on a leather sofa and sucked on his cigar while the two bodyguards loitered nearby, watching Sansi.

"Well?" Bikaner rumbled.

"I have a message from Paul Kapoor," Sansi began.

Bikaner's scowl of suspicion never changed. "Why you?"

"He's made an offer to the police department . . . and to you. If you're interested."

"He's back in Bombay?"

"Yes."

Bikaner nodded. "What does he want?"

"A truce. For two years. He says he's getting out of Bombay . . . but he won't be pushed out. He says you can have it all in two years, without a fight, if that's what you want. But he isn't ready to go yet and if you keep poaching on his territory he says he'll fight."

Bikaner hawked a globule of phlegm into his mouth and swallowed. "That little shit. He's finished now and he knows it. He's lucky he got this far. He has no style. He's always been *salah*. Why should I make a deal with him?"

"If you don't, he says he'll turn Jackie Patro loose." Sansi deliberately used Kapoor's words. The image of Patro unleashed was not an idle threat. "He said Patro wants you. Personally."

Bikaner seemed unimpressed. "What does Jamal think of all this?"

"He doesn't want another gang war." It was the truth but Sansi wasn't going to explain why.

"How much is Kapoor paying you to be his messenger boy, Sansi?"

Sansi suppressed the sudden flare of anger. Normally he had little difficulty in putting distance between himself and his emotions when it came to hoodlums. But Bikaner was different. Bikaner was malign and obscene. Kapoor's criminality was tempered by the charm of eccentricity. Bikaner had nothing—only ugliness. An ugliness that spilled outside the boundaries of his world and harmed innocent people. Bikaner didn't care who he hurt. And his sexual appetites were known to include children of both sexes. Sansi chafed because he had been put in a position where Bikaner could talk to him like this. What he wanted to do was to go back downstairs to his car and radio the tactical response group to come and take Bikaner now and worry about charges later.

"I don't take money from scum," Sansi answered.

If Bikaner picked up the nuance it didn't register in his expression. Bikaner rephrased the question. "What do you get out of this?"

"Kapoor saves us the trouble of kicking him out of Bombay again. This time he doesn't come back. He leaves Patro to run things for two years. There's no gang war. All we have to worry about is you."

Bikaner smiled for the first time. It was only a slight curling of the lips but it was a smile, nonetheless. "I think it smells," he said.

"*Acha.*" Sansi nodded. "That's the deal." He was sick of the sight of Bikaner. He got up to go. "Kapoor said he'd do nothing for forty-eight hours. Forty-eight hours from midnight last night. After that . . ." He shrugged.

Bikaner stayed where he was, lounging on the sofa. Sansi headed for the door. Bikaner's bodyguards closed in on him.

"Two years?" Bikaner said.

"Two years."

Bikaner got up with a grunt, stepped outside onto the terrace, hawked and spat over the balcony.

"Tell him I'll think about it," he said.

"VIP Escort Service." It was a woman's voice, silky with promise.

"Ah, yes, ah, good evening." Sansi didn't have to feign awkwardness. He had never been a proficient liar. "I am calling to inquire about the type of service your agency provides."

"Certainly, sir," the woman answered. "We have a number of young ladies and young gentlemen available for various occasions, social and personal. Perhaps you would like to tell me what you are looking for?"

Sansi coughed. "It is, ah, not something I would care to discuss on the telephone. I, ah, wonder if it might be possible to . . . see someone."

"Certainly, sir. We provide a most discreet service. We can arrange for someone to call at your home, at your apartment or your hotel to discuss your requirements. We have a large number of very nice young ladies and gentlemen, very well mannered, very clean. Privacy is—"

"That would not be possible," Sansi interjected. "I do not need . . . I am looking for an arrangement . . . I hope you understand. I would like to come and talk to someone at your office."

There was a pause. Sansi didn't think she was going to go for it.

"May I ask where you obtained our telephone number, please, sir?"

"Yes, ah, there was an advertisement in a magazine . . . *Bombay Tonite.*"

"Thank you, sir. When would it be convenient for you to call and discuss your requirements?"

"Tomorrow perhaps? Around five o'clock?"

"That would be fine, sir." She gave Sansi an address not far from the Taj Mahal hotel in Fort Bombay and hung up.

"Very good, sahib," Chowdhary applauded Sansi's performance. "Very convincing."

Sansi looked at him. He wasn't used to jokes from Chowdhary.

"I don't do it all the time," Sansi said.

"Oh no, sahib. Certainly not, sahib."

It was almost nine o'clock and Sansi was close to exhaustion. After his meeting with Bikaner he had returned to his office and spent the rest of the day with Chowdhary going through the names and numbers in Nayak's address book. There were twenty-three numbers in all. Six of them were traced to supposedly respectable businessmen, five of them to senior public servants, two of them to escort agencies and the rest to a handful of small-time actors. There were no numbers for Europeans or Americans. The numbers that stood out most were those for Pratap Coyarjee—and another that was identified only by the initials *N.K.* The number turned out to be the private residence of Noshir Kilachand.

Sansi had decided to make one more call before he was finished for the day. He needed just a little more information with which to confront Coyarjee and Kilachand.

"Come on, Sergeant," Sansi announced, getting wearily to his feet. "We're going to see the good people at the VIP Escort Service."

"Now, sahib?"

"Yes, while they aren't expecting us."

Khalia hit the curb with a rending screech of metal and stopped in front of a twenty-story high-rise lit up like a Christmas tree. Sansi and Chowdhary climbed out of the car and walked across a scrubby patch of grass toward the entrance. The night was stiflingly hot and humid. Light and noise poured from every open door and window: television sets, radios, people laughing, shouting, arguing, crying. Somewhere in that Tower of Babel, Sansi knew, the VIP Escort Service was just one of a hundred illegal businesses.

They got out of the elevator on the eighteenth floor and went to apartment 1805. The man who answered the door wore a mauve suit and a smile that evaporated the moment he saw Chowdhary's uniform. Sansi waved his police ID and pushed inside before the man could recover enough to protest.

They found themselves in a hallway with a couple of closed doors and a desk at the far end. A fat middle-aged woman wearing a sari and a lot of expensive jewelry sat at the desk, speaking into a phone. Sansi recognized the soft, silky voice. When she saw them, she mumbled something quickly into the mouthpiece and hung up.

"Inspector Sansi from Crime Branch. This is Sergeant Chowdhary. We'd like to speak to the manager . . . please." Sansi's voice was polite but firm. He preferred to keep it cordial but he also wanted them to know that they had no choice.

The woman looked miserable but recovered quickly. "Please, come through." She stood up with a rustle of silk and gave Sansi an ingratiating smile. Her figure was nowhere near as beguiling as her voice. Sansi put her weight at close to three hundred pounds.

"My name is Ashwin," she said. "Would you like some *chai*, gentlemen?"

They walked past the desk and into a small, blandly furnished living room. Sansi looked around. The apartment didn't look lived in. It seemed to be used solely for business. The three of them sat down and the woman spoke quickly to the doorman. She ordered tea and asked him to send in someone called Vinod.

"Vinod is my brother," she explained to Sansi. "We manage the business together."

A moment later a huge man in a three-piece pinstripe suit with a lot of gold rings on his fingers and a worried look on his face maneuvered himself sideways through the open door.

Sansi stared, first at the man and then back at the woman.

Twins, he realized. Twin grotesques.

"Good evening, gentlemen." Vinod bluffed his way through the introductions. He had the oily manner of his sister and the same anxious look in his eyes. He sat down on the sofa beside his sister and a wave of foam rippled across the seat cushion and slapped against the bulwark of her thigh. They were the same height, the same build, they had the same mannerisms and identically shaped faces. Sansi felt as though he had just been introduced to Tweedledee and Tweedledette.

"If it's about the premises . . ." Vinod began.

"No," he sought to reassure them. "We're here for information." Sansi preferred to enlist their willing cooperation and hoped self-interest would prove to be the best coercion.

Brother and sister nodded in unison.

"I want some information about a few of your clients," Sansi said.

"We're a respectable agency. . . ." Ashwin began.

"We're members of the chamber of commerce. . . ." Vinod stressed.

"We provide an executive service. . . ." Ashwin added.

"We have a very respectable client base," Vinod concluded.

It sounded like a routine. Brother and sister in psychic harmony, taking it in turns to deliver the same thought. It was like speaking to two halves of the same person. Which, Sansi realized, was precisely what they were.

He pulled an envelope from his jacket pocket, produced the photograph of Sanjay Nayak on the beach at Juhu and passed it to the twins.

"Do you know him?"

The twins examined the picture, looked at each other, then back at Sansi. They both nodded.

"That's Sanjay. . . ." Ashwin said.

"Sanjay Nayak," Vinod added.

"He worked for us last year. . . ."

"He was very popular. . . ."

"He left us at the end of November."

Sansi nodded. "I need to know which clients he serviced."

The twins looked at each other.

"Please . . ." Vinod began.

"Inspector . . ."

"This is a VIP service. . . ."

"We have client confidentiality. . . ."

"I'll close you down and seize every file in your possession," Sansi said. "Tonight."

"He had regular clients. . . ." Ashwin said.

"He wouldn't do Arabs. . . ."

"I can remember most of their names," Ashwin added.

"Good," Sansi said and took out his notebook.

Most of the names sounded familiar. Sansi guessed they were all in Nayak's address book. There was one notable exception.

"What about Noshir Kilachand?" Sansi asked.

The twins looked at each other, then back at Sansi. They both shook their heads.

"We know who he is. . . ." Vinod said.

"We've heard things. . . ." Ashwin added.

"But he was never a client of ours."

"How long was Pratap Coyarjee a client of yours?"

"A long time . . ." said Ashwin.

"Eight . . . nine years."

"And he saw Sanjay Nayak regularly?"

"He took Sanjay away from us," Vinod said.

"I'm sorry?" Sansi looked puzzled.

"They made an arrangement outside the agency," Vinod said.

"It happens sometimes," Ashwin added.

"That's why Sanjay left us. . . ."

"He said he didn't need us anymore. . . ."

"He said Pratap was going to take care of him from now on. . . ."

"We were very upset. . . ."

"He was a beautiful boy. . . ."

"One of our most popular . . ."

"Why . . . ?" Vinod asked.

"Has something happened to him?"

Sansi closed his notebook and got up to leave. "I don't think Pratap Coyarjee took very good care of him," he said.

The twins followed their two official visitors to the front door.

"If there's ever anything we can do for you, Inspector . . . ?" Ashwin called after him.

Sansi glanced at Chowdhary. The sergeant looked away, his face expressionless.

13

Pratap Coyarjee was sweating again.

The only time he had ever seen a police interview room before had been on a set at Film City. The real thing was much worse. It smelled of fear and urine. And some of the stains on the wall looked like blood. Real blood.

He had been on his own for three hours, ever since Sergeant Chowdhary had called for him at his apartment that morning. Apart from the initial information that Inspector Sansi wanted to ask a few questions, Chowdhary had volunteered very little. Coyarjee had made a quick call to Film City to say that he would be late, then he had been brought in to police headquarters and left in the interview room to stew for a while. And it was working. No one had charged him with anything. He ought to be free to go, he realized. Then why was he afraid to just get up and leave? Why had it come to this?

The door opened and Sansi appeared. He looked cool and fresh in a plain white suit. Coyarjee felt used and stale just looking at him. He shuffled on his chair. One chair leg was shorter than the others and it rocked. There were only two other pieces of furniture in the room. A table and a chair. Sansi pulled up the chair and set a notebook and a pen on the table in front of him. Then he looked at Coyarjee for a long time and something in his eyes told Coyarjee that Sansi knew.

"Pratap," he began. It sounded familiar and friendly. Sansi had never used his first name before. "You are aware that under Indian law, acts of indecency between males are punishable by jail terms of up to fourteen years? Aren't you?"

Coyarjee flinched. There was no answer. A gelatinous globule of sweat and gel trickled down his left cheek. Everything itched. He poked a fingernail delicately through the carefully arranged strands of hair on his head and scratched the bare skin underneath.

"How long had you and Sanjay Nayak been lovers?"

Coyarjee sniffed and wiped his nose with the back of his hand. "Is that who it was?"

"You know that's who it was," Sansi said softly.

Coyarjee hesitated a moment, then heaved a sigh of resignation. "I warned him. I told him to be careful. I told him he was getting involved with people, with things he didn't understand."

"With people who would kill him?"

Coyarjee gave Sansi the kind of pleading look he saw from a hundred beggars every day.

"I had nothing to do with Sanjay's death, Inspector. I swear. I tried to be his friend. I tried to give him advice, good advice. But he was so arrogant. You know what the young are like. They think they're invincible. They think they're going to live forever. He thought he could get away with anything . . . because he was young and beautiful."

Sansi never took his eyes off Coyarjee. "How long were you lovers?"

"Not quite one year," Coyarjee admitted, his voice weaker.

"How did you meet?"

Coyarjee looked at Sansi. He had no way of knowing how much Sansi knew. "Are you going to charge me with anything, Inspector?"

"At this moment, Pratap, that is entirely up to you." Sansi's tone was reasonable, sympathetic.

Coyarjee sighed. He looked wretched. Sansi felt nothing. Nothing but a determination to wring out of him everything he knew.

"I used to go to a couple of escort agencies in town,"

Coyarjee said. "I met Sanjay through the VIP Escort Service. He was new to Bombay. He was different, better than the usual boys they sent. He was . . . extraordinary."

"In what way?"

Coyarjee's throat suddenly went dry. Sansi ordered a constable waiting outside to bring a glass of water. The studio manager took a long drink and then looked oddly at Sansi.

"I don't know that someone like you would . . . understand," he hedged.

"You're going to have to try," Sansi responded.

Coyarjee took a deep breath. "Sanjay wasn't just beautiful," he began. "He was . . . he needed to be told, constantly, how beautiful he was. He wanted to be worshiped. As long as you worshiped him, he was happy. But as soon as he had won your devotion, he would get bored. He needed new people all the time. New people to conquer, to tell him how beautiful, how perfect he was. That was the only thing that made him happy. In the beginning it was enough that you were someone new to him. And his virility could be . . . extraordinary. He drew power from the devotion of others. He could stay hard for hours . . . and even when you were tired he still wanted you to touch him. To stroke him. To worship him. I remember . . . he loved mirrors . . ."

Sansi recalled the mirrored doors on the walk-in wardrobe in Nayak's bedroom.

"In the end he would only let me touch him. He liked me to stroke him in front of the mirror. He never grew tired of that. He could come and come and . . . he never grew tired. Worship was his aphrodisiac."

Sansi listened impassively. Just enough truth. Just enough lies. The key was to know which was which.

Coyarjee took another sip of water. "He got tired of me. The only way I could keep him was by introducing him to new people. I promised to build him a career in the movie business, to make him . . . a star."

Coyarjee gave Sansi a wan smile. "It wasn't difficult. He

had the looks. All I had to do was to put his name on the lists. He wasn't much of an actor but that doesn't matter. He could be so charming. People liked him. And he was ambitious. If he had been successful he would have been the most voracious movie star who ever lived. He would have consumed his audience. He was the kind of person who is made for the movie business."

"What went wrong?"

Coyarjee's gaze wandered and it was a full minute before he found his focus again. "Trying to hang on to someone by giving them their freedom is a self-defeating philosophy, Inspector. They don't come back, you know. Sanjay simply did not need me anymore. He met new people. One of them killed him."

"Who?"

Coyarjee looked directly into Sansi's eyes. "I don't know, Inspector, I swear. In the end I hated him. I loved him and I hated him. But I didn't kill him. And I don't know who did." His voice sounded flat and empty.

Sansi stared at Coyarjee in his loud silk shirt and his tawdry jewelry, at the ridiculous subterfuge of his hair, and saw a pathetic, ravaged man whose whole identity rested on a world of illusion. He didn't see a murderer. Coyarjee didn't have it in him. But he could still point in the right direction, Sansi was certain of that much.

"Did Sanjay have any white lovers?"

Coyarjee looked confused. "What, you mean . . . ?"

"Foreign businessmen, diplomats. Americans, Britons, Germans, Russians?"

Coyarjee shrugged. "It's possible. I told you, I don't know. He shut me out when he didn't need me anymore."

"What about Noshir Kilachand?"

The dullness in Coyarjee's eyes was lit by an unmistakable spark of alarm.

He shook his head. "I can't. Noshir wasn't . . ." He faltered and stopped.

"Pratap." Sansi leaned forward on the table. "You aren't leaving here until you tell me."

"I . . . if . . ." Coyarjee fumbled. He looked pleadingly at Sansi. "You can't tell him. You must never, never tell him I told you anything."

Sansi shrugged. "That depends."

Coyarjee looked around the ugly, windowless room. There was no comfort for him anywhere.

"Noshir was . . . another victim," he said at last. "That's all. Like me."

Sansi asked the obvious. "How long has Kilachand been bisexual?"

Coyarjee gave a tired laugh. "He's never been bisexual."

"He has a wife, three children," Sansi recalled.

"What difference does that make?"

"How long have you known?"

"Ever since we went to school together. He never came out, that's all. He was afraid. He was convinced it would ruin his life. You can hardly blame him."

"Didn't anybody ever suspect anything?"

"Did you?"

"How many people knew?"

"Not many. Me. Sanjay, of course. There were a few others over the years. Noshir was always very discreet. I usually found boys for him. I let him use my apartment."

"He would have been the perfect target for blackmail, wouldn't he?"

"Noshir didn't kill Sanjay."

"Who did?"

"I told you, I don't know. But it wasn't Noshir. He couldn't do something like that. You saw what he was like at the lake. He couldn't even look at the body."

"It didn't seem to upset you quite so much."

Coyarjee slowly shook his head. "I wasn't surprised. I knew that something had to be seriously wrong when he didn't come into work and I didn't hear from him. Nothing would have kept him away from a film set."

"Why didn't you tell me then that you knew who it was?"

Coyarjee evaded Sansi's gaze. "Because I didn't know,"

he said. "Neither of us knew then. I thought . . . I couldn't be sure. I think part of me didn't want to believe it. There was still a chance it could have been someone else. Noshir didn't want me to draw attention to Sanjay. I think it's obvious why."

Sansi nodded but his eyes looked unconvinced. "A moment ago you said Noshir was a victim, like you. Another victim of Sanjay. Why did you say that?"

Coyarjee shrugged. "People like Noshir and me make easy victims, Inspector. We're old men. Old and ugly. What do we have to offer someone like Sanjay? Money? Power? That's all. We enjoy his youth and his beauty. He uses us in return to get what he wants. Noshir is an important man, much more important than me. Sanjay wanted to use him too. Noshir knew that. He knew he could never trust Sanjay. That's why Noshir only saw him two or three times. He was falling in love. Like me. He couldn't afford to let that happen. Sanjay hurt him too and didn't even know it."

Sansi remained impassive. "Did Noshir ever go to Sanjay's apartment?"

Coyarjee shrugged. "I don't think so. I don't know. How would I know?"

Sansi looked at Coyarjee for a long time, then wrote something in his notebook, closed it and leaned back in his chair. *"Acha,"* he decided. "You can go now."

Coyarjee looked miserably back at him but said nothing. He got up to leave.

"Just one thing, Pratap," Sansi added, "don't plan on leaving town in the near future, will you?"

"I want a warrant for the arrest of Noshir Kilachand."

Joint Commissioner Jamal blinked across his desk at Sansi. "You think an arrest warrant is justified now? Why not bring him in for questioning, like Coyarjee?"

"Because I think I can get through to Kilachand faster this way. Coyarjee is a lot tougher than Kilachand. Coyarjee didn't turn a hair when he saw the body.

Kilachand could hardly stand up, he was so sick. In his own way, I think Coyarjee is smarter than Kilachand. He's still holding something back—and I think I can get at him faster if I crack Kilachand first. An arrest warrant will help me do that. It will shock Kilachand to the core."

"It will ruin his career, you know. It will be in all the papers. He will be finished."

"He's been withholding important evidence in a murder inquiry, sir."

"What evidence?"

"That he was a sexual partner of the murder victim. He might deny that he knew the body at the lake was Nayak, but he'd be lying, just like Coyarjee."

"You don't think either Coyarjee or Kilachand killed Nayak?"

"No, sir." Sansi gave Jamal a summary of Rohan's forensic findings, including the information about the blond pubic hair.

"But you think Kilachand is involved?"

"I'm certain of it, sir. Kilachand and Coyarjee shared the same lover. Coyarjee won't admit it but he pimped for Nayak at Film City. He supplied prostitutes to homosexual cronies like Kilachand. I think it's more than likely that Coyarjee introduced Nayak to some foreign visitor at Film City, a European or an American . . . and that's the man I'm looking for. I'm quite sure that both Kilachand and Coyarjee know who he is."

Jamal scratched absently at his neck. "Old Noshir a closet queen, eh?" he murmured. "The crafty old beggar called me so it would make him look all the more innocent. And all the time he was trying to make sure that when an investigation started, he would have a line open to me so he could try and keep it quiet. I'm surprised I haven't had another call from him."

"I don't think he knows yet, sir."

"It won't be long."

"That's why I want your approval to apply for an arrest warrant, sir. I want to pull him in today. Now."

"You can't arrest a man for sneaking around and telling lies, Sansi. The entire city would be under arrest."

"I only want the warrant on the withholding of evidence, sir. That will enable me to hang on to him for a while. If he's involved, as I know he is, a conspiracy charge will follow."

Jamal nodded. "I don't want you to apply for the warrant yet," he decided. "Bring him in for questioning. That's fair. If you get something concrete, charge him."

"But, sir—" Sansi protested.

His sentence was cut short by a flashbulb going off in Jamal's windows. At the same moment, both windows exploded inward in a shower of glass. A blast of hot air invaded the room, followed by the deafening crack of an explosion.

Sansi and Jamal threw themselves onto the floor in an effort to put Jamal's heavy desk between them and the blast. The office filled with dust and Sansi heard glass and other debris pattering down around them. The concussion ebbed away and all that was left was an unpleasant ringing sound in his ears.

"Bhagwan," Jamal swore. "Sansi, are you all right?"

Sansi tried to answer but the dust rushed into his nose and mouth and clogged his throat. He coughed and got shakily to his feet, peering through the murk to find Jamal.

The veranda outside echoed to the sound of running footsteps and men shouting. The office door burst open and someone called Jamal's name. Then Sansi felt someone take hold of him and guide him gently but firmly toward the open door.

The air cleared the moment Sansi stepped outside. He blinked the dust from his eyes and took in a series of disjointed images: Jamal, coated in dust and glass, surrounded by anxious police officers. Policemen in torn uniforms helping injured civilians down the stairs. A man lying on his back, surrounded by a spreading pool of blood, two constables trying to help him.

"Are you all right, sahib?"

It was Chowdhary who had rushed up from downstairs.

"I think so," Sansi answered tentatively.

He shook the dirt and glass from his hair, afraid of catching splinters in his eyes. When he moved his arms he felt a stab of pain in his middle back. He must have wrenched it when he threw himself to the floor in Jamal's office. He caught his breath and looked around.

A pall of dirty gray smoke loitered over the parade ground. The usual battery of parked vehicles had been transformed into a scrapyard. Not a single car or truck appeared to have escaped undamaged and several were on fire. At the far end of the parade ground, at the epicenter of the blast, there was a blackened crater filled with a tangle of smoldering metal. Every window in every building that faced the parade ground had been shattered. The elegant facade of the Crime Branch building had been peppered with fragments of flying metal and masonry. All around the parade ground people were running. Sansi glimpsed a few bodies on the ground, some moving, some still. In the distance he heard the first ambulance sirens.

"Car bomb," Jamal said.

Sansi looked around to see his boss leaning against the wall, surveying the carnage below.

"Bloody terrorists. Sikhs, Kashmiris . . . Punjabis. Somebody will claim responsibility before the end of the day."

Sansi gingerly brushed himself down. A pocket had been torn loose and a few slivers of glass glinted in the threads of his jacket.

"How the hell are we supposed to run an effective crime-fighting organization when we can't even stop people from blowing us up?" Jamal muttered, mostly to himself.

"Sir?" Sansi asked.

"Yes?"

"I'd still like that warrant, sir."

Jamal looked at him for a moment. "You really are quite determined about this one, aren't you, Sansi?"

"I saw the body, sir. Sanjay Nayak may not have been much of a human being. But no one deserves to die like that. Whoever killed him has to be caught. Soon. Before he kills again."

"You expect more like that?" Jamal asked.

"I've never been more certain of anything in my life, sir."

The noise and confusion around them seemed to fade as the two men studied each other. It was as though they had manufactured an oasis of calm at the eye of a storm.

"Acha," Jamal decided. "You can file for your warrant, Sansi. I don't think Kilachand has to worry about being on the front page tonight."

It was five o'clock before Sansi and Chowdhary pulled up outside Kilachand's office building on Madame Cama Road.

In the aftermath of the bomb blast at police headquarters, it had taken Sansi two hours to find a magistrate who would sign his warrant. Sansi had been glad to get away. First reports suggested it had not been as bad as it looked. Only one confirmed dead, twenty or thirty injured, including several visitors and civilian employees. Damage to police property had been considerable. Sansi counted himself fortunate that Khalia never parked on the parade ground. His car had been spared. Jamal's car was one of those destroyed.

"I'm sorry, was Mr. Kilachand expecting you?" the receptionist asked.

Sansi showed his ID, though he kept the arrest warrant in his pocket. That was for Kilachand's benefit. He wanted to go right into Kilachand's office, to the heart of his power, and to take him away to a dingy police interview room where no one could help him—where his power, his influential friends, his bureaucratic cunning and his refined, gentlemanly charm would do him no good at all. To a man like Kilachand, a gesture like that would be better than twenty-four hours in an isolation cell.

Ordinarily Sansi might have felt sympathy for Kilachand. But the Film City mogul had deceived him, lied to him, held back valuable information. If his life of deceit was finally going to catch up with him, he only had himself to blame.

"I'm afraid Mr. Kilachand isn't here," the receptionist added. "He went home early today. He said he was feeling ill."

Sansi felt a stab of apprehension. Kilachand knew. Too much time had elapsed between Coyarjee leaving headquarters and Sansi getting his warrant. That damned terrorist bomb! Kilachand was going to get away.

It was another hour before they were able to battle through city traffic to the quiet, leafy enclave off Desai Road where Kilachand lived. On the way, Sansi radioed headquarters to put an airport watch on Kilachand and to stop him if he tried to board a flight out of the country.

Mrs. Kilachand was surprised to see them. Sansi heard the voices of children playing in the garden. Two girls and a boy, Sansi recalled, seven, nine, and thirteen. It was an exquisite summer's evening with just enough of a breeze off the Arabian Sea to rustle the leaves in the trees. It all seemed so restful and calm, Sansi thought. So perfect.

"He's in his study," Mrs. Kilachand explained, puzzled. "He always brings his work home with him, Inspector. I do hope it's nothing serious; he's been so tired lately. He did tell me that he didn't want to be disturbed."

"Where is his study?" Sansi asked, his voice escalating to a pitch that was just enough to prompt a look of alarm on Mrs. Kilachand's face.

"Down this way, at the end of the . . ."

Sansi pushed past her, followed by Chowdhary. They both ran down the long, elegantly furnished hallway to the farthest wing of the house. The door was locked.

"Mr. Kilachand, sir. It's Inspector Sansi from Crime Branch. Please open the door, sir."

There was no answer. Sansi knocked loudly.

"Please, Inspector . . ." Mrs. Kilachand said behind them.

Sansi looked at the door. It looked as though it was made from solid oak.

"Sergeant!"

The two of them slammed their shoulders hard against the door in unison. Sansi winced as the pain in his back flared anew. The door didn't budge.

"Damn," Sansi swore.

"Mr. Kilachand, please," he tried again. "If you can hear me, open the door."

Still there was no answer.

Sansi turned to face Mrs. Kilachand. "Quickly, please. Is there another way into the study?"

Sansi's urgency was contagious. "Around the back," Mrs. Kilachand said. "The study has its own courtyard. There's a gate. . . ."

The *bai* and the cook stared as Sansi, Chowdhary and Mrs. Kilachand hurried through the kitchen. Mrs. Kilachand pointed to a narrow stone footpath and Sansi took it at a run. It took him around the house to a high brick wall with a narrow green gate. Sansi didn't slow his pace. He ran at the gate and kicked the lock hard. The gate flew open and Sansi rushed through to a small, paved courtyard, prettily embellished with vines and blossoming red bougainvillea. He stopped abruptly with Chowdhary right behind him.

"Don't let her. . . ." Sansi began.

Chowdhary turned to prevent Mrs. Kilachand from following them into the courtyard but it was too late. She looked over to the open French windows and saw her husband. She began to scream.

Noshir Kilachand hung from a crossbeam, a length of knotted rope around his neck. He rotated slowly in the breeze, like a giant chrysalis.

"Take your shirt off," Annie Ginnaro said. "I'll give you a massage."

Sansi suddenly felt self-conscious.

"Don't worry," she chided him. "I'm not making a pass at you. I'm a little more subtle than that. I took remedial massage at USC. I'm from southern California, remember? As long as you haven't torn anything, I can probably help you get some of the tension out. It might help you sleep tonight."

The idea of a good night's sleep appealed to him. Sansi hadn't slept much the previous night, despite the consumption of half a bottle of whiskey. The bomb blast at HQ, the sight of Noshir Kilachand hanging in the French windows, the looming possibility of a gang war—his mind had skipped from one nightmarish scenario to another.

It was only a few hours before Kapoor's forty-eight-hour deadline expired and still Sansi hadn't heard from Bikaner. Sergeant Chowdhary was watching the phones at HQ in case a call came through, and he knew how to get in touch with Sansi. The only reason Sansi had kept his dinner date with Annie was because her apartment was a few minutes' drive from his office and it was better than twiddling his thumbs beside a telephone all night.

Besides, he needed the break. Sansi felt as though he had spent the last few days on a roller coaster. His mood had veered from optimism and expectancy to gloom and despondency. No matter how hard he worked, no matter how fiercely he fought, it seemed he could never make any headway against the engulfing tide of chaos and corruption. Sansi worried that he was losing heart for the struggle. He had begun to feel as if he were drowning in the madness, in the perpetual turmoil that was India. Was it really any worse, he wondered, or was it only that he was getting older?

Sansi smiled. He recognized the symptoms. He was beginning to feel sorry for himself. Perhaps Annie was right. Perhaps all he really needed was a soothing massage at the hands of a beautiful redhead from southern California.

Dinner had gone well. He had picked up a few dishes of *tikki* and *tandoori* at the Delhi Durbar and Annie had provided a pitcher of vodka martinis and a couple of bottles of good chablis. Her apartment was a small one-bedroom flat on the ninth floor of a new complex at Nariman Point. Its most expensive feature was the view over Back Bay, which at night included the illuminated crescent of Marine Drive.

"Alimony." Annie had answered his unspoken question when they had stepped out onto the balcony with their drinks.

She had dressed all in white in a loose cotton blouse and a pair of baggy drawstring pants. The effect was to make her look darker, more Indian. It seemed to him that she had deliberately avoided shoptalk all evening, although that was supposed to be the reason for their meeting. Instead, they had talked about childhood, about parents and friends and lost innocence, about southern California, England and India. Despite some initial misgivings, they had found it surprisingly easy to talk to each other. Annie said she had expected him to cancel when she heard about the bomb blast at police headquarters. She seemed flattered that he had come anyway.

Now they sat opposite each other in her tiny, prettily decorated living room. He sat awkwardly in a thickly cushioned wicker chair. She studied him from a small, two-seater sofa where she sat with her bare feet tucked underneath her, a half-finished glass of wine in her hand.

"It's been killing you all night, hasn't it?" she said.

"I'm sorry?"

"Your back. It's been giving you hell all night. I can see it on your face."

Sansi tried to make light of it. "I think I pulled something, that's all. It will probably go away in a few days."

She made a face. "Why suffer? Come on, take your shirt off. I promise not to swoon at the sight of your manly chest."

Sansi fidgeted for a moment, then got up. She was right. His back had nagged him nonstop since the blast. Discomfort overcame embarrassment. He began to unbutton his shirt.

Annie got up, brought a large towel from the bathroom and spread it out on the carpet.

"There," she said. "Lie facedown, arms over your head . . . and try to relax."

Sansi did as he was told. Annie disappeared into the bathroom again and reappeared a moment later with a bottle of baby oil. Then she sat astride his legs, poured some of the baby oil into her hands and began to smear it across his back. It felt cold and slick. Sansi gave an involuntary twitch.

"My friends and I used to do this for each other all the time when I was at USC," she said. "Total body massage. Total turn-on."

Sansi didn't respond.

"You're not shocked, are you?"

"No," he answered truthfully.

"Maybe they were more conservative at Oxford."

"No . . . it was just colder."

She laughed softly. "There's a lot of the Brit in you, isn't there, Sansi?"

"My father was very English."

"He was in the army, wasn't he? What did he do?"

"He was a general."

"Jesus," she breathed. "That's . . . brass. Real brass." She finished spreading the oil and then began to probe and prod with her fingertips around the muscles of his back, gently in some places, more firmly in others. "How did he meet your mother?"

"At a party at Government House. He was with his wife when he fell in love with my mother."

"My God," she laughed. "Is that true?"

"That's what he told me. Love at first sight."

"How did they, ah, get together?"

"You mean how did I get into the picture?"

"Well . . . yes."

"My mother became his mistress."

Annie gasped and leaned back on her haunches. "I love it!" she exclaimed. "Pramila was the girlfriend of a stuffy British Army general. My God, it's like something out of Kipling. It's so . . ."

"Romantic?"

"Well, yes it is. Stop laughing at me." She leaned forward and began probing his muscles again for the hidden knots of tension, the raw sinews and tender muscle fibers.

"It wasn't romantic for very long."

"How long were they together?"

"Two years, I think. They met in 1945, at the end of the war. I was born in 1947, the year of Indian independence. My father went home with the rest of the British Army. My mother was left on her own with a child to bring up."

"Weren't her family any help?"

Sansi chuckled drily. "You must be joking. Her father, my grandfather, wouldn't have anything to do with her. When he knew she was sleeping with a British Army officer he threw her out of the house, disowned her, disinherited her."

"Why? Because of this caste bullshit? Because she was damaged goods?"

"Partly," Sansi said. "At least, that was the excuse he gave."

"Well ...," Annie paused, fascinated. "What was the real reason?"

"Extreme bad timing. British officers had been taking Indian women as their mistresses for two hundred years. There was nothing new in that. For a while it was even an advantage for an Indian girl to be kept by a British officer—the more senior, the better. It could benefit the whole family. Some officers used to steer big army contracts to the families of their girlfriends. A lot of Indian merchants grew rich by exchanging a daughter for a good trade deal.

"My mother's problem was her timing. She met my father just when the British were coming to the end of their reign in India. Everyone was a nationalist after the war. Everyone followed Gandhi, whether they believed in him or not. It was the thing to do if you wanted to survive in an independent India. My grandfather was a shipping broker and he couldn't afford to have a daughter sleeping with a

British general just when the country was getting its independence. It would have been bad for business. My mother said he was courting all the bigwigs in the Congress Party at the time, hoping to find favor with the new government. He absolutely forbade her to see the general. You've met my mother. You know how she reacts to threats."

Annie smiled. "So she was thrown out on the street, with nothing?"

"Not quite. General Spooner bought her the apartment on Malabar Hill before he left. And he gave her some money. I think it was quite a lot of money. His wife was rather upset with him."

"Spooner, that was his name?"

"General George Spooner," Sansi said.

"So that's where the George comes from."

"Forever cursed," Sansi added. "Half English, half Indian."

"My God." Annie shook her head. "What a story." Her hands had fallen still on his shoulders. She pulled herself back into focus and tried to concentrate on what she was doing. Her fingers resumed their exploration of his spine again, then moved across his shoulders and around the fibrous mass of the trapezius at the base of the skull.

Neither of them spoke for a few minutes.

"Okay," she said at last, "I've got it." Her right hand moved lightly down to his lumbar region and traced an ellipse across his skin.

Sansi winced.

"That's it, isn't it?"

"Yes."

"There's no bruise but you obviously pulled it when you hit the floor. Must have twisted as you fell."

"Yes." Sansi recalled the way he had thrown himself sideways off the chair.

"All right," she said. "I'll work around it, soften you up for a while. Your sternomastoid is like a boulder. You've got a lot of tension in there, George."

Sansi smiled at the way she used his first name. "My what?"

"Your sternomastoid. That's where your neck latches onto your shoulders. Always a great trouble spot. If you're feeling really tough I could stand on it for you."

"Perhaps another time."

"What a wimp." She smiled. "All right, I promise I'll be gentle."

She started around the shoulders, working her fingers gradually into the tightly clenched mass of muscle fiber, pushing and massaging as the muscles responded and relaxed. Sansi groaned. It was half agony, half pleasure.

"Is your father still around?" she asked after a while, unable to suppress her curiosity.

"Yes," Sansi answered. "He's getting on a bit. He's in his eighties now. He lives quite near Oxford. A delightful old man. He really loved my mother. That was the tragedy of it."

"Is his wife still around?"

"Audrey Spooner died a long time ago. She hated India. She only came out once, stayed a year and went home. The general first came out in 1933 when he was a young lieutenant. Apart from a couple of years back in England, I think he was in India most of his married life. That's why it was so easy for him to take a mistress. Audrey didn't mind, as long as he never brought any scandal home with him. His other children hated it."

"His *other* children? You have . . . brothers and sisters?"

"Oh yes," Sansi said. "One of each. Eric and Hilary. Both white, very County. You can imagine what they make of me."

"I take it you don't get along."

"Audrey Spooner had all the money in the family. When she died, it passed to my father. He spent some of that money on me. Eric and Hilary resented that. He paid for me to be educated at Oxford. He thought a law degree was the best present he could give me. I don't think it was the money that bothered Eric and Hilary so much—it was the thought that he was desecrating their mother's memory by bringing his bastard into the family fold. It probably didn't help that I was a black bastard. That never bothered my father. Obviously a lot of what he did for us was because he felt guilty. But I think most of it was because he happened to be a good man."

"How much time have you spent with him?"

"The first time I met him was . . . 1959. He came out to see us. Audrey had died the previous year so I suppose he felt free to do as he liked then. He stayed for a month. I remember thinking what an old man he was to have been in love with my mother. It was impossible to see what she saw in him. She was so beautiful."

"She still is."

"My mother said he was the kindest man in the whole world. That's why she loved him. After a while I saw what she meant. He took the time to get to know me; it was the first time anyone, apart from my mother, had really taken an interest in me. I didn't see him again until I went to Oxford. I lived at Goscombe Park for a year."

"Goscombe Park?"

"The Spooner family home."

"It sounds pretty grand."

"It was. It still is. He lives there with Eric and his wife and children. Hilary married and moved away years ago. Eric will inherit the estate when my father dies."

"If the general loved Pramila," Annie said, "why didn't he just say 'To hell with it' and leave his wife? It doesn't sound like he had much of a marriage anyway."

Sansi smiled. "That's a very American way of looking at things," he said. "It was never that easy in England, especially in the class to which my father belonged and especially at that time. It was all bound up with duty and family honor. You could have a mistress on the side, you could be a gambler, a drunk, you could chase choirboys around the church, you could be as much of a hypocrite as you liked—as long as you did it behind closed doors. It was very much a class thing."

"Caste and class," Annie murmured. "No wonder the British lasted so long in India. Underneath all the bullshit about colonialism and independence, you're both exactly the same."

"Yes," Sansi agreed. "I think we probably are. And that is why I have never been able to hate the English."

"What's that?" Annie asked abruptly.

"What's wha—?"

"That." She passed her finger along the ridge of a scar on his lower left side.

"An old scar," he said.

"What from?"

"A knife, actually."

"Actually?"

She made him smile again.

"How did you get it?"

"A terrorist. A long time ago, when I was a young constable."

"What happened to him?"

"Her."

"*Her?* It was a woman?"

"A girl, actu—" This time he stopped himself. He had noticed that she found the Anglicisms in his speech and manner much more amusing than the Indian.

"A young girl. About sixteen or seventeen, I think."

"What happened?"

"I shot her."

"You killed her?"

"Yes."

Annie paused. "I can't imagine ever being in a situation where I might have to do something like that," she said.

"This is India," Sansi answered. It was the only explanation he could offer.

Wordlessly, Annie returned to the massage. Her need to know more about Sansi had only been awakened. But instinct told her that for now, he had no more to give. Instead, she decided to give to him.

Inch by inch she worked through every nervous muscle

and tendon in his body, feeling for the pain as though it were written in Braille, kneading and pushing, exorcising the tensions locked beneath his skin.

After ten minutes she thought she heard something. She stopped and listened. Perspiration clung like dew to her skin and she was breathing heavily. She held her breath. Then she heard it again. He was snoring.

Annie smiled. She leaned away from Sansi's sleeping body, then got up and stepped into the bathroom to get a towel for her hands. When she returned she sat on the sofa for a while and watched him sleep. Then she got down on the floor and lay down beside him, her head cradled on her arm, her face only inches from his. She lay still for a long time, watching him. Then her eyes closed and she too drifted comfortably off to sleep.

At that moment, six blocks away, Jashwal Bikaner left his penthouse apartment, flanked by two bodyguards. They rode the elevator down to the lobby in silence. Two more guards waited at the entrance to the building with the security men who patrolled the grounds. There were two cars parked at the curbside, their engines already running. The lead car was a sleek black armor-plated Mercedes that Bikaner had bought cheap from the chairman of one of Bombay's biggest companies. The second car was a Contessa. Two more armed bodyguards stood by the Mercedes, waiting for Bikaner to arrive.

Bikaner walked quickly down the short pathway to his car. He was dressed in an expensive fawn-colored Italian suit. He wore white shoes and a turtleneck shirt of creamy white silk. Somehow so much white only made him look dirtier.

A guard opened the rear door of the Mercedes and Bikaner slid in without a word. His two closest bodyguards followed, one beside him, one in front beside the driver. The others climbed hurriedly into the car behind. A moment later the Mercedes pulled out onto Marine Drive and joined the flow of traffic heading north.

It was a little after eleven o'clock. Bikaner was headed for his safe house. Everybody in Bombay knew about the penthouse, but he was certain that no one, especially not Kapoor, knew about the house out by the racecourse. Bikaner would bunker down there for a few days while he orchestrated his next move against Kapoor. There was still an hour left before the deadline on Kapoor's offer. Bikaner would make the call to Sansi, agreeing to accept the truce. But he would make them sweat first. He would show them he was not a man to be manipulated. He would wait till an hour or two after midnight and then he would let them know his decision. He wanted to lull Kapoor into a false sense of security and then, in a couple of days, he would strike. But like all big cats, Bikaner would toy with his victim for a while. And there was something else on his mind. He would stop off at Nana's place to look over the new girls and decide which ones he would take home with him for the night.

"Madarchod." The driver swore, wrenched down on the wheel and stamped on the brake all at the same time. Bikaner growled and braced his arm against the seat in front to stop himself from being thrown forward. His two bodyguards peered nervously through the smoked-glass windows. The car in front had stopped without warning and the Mercedes had fishtailed halfway out of its lane before coming to a halt. Other cars swarmed past, horns blaring, drivers waving angrily.

Bikaner swore softly to himself. He could feel the anger building inside. Didn't these peasants have any idea who he was?

There was a deafening bang at the rear of the Mercedes and the car lurched forward so that it rammed into the stalled car in front and held fast.

"Shit . . ." The bodyguard sitting beside Bikaner fumbled for the gun in his shoulder holster.

Shots sounded right outside the car. Everybody in the Mercedes began shouting at once.

"Keep the doors locked," Bikaner yelled. "Keep the doors locked and they can't touch us."

There was a loud crack at the front of the car and the windshield starred and buckled. Bikaner stared. It was supposed to be blastproof glass. Another crack and this time the windshield disintegrated in a welter of flying shards. Everyone ducked. Everyone but Bikaner. He could see someone silhouetted against the streetlights. A short, stocky man with a shaven skull. He was holding a sledgehammer. And grinning. Jackie Patro was grinning at him. A growl of pure rage formed in Bikaner's throat.

Patro disappeared and was replaced by two men holding AK-47s. They fired in unison and a twin stream of bullets scythed through the interior of the car, shredding flesh and bone and metal. The four men in the car jerked and spasmed like puppets as the bullets tore into them until both ammunition clips were exhausted. Only then did their assassins hurry back to two waiting cars and drive off, leaving a mangled, bloody traffic jam behind them.

Jashwal Bikaner sprawled in the back of the Mercedes, head flung backward, eyes open, blood oozing thickly from his mouth and throat. His body had been ripped by bullets from head to toe and the blood poured from him in rivulets, painting broad stripes across his beautiful Italian suit. In the eerie amber streetlight the stripes coalesced into a bizarre pattern. Like the stripes of a slaughtered Bengali tiger.

The ambulances were coming again. Sansi could hear the clanging of their bells as they roared through his dream.

He awoke and realized it was the telephone. Annie Ginnaro's telephone. He had forgotten where he was. His eyes blinked open and he found himself staring into Annie's face. She opened her eyes and saw him too and a warm smile formed on her lips.

"It could be for me," Sansi said.

She jumped up, ran to the kitchen counter and picked up the phone. Sansi got self-consciously to his feet and looked around for his shirt.

"It is for you," Annie said and held out the phone. "A Sergeant Chowdhary."

Sansi pulled on his shirt and took the phone. He listened for several minutes. Annie watched the tension creep back into him like a darkening cloud and her spirits sank. It had been nice for a while. A small peaceful interlude for the two of them. Despite her misgivings, they hadn't come together as professional antagonists at all. They had come together as a man and a woman.

"I'm only a few blocks from there," Sansi said. "Call for me in the car on the way."

He gave Chowdhary the address of Annie's building and hung up. She stared at him while he fumbled with the buttons on his shirt and hunted for his shoes.

"What's wrong?" Annie asked, the concern in her voice unmistakable.

Sansi hesitated and looked at her. "Have you heard of Jashwal Bikaner?"

"A gangster, right? Big time?"

Sansi nodded. "He was murdered less than half an hour ago, six blocks from here. Ambushed in his car on Marine Drive. It looks like a gangland execution. Eight dead, including Bikaner."

"My god," she gasped. "This place is like Chicago in the twenties. It's worse . . . it's people killing each other to see who's going to take over the sewer. It's—"

"It's India," Sansi interrupted. He took a step toward the door, then hesitated and looked back at her. "Get your things and come with me," he said. "It's time you saw what it's really like."

14

THE MILKY DAWN of a sultry, overcast day crept over Chowpatty Beach like a bad omen. As always, ten-year-old Hiraldar was the first on the beach to wake up. He crawled out from under the plastic sheet that had been his home since he had come to Bombay with his family six weeks before from their village in distant Karnataka.

It was Hiraldar's favorite time of the day, the time when he had the beach to himself and he could pretend he was the sultan of Chowpatty for a while, before joining his brothers and sisters begging from cars stopped at the traffic lights on nearby Subhash Road. He slipped away from his family and walked down to the water, bare feet scuffing against the sand. He had heard that it wasn't safe to play in the sea, that the water here was polluted and you could get diseases in your eyes and your ears if you ducked your head under. It was true that his skin sometimes felt slick and greasy after he had waded through the shallows, but he liked the coolness of the water and it still smelled like the sea. He also liked to wake up the seagulls who squatted along the waterline, running through the midst of them, yelling and waving his arms, scattering them into the sky in a flurry of beating wings.

But this morning they were up before him, diving and playing in the shallows, swooping and picking at something floating a few yards out from the shore. The air was so still there were no waves and the water had a sinister, linoleum sheen. Even in the shallows it was impossible to see the sand on the bottom. Hiraldar stepped into the water and waded out until it reached his thighs. It felt cold and oily. He stopped and tried to see the thing in the water. The gulls grew angry with him and scolded him for interfering with their game. Then he realized he was looking at a corpse. A current of terror coursed through his body and he struggled backward out of the water in a panic, fleeing its cold, cloying embrace.

A large crowd had gathered on the beach by the time Sansi arrived. Sergeant Chowdhary helped him push his way through the mass of onlookers to the police cordon near the water's edge. The first person Sansi recognized was Dr. Vyankatesh Rohan, deputy coroner of Bombay.

"How did you get here before me?" Sansi asked. "I only got the call twenty minutes ago."

"I know," Rohan answered, looking at Sansi through red-rimmed eyes. "It was me who told them to call you. I was at the mortuary when the report came in. I've been up all night, working. I thought I might as well come down myself, see the recovery site for myself, get a breath of fresh air. When I saw the body I decided we shouldn't move it until you got here. I think you're going to find it interesting."

Sansi looked at the bundle on the ground, hidden beneath a green plastic sheet.

"Come here," Rohan beckoned him.

The deputy coroner bent down and lifted one flap of the sheet so Sansi could see underneath. The body lay on its side, facing Sansi. It was naked; it had been tied with rope at the hands and feet and it had three massive wounds. One to remove the genitalia, another two to remove the breasts.

Sansi looked at the face. The gulls had already taken the eyes. But the mouth was open wide, set in the rictus of terror, a silent testament to unimaginable pain. The head was bald except for a thin rind of hair that hung longer on one side than the other: the hairstyle of a man trying to conceal his baldness, though the indignity of death had robbed him of even that small vanity.

Sansi nodded to Rohan to drop the sheet. He stood up and looked at the deputy coroner.

"You know him?" Rohan asked.

Sansi nodded. "It's Pratap Coyarjee," he said. "He's the studio manager from Film City. He was the only lead I had left."

The day ended as it had begun. With a brooding, sunless sky and an ominous sense of worse to come. It suited Sansi's mood perfectly. He sat in his favorite chair on the terrace at Malabar Hill, feet crossed on the parapet wall, whiskey and soda in his hand, watching the sky darken.

The weather was changing. The clouds meant the monsoon was on its way. But they weren't rain-bearing clouds yet; they were only portents of rain: the first layers of alto-stratus, thick enough to blot out the sun and low enough to trap the heat and add to the suffocation on the ground. If the monsoon was late, it would get worse in the following weeks. Lethargy would set in, tempers would fray, crimes of random violence would increase as the gloomy, stifling heat continued. Everyone would be waiting for the cool, cleansing deliverance of the monsoon. Some would handle it better than others.

"You look tired." Sansi's mother appeared on the terrace. It was a little after seven and she had just returned from a lecture at the university.

Sansi shrugged but said nothing. Pramila took her cue and disappeared back inside to unpack her briefcase and talk to the *bai*, Mrs. Khanna, about dinner.

She reappeared half an hour later, a glass of white wine in her hand. "Ready for a little company yet?"

Sansi smiled. Only his mother could make him feel that his need to be alone was unreasonable. But it was her terrace too, he realized. The whole apartment belonged more to Pramila than it did to him. Someday soon he would have to move, he knew. If only he wasn't so comfortable at home.

Pramila pulled up a chair and sat down beside her son so they could both watch the lights of Queen Victoria's Necklace switch on along the shoreline. She said nothing for a while, then reached across to him and rested her hand gently on his arm. It felt warm, soft and comforting.

"What's wrong, darling?" Her voice was so tender so filled with genuine concern, it was impossible not to respond.

Sansi tried to shake off the darkness. He turned and looked at his mother, saw her small, lined face, her nest of gray hair and her calm, questioning gaze. And he saw the beauty, the wisdom and the strength that he had always seen there. As kind as the General was, Sansi had never missed his father.

"Work," Sansi answered. He hoped that was sufficient. He could not begin to explain all that had gone wrong in the preceding few days or the mood of hopelessness and futility that threatened to engulf him now. He thought it better she didn't know.

"Can I help?"

Sansi slowly shook his head.

"Is it this business about that gangster Kapoor?" she asked.

Sansi smiled inwardly. His mother had read the newspapers . . . and it was clear she wasn't going to give up that easily.

"No," he said. "That's part of it. Not all of it. Kapoor made a fool of me but at the same time he got rid of Bikaner and, as far as I know, he's left Bombay again. And it doesn't look as if there's going to be a gang war. So it may not be exactly the way we expected it, but . . . he's done us a favor. Jamal will find a way to rationalize it to Cabinet. And I'm not so proud I can't live with a little . . . embarrassment."

"What, then . . . Annie Ginnaro?"

Sansi looked at his mother in amusement. "What about Annie Ginnaro?"

Pramila smiled. "How did your dinner go the other evening?"

"Very well, until Kapoor brought it to a rather unpleasant end."

"She's a very attractive girl."

"Yes." Sansi nodded. "But she's not a girl. She's thirty-one years old. And divorced."

"That doesn't matter," Pramila answered lightly. "She's very funny, too."

"Funny?"

"Oh yes," Pramila said. "She has a lovely sense of humor. Very vulgar. Haven't you found out yet?"

Sansi stirred. He felt needled, as though his mother had told him something obvious that he had missed.

"She's got some funny ideas about India," he answered.

"You sound just like your father when you speak like that," Pramila chided him.

"Just becau—"

"I think she's rather brave," Pramila interrupted. "She had a very spoiled life in California, you know. A lot of American women only think they're strong. She decided to put it to the test. I admire her for that."

"She wasn't ready for some of the things she saw the other night," Sansi said. "I think she's only now beginning to realize that she might be out of her depth here. At the very least she could be making a big fool of herself."

"That's only a male concern," Pramila said dismissively. "Most women are so ecstatic to be doing something exciting they couldn't care less about failure. I think she likes India. I've seen all kinds of people come out over the years and I have a pretty good idea who is going to make it and who isn't. Her appetite for adventure has just been awakened and, underneath, I think she's quite tough. I think she'll stay."

"She told me she's only here for a year."

"Perhaps." Pramila shrugged. "I think that will change."

They sipped their drinks in silence, listening to the cicadas, feeling the night descend like a hot, vaporous cloud.

"Will you be seeing her again?" Pramila asked.

"I expect so," Sansi answered, his voice noncommittal. "It will be difficult to avoid her if she's going to be one of your friends."

"She is," Pramila said, her voice light but definite.

He wondered if his mother was finally making an effort to get rid of him. It was unlike her. Sansi had met many interesting women over the years through Pramila's worldwide network of friends, but she had never tried to match him up with any of them before. Perhaps it was a symptom of age, he thought. Even though she enjoyed superb health, Pramila was approaching seventy. Perhaps she simply didn't want him to grow old alone. It was a melancholy notion but quite in keeping with his mood.

"What, then?" Pramila intruded on his thoughts again.

"What . . . ?"

"What are you brooding about?"

Sansi sighed. "Mother, I doubt you can help."

"Is it something to do with this Film City case you've been working on?"

He remained silent.

"I met Noshir Kilachand several times, you know," she added.

Joint Commissioner Jamal had been wrong about Kilachand not making the newspapers the day of the bomb blast at police headquarters. The suicide of the state film industry's chief executive was big enough to command equal billing on the front pages of most of the big dailies.

Sansi looked at his mother.

"I can't say I knew him terribly well," she went on, "but enough to wonder about him. He was a very able administrator and genuinely committed to the arts. He could be quite charming too—but there was something about him that never seemed quite right. You always had the feeling that he wasn't being absolutely honest with you, that he was holding something back. I put it down to bureaucratic paranoia. Is it true that he was homosexual? The newspapers only said something about pressure of work."

Sansi had not discussed the investigation with Pramila. Not because he had a rule against discussing cases at home but because he was naturally discreet and also because he preferred to leave the most sordid details of his work at the front door. But there was no need to worry about protecting Noshir Kilachand from anything anymore.

"It looks that way," Sansi conceded.

"Is that why he killed himself?"

"He killed himself because he knew he was about to be exposed."

"*Are Bapre,*" Pramila muttered. "Does his wife know what he was? What about his children?"

"They'll know in time, if they don't already," Sansi shrugged.

"Poor, ridiculous man," Pramila muttered. "Why couldn't he be honest about what he was?"

"Oh, he knew what he was." Sansi smiled. "But he was ashamed of it. And he couldn't bear to let the rest of the world find out. He might have been a great success in his professional life: powerful, respected, all of that. But his personal life was built on a foundation of lies. There are a lot of men like that, you know. Men who would rather die than have the world discover what frauds they are."

Pramila shook her head. "Such a cowardly thing to do. And he is connected to this murder you've been investigating?"

"I think so."

"You don't think Noshir . . . ?"

"I don't think he was the murderer, no. He was at Lake Vihar when we recovered the body and he was very distressed. Genuinely distressed, I believe. I don't think he had the stomach for murder. But he was involved in a homosexual prostitution racket that operated out at Film City. The racket was controlled by a man called Pratap Coyarjee, the studio manager. Coyarjee never hid his homosexuality. He and Kilachand were friends at school; they had known each other all their lives. Coyarjee knew Kilachand's secret and used to keep him supplied with boys—it was a good way for him to control Kilachand and to protect his job. But Kilachand was only one of Coyarjee's many clients. I think it was Coyarjee who knew the murderer, because it was Coyarjee who supplied the murderer with boys too.

Kilachand was connected to the murderer only because they shared the same boy for a while—Sanjay Nayak, the boy we pulled from the lake. The forensic evidence suggests very strongly that it was a European male who was with Nayak at the time he was murdered."

Pramila's brow furrowed and Sansi had to explain briefly how Rohan's enzyme tests could differentiate between Indian and white males.

"You can do that now?" she asked, incredulous.

Sansi smiled. "We have many of the tools of justice," he said. "Even if we do not always have the will to use them."

He went on. "I think Coyarjee had a European client, somebody who went out to Film City as a visiting VIP—a businessman, a diplomat or something. Kilachand might even have met him at some point, but I am reasonably sure he was not involved in the murder. It was Coyarjee who was my link. It was Coyarjee who manipulated Kilachand into contacting Crime Branch so they would all appear so concerned and cooperative. Once the body had surfaced, Coyarjee knew it was only a matter of time before we established the identity and came looking around Film City. They were trying to throw us off the scent from the beginning, to discount them from the investigation early. Citizens above suspicion and all of that.

"Kilachand certainly had the motivation to try to deflect the investigation. His life, his career, everything depended on his ability to protect Coyarjee, even if he didn't know the identity of the real murderer. I must say, it was a very clever move by Coyarjee. I'd already talked to him once and I knew he was lying—but I didn't know how much. I knew that the way to break him was through Kilachand. I knew Kilachand would be much easier to crack. So did Coyarjee. He must have called Kilachand as soon as he left headquarters. He knew what effect the information would have on Kilachand. If only we'd been able to move faster. If only Jamal had agreed to a warrant straightaway. If only that damned terrorist bomb . . ." He let the sentence trail away.

"You don't think this man Coyarjee could have committed the murder?" Pramila asked.

Sansi finished his drink and set his glass on the floor. "He was closely involved, I know that. He knew the identity of the murderer. He may even have helped. But I don't think he was the prime motivator. I think Pratap Coyarjee got involved with someone who wanted to go far beyond anything he'd ever done before."

"You can still talk to him?"

Sansi shook his head. "We found his body this morning on Chowpatty Beach."

Pramila stared.

"Coyarjee was clever," Sansi added. "But he wasn't clever enough to protect himself from the real murderer. Whoever killed Nayak also killed Coyarjee. To stop him talking. To put a stop to my investigation. And . . . because he likes killing."

Pramila looked at her son but said nothing.

"What bothers me . . ." He hesitated, then corrected himself. "What *frightens* me . . . is that I feel I've just come in at the end of something. There are more victims out there, I'm sure of it. Other people, other boys who have been killed by the same murderer but whom no one has missed . . . because they don't matter. There is a pattern here: the beginning, the middle, the end of a pattern . . . something. Everything about these killings suggests they have been committed by someone who knows what he is doing, someone who has done it before. All that we're missing is . . . the other victims."

He turned to his mother. "Where do you think would be the most perfect place in all the world to commit murder?"

Pramila thought for a moment, then shrugged. "I don't know. I would assume that would depend on the murderer . . . and the victim."

"Exactly," Sansi said. "But what if the murderer doesn't know his victim? What if it is a crime of . . . controlled passion? What if the murderer is a psychopath?"

"I don't see what difference . . ."

"It makes a world of difference," Sansi interrupted. "Just look around you. This is India. What do you see?"

Pramila hesitated. "What I've always seen: beauty, tragedy, poetry, ugliness . . ."

"Poverty . . . injustice . . . ?" Sansi finished the sentence for her.

"Yes, but I try not to dwell too much on those things. I prefer to—"

"And *victims*," Sansi interrupted again. "Think of it. You only have to look at the streets of Bombay. They're awash with people, thousands and thousands of people. Faces without names—millions of them, all over India. Docile, submissive, trained from birth to be victims. India is a country filled with victims. So where is the perfect place to commit murder? Why, the place which offers the most perfect victims, of course."

"India?"

"It is the only country in the world where you can kill someone and know that even if the body is found, no one will care. There is a very good chance that it won't even be noticed amid the daily toll of the dead. We pick dozens of bodies up off the streets every day and nobody cares. We can't investigate them all. People go missing all the time and we never hear about it. India is a country where a million people could go missing and the government wouldn't notice. India is the perfect place for the psychopath who kills for pleasure. Choose your victim carefully, someone you're sure is unimportant, someone without friends or family, someone so insignificant that the police won't bother to waste investigation time on him. He's the perfect victim. He may be a nobody but he's still flesh and blood. He shows fear. He feels pain. He still gives pleasure. India is a paradise for the psychopath. It always has been. What is ironic is that Kilachand and Coyarjee may have done us a favor. Their fears drew our attention to a victim that no one might otherwise have cared about. A nobody, a male prostitute without friends in a strange city."

He paused. "There's something else too."

Pramila waited.

"My murderer may have stopped me for the moment . . . but he's left other victims out there, other clues. I'm sure of it. All I have to do is keep looking. . . ."

"Why do you think he likes it?" Pramila asked softly.

"What?"

"The man you're looking for, this European. Why did you say that he likes to kill?"

Sansi shrugged. "The profile . . . it's unmistakably psychopathic."

"You're not telling me everything."

Sansi hesitated. "Mutilation," he said finally. "Both bodies were badly mutilated and in exactly the same way."

"In exactly what way?"

"Mother . . ."

This time it was Pramila's turn to interrupt. "Stop trying to protect me from the world, darling."

Sansi heard the tone in her voice. He sighed. "The genitals had been removed. Completely. Genitals and breasts."

Pramila's face remained still and composed.

Sansi stood up. "Would you like another drink? I didn't want to . . ."

"Your father," she said abruptly.

Sansi leaned against the terrace wall and looked at his mother. "What does my father . . . ?"

"He's seen something like this before."

It was Sansi's turn to stare.

"It was something that happened during his first years in India," she said. "When he was in New Delhi in the early thirties, long before he met me. You must remember, your father loved India. He was fascinated, absorbed by India. He would have stayed here if he hadn't felt honor bound to return to England. We often talked about the things he saw. I was one of the few people who would listen, really listen to him."

Sansi smiled. "It can't be the same. Similar, perhaps, but not the same. Mutilation of murder victims is not uncommon in India. I've already been through all the files in Modus Operandi Branch."

"That doesn't mean a thing," Pramila said. "Your father told me himself that the British took everything of importance when they left India, including all their grubby little secrets: the political murders, the beatings, the tortures. It all went on under the British, you know. They only left the records they wanted to leave. Anything that might prove the slightest bit embarrassing they either burned or took with them."

"Acha." Sansi nodded. "Politics is one thing, but why would they want to protect a common murderer?"

"Because he was English," Pramila said.

"What?"

"The man who committed these murders was English, a bigwig of some kind. They shipped him home to avoid a scandal. The thirties were a very bad time for the British in India, you know. They couldn't take the chance that a trial might be the focus of more unrest. Your father told me it was the most shameful thing he had ever seen in all his years in India. He said it made him ashamed to be British."

Sansi sighed. "You're sure the murders were the same?"

"I'm not an expert," Pramila said. "But your father said the man who did it was sick. I remember that. The victims were male . . . and they all had their penises cut off. That's what you're talking about, isn't it?"

Sansi shook his head, perplexed. "It's not possible," he said. "It's a coincidence. It has to be. The dates . . . you're talking about fifty years ago. It can't possibly be the same murderer."

"Talk to your father," Pramila said. "What harm can it do?"

Sansi nodded but said nothing.

"There's something else you could try," she added.

Sansi waited.

"The police aren't the only people who kept records of the British in India, you know."

15

THE DAVID SASSOON Library at 152 Mahatma Gandhi Road was one of the city's hidden treasures. Founded in 1847 by an Iraqi Jew who became one of Bombay's greatest benefactors, it was a haven of peace in an urban maelstrom.

Its entrance was a single doorway set in a street of dingy shops and offices fronting onto Jehangir Circle. The door opened into a short, high-ceilinged corridor that led to a small lobby containing a reception desk, a life-size statue of Sassoon in robes and turban, and a spiral staircase that wound up to the library and reading rooms on the second floor. At the rear of the building was another door that led out to a peaceful garden shaded by jackfruit and mango trees. Each morning at dawn, the dirt pathways were raked into a mysterious calligraphy of whorls and swirls known only to the groundskeeper. Scattered beneath the trees was a handful of dilapidated chairs and benches where members could read in the shade.

Pramila had been a member for thirty years and had sponsored her son's membership on his return from Oxford. For a while it had been one of Sansi's favorite hiding places. He had spent many peaceful afternoons in the garden of the Sassoon library, absorbed by the therapy of aimless scholarship, while he waited for yet another law firm to reject his application for employment. Inevitably, once he had committed himself to a police career, the library had slipped into his past.

As he climbed the spiral staircase and was assailed by the smell of old books, he was reminded once more why he

had liked it so much. It wasn't only because the David
Sassoon Library was the largest private library in Bombay.
It was the sensation of stepping back in time. The library
was a living thing that had been in use for every day of its
150 years. There was a feeling of being part of a contin-
uum, a sense that Sansi could reach back and touch history
there.

A couple of university students glanced up from their
books at the teak slab reading tables when Sansi creaked
into view. Fat-bladed ceiling fans ruffled the pages of the
open books. Three French windows opened out onto a wide
veranda where a number of middle-aged men sat reading
newspapers, legs splayed comfortably over the extended
arms of their rattan chairs. Sansi slipped quietly into the
shadows between the rows of high-shouldered bookcases
and let his eyes wander over the titles of books that rivalled
the gems of the British Museum for antiquity and eccentricity: *The Private Memoirs of a Justified Sinner, The Super-
human Life of Cesar of Ling, The Legendary Tibetan Hero,
The Titanic and Other Ships, The Private Life of Helen of
Troy, The Last Englishman.*

Sansi wanted to read them all. But not today. He was
looking for something special, something that might give
him the clue he needed so badly. He had no particular book
or title in mind; it might be a memoir, an archive, an item
in an old newspaper report, something buried in the records
of Maharashtra. He was sure his mother was mistaken: the
murders could not be identical. But if there was a possibility that the killings could be the work of a bizarre cult—
even if it meant his theory about a lone psychopath was
wrong—there had to be a link somewhere. If a deranged
Englishman had been involved and the British had tried to
cover it up at the time, it was unlikely that the murders
themselves would have gone unrecorded. Somewhere in the
long and bloody history of the British occupation of India,
he knew, there was another clue. A bloodstained thread that
bound history together. Something that would point from

the past to the present and give his investigation the fresh impetus it so badly needed.

Sansi spent the entire morning examining every newspaper published between 1930 and 1936. He found references to uprisings, riots, massacres and all manner of emergencies, but nothing about a series of unsolved mutilation murders. He skipped lunch and spent much of the afternoon leafing through volume after volume of old government reports. He found statistics on the number of deaths caused by famine, flood, outbreaks of cholera, leprosy and typhoid, but again he found no mention of the type of murder he was looking for.

It was a little after four in the afternoon when he carried another pile of books out onto the veranda. They were his last hope, a selection of memoirs by British military and police officers who were active in India between the turn of the century and the beginning of the Second World War. Sansi picked a chair, sat down, draped his legs over the extended arm slats and plucked the first book from the pile on the floor. It was a thick, heavy bound volume with a green cover and a cracked spine. *Life on the Northwest Frontier.*

Sansi made himself comfortable and opened the book. The smell of the past wafted up from the yellowing pages to fill him with a strange nostalgia for a world he had never seen. In a moment the furious roar of the traffic on Jehangir Circle faded into a distant murmur and Sansi drifted back to the lonely mountain passes of the Northwest Frontier and the clatter of horses' hooves on barren rock as a single British police officer set out on mounted patrol with a dozen native sepoys from the Khyber Rifles.

Four hours later it was getting dark, the library lights had been switched on and Sansi's feet were back on the floor to stop their going to sleep. There were two piles of books beside his chair: one of unread books, one of those he had read. Although "read" wasn't entirely accurate; he had started skimming, knowing that he couldn't possibly finish them all before the library closed for the night. There was a danger he might miss something, but he had little choice. He had a meeting with Jamal in the morning and he was loath to go before his boss with only more failure to report.

Sansi looked at his watch and calculated that he might be able to flick through two, maybe three more books before ten o'clock. His eyes hurt, his back ached, his stomach was rumbling, and his head was reeling after ten hours of immersion in the musty records of the past. He closed his eyes for a moment, then picked up a black book with faded silver lettering: *British India: A Policeman's Memoir.* The author was a former detective superintendent in the Indian police service, a man by the name of E. L. Howe. Detective Superintendent Howe had apparently served in India from 1921 until 1935.

Sansi leafed through the first few pages, enough to assess the florid, self-serving literary style and ascertain that Howe had considered himself to be yet another unsung hero of the Empire and that his book was an attempt to rectify such an unconscionable oversight. The first few chapters held nothing much of interest. Sansi stifled a yawn. He was midway through a chapter on the author's experiences in Jaigapur when something caught his eye. He stopped, flicked back a few pages and read the same passage again, slowly this time. Gradually, somewhere in a cold, dark corner of his gut, Sansi felt the first electrical thrill of anticipation. He forgot about his tiredness and the ache in his lower back. He sat upright and studied the passage carefully:

In September 1931, duty compelled me to forsake the comforts of Delhi once more in order to journey by train to Jaigapur, some three hundred miles to the southeast, on the edge of the Great Indian Desert. A series of gruesome killings had taken place in the countryside around Jaigapur and the local authorities were without explanation. When I arrived I swiftly ascertained that there had been five such killings in the space of one year and all were identical. The victims were young males and all had suffered the most grievous form of mutilation to their bodies and their private parts. I commenced my investigation with vigor but quickly encountered that customary native hostility which bedeviled so much of the policeman's work in India. The Hindu mind seemed unable to grasp the simple truth that officers of the Crown, such as myself, were there to guarantee equal protection under the law. Nor could I be entirely sure of the faithful cooperation of those native officers who were assigned to assist me in the course of my investigation. Indeed, there were several occasions when I could not be certain that my interpreters were translating all my inquiries faithfully.

The mood in Jaigapur was most unfriendly and I gathered the impression that there was much mistrust between the British regional administration and the local population, which included the Maharajah of Jaigapur. I only had occasion to meet the Maharajah once but found him to be bellicose in nature and hostile to the Collectorate. The Collector himself informed me that the Maharajah had a large number of concubines and was believed to have become deranged through syphilis.

Despite native antipathy and the many obstacles placed in my path I persevered with my investigation. Mutilation murders were not uncommon in rural India. The gouging out of eyes, blinding by the inserting of firebrands into the eyes and the slitting or cutting out of tongues were quite common. The amputation of limbs in children was a common practice among beggar gangs. Castration of young males was employed by certain primitive sects, which included the eunuch society known as the Hijdas.

I deduced that the Jaigapur killings were the work of a Hindu cult. The mutilations were so peculiar in nature, so barbarous and cruel, that they were indicative of the kind of depravity that manifested itself all too often in the Hindu personality. This would explain the reluctance of the local population to cooperate with the British authorities. The peasant peoples of India came from primitive stock and were susceptible to teachings which those of us of civilized intellect would swiftly dismiss as bogus or absurd. It was apparent to me that the population of Jaigapur had been duped and cowed into silence by the activities of a particularly unpleasant sect.

Unfortunately, events conspired to prevent my pursuing my investigation further. After six weeks in Jaigapur I was recalled to Delhi for urgent assignment elsewhere, precisely at that point at which I might have expected my investigation to bear fruit. I could only surmise that there had been some apprehension in government that my inquiries could exacerbate further the difficult relations that existed between the British and the native population at that time. This was not the first time that political considerations had taken precedence over police matters. What small satisfaction I derived from this unhappy episode was furnished by the news, some years later, that the killings in Jaigapur ceased abruptly, following my visit, and never resumed. It was further evidence to me that I had been on the right track after all and that the pressure I had been able to exert through my investigation had forced the cult to move on. The irony of this would have been lost on the natives of Jaigapur, of course. For it was the presence of the very Crown they despised which had ultimately assured their peace and security, however ungrateful or ignorant of that fact they may have been.

Sansi reread the passage several times, then leaned back in his chair and stared, unseeing, at the moths that fluttered around the electric light bulbs. It was a familiar tale. The memoir of a man whose ego had not been satisfied by the modest accomplishments of his best endeavors. Self-aggrandising, unctuous, petulant, racist, banal . . . and ultimately stupid.

Detective Superintendent Howe could not have been

more wrong about the killings at Jaigapur, Sansi realized. Even now, half a century after those words had been written, the hidden message simmered unmistakably between the lines. Howe had not been recalled to Delhi because his investigation had threatened the balance of an uneasy peace between the British and the native population in Jaigapur. He had been recalled because he unwittingly posed a threat to the British authorities of the day—to the authority of the Crown he represented.

E. L. Howe had stumbled onto something he did not understand and because he did not understand it he had fallen back on the comfortable prejudices of the colonial policeman. But someone had known. Someone in Delhi had understood the truth of what was happening in Jaigapur, and knew that it had nothing to do with the barbarism and depravity of the Hindu personality. Someone highly placed in the Raj, who had ordered Howe's recall from Jaigapur before he could make the situation worse. Before it became irretrievable.

Sansi closed the book and set it carefully on the floor, separate from the others. He looked around and realized he was alone on the veranda. It was almost ten and there was a light breeze disturbing the restless shadows. The thrill of anticipation inside his stomach had congealed, frozen, turned into something else. Sansi shivered.

It was the same murderer. It had to be.

But that was impossible. The first murders had been committed in Jaigapur, fifteen hundred miles away in Rajasthan—more than half a century ago.

How could the same murderer return from the past to begin killing all over again?

"You're a very lucky man, Inspector."

Joint Commissioner Jamal sat back in his chair and waited.

Sansi wouldn't bite.

"It wasn't too difficult to persuade the Cabinet that Jashwal Bikaner was no great loss to the community,"

Jamal went on. "I even managed to persuade them that we had been successful in averting a gang war. It wasn't quite so easy to explain how Paul Kapoor could get in and out of the country without us knowing about it."

Sansi waited.

"So," Jamal added, "I thought it better not to try. I presented it in such a way that they now believe we had Kapoor under observation the whole time and we made a political decision to allow him to conclude his little vendetta against Bikaner without interference from us."

Jamal smiled. "I don't think there is any need for them to know otherwise, do you?"

"No, sir." Sansi smiled back at his boss, content to play the game.

He knew he could rely on Jamal to present disaster as a victory to the state Cabinet. But they were both lucky. If the Cabinet hadn't bought Jamal's explanation, they might both be staring at demotion. Instead, Cabinet had been left with the impression that the Joint Commissioner of Crime Branch was a very shrewd fellow indeed, and just the man they needed to continue to outsmart the criminal masterminds of Bombay.

"Now I have to see what I can do to salvage something from this other disaster of yours," Jamal added. "Cabinet was very upset about Noshir Kilachand. He was known to all of them. The chief minister in particular. I think it would be very embarrassing to the government if it were to come out that Kilachand was involved in a homosexual prostitution racket out at Film City. Still, Inspector, that is no reason to shirk our higher responsibility to the public good, is it?"

There were times when Sansi couldn't tell whether Jamal was satirizing himself or not.

"No, sir," Sansi answered.

"What have you got that's new?" the joint commissioner asked, suddenly all business again.

Sansi pulled his case diary out of his pocket and quickly ran through the progress of his investigation. When he came to Rohan's forensic evidence he was careful to stress the connection to someone of European or North American background.

"Rohan has been able to establish that the semen on the sheets we took from Nayak's bedroom came from Kilachand. That fits in with what we already know about Kilachand's relationship with Nayak. But we've found nothing to connect Kilachand to the murder scene at the temple."

"Good." Jamal nodded.

Sansi thought his boss would be pleased. If they could lay all the blame for the murders at the feet of a foreigner it would shift the focus of impropriety away from the government and its agents. He was sure that Jamal could present Kilachand as a pathetic victim caught in the lethal machinations of a foreign national if it would make the government feel better. When he came to the new information about the killings in Jaigapur in 1931 and the similarity of the modus operandi he saw the joint commissioner frown.

"You've gone off the track, Inspector," Jamal said. "Even if there was a cover-up by the British fifty years ago, we aren't in the business of solving ancient crimes. It couldn't possibly be the same murderer. So what relevance could a series of murders committed so long ago have to this investigation?"

Sansi was ready. "At this point the strongest theory I have is that we may be looking for a copycat killer. But a copycat with a difference. He has taken a series of long-forgotten murders as his model. It's as though someone in London had decided to copy the murders of Jack the Ripper all over again. The only difference is that, in that case, everyone in England knew about Jack the Ripper. He was the most famous murderer in English history, even though his identity remains unclear to this day. In this case, however, there were very few people who knew about these old murders. And yet they were almost identical to the murders we are seeing today in Bombay. It is most unusual, is it not, sir?"

Jamal grunted but looked skeptical.

Sansi continued: "I don't think we can discount the possibility of a copycat killer only because it is bizarre, sir. We know that a person of European background was involved in Nayak's murder. Given the identical nature of Coyarjee's wounds and the importance of Coyarjee to the investigation, we can assume with some certainty that the same killer was involved in his death. We know that the modus operandi that was employed in the killings in Jaigapur was the same as the modus operandi employed in these killings today. I think I have to go to Jaigapur, sir—to Jaigapur and New Delhi—to see who else has had access to this same information. And to see if there are any more recent victims."

Jamal's skepticism had been replaced by something closer to intrigue. "You think there might be others?"

"Oh, yes, sir," Sansi added. "I am certain of it."

"Why?"

"Because what we are looking at here is a pattern, sir. The pattern has only been disturbed by the killing of Coyarjee. He was killed to keep him from talking. The wounds were a message that the killer is too clever for us. It is characteristic of the arrogance of the psychopathic personality, sir. And I am sure that there are other bodies out there somewhere. Other victims we have not found yet, sir. All we have found so far are fragments of a pattern, perhaps two patterns. One old, one new. We have to find the other pieces of the pattern, sir. I think I have to go and look."

16

SANSI DIDN'T TRUST Indian Airlines, the domestic airline of India, so he flew the internal leg of an Air India flight from Bombay to New Delhi and enjoyed the superior service. He stayed overnight at a creaky but charming relic of the Raj called the Imperial Hotel and got up before dawn the next morning to catch the 6:05 train to Jaigapur.

The journey was expected to take at least twelve hours. Sansi took a flask of tea and a box of sandwiches provided by the hotel and paid a porter fifty rupees to find him a compartment that was only half full. He was shown to a window seat in a compartment with only four fellow passengers: a doctor who was going to Jaigapur to take up substitute duty for a colleague, and a woman with two small and surprisingly well behaved girls who were returning home after a visit to relatives in New Delhi. When all grown-up conversation had been exhausted and the girls had become bored and quiet, Sansi contented himself by watching the passing scenery. It had been years since he had taken a long trip into the countryside. These days he preferred to take his vacations outside India. Nothing had changed, he realized. India presented the same timeless landscape, a panorama of dusty brown fields stubbled with corn and punctuated every few miles by villages that looked like ruins. Each village was surrounded by a skein of ditches carrying water and untreated sewage to the fields.

After four or five hours the fields gave way to open plains and the occasional cluster of conical, thatched huts that looked as though they ought to be in Africa. And everywhere the absurd, jumbled images of India. A sign on a brick wall: *For VD, see Dr. Khan.* A holy man in the middle of nowhere, angrily brandishing his staff at the passing train. A small boy crouched behind a defecating bullock, collecting the droppings to dry for fuel. And then, one mad, magnificent image: a man on horseback racing the train ... a Mogul warrior in flowing white robes and matching turban, astride a snow-white stallion galloping at full speed alongside the track. And then he was gone, as completely as a mirage.

Gradually the plains yielded to the first probing fingers of the desert until soon there was only a raw expanse of sand, an ocean relieved occasionally by sawtooth ranges of ragged quartzite that poked through the earth's crust like broken ribs. Sansi had never been to Jaigapur but he had seen country like this before. This was Rajasthan. Harsh, barren, dramatically beautiful. The women of Rajasthan were famous for the colors they wore to compensate for the monotony of their environment.

Twelve hours passed and still there was no sign of Jaigapur. At seven o'clock the sun went down in a brief, brilliant fusion of violets and reds. It was another two and a half hours before the train pulled into Jaigapur Station. The city was invisible in the darkness.

All Sansi knew about Jaigapur was that it was one of India's oldest fortified cities, the former capital of a vanquished desert kingdom. Built beside a small lake in the bowl of a mountain range, it had once been a crossroads, a meeting place for the trader tribes of the Great Indian Desert. The Moguls had built a fort there to command the mountain pass and successive Maharajahs had erected three splendid palaces. Only one of those homes was still occupied by the Maharajah of Jaigapur. One was a museum and the third was a hotel.

The train had barely stopped before it was besieged by a clamoring crowd. Porters, taxi drivers, rickshaw drivers, hawkers, peddlers and beggars, squabbling and fighting each other to get at the people on the train. Sansi helped clear a path through the chaos for the lady with the two girls until she found her husband. Then he struck out on his own toward the exit. In the midst of the struggle he noticed half a dozen policemen watching idly from a distance. There was no reason for them to intervene. It was only the usual riot that accompanied the arrival of every train.

Once outside, Sansi threaded his way between the logjam of taxis and motor rickshaws until he found an ancient police Ambassador with a small, neatly dressed man in civilian clothes and a driver in uniform leaning against the hood. Sansi introduced himself. Inspector Krishna Parmar from Jaigapur Crime Branch had been waiting for Sansi since six o'clock, when the train was supposed to arrive.

Half an hour later, Inspector Parmar had delivered his guest to the white marble palace that was now owned by the Sheraton hotel chain. Sansi was tired, disheveled and in need of a hot bath, but before he saw the inside of his room he wanted to talk to Parmar. Once he had checked in, he invited the inspector to join him in the hotel lounge for a drink. Sansi couldn't afford to waste time. He had allowed himself only three days in Jaigapur. And, unlike author-detective E. L. Howe, Sansi intended to secure the cooperation of the local police.

After five minutes of conversation it was apparent that Parmar had no idea why Sansi had come to Jaigapur. He said his instructions were only to provide transport and local police support. It was just as Sansi had requested. He had not wanted anyone but the commissioner in Jaigapur to know what he was looking for until he had arrived.

Sansi studied Parmar carefully. The small, quiet Rajasthani was polite and helpful and had an underlying reserve that Sansi found reassuring. He was inclined to trust Parmar.

"We had a rather unusual murder in Bombay last month," Sansi said at last.

Parmar sipped his beer and listened, his face expressionless.

"The evidence so far suggests that the murderer is a foreigner, a European. I think there is a connection between the murderer and Jaigapur. I think the murderer may have been here at some point . . . in the past."

Sansi did not tell Parmar how long ago in the past. He went on to summarize his investigation thus far, beginning with the discovery of Nayak's body in Lake Vihar and ending with the murder of Pratap Coyarjee. It was only when he described the mutilations of both corpses that he saw a flicker of interest in Parmar's eyes. It could have meant anything. The inspector waited patiently for Sansi to finish.

"What I want to know," Sansi had concluded, "is if your department has seen anything, anything at all, with a similar modus operandi, at any time over the past five, ten, twenty years or so."

Parmar nodded and finished his beer. "More recent than that," he said blandly.

Sansi waited.

"Two years ago," Parmar continued, "we pulled a body out of Lake Jaigapur. It had the same mutilations you described."

The fatigue, the exhaustion, the despair, that had threatened to swallow Sansi lifted like a veil. He struggled to keep his voice level. "Two years ago?"

Parmar nodded.

"You're sure the mutilations were the same? Exactly the same?"

"I never saw the body," Parmar shrugged. "But you said both breasts and genitals had been removed. It sounds the same to me."

"Did you get any leads?"

Parmar shook his head. "Like you, we assumed at first that it was part of some strange ritual, perhaps even a revenge killing. But the investigation never came to anything. It was classified as a random homicide. I always thought the wounds were to cover up the real motive for the murder. But no one in town knew anything. All our usual sources, our informers . . . nothing. I had forgotten it until you mentioned it. There has been nothing like it since."

"You found nothing in Modus Operandi?"

Parmar grimaced. "Our records only go back to the 1950s. Anything that predates Independence is very unreliable. The British didn't leave much behind when they left Jaigapur. As far as we can tell, there has been nothing like this before ... or since. It's in Modus Operandi now ... one of a kind."

"Was the victim a local boy?"

Parmar nodded.

"Young? Homosexual?"

"Yes."

"Male prostitute?"

"Sometimes. He made a living selling things to tourists. Souvenirs, escorted tours, himself. How did you know?"

Sansi leaned back in his chair. On the outside he looked exhausted and there were dark puddles of fatigue beneath both eyes. Inside, his adrenaline was surging.

"And you say there's been nothing like this in Jaigapur before?"

"Not to my knowledge, but as I told you, our records—"

"You've got a library in Jaigapur?" Sansi interrupted.

Parmar nodded.

"Public archives? A museum?"

"Yes."

"*Acha.* I want to see any newspapers, records or files that tell us about Jaigapur in 1931. Can you do that?"

"Nineteen thirty-one?" Parmar looked baffled. "But I thought ..."

"I want to know the name of the Collector at that time, the military commander and all other senior British officials in the local administration. I want to know the names of everyone of importance who was connected with the Maharajah. Everything."

"I understand," Parmar said. The expression on his face said otherwise.

"Are there any residents of Jaigapur still alive today who were alive in 1931?"

Parmar smiled. "The Maharajah's mother . . . there must be others."

"*Acha,*" Sansi said with an air of finality. "I want to speak to the Maharajah, his mother, and any others you can find."

Parmar's eyes shadowed. "I doubt you will be able to speak to the Maharani," he said. "She is very old, very sick. No one has seen her or her son, the Maharajah, in years. They speak to nobody. I don't think they will agree to see us."

"Ask," Sansi said flatly. "Tell them I have come from Bombay. Tell them it is state business. If that doesn't work, tell them I will send to New Delhi for a federal warrant. That should do it. They've been frightened of the government ever since Indira took their pensions away."

Parmar gave an odd, embarrassed smile. He had no idea whether Sansi was bluffing or not. But if he didn't know—the Maharajah and his mother might not know either.

Sansi spent the following day studying the local coroner's report and speaking to the officers who had investigated the mutilation murder of Jitendra Macwan two years before. He found little that was new but the parallels between Macwan in Jaigapur and Nayak in Bombay were inescapable. Both were young, attractive and homosexual. Both sold their sexual favors. Both were alone in the city, without real friends or families. And both had met their ends in the same way. The only differences were that Macwan was eighteen years old; he operated alone and procured most of his customers from the foreign tourists who stayed at the major hotels.

Inspector Parmar called at the fortress-palace that was home to His Highness the Maharajah of Jaigapur and his mother, the Maharani, and asked for an appointment on Sansi's behalf. By the end of the day there had been no response. Sansi told Parmar to go back in the morning, and this time he was to use threats if necessary. . . .

Sansi spent most of his second day at the museum. He finally found something in the records of the assize courts that had been conducted in Jaigapur under British rule from 1836 until 1946.

In 1931 the Collector of Jaigapur was a man called Cardus. Antony Cardus. What was interesting was that he had enjoyed the shortest tenure of any Collector in the history of Jaigapur. Cardus arrived in June 1930 and left in November 1931, the year of the five original mutilation murders and not too long after Detective Superintendent E. L. Howe had conducted his inconclusive investigation. Cardus's tour of duty lasted barely eighteen months. Other Collectors had stayed in Jaigapur an average of six years or more. What possible cause could have compelled Cardus to give up his post so abruptly? Sansi wondered.

On the morning of the third day Sansi was handed a written message by a clerk at the hotel's front desk. It came from someone who identified himself as Mr. Ahbay, the Maharajah's personal secretary. The note invited Sansi to present himself at the main gate of the palace at two o'clock that afternoon. The desk clerk seemed impressed.

Parmar called at the Sheraton for Sansi at a quarter to two. It wasn't a long drive to the palace. They could see it from the front lawn of the hotel, a majestic cluster of towers, turrets and battlements commanding the mountain pass two miles away, as dramatic and as improbable as a picture in a child's storybook. They skirted the city center and followed a potholed road across the lower mountain slopes through a suburb of big and impressive houses, many of them painted blue to denote the superior caste of their Brahmin occupants. They came to a fork in the road where there was a soda stand and a dozen or so tourists with cameras who had come up from Jaigapur to get a closer look at the Maharajah's official residence. The lower fork of the road led back into Jaigapur. The upper fork led to the palace, but was barred by a candy-striped security gate. Three uniformed security guards lounged around a gatehouse to discourage uninvited visitors.

The police car stopped at the gate and they waited while one of the guards checked Sansi's name on a clipboard. He signaled to his colleagues, the gate lifted with a rusty squeal and the car bumped forward onto the Maharajah's private road. The road was wide enough for only one car and was paved with enormous flagstones that had once been smooth and even but had not been repaired for years. With time, they had warped, cracked and risen like disintegrating ice floes and the driver had to proceed slowly so as not to damage the car's undercarriage. The road snaked up the mountainside for half a mile, a shadowed gully with a low, embrasured parapet to their right and a sheer rock face to the left.

The road turned one last time and bellied into a high-walled courtyard commanded by a pair of massive arched gates armored with brass. There was room for a dozen cars and a series of parking bays had been painted on the flagstones to the left of the gates. As the car stopped, a sentry's door opened in the big gates and a man appeared wearing the turban and tunic of a servant.

Sansi and Parmar climbed out of the car and brushed the creases self-consciously from their clothes. There was something about meeting royalty that made everyone feel underdressed.

"Please," the servant called to them, "tell your driver he can wait inside. He can have a cup of tea while you meet with Mr. Ahbay."

Parmar beckoned his driver to follow and the three of them filed through the sentry's door after the servant. They found themselves in a gloomy, high-arched tunnel flanked by the empty shops of what had once been the palace bazaar. This was where the Maharajah's wives and concubines, as many as two hundred of them, would once have shopped for jewelry, perfumes and silks. The tunnel smelled of age and neglect.

The servant ushered their driver into a gatehouse where two more servants were drinking tea, then led the two police officers out of the tunnel and into a wide, sunny courtyard covered with pink gravel. The courtyard was shielded by massive battlements on all four sides. But the great stone walls were crumbling and weeds could be seen sprouting from the cracks. One wall comprised a series of massive arches, all but one boarded up.

"Stables," the servant explained as they crunched across the gravel. "Elephants, camels, horses . . . now only motor-cars."

They passed through another arched gate into a smaller courtyard surrounded by high walls and colonnaded walk-ways. The courtyard grounds were divided into lush green lawns and well-tended flower beds that were startling after the dusty browns and pinks of the desert outside.

Sansi looked around. The doors and windows of many apartments were visible through the shadows of the colon-nades but most were closed and shuttered. Many of the arches and columns of the walkways looked fragile and unsafe. There was a sadness about it, Sansi thought, a per-vasive mood of faded grandeur.

The servant led them to a corner turret where the win-dows were open and Sansi could see curtains, wallpaper and a sliver of a painting. It was exactly as he had been led to believe it would be. The fortress may have sprawled over fifty acres of mountainside but ninety percent of it was ruined and uninhabitable. Like most privately owned pal-aces in India, it was a mere echo of its former glory. Sansi guessed that the royal apartments comprised no more than a dozen rooms. All the others would have been stripped of their furnishings long ago and abandoned to the scratchings of mice and cockroaches.

"Harem." The servant interrupted his thoughts and ges-tured at a line of shuttered doors and windows down one side of the inner court. "No more use for harem," he added with a wry smile.

He opened the heavy wooden door to the corner turret and stepped aside. Sansi and Parmar found themselves in the reception hall of an English country manor. The hall was paneled with polished teak, there was an antique table with a vase containing an arrangement of fresh flowers, a hat stand and an umbrella stand, both bare. On the walls hung two paintings depicting burly, mustached men in gorgeously jeweled costumes, former occupants of the castle, Sansi assumed. There were also three doors, all closed.

The servant tapped lightly on one of the doors. A moment later it opened and a distinguished-looking man in his early fifties appeared, wearing the black jacket, white shirt, dark tie and discreetly striped trousers of an English butler.

"Good afternoon, gentlemen," he welcomed them. "I am Mr. Ahbay, personal secretary to their Highnesses the Maharajah and Maharani of Jaigapur. Please, come in."

Sansi had not heard English spoken so elegantly since he had been at Oxford. Mr. Ahbay was Indian but his bearing was entirely English. Clearly he had been trained by one of the better London agencies.

The two policemen stepped into Mr. Ahbay's room. It was also paneled with teak and was half drawing room, half office. The furniture looked early Victorian and was probably the real thing, Sansi realized. Most of the Maharajahs furnished their palaces direct from London once the British had arrived. The only contemporary touches were a telephone, a fax machine and an intercom.

Ahbay glided behind an enormous desk and gestured his guests toward two high-backed armchairs. "Can I offer you some tea, gentlemen?"

Sansi declined with equal politesse. He felt as though he was about to be interviewed for a job by the manager of an English country estate.

Parmar looked uncomfortable. Clearly it was the first time he had been inside Jaigapur Fort.

"Well, gentlemen." Ahbay smiled. "What can I do for you?"

Sansi knew what was going on. An appearance of polite cooperation that would lead them nowhere. The velvet curtain in front of a stone wall.

He explained the purpose of his visit to Jaigapur and his reason for wanting to speak to the Maharajah. Ahbay listened politely, nodding occasionally, never interrupting. The picture of reason. When Sansi had finished, he smiled.

"I'm frightfully sorry, Inspector," he said. "But it simply is not possible for you to meet with the Maharajah in person. His Royal Highness has been ill for a very long time. He is not able to receive visitors. I am most frightfully sorry. Perhaps if you were to direct your questions to me?"

Sansi smiled back. A battle of manners. "I would be happy to speak with Her Highness, the Maharani."

Ahbay shrugged his shoulders as though he would like to help but what Sansi had requested was simply not within his power to grant.

"The Maharani is very advanced in years, Inspector." He said it as though he was explaining the facts of life to a simple child. "Her Royal Highness never sees visitors. She tires very easily. Her Highness is taking a nap at the moment. She couldn't possibly be disturbed."

"Mr. Ahbay," Sansi persevered. "I have proceeded on the understanding that their Highnesses would be pleased to assist the police in this matter. I am sure they would not wish to obstruct the progress of a murder inquiry. I do hope you will not require me to return to New Delhi to seek an instruction from a federal judge."

"I have already spoken to your superiors in Bombay and New Delhi." Ahbay smiled. "I assured them that we would do everything we could to assist you. Within reason."

Within reason? Sansi turned over the words in his mind. He hadn't come this far to be bluffed by a butler.

"Mr. Ahbay, I'm reassured that you took the precaution of checking with my superiors. But perhaps I ought to explain something to you about the function of the police." He paused to give Ahbay a moment to reflect that it was his turn to be lectured about the facts of life. "I have the discretion to decide whether I should return to New Delhi to seek an injunction from a federal court requiring either or both of their Royal Highnesses to cooperate with my investigation, in person, on pain of contempt. My superiors may or may not approve of this course of action but that is beside the point. It is entirely within my power to do so. The legal process exists to allow me to do so. You must feel free to call the office of the prime minister if you wish, Mr. Ahbay. But I can assure you that if you try to obstruct me, I will go to New Delhi, seek a federal injunction to force compliance, and return here within three days to serve that injunction on you and both their Royal Highnesses."

Ahbay frowned. But he was tougher than he looked. "With respect, Inspector, I really don't think you understand. It is not a matter of obstruction at all. It is a very real question of inability. His Royal Highness is simply not able to receive visitors."

"Why not?"

Ahbay sighed. "His Royal Highness has been ill for a very long time. . . ."

Sansi nodded. He was beginning to get angry. "Tell me, Mr. Ahbay, what is the nature of his illness? I want you to tell me . . . precisely."

"He's dotty."

The three men started as the strangely metallic voice filled the room.

Ahbay fidgeted and looked at the intercom on his desk. "Please, memsahib . . ."

"He's dotty," the disembodied voice reverberated around the room again. *"Dotty . . . crackers . . . bonkers."*

It was the thin, high voice of an old woman. An old woman who was supposed to be too infirm to be interviewed but who now sounded dauntingly alert.

"That's why nobody can talk to him," the voice continued. *"Nobody's had any sense out of him in years. Fell on his head playing polo. I told him it was a stupid game, but . . ."* The voice faded, then surged back again. *"If it's a murder investigation you had better come up and see me, Inspector."*

"Please, memsahib . . ." Ahbay protested but the old lady upstairs cut him off again.

"Send him up, Ahbay. He sounds perfectly reasonable to me."

There was a soft click and she was gone. Sansi realized

that the Maharani had been listening all the time, deciding
for herself whether she wanted to speak to him or not.

Ahbay raised his hands in a gracious gesture of defeat.
"Her Highness the Maharani will see you now," he said.

Sansi found it difficult to conceal his pleasure. He had
only requested an initial interview with the Maharajah in
order to get to his mother, the Maharani. Until now there
had been no way of knowing that it was the Maharani who
really ran the household. Not her son, the playboy-
maharajah who had to be closeted away, his brain damaged
beyond all hope of recovery and unable to communicate
with the outside world. Parmar stayed behind while Ahbay
escorted Sansi to the Maharani's quarters.

One of the doors in the entrance hall concealed a small
lift. It carried the two men to the third floor and stopped
with a soft wheeze.

"This is most unusual," Ahbay bleated. "She's bedrid-
den, you know. She never sees anyone. It is most unusual.
Most frightfully, frightfully odd."

He led Sansi down a long, teak-paneled corridor hung
with more portraits of mustached and turbaned men and a
few black-and-white photographs from the past. Sansi
glimpsed a picture of a handsome, robust young man in
polo shirt and jodhpurs accepting a trophy from the young
Queen Elizabeth. The young Maharajah before the accident.
His face full of life and confidence.

There was a single door at the far end of the corridor and
Ahbay asked Sansi to wait while he stepped inside for a
moment. He quickly re-emerged, his face filled with dis-
may.

"Ten, fifteen minutes at most," he warned, trying to cling
to some vestige of his power. "But for heaven's sake, don't
believe everything she says." He wandered back down the
corridor, shaking his head.

Sansi opened the door and stepped back a hundred years
in time. The room was large, with white walls, high,
vaulted ceilings and fluted columns crowned with gold leaf.
The furniture was old, opulent and dark. One wall was

curved and accommodated a series of small windows that gave a breathtaking view of the mountains, the lake and the sprawling blue city of Jaigapur below.

The windows were bordered by heavy damask curtains tied back with tassled golden sashes, the floor covered in richly patterned carpets. The whole room smelled of money, age and camphor. And it was dominated by the biggest bed Sansi had ever seen: an early Victorian four-poster with columns of burled mahogany that could have supported a house and a canopy that reached to the ceiling.

A step had been built on one side of the bed to assist its occupant, who remained invisible beneath layer upon layer of silk coverlets. Propped against the carved mahogany headboard was a nest of snowy pillows; somewhere at the bottom of them, Sansi thought he could see a tiny gray head.

There was an empty chair and a table next to the bed. The table was covered with bottles of pills and assorted lotions and potions . . . and an intercom.

"Come in and sit down, Inspector," a voice commanded from the nest of pillows. It was weaker than it had been when amplified by the intercom.

"What did you say your name was? Fancy? Sansi? Nancy? What kind of a silly name is that?"

Sansi smiled and crossed the room. The pile on the carpet was so soft and deep he felt as though he were walking through sand. He stood by the side of the bed and the two of them studied each other for a minute.

He saw a thin, withered stick of a woman with a floral flannel nightdress buttoned primly to the throat and a red kashmir shawl across her shoulders. She wore a gold stud in her left nostril and there was a tiny red teardrop in the middle of her forehead, identifying her as *Kshatriya*, the ruling caste. Her hair was gray and plaited into a thick rope that disappeared into the pillows. She stared back at him through thick-lensed glasses.

"You've got blue eyes," she said.

He smiled and thought of Annie Ginnaro.

"Sit down," the Maharani ordered. "Make yourself comfortable."

Sansi did as he was told.

"I can tell by your accent that you're well educated," she said. "Did you go to university?"

"Oxford," he said.

"Very impressive," she observed drily. "But you're not full caste. What are you?"

"My mother was *Gujerati* by birth. Her father's caste was *Vartak*. He owned a shipping company. My father was English. A general in the British Army. That's why my name is half Indian, half English. If you include my middle name, it makes me more English.

"What is it?"

Sansi smiled self-consciously. "It's Louis. After Louis Mountbatten. My mother wanted to remember the British and India's independence both at the same time. Mountbatten was Viceroy during independence."

"I know," she answered sharply. "I met him. Charming man. Bit of a fool though, thought he could rush things. What a mess he made of it. What a botch-up the British finally made of it all, eh? What do you think?"

Sansi smiled again. He found himself being charmed. "I agree," he said. "It was a terrible botch-up."

"Still," she wheezed, "that's the British for you: the best of intentions and the worst of consequences. Heaven knows how they managed to build an empire. Only because we were more incompetent than they were, I suppose."

Sansi tried to guess the Maharani's age. She had to be at least in her early eighties. She reminded him of an exotic bird, the last of a rare species, now bordering on extinction. Alone in her faded plumage, waiting to die. Only the sharpness of her eyes indicated the precious memories stored within.

"This used to be the *zanana*," she said, reading his mind.

The *zanana* was a gilded prison where the wives and daughters of the Maharajah spent most of their lives, governed by the ritual of *purdah*, which meant that no man but those in their immediate family could look at them—a ritual that endured until after the Second World War.

"I started my life in *purdah* right here in this tower," she observed. "I think it rather appropriate that I end my life here."

Sansi felt humbled by the immensity of all she had endured in her life and the fact that somehow, she still kept her wit.

"My father was a dreadful man," she went on, enjoying the rare opportunity for conversation. "He was very big and very strong. He loved to wrestle; he was good at it, too. He liked to go down into the city in one of his Rolls-Royce touring cars and challenge the biggest men he could find to wrestle him."

"He must have been an extraordinary character," Sansi said lamely.

She chuckled softly to herself. "An extraordinary bore. 'A man's man' used to be the expression, before it came to mean something else. I hardly knew him. I don't think he even knew who I was. Officially he had four wives and eleven children. Unofficially he had at least six concubines and the same number of illegitimate children all over again. I was just another girl who lived in the palace. I was lucky he never tried to sleep with me. He was always getting confused, especially when he got older. Everybody mourned when he died but nobody was really sad. Do you know that at one time he owned seventeen Rolls-Royce cars? Seventeen! He never stepped inside half of them. He used to have them lined up in front of the stables to show off to visitors. No wonder we had no money left when he died."

Her voice was growing fainter and Sansi was afraid she might exhaust herself before he could ask any questions.

"Your Highness," he said, "may I ask you something?"

She looked at him curiously over the top of her glasses. "What is it?"

"May I know how old you are?"

"Acha." She smiled. "You want to get down to business. Yes, all right, it's what you're here for." She paused for a

moment and he could see her trying to calculate. "Eighty-one or eighty-two, I think. Yes, I, no . . . eighty-two. That's right, eighty-two. I was born in 1909. I was the youngest of the Maharajah's official children. That is why I am now the Maharani: I outlived all my brothers and sisters."

Sansi did some quick calculations of his own. She would have been twenty-two years old in 1931. If only she could remember.

"Your Highness, do you remember when a man called Cardus was Collector of Jaigapur from 1930 to 1931?"

Her face sagged. There was a long pause and when she spoke again her voice sounded flat and disappointed. "Don't tell me you're looking into that sorry old business," she said. "Nothing was done about it then—I can't imagine that anybody would want to do anything about it now."

Sansi leaned forward on his chair. The focus of his attention had narrowed to one tiny prism, a sliver of living history that held him and the Maharani in fleeting suspension. For a moment they could make the past come alive in this room. He could feel it: he could hear it breathing faintly, he could sense its fragile heartbeat. The old lady on her deathbed was the only person in the world who could reach across time and hand him the one precious clue that he needed. Karma. Destiny.

"What business do you mean, Your Highness?"

"That Cardus affair," she answered irritably. "An awful business. It was the British at their worst. No one in Jaigapur trusted them ever again after that."

"Please, Your Highness, this is very important. I need you to tell me what happened."

The Maharani lay back in the pillows and closed her eyes. For a moment there was only the sound of her breathing. When she spoke again it was with her eyes still closed, as if she was describing images that only she could see, flickering inside her eyelids like pictures from a silent newsreel.

"I can remember the first time I saw him," she began. "It was soon after he had arrived in Jaigapur to take up the

Collectorate. He had come to pay his respects to my father in the main hall. I watched with my sisters from a balcony. We weren't supposed to be there but one of the guards let us out of the *zanana* and we crept onto the balcony with veils over our heads to watch the show. My father liked to tease the British. It was another kind of contest to him, a contest of wills. I remember the new Collector was wearing a white suit with gold thread on the shoulders and he had a very high hat with feathers on it under one arm. He was a small man but he stood very straight to make himself look taller. I still remember how ordinary he looked. Even the uniform couldn't make him look important. He was thin and small and losing his hair, and he had a mean face with an ugly little mustache. Not the kind of big, fierce mustache that my father and the other men in the palace used to have. He was such an unimpressive-looking man. It was almost as if it was an insult to send a man like that to be the Collector. He was not the sort of man you would expect to represent a great empire. That was why it was so hard to take the British seriously all the time. They kept sending us such unimpressive little men to tell us what to do."

She paused for a moment and Sansi asked if she was all right. She asked him to pour her a glass of water from a pitcher on the table. When she had taken a sip he replaced the glass and waited.

"We knew there was going to be trouble," she said. "Right from that first time. It was the way he spoke to my father. Talking down to him, as though he was a servant and not the titular ruler of Jaigapur. Cardus had no manners, no grace. He wasn't a gentleman. I think he must have come from a bad family, or perhaps he did not have a good education in England. The British made a mistake sending him here. It was something they did often. India was too big for them, you see. They didn't have the numbers or the talent to service the administration; they kept sending out people who were nobodies in England to fill important positions in India, positions for which they were not remotely qualified. I tell you, Inspector, they were scraping the bottom of the barrel when they sent that Cardus man to be Collector of Jaigapur.

"My father was very angry when the new Collector left that day. I think we all knew that bad things would come. I did not hear anything about him for many weeks. He did not call for tea or bother to keep my father informed of the various goings-on, as had been the habit of the other Collectors. My mother told us what was happening. She said the people in the town were very unhappy; the new Collector was a cruel man, they said, and a bad magistrate. People said he drank too much whiskey every night and went to court the next day in a bad temper. He put people in jail for nothing. He had men flogged for stealing. No one had done that in Jaigapur in my father's lifetime.

"My mother said he called our people niggers. I had not heard the word before. My mother said it was a word the British used for people with dark skin. Things went on like that for a long time. And then . . ."

She paused for a moment, as if gathering her strength to voice what she was about to reveal.

"Then some very bad things happened. The Collector was supposed to be married but he did not bring his wife with him. People said he did not like women. He liked men—not men . . . boys. Young boys. People came to my father and said their sons had been charged with crimes they did not commit. When they were in jail some of the boys were taken to the Collector's house for his . . . entertainment. My father was shocked. He did not know what to do; it was like nothing he had ever had to deal with before. Jaigapur was quite isolated in those days: the train came once a week. There was a small garrison of troops under the command of a British officer who was a friend of the Collector. They drank together and played cards. My father sent a message that he wanted to see the Collector but Cardus ignored him.

"Things began to get worse. Boys went missing. Bodies were found in the lake and in the countryside. People said parts of the boys were missing . . . their male parts. Some

people said the Collector was responsible. That he was sick
in the head . . . crazy. There was so much fear in Jaigapur.

"My mother said my father decided to kill the Collector.
He said he would bring Cardus to the castle and poison
him. My mother said that would only get us in trouble with
the British, and told my father he should go to the authorities
in Delhi. She believed in British law. She was sure that once
they knew what was going on, they would be angry too and
they would arrest the Collector. So my father sent a message
to the Governor in Delhi, telling him about the murders and
saying the British should come and see for themselves.

"The British sent one policeman. He stayed at the Collector's house. They were all down there drinking together
and having a high old time of it. The policeman talked to
a few people but everybody was too afraid to tell him anything. My father was going mad with frustration. The policeman was living with the murderer and *still* couldn't find
him. The policeman spoke to my father only once and my
father lost his temper and shouted at him. The policeman
said my father was mad. That was the last straw for my father. He sent another message to the Governor and this time
he spelled it out for them so there would be no mistake. He
came right out and accused the Collector of committing
murder. That did the trick."

A faint smile played around her lips.

"The policeman went away and a month later the Collector was replaced. But nobody was ever charged; there was
never a trial, not even one of their ridiculous inquiries. The
commander of Jaigapur garrison was transferred soon afterward and that was it. The new Collector never mentioned
a thing about it to my father. The British hushed it all up
and pretended it had never happened.

"My father was very bitter. He said we had all seen what
the British were really like. They might boast about their
great laws and their tradition of justice . . . but they really
had very little to be proud of. In the end we all knew. They
had nothing to teach India. They were bandits in fine
clothes. Worse—they weren't even honest about it."

She stopped and lay very still. Sansi thought that she must finally have exhausted herself and drifted off to sleep. Then her eyes blinked open and she looked at him.

"That was it, Inspector," she said. "The Cardus affair. One of the great, dirty secrets of the Raj. And you think you can do something about it now? After all these years, when all the people are long gone? What a fool you must be, Inspector. No one can go back in time and correct the crimes of history."

Sansi's gaze wandered over to the windows and the old worn city far below. "Perhaps he hasn't gotten away with it," he said softly. "Perhaps he's come back for more. Perhaps this time I can catch him."

Sansi was silent during his journey back from the past as they bumped down the hill from Jaigapur Fort and back into the sunlight of the present day. It was only when they rejoined the snarling clamor of the city traffic that he was jolted into a new awareness of his surroundings.

"I want to check the records of every hotel in Jaigapur," he told Parmar suddenly. "Going back two years."

They started with the registers of Jaigapur's best hotels and proceeded with the intent of working gradually downmarket. Sansi had a hunch.

He didn't have to look far. He decided to check the register of the Sheraton Jaigapur himself. It was the only five-star hotel in the city. He was on his own in the manager's office, working his way down the column of names for those guests who had stayed at the Sheraton the first week in March 1989.

The name leapt out of the register as though lit in neon.

Tony Cardus. British High Commission, New Delhi.

He had charged his accommodation to his American Express card. Sansi made a note of the number. In the right-hand column was an elegant, elongated signature. The signature of a murderer.

A murderer from the past.

17

SANSI PUT HIS stopover in New Delhi to good use on his way home to Bombay. He spent most of the day at Crime Branch comparing the records of every murder that had taken place in the northern states of Haryana, Uttar Pradesh, Bihar, Madhya Pradesh and Rajasthan over the previous two years. It was the mind-numbing, time-consuming kind of work that no other policeman had bothered to do.

He found two more murders with the same modus operandi. The victims were both young, homosexual males. Both were subject to the same pattern of mutilation. Both had been murdered between the months of March and May 1988. One of the victims was a male prostitute in New Delhi. The second was a youth in Agra, site of the Taj Mahal, the most popular tourist destination in India. Sansi knew that when he investigated further, the youth in Agra would also turn out to be homosexual.

Still, he was perturbed. He could find nothing more recent than 1989, which fitted in with the pattern of activity that would include Jaigapur in March 1989. All the cities were on the well-trodden tourist path, where any foreigner would blend in easily with the teeming crowds of visitors. But as Sansi knew all too well, his murderer had been active in the past few weeks in Bombay. Yet there was nothing to suggest there had been anything more recent than 1988 in the other cities of New Delhi, Agra and Jaigapur.

Sansi froze. Somewhere out there in New Delhi, he realized, there were almost certainly other victims, whose bodies were waiting to be discovered.

Because Cardus seemed to prefer Sheratons, Sansi checked with the Sheraton Maurya in New Delhi first.

Cardus had been a guest there too. And recently. He had stayed for five days, and checked out only eight days ago. He had also stayed at the hotel for a week in April 1988.

Sansi checked the Mogul Sheraton in Agra and found Cardus had stayed there one week before the body of the Agra victim had been discovered. The dates of his visits all corresponded with the dates of the murders.

There would be other victims too, Sansi was certain. In other cities, in other parts of India. All neatly separated by time, distance and the unbridgeable gulf created by the lack of coordination between the different departments of the Indian police service.

There were no computers to make Sansi's job any easier. It was impossible to run speculative cross-checks of police records in anything approaching real time. Everything had to be done by hand through the laborious process of tracking down the right files and scanning page after page of typed or handwritten reports in half a dozen different languages. If an investigator didn't know what he was looking for, it was impossible for a pattern to emerge by itself. It was only because Sansi had found a few fragments of the same puzzle and had managed to put them together that the pattern of murder had become apparent.

The closer he got to Cardus, the angrier Sansi became at the arrogant simplicity of his approach. Cardus was so smug, so sure of himself, he had not even bothered to cover his path by using an alias. There was no need. No one was looking for him. No one until now.

What angered Sansi most was that whoever this new Cardus was, he was right. He was safe in India—as safe as his murderous predecessor. Like the Collector of Jaigapur, who bore the same name, the new Cardus had been protected by the corrupt and compliant character of the country on which he preyed. By universal indifference to the disappearance of a few more nobodies among millions. By the lack of sophistication in the Indian police service. By the perpetual chaos of India.

Sansi had one more move to make before he was finished in New Delhi. He borrowed the office of a colleague, closed the door and placed a call to the British High Commission. When the switchboard operator answered he gave a false name and announced himself as a journalist from the *Times of India*. He asked to speak to Antony Cardus of the Foreign Office.

After a few minutes, the operator returned with the information that there was no one with that name at the High Commission. Sansi pressed her, insisting he was right. It was a dangerous game. The last thing Sansi wanted to do was talk to Cardus, if he was there. All he wanted was to be sure.

The operator returned and said she would pass him on to a gentleman in the Commercial Management and Export Department.

A moment later a man's voice came on the line. "Miles Woolley here. How can I help you?"

Sansi repeated the false name and said he was a financial journalist who had been referred to Antony Cardus for some information about trade figures.

"Tony Cardus doesn't work here, I'm afraid. Perhaps I could ask our press liaison officer to give you a call. Could you give me a number, please?"

Woolley knew Cardus. Sansi was sure of it.

"I'd be happy to give you my number," he lied. He fumbled hurriedly through the pages of the telephone book looking for the number of the *Times of India* office. "But I'm returning a call to Mr. Cardus. He asked me expressly to get back to him. Have you any idea how I might contact him?"

"Not unless you want to ring him in London, old chap," Woolley answered breezily.

"London?"

"Yes . . . London." The voice sounded just a trifle supercilious.

"Well," Sansi responded vaguely, "I suppose I could do that too. Where should I contact him in London?"

"The Foreign and Commonwealth Office, of course. Ask for the Commercial Management and Export Department, old chap, just as you did here."

Sansi smiled. "Won't he be coming back to New Delhi soon?"

"Shouldn't think so," Woolley answered. "He's just left. He was here for six weeks. He only comes out every two or three years. It's a working holiday for him. If you really must speak to him you'll have to ring him in London . . . or I might be able to pass a message on to him."

"Oh, thank you very much, that won't be necessary," Sansi said. "I think I will give Mr. Cardus a ring in London."

"No problem at all, old chap. Any other queries just be so kind as to give our press liaison chappie a call first, would you?"

"Oh, most certainly," Sansi answered, sliding into an even thicker Indian accent. "I would be most willing to give your press liaison chappie a call. I have always found the High Commission to be full of very helpful chappies. Thank you, sahib."

"Yes . . ." The reply was a long uncertain drawl.

Sansi put down the phone, pushed his hair out of his eyes and stood up. He shoved his hands into his trouser pockets and paced back and forth across the small office. He felt nervous, elated and newly apprehensive all at the same time.

Antony Cardus, trade liaison officer with the British Foreign Office, was his man. His murderer from the past. A direct descendant of Antony Cardus, former Collector of Jaigapur. A grandson, a great-grandson or a nephew. A man who had inherited his forebear's murderous characteristic. An appetite for murder and mutilation.

It was the breakthrough Sansi had been looking for. The

breakthrough that could close the case. At the same time, it was enough to drag his investigation into a political imbroglio involving government departments in London and New Delhi. A treacherous political morass which would allow the new killer to escape, just like the first, with the connivance of amoral politicians who didn't want the world to know what monsters their system sheltered.

Sansi wasn't prepared to let that happen.

It was a little after midday when Sansi's Air India flight touched down at Sahar International Airport in Bombay. He took a taxi straight home.

For twenty-four hours he told no one of his findings. Not even Pramila. He did not go into his office and he did not tell Jamal what he had uncovered in New Delhi and Jaigapur. All his instincts told him that Antony Cardus was a serial killer. His evidence was compelling—but it was still circumstantial. It was more than enough to convince another policeman. But was it enough to convince a judge and jury—or even guarantee an extradition order? As Jamal would almost certainly remind him, that was a different game. But it was the game that mattered.

Sansi had other reasons for not calling Jamal immediately. He had few illusions about his superiors. He knew that Jamal would do nothing with the new evidence until he had considered every possible political implication. He might raise it with the commissioner, the chief minister, even state Cabinet. And if it became politically expedient, for any reason, Sansi knew the investigation would be taken away from him and shut down. Slowly but surely the wheels of a new cover-up would grind into place, engineered this time by an Indian government anxious to spare itself the embarrassment of a diplomatic incident involving one of its most important Western allies. India still needed Britain. For all its sins, Britain was still the head of the Commonwealth and a major trading partner. More important since the collapse of the USSR, it was the source of much of India's high-tech defense needs, including warships, aircraft and missile systems. Sansi knew his government would not fret over the deaths of a few male prostitutes if they decided it was in their country's better interests to avoid an ugly extradition battle with the British: a battle which had the potential to attract enormous publicity and to do great harm to the reputations of both governments.

Within twenty-four hours of his arrival back in Bombay, Sansi had to put together his case in such a way that it would acquire a momentum all its own. A momentum so powerful that no one, not even the most senior political figures in Maharashtra, would dare interfere with it—without putting their careers at risk.

Sansi had already made up his mind on the flight back from New Delhi that if his investigation were to be stalled now, for any reason, he would exercise an option of consummate irony. He would give all his evidence to Annie Ginnaro, and drop the bombshell that would explode across the front pages of every newspaper in India. There was nothing the media liked better than a government cover-up, especially when it involved sex, movies, murder and intrigue in high places.

Sansi spent the rest of his first day back going through the registers of Bombay's leading hotels. He started with the Oberoi, then moved to the President, the Taj Mahal Inter-Continental and then the original Taj Mahal next door on Apollo Bunder. By midafternoon of the following day, he had almost everything he needed.

He also placed a call to Film City and spoke to a man who was able to answer several questions. When Sansi hung up the phone he smiled. Antony Cardus had visited Film City in 1988 as a VIP guest of studio manager Pratap Coyarjee.

Sansi walked back to the kitchen table and surveyed the mass of papers one last time: interview reports, copies of the coroner's report and police reports from Jaigapur and New Delhi, copies of hotel registers, credit card receipts, his overflowing case diary.

Antony Cardus had stayed at the Taj Mahal in Bombay

on two separate occasions between April 2 and May 14 that year. His April visit lasted for ten days, his May visit for five. Like the hotel registrations in New Delhi and Jaigapur, Cardus described his status as "diplomatic" and gave his address care of the British Foreign Office.

The dates of both stays in Bombay corresponded with the murders of Sanjay Nayak and Pratap Coyarjee. Taken in conjunction with the material he had acquired in Jaigapur and New Delhi, as well as Rohan's compelling forensic evidence, Sansi believed he had enough to place Cardus at the locations of five separate murders in five separate cities on five separate dates. With the additional evidence that Cardus and Coyarjee knew each other and with Rohan's forensic evidence of a homosexual link, Sansi believed he had enough. He knew it was still largely circumstantial. But it was enough to convince even the most cynical politician that the case had progressed beyond the point of no return and that to interfere now would be to risk political embarrassment.

He hoped it was enough to convince Jamal that he ought to make one more trip. To London. To close the final chapter of the Cardus affair . . . after more than sixty years.

"There's something missing," Jamal said.

Sansi waited.

"If we could be sure that a jury would bring in a conviction on circumstantial evidence alone, then I would file the extradition order myself. But it probably won't even get as far as a trial here. The first thing this Mr. Cardus will do is to engage a lawyer to fight the extradition order. A clever London lawyer might be able to convince a sympathetic judge that Mr. Cardus only had an unfortunate knack for being in the wrong place at the wrong time."

"Five times? In five different cities? On five different occasions?"

"It is not me you have to convince." Jamal smiled. "I agree, you have enough to go on with the case. But that is all. It is not enough to justify an extradition order. Not yet."

Sansi sighed. "Do I take it that I have your approval to go to London?"

Jamal shook his head. "Not yet, Inspector. There is much more to be considered here before I give you permission to spend the department's money on an expensive trip to London."

It was just as Sansi had feared. Jamal wouldn't do anything until he had considered the political fallout first.

The joint commissioner changed direction.

"What do you make of this business in Jaigapur?" he asked. "This Collector fellow with the same name, all those years ago? This is a most curious twist, is it not? Do you really think the two are connected?"

"I think I could prove they are connected if I go to London, sir."

Jamal smiled thinly and leaned back in his chair, hands behind his head, gold Rolex glittering on his left wrist.

"It is not that simple, Inspector," he said, his voice and manner soothing. "If you do go to London, we will have to arrange powers of arrest through the metropolitan police. Before we do that, we have to have an extradition order prepared and ready to lodge with the British government at the moment of arrest. That means we have to go through New Delhi and then through the High Commissioner in London. We will have to retain our own counsel there to support the extradition proceedings in court. And then the whole thing could fall flat on its face if the judge decides that it all sounds very nice as far as it goes but it doesn't go far enough. Because if you are going to extradite a British subject to India to face a murder trial that could result in him getting the death penalty—because that is what he would be looking at here—then you're going to have to come up with something a little stronger than a string of coincidences.

"Just think of what the British newspapers would make of this." Jamal leaned forward and arched his eyebrows at Sansi. "Capital punishment was abolished in Britain years ago, you know. Just the idea of extraditing a British citizen to a country where he could go to the gallows would be enough to bring all the civil libertarians out onto the streets. This case of yours is not a conventional murder inquiry anymore, Sansi. It is the kind of case that could result in questions in both the British parliament and ours. It has become political. I'm sorry, but it is no longer something only I can decide upon. You know what is involved, Inspector. Before we begin something like this, we have to be sure we can control it—otherwise it will get away from us and the result will be a disaster for all of us."

"I'm not looking for an extradition order," Sansi answered softly. "Not yet."

Jamal waited.

"I know there is more work to be done. But it has to be done in London."

"What are you suggesting then?" There was a note of exasperation in Jamal's voice, as though he resented the possibility that he might be cheated of the chance to play power politics again with something new.

"All I need is your approval to continue my investigation in London," Sansi said. "If I can gather the additional evidence I need there, then we can look at an extradition order. I promise you, sir, I won't ask you to extradite unless I have the evidence that will guarantee a conviction."

"What evidence are you going after, Sansi?"

"Blood."

Jamal gave Sansi a wry smile. "Blood?" he echoed.

"Bad blood is supposed to be passed on from generation to generation, isn't it?"

"It's a theory," Jamal observed drily. "But suspecting it and using it to prove murder are two separate things."

"All I need is a hair of his head," Sansi pressed on. "From his barber. From the dry cleaner where he takes his clothes. From his pillow. From his lover. From a search warrant if the metropolitan police will help me get one."

"And what good will that do you?"

"We have a fragment of pubic hair taken from the colon of Sanjay Nayak, remember?"

Jamal nodded.

"There is only one way it could have got there. Rohan has taken a clear enzyme pattern from it. If I can put my hands on just one fragment of my murderer's hair and the two samples match . . . we've got him. No two human beings have the same blood enzyme pattern. It's more reliable than DNA analysis."

Jamal shrugged. "All that proves is that Cardus committed buggery with Nayak before he died."

Sansi shook his head.

"*Moments* before. The pubic hair has the same enzyme pattern as the semen we found in Nayak's colon. Nayak had no time to expel either from his bowel before he was killed. Our man was there. The sex was part of the murder. Part of the fun."

Jamal remained silent, thinking. "You're asking the department to spend a lot of money on a chance," he said.

"I would think that money invested in the apprehension of a mass murderer is money well spent, sir."

"Don't be insolent," Jamal responded, his voice ominously gentle.

"Sir . . ." Sansi hesitated. He had made the speech many times in his head but he had never delivered it to Jamal before. "We're talking about a man who has killed five of our people . . . for pleasure. A man who believes he can repeat the crimes of history. A man who follows the dark inspiration of his predecessor who walked away, unpunished, because of who he was and because his crimes were so great that the powers of the day feared to make them public. And all of it was made possible because no one really cared. Because all the victims were worthless. Now a new killer has returned to commit the same crimes by exploiting the same prejudices. Back then, we had no choice. It wasn't our country. Today we do have a choice. We can choose to bring to justice the man who preys on the most wretched of our people. It doesn't matter that they were all nobodies; it doesn't matter that they were beggars or thieves or homosexuals or prostitutes. If India is to mean anything, we have to get justice for all our people, even the lowest of the low. Especially them."

Jamal shifted in his chair. "You are the only officer in my whole department who can throw Gandhi at me," he said.

Sansi smiled. No one paid anything more than lip service to the teachings of the Mahatma anymore.

"Acha," Jamal decided. "The department owes you some leave. Take a couple of days off, Sansi. Don't talk about this to anybody. I'll call you."

18

SANSI WAS AT home when the call came through. It wasn't Jamal, it was his personal aide. The joint commissioner would meet Sansi for lunch at noon the following day at The Willingdon Club. They would be joined by the governor of Maharashtra.

Sansi hung up, disappointed. It was a bad sign. The wheels of government did not turn that quickly when it was good news. The fact that Jamal wanted him to meet the governor indicated that the investigation was to be dropped and Sansi was to be subjected to some sophisticated intimidation. A nice civilized lunch, some pleasant conversation, a little gentle persuasion, the odd veiled threat or two and just a hint of some unspecified future reward for his cooperation. That the meeting was to take place in a discreet civilian location away from any official forum only confirmed Sansi's suspicions further. It was how the system worked.

Sansi was there early. His taxi dropped him at the main entrance to The Willingdon Club at eleven forty-five. The sky was darkly oppressive though there had still been no rain to herald the coming monsoon. Everyone had been complaining how the monsoon was much later this year and how much hotter the weather had been and how the greenhouse effect could only be making it worse.

Sansi waited at the top of the steps beneath a grand, white marble portico and watched dust dervishes chase each other along the drive. He shook the creases out of his jacket and straightened his tie. His shirt collar was damp and tiny rivulets of sweat itched down his back. The cool marble interior of the club yawned invitingly behind him: a large, open vestibule paneled with English oak, a majestic double staircase leading to the second floor, a reception desk and an eclectic collection of antiques donated by long-dead gentlemen or scavenged from long-dead gentlemen's clubs.

Sansi knew The Willingdon Club well. His father had been a member and so had Pramila. Sansi had played tennis and squash there and drunk sweet limes on the front lawn before he had gone to Oxford. He hadn't been back in twenty years.

The club was founded in 1917, as a social forum where high-caste Indians and British gentlemen could meet as equals, away from the snobbery and racism that marred other clubs of the time. The original grounds had encompassed two polo fields, though they had long since been replaced by an eighteen-hole golf course, which was now used mostly by visiting Japanese businessmen.

The vestibule was dominated by portraits of the club's founders, Lord and Lady Willingdon. Lord Willingdon looked like a weed but his wife could have sat for a portrait of Britannia. It was part of her legend that she had extorted a fortune in jewelry from the Indian princes who visited the club in the early days. It was her practice to express loud and profuse admiration for some Nawab's necklace or brooch to the point where the embarrassed potentate had little choice but to offer it to her as a gift. The princes grew wise to her scheme and whenever they were invited back to The Willingdon Club they made sure their jewels were paste imitations.

Jamal's Contessa pulled up at the bottom of the steps. The joint commissioner emerged, wearing a beautiful cream-colored suit and looking as though he had just stepped from the pages of a men's fashion magazine. He trotted elegantly up the steps to join Sansi. There wasn't a bead of perspiration on his face.

"A bit more pleasant than business at the office, wouldn't you say, Inspector?"

Sansi thought he saw the trace of a smirk on Jamal's handsome face. Just enough to make Sansi even more apprehensive.

"Why here?" he asked, his voice artificially cool.

Jamal shrugged. "The governor is a member of the club. He likes it. He felt like a little outing, I suppose. He wanted us all to relax, have a nice lunch."

Jamal chatted on amiably as though they were there to discuss the rules for an upcoming gymkhana rather than the extradition of a British government official on charges of mass murder. Sansi checked his watch against the grandfather clock in the vestibule. According to his watch, it was 12:03. The clock said 12:06. Sansi decided the clock was wrong.

A moment later, the governor's Daimler appeared in the driveway, twin pennants fluttering regally from each fender. The car came to a graceful stop and almost by magic the club secretary materialized at the bottom of the steps to greet the state's head of government. Governor Girja Shankar Jejeebhoy climbed slowly down from the Daimler, exchanged a few pleasantries with the secretary, then struggled up the steps with a silver-topped walking cane in one hand and his chauffeur supporting the other.

Governor Jejeebhoy was a vastly overweight man in his sixties. He had a big, fleshy face, a neat, white mustache and gray hair brushed straight back from his forehead. His pale blue safari suit was cut large to accommodate his massive gut. He walked slowly and stiffly because his great weight had long since pulverized the cartilage between his knee joints. Sweat glistened in the dark creases around his neck and there was a damp half-moon beneath each armpit.

"Afternoon, Jamal," he grunted in a deep friendly bass as he reached the top of the steps. "Inspector Sansi." The governor leaned on his cane with one hand and offered his free hand to Sansi. It felt like a hot, wet towel. "Let's go inside, shall we, gentlemen?" the governor huffed. "Before I die right here in the lobby."

Governor Jejeebhoy struggled ponderously toward the dining room with Sansi and Jamal respectfully marking time alongside. A government aide hovered silently in the background. Sansi felt as though he were part of a funeral cortege. It took them nearly five minutes to get from the lobby to the dining room and another five minutes to lower the governor into a chair. The club secretary and the governor's aide fussed around for a few minutes and when both were satisfied that the old boy was comfortable, they disappeared.

"Anyone for tennis?" the governor asked, cocking an eyebrow at Sansi.

Sansi smiled. Governor Jejeebhoy was one of the greatest political survivors in the modern history of Maharashtra State. He had been a politician since Independence and his fortunes had peaked and slumped many times over the years. To endure and prosper for so long in the maelstrom of Indian politics a man had to like the game for its own sake. Jejeebhoy loved it. He was good at it too, and at that moment he was at the summit of his political powers. Unlike other nations which had inherited the framework of the Westminster system, state governors in India carried more authority and were more politically active than their counterparts in other Commonwealth countries. Governors influenced the state government, had the power to approve the appointment of chief ministers, and presided over every high-level decision that involved state and federal jurisdictions.

Sansi couldn't help but be impressed. Jamal's contacts reached much higher than he had suspected.

Half a dozen white-jacketed waiters descended on the table like a flock of cockatoos. The governor and Jamal both ordered whiskey with soda. Sansi ordered a salt lime. The cockatoos dived and swooped, plates and glasses disappeared, reappeared, and were supplemented with menus on small white cards, each bearing the club's crest, a *W* in the shape of a crown.

Sansi glanced over the food selection. It was the same eccentric selection of European and Indian dishes the club had always presented, most of them misspelled: Cabbage Chowder, Mutton Moussaka a la Greeque, Chicken Do Piaza and Rice, Spicy Baked Beans, Tandoori Pomfret and Butter Nan, Tandoori Vegetable Mixed Grill.

Sansi wasn't particularly hungry. He put the menu down and looked around the grand open-sided dining room with its white marble columns and views of the golf course. It was almost empty, except for a party of middle-aged Indian women and a young Japanese couple in loud, checkered golfing shorts. Times may have changed, Sansi thought, but everything else looked the same. The tables and chairs, made from opulent Burma teak, the wide-bladed fans from the Byculla Club that still spun lazily in the ceiling. The starched white tablecloths and heavy silverware with the club crest embossed on the handles were still the same. Everything looked the same. Yet everything was different.

When Sansi had first visited the club, as a young boy with his mother, he had been awed by its grandeur. There were many British expatriates still living in Bombay then, the only people who had not ostracized Pramila, and it had been possible to feel the breath of Empire still wafting through the grand marble halls. Now, even that faint breath had expired. With its bone-colored shell and rib-like pillars, The Willingdon Club was the exoskeleton of Empire. The great armies of redcoats, the corpuscles that had once sustained it, were gone. All that remained was the white carapace of a once-great beast that had cowed and colonized half the globe but was now extinct.

"So," the governor interrupted Sansi's thoughts, "you're going to London to bring back a murderer."

Sansi stared at him. "I am?"

"That is what Narendra tells me."

Sansi looked from one man to the other. He saw Jamal looking back at him, an amused gleam in his eyes.

"You look surprised, Inspector," the governor observed.

"I wasn't expecting a . . . positive reply . . . so soon," Sansi blustered.

The governor thoughtfully pursed his lips, as though personal caprice and political intrigue were characteristics which played no part in his life. "I think Inspector Sansi is a cynic," the governor remarked to Jamal.

"Worse," the joint commissioner replied. "He is an idealist. Inspector Sansi believes he is the sole custodian of the community conscience. He thinks that the rest of us, especially those in government, are too interested in hanging on to power to care about real police work."

"Really?" Jejeebhoy arched his eyebrows as though he had never heard of such a thing. "Well," he went on, "now you have to tell us, Inspector, and tell us truthfully, if you go to London can you get this man, this . . . ?"

"Cardus . . . Antony Cardus," Sansi said.

"Antony Cardus." The governor repeated the name slowly. "Such strange names the English have, don't you think?"

Sansi and Jamal both smiled.

"Are you sure you can get the proof you need, Inspector? First, to convince our government that an application for his extradition is justified, and second, to convince the British that they have no choice but to give him up? I understand Joint Commissioner Jamal has already told you that there is no point in going ahead with any of this unless there is a very real prospect that we can bring this man back to Bombay. Is there, Inspector?"

"Yes, sir," Sansi replied. "I'm sure I can bring him back."

"What makes you so sure?"

"As you may know, sir, I have family in England. I lived there for several years. I know London. I can operate there very well, with or without the assistance of the metropolitan police. I have reason to believe my father might be able to help too."

"Oh." Jejeebhoy looked intrigued. "Why?"

"My mother thinks he knows something about the original murders in Jaigapur."

"The business with the Collector?" Jamal interrupted.

Sansi hadn't told Jamal about the connection to his father. He had been saving that in case he had needed to go to London without official permission.

"Yes," Sansi acknowledged. "My father was a colonel in New Delhi at the time the original murders took place. My mother seems to think he knew something about the cover-up that followed. He wasn't very happy about it."

The waiters arrived to take their food orders. Jejeebhoy tore a bread roll in half, stuffed it in his mouth and moistened it with whiskey and soda. Sansi paused until the waiters had gone again.

"My father still has many useful contacts in the British government," he continued. "I think he can help give me some of the hard background I might need to convince the British that this is something that finally needs to be put right."

"You'll need more than that," Jejeebhoy said.

"Yes, sir," Sansi acknowledged. "I'll get it."

"How?"

"By whatever means necessary."

The governor smiled faintly. "You will keep it legal, won't you?"

"The weight of forensic evidence we've accumulated will close the case," Sansi went on. "I'll get a tissue sample from Tony Cardus if I have to drag him to a blood donor clinic myself. I'll find a way. A legal way."

"If you get it through trickery it won't stand up in court, you know," Jamal added.

"Hair, blood or semen," Sansi said. "A man parts with all three constantly. All I have to do is to be there. I'll watch him twenty-four hours a day if I have to."

The governor and Jamal glanced at each other.

"Perhaps we might change the subject until after lunch," Jejeebhoy observed.

Sansi did not return to the case again until the governor

had finished his second dish of chocolate ice cream and the waiters had cleared the last of the dishes and brought the coffee. The governor ordered port and cigars. It was three o'clock in the afternoon. Sansi declined.

"Forgive me for asking," Sansi said, "but I must say, I expected to face a great deal more difficulty than this in persuading the government to pursue this case."

"The government doesn't know ... yet," the governor said. "I don't think the government needs to know until you've been in London for a week or two. That should give you enough time, shouldn't it?"

Sansi suddenly heard the wheels and cogs of political machinery grinding all around him. It wasn't as straightforward as it had first seemed. Only three people in positions of authority knew what was going on. Himself, Jamal and Governor Jejeebhoy.

"The Cabinet is a little nervous after the Kapoor affair," Jamal interjected smoothly. "Neither the governor nor myself has any doubts about the importance of the case. I think the Cabinet would be greatly reassured if we could present it to them as a fait accompli."

The governor nodded.

"When you are ready to close the case," Jamal went on, "you will call me first. The extradition papers will be ready and waiting. I will call the Indian High Commissioner in London myself. Then I will inform the chief minister and he will inform the Cabinet. I think the Cabinet will be very relieved to know that a foreign national is responsible for the unfortunate set of circumstances that led to Noshir Kilachand's suicide."

"And the murders of Sanjay Nayak, Pratap Coyarjee and the others in New Delhi, Jaigapur and Agra," Sansi added.

"Of course," Jamal concurred.

The governor nodded his approval. "There's a certain poetic irony about all of this, don't you think, Inspector?"

"Sir?"

"Your going to London to arrest an Englishman for killing Indians," Jejeebhoy explained. "A legal ambassador from the former colony going right into the heart of the old empire to show them how justice is done. Rather poetic, wouldn't you agree?"

"Yes, sir." Sansi nodded.

At least some of his suspicions had been right. The government was more concerned with deflecting the blame for the scandal that surrounded Kilachand's death than it was in seeking justice for the murder victims of Antony Cardus. And he could see what Jamal would get out of it. If Sansi arrested Cardus, Jamal would get all the credit, the government would have been spared further embarrassment, justice would have been done and Jamal would have the governor's approval when he made his own move for the chief minister's job in a couple of years. It was perfect, Sansi realized. Jamal was a master strategist. He had taken a difficult case and a potential political disaster and turned it into a springboard for personal triumph. If Sansi failed it would be his fault and no one would ever know ... because his visit to Britain was unofficial. And it would not become official unless he was assured of success.

The port arrived and the three men waited in silence while the waiters filled glasses and lit cigars. When they were alone again, the governor raised his glass in a toast.

"To justice," he said.

Jamal raised his glass and echoed the toast, a small smile on his lips.

Sansi drained the last of his salt lime and took one last look at the club. Perhaps nothing had changed after all.

"I'm leaving for London tomorrow," Sansi told Annie Ginnaro. "I wanted to see you before I go."

Annie stepped aside to let Sansi into her apartment. It was the first time they had seen each other since the night she had massaged him to sleep, only to be awakened later by the phone call bringing bad news. They had parted later on a city street splashed with blood and littered with broken cars. He had given Annie her story. They had spoken on the phone several times since and she had never asked him another question about his work, though her name had appeared more prominently in the pages of the newspaper in the intervening weeks.

"I'm glad you made time," she said, "I'm flattered. Won't Pramila wonder where you are?"

"She knows where I am," Sansi smiled.

"I mean . . ."

"I'm being selfish," he explained. "I wanted to unwind before I go home. It's getting harder and harder to do that there."

Annie nodded and decided not to probe further.

"Drink?" she offered.

"What do you have?"

"I got some Gallo burgundy in earlier this week," she said. "It's not subtle but, like the Gallos say, it's good drinking wine. Gallo wine and Acapulco Gold got me through college."

"Acapulco what?"

"Never mind. You're a policeman. You're not supposed to know these things."

Sansi draped his jacket over a chair and walked over to the balcony. The sliding doors were wide open but there was hardly a breath of air from outside. It was a little after nine and the night was so dark and dense it was like living in a steam bath. Annie had two small fans going to rearrange the humidity.

She came out of the kitchen and handed him a glass. She was wearing shorts and a white cheesecloth blouse. When she sat down the blouse molded damply to her breasts. A few strands of hair clung to her forehead. Her face was covered with a sheen of perspiration.

"So," she asked, "why are you going to London?"

Sansi sat on the couch opposite. "You remember the Film City murder?"

"I remember," she said.

"And the body washed up on Chowpatty Beach, the studio manager? And the suicide of Noshir Kilachand?"

"Yes."

"They're all connected."

"Where does London fit in?"

"The man responsible lives there."

Annie sipped her wine but said nothing more.

"You've never pursued the case with me," he observed. "Not since the last time I was here. Why?"

"It didn't seem right," she said with a small shrug.

"It didn't stop you before. What kind of reporter are you?"

She smiled. "Probably a very bad one. I have this unfortunate habit of feeling sympathy for my victims. It's fatal in this business. I know I'd never make it in television."

Sansi looked at her. "Seriously," he said. His tone was soft but earnest.

Annie looked away and gave a deep sigh. "I don't know. It's you, I guess," she said. "It's something about the way you are. I think you're probably the most focused . . . the most moral man I've ever met, Sansi. And you do it here, in the midst of this perpetual bloody . . . chaos. It awes me. It makes me want your respect. And it makes me want to respect myself. That's part of the reason I'm here."

"My mother admires you."

Annie eyed him skeptically. "Your mother is a great woman. She has a lot of time for everybody."

"She thinks you'll stay in India," Sansi said.

"Hah." She gave a dainty snort and looked archly at him. "I doubt it. I've had a lot of trouble getting this far. Right now I think what I'd like most in all the world is a thick shake, a party pack of Doritos and a toilet that knows it's a toilet and not a fountain. It might look like I know what I'm doing but inside, believe me, there's a bimbo trying to get out."

"My mother says you have courage. Real courage. Because you do things even when you are afraid."

Annie looked at him. "She really say that?"

He nodded.

She leaned toward the coffee table and lit a cigarette. "That's nice," she said. "That's good to know."

They sat and drank their wine in silence.

Sansi spoke first. "Now," he said, "you've made me feel guilty."

She looked at him.

"Because you think I'm so . . . moral. It's too much responsibility to bear," he smiled. "The real reason I came to see you is because I have a story for you."

Annie laughed softly. "Okay," she said. "This is more like it. Being used is familiar territory. Hell, I might even start trusting you next."

"The only catch is that you have to promise me you won't use it until I say it's okay."

She shook her head. "No deal. When I'm chasing a story I'm willing to make a deal. But you give it to me, I use it when I want."

"I can't do that," he said.

"Okay," she shrugged. She emptied her glass and got up to retrieve the bottle from the kitchen. When she returned a moment later she looked at him, her eyes already contrite.

"I'm being just a little bit of a bitch, aren't I?" she said, slumping back down on the sofa, her legs curled underneath her. Sansi noticed how long and brown they were and how there was a rash of dark freckles on the outside of her left thigh.

"A bit," he agreed.

She sipped her wine. "Oh, all right," she sighed. "Tell me the fuc . . . tell me the deal."

Sansi smiled. And then he told her everything. He told her about the gay prostitution ring at Film City, he told her about the trip to Jaigapur and his visit with the Maharani, he told her about the Collector and he told her about Cardus. He even told her about his lunch with Jamal and the governor two days before. When he had finished he looked searchingly into her eyes.

"I want to leave copies of all the evidence with you," he said. "If Jamal or the government does anything to stop my investigation, I want you to run the whole story. Whatever happens, Annie, you will have the story of the year. Before anyone else. But you must promise me to wait until I say it is all right." Sansi took a long swallow of wine then sat back and waited.

Annie didn't look at him. Instead she sat and stared for a long time through the balcony doors and into the sweltering darkness outside. When she did speak it was with customary directness.

"You make me feel like such a jerk," she said.

He stared at her. Then he saw the trail of a tear on her left cheek.

"Here I am," she went on, her voice wavering, "trying to be so smart and sophisticated and take charge of the situation and then you go and spill your guts and I know damn well that you're putting your job, your career, your whole goddamn life on the line and oh, shit . . ." She stopped to wipe her eyes and nose with her sleeve.

Sansi got up, crossed the room, sat on the couch facing her and put his hands lightly on her shoulders. "I wouldn't have done it if I didn't think I could trust you," he said.

"I know," she said and made a sound that was part sob, part laugh. "That's why I feel so goddamn shitty."

"I trust you more than I would trust the governor of Maharashtra," Sansi said gently. "More than Joint Commissioner Jamal."

"They're helping you get what you want," she said.

"Yes." Sansi nodded. He was so close their heads were almost touching. "But for all the wrong reasons, Annie. They're doing it because it suits them politically to do it. Justice is a whim with them. They could change their minds in a moment if they wanted. And I'm afraid they will. That's why I need you . . . to print the truth."

She lifted her face to look at him. Their eyes locked and suddenly it seemed like the most natural thing in the world for Sansi to kiss her. He tilted his face close to hers and kissed her lightly on the lips. Then he drew back and looked at her. Her hands went up to his face so she could draw him back and kiss him again. This time her mouth opened and he felt the tip of her tongue sliding between his lips.

They kissed for a long time, savoring each other, savoring the moment. He moved his hands down her sides, feeling the lines of her body, the gentle inward curve to her waist and the seductive bell of her hips. Her blouse clung to her skin like damp tissue paper. He held her breast in his right hand and she sighed and pressed closer to him. Her tongue performed a lewd ballet in his mouth, teasing, caressing, sucking him into her. He tried to loosen the buttons of her blouse but he fumbled and she pulled back slightly and opened them for him. All the time she stared into his eyes, her face solemn with anticipation. She threw her blouse onto the floor then leaned back on the couch and pulled him down to her. Her breasts swelled across her chest. He looked down at her and smiled. There was a cluster of dark freckles between her breasts. He bent his head and took a nipple in his mouth. It was hot and spongy and tasted of sweat. Annie moaned and pulled his head up so she could kiss him again. After a moment she squirmed out from under him and quickly threw off the last of her clothes. Then, with cool and deliberate passion, she slowly undressed him. And when he was naked she knelt in front of him and took him into her mouth, sucking him and tracing the urgency of his need with her tongue. Then she lay back on the floor, pulled Sansi on top of her and guided him inside her.

Outside in the darkness the first fat drops of rain splashed onto the dirty streets. A flash of lightning darted across the sky and a few seconds later there was the grumble of distant thunder. The rain intensified quickly into a drumming downpour. Soon it was no longer rain. It was a waterfall that spilled in an unrelenting torrent through the fissures of the clouds overhead.

Annie noticed it first. Sansi was on the verge of a delicious lovers' slumber when she whispered urgently in his ear.

"Wake up," she said. "It's raining."

Sansi stirred and pulled her closer to him. Just then the whole apartment filled with a silver-blue light that was followed almost instantaneously by a deafening clap of thunder.

"Come on," Annie urged him. Sansi didn't understand the urgency but he allowed her to pull him to his feet. He watched, bemused, as she switched off all the lights. Then she stepped out onto the balcony, still naked.

"Come on," she coaxed him. "It's the monsoon. Come and feel it. It's wonderful. . . ."

Sansi smiled and followed her timidly onto the darkened balcony, afraid that he might be seen. Annie did not seem restrained by any such inhibition. She put her hands on the balcony rail, stood on the tips of her toes and lifted her face to the sky, her body stretched taut to receive the rush of warm, cleansing rain. Sansi stood a few feet away and watched, hardly aware of the rain on his own body, entranced by Annie's exuberant sensuality.

There was another flash of lightning and for one fleeting moment she was drenched in luminescence, a sight so mesmerizing Sansi forgot to take a breath. Her body looked like sculpted marble. Her hair was plastered closely to her skull, shaping and streamlining her profile. Her eyes were closed and her lips open in a frozen gasp of ecstasy. The rainwater streamed down her face and neck, poured in torrents across her shoulders and spooled like strands of pearls from her swollen nipples.

The lightning vanished and everything was plunged into blackness again, leaving the outline of the moment engraved forever on his mind's eye.

She turned, reaching out to him, and pulled him to her. They clung to each other tightly, letting the monsoon wash over them, drowning them in a baptism of fresh innocence.

She lifted her face to his in the dark and shouted above the tumult. "I'll do anything you want me to do."

19

IT WAS RAINING when Sansi's British Airways 747 took off
from Sahar Airport and banked low over the city before
wheeling westward over the Arabian Sea. Sansi had one
brief glimpse of Bombay before it was snatched away by
the cloud. The scab of brown dirt that had encrusted the
city all summer had been dissolved by the rain and flushed
through the flooding creeks into the ocean, where it spread
now like a giant, rust-colored question mark in the shallows
of Back Bay. The white apartment buildings along Marine
Drive looked clean and freshly scrubbed. Sansi was reminded of blocks of Styrofoam floating in a sewer.

It was still raining when the plane touched down at London's Heathrow Airport, eight hours later. Sansi wondered
idly if the monsoon had followed him to London. He used
his British passport to bypass the congestion at the gates for
foreign nationals and was only delayed momentarily by an
immigration officer who had difficulty believing an Indian
would have blue eyes.

Sansi stepped through the sliding glass doors of Terminal 2 and wrinkled his nose. London smelled bad—of damp
and rotten eggs. Sansi wondered if there was anything more
miserable in all the world than a wet Sunday afternoon in
London. He shivered, stepped back inside the terminal and
opened his suitcase. He pulled out a sleeveless brown
sweater and put it on under his suit jacket. Immediately, he
realized, he looked like the archetypal Indian migrant: rumpled suit, pullover, tie and suitcase. Sansi never felt more
Indian than when he was in England.

He had an hour to wait before the express bus to Oxford arrived and he decided he ought to call his father at Goscombe Park. Sansi had an open invitation to visit whenever he liked, and Pramila had already written to the General to tell him their son was on his way. But it had been three years since Sansi had last seen his father and he felt uncomfortable about dropping in unannounced. The old man had been eighty-four then and, although his mind was still sharp, his health was failing. Sansi wondered how much his father might have declined during the intervening years.

A woman's voice answered the phone. It was Joyce, the wife of his half brother Eric. Joyce did not share her husband's hostility toward Sansi. Eric Spooner saw Sansi as a direct threat to his share of the family inheritance. A fifty-fifty split between Eric and his sister Hilary was one thing, but the prospect of a three-way split involving Sansi was intolerable. It made for a great deal of unnecessary friction whenever Sansi visited. Sansi didn't care whether he received a penny from his father's estate. Ironically, that only seemed to make Eric angrier.

"Joyce, it's George," Sansi said. "Is my father able to come to the phone?"

"George?" Joyce sounded vague. "George who?"

"George Sansi? Your half brother? In-law? From India?"

"Oh ... Bombay George," she said.

"Yes," Sansi answered. "That's right. Bombay George. Now, is my father there, please? Can he come to the phone?"

"He's sleeping."

"All right." Sansi hesitated. "When he wakes up, tell him I'm on the way, would you? I should be there around six."

"Tonight?"

"Yes."

"All right, George. Oh, just a minute, would you? Eric wants to know something."

Sansi waited.

"How long will you be staying?"

Sansi smiled.

"Tell him six months. Tell him I'm on my honeymoon and I've brought my wife and all her relatives."

He heard a muffled giggle on the other end of the line. "Tell him yourself," she said and hung up.

The bus trip to Oxford took a couple of hours. Sansi shared the bus with a half-dozen newly arrived American tourists. An hour after they had left London the rain dropped behind them like a falling curtain and they found themselves spotlighted in the bright sunshine of a spring day. The mood inside the bus lifted with the clouds and the tourists began chattering to each other in that loud, amiable way that Americans have. Sansi thought of Annie Ginnaro and their last night together. It already seemed too far away. He had never met a woman like her: confident but afraid, worldly but naive, vulnerable but brazenly uninhibited. They had a lot to learn from each other.

Sansi stared at the passing countryside, so green and tidy after the sprawling, monochromatic browns of India. A sudden gust of wind buffeted the bus and rippled the surrounding wheat fields with bright, shiny waves. Sansi felt more optimistic than he had felt in a long time. The world never would be a perfect place, he knew. There were simply too many people fighting each other and all of them willing to cheat and steal to get what they wanted. Perhaps Jamal, for all his calculating cynicism, was right. Perhaps Sansi was an idealist. Annie might be right too: justice was still justice, however you found it. Maybe the end did justify the means . . . as long as you didn't get your hands too dirty along the way.

The bus had to go right past the entrance to Goscombe Park on its final swing into Oxford. Sansi asked the driver to let him off at the gates. It meant a long walk to the house but his suitcase wasn't heavy and Sansi felt he needed the break to steel himself for whatever lay ahead. The bus pulled away and left Sansi alone at the gates, a strange, solitary figure at the entrance to a stately English home. The gates hung from pillars of mossy stone. A white sign with green lettering proclaimed: *Goscombe Park. Strictly private. Trespassers will be prosecuted.*

The driveway curved gently to the right through an avenue of feathered elm trees, and was flanked on either side by neat fenced fields filled with cattle: black and white Herefords. They watched Sansi pass with the same beaten eyes he had seen on beggars in his homeland.

After twenty minutes the house came into view at the end of the drive, a grand Georgian manor studded with high chimneys and twenty-two attic windows. He had counted them when he first arrived to study at Oxford.

Sansi was eighteen years old when he first saw Goscombe Park. It was the first time he had been out of India and he had been utterly intimidated. He could not believe he belonged there—neither could his half siblings. Fortunately for him, the house was big enough to accommodate everyone with room to spare, and their petty jealousies were dissipated in the distances they were able to put between each other. When the time came for Sansi to leave he had become as comfortable and as familiar with the big house as if he had always lived there. His father made him feel that he belonged.

"Oh, God."

Eric was in the drawing room when he glanced through the window and saw Sansi trudging up the drive. "He looks like some little wog salesman with a suitcase full of silk scarves."

His wife looked up briefly from the magazine she was reading. "Be nice to him, darling," she said. "I'm sure he's only here to see the old man. You know he never stays for long. He knows how you feel about him."

"I don't think he has the faintest idea how I feel about him," Eric grumbled.

Sansi walked up the wide stone steps to the front door and pushed the button for the doorbell. Eric turned his back to the window and ignored the loud ringing.

"Darling?" Joyce looked at him.

Her husband shoved his hands in his pockets and looked away. Joyce started to get up but then saw Mrs. Chappel, the housekeeper, hurrying to answer the door. Mrs. Chappel had been the Spooners' housekeeper for twenty years and knew Sansi well. She gave Eric a dirty look as she passed the open door to the drawing room. They heard the front door open and the sound of Sansi's voice.

"Such a lovely surprise when I heard you were coming," Mrs. Chappel welcomed Sansi. "The General is over the moon."

"How is he?"

"Oh, he's well," Mrs. Chappel reassured Sansi. "Spring has been a real tonic for him. Says he might lead the Goscombe hunt this year. You just go and say hello to Mr. and Mrs. Spooner in the drawing room and I'll tell the General you're here. Leave your suitcase. Brian will take it up to your room later." Brian was Mrs. Chappel's son, who had taken over as the estate's handyman when her husband had died. "Can I bring you something? You're probably dying for a nice cup of tea. Take away the taste of that dreadful airline food."

Sansi thanked Mrs. Chappel and she bustled off back toward the kitchen. A moment later Sansi appeared in the doorway to the drawing room.

"Joyce . . . Eric," he greeted them.

"Hello, darling." Joyce got up, crossed the room and kissed Sansi lightly on the cheek.

Eric nodded to Sansi but remained standing by the window, hands in his pockets. "What brings you this time?" Eric asked, barely polite.

"Business." Sansi answered with the same coolness in his own voice. He had learned the art of bad manners at Goscombe Park. "And I wanted to see my father."

Eric nodded but said nothing more. Instead, he wandered across the room to the liquor cabinet and splashed some whiskey into a glass without asking Sansi if he wanted a drink.

"Would you care for a drink, George?" Joyce offered, embarrassed.

"Mrs. Chappel is bringing some tea," Sansi said.

"Don't mind if we catch up with the news, do you, old chap?" Eric asked and switched on the television set before Sansi could answer.

It suited Sansi. Joyce was sweet in a cheerfully vapid, middle-class way but he and Eric had very little to say to each other, as always. The room filled with the fluted tones of a BBC newsman. Sansi was glad of the noise to fill the void between them all. He picked out a chair and sat down to wait. He was good at waiting. Joyce looked uncomfortable and tried to make small talk. Sansi almost felt embarrassed for her.

A moment later Mrs. Chappel arrived with Sansi's tea on a tray. "Your father's just getting ready," she said. "He was having his nap till a few minutes ago. He wants to see you in a minute."

"Should I come and help?" Sansi offered.

"No, it's all right. He's just down the hallway. We moved him downstairs the year before last to save his legs. His arthritis has been giving him a lot more trouble the last year or two, especially his knees. We turned the music room into a bedsitting room for him. It's got a lovely view from the French windows. There's a big fireplace and he can get out onto the back terrace quite easily. He's still an outdoors man, the General. Still likes to sit in the fresh air whenever he can. You just enjoy your tea now and I'll come and fetch you in a minute, when he's ready."

Mrs. Chappel poured Sansi's tea and bustled out again. The tea was strong and scalding but exactly what he needed. He was about to pour a second cup when Mrs. Chappel reappeared.

"He's ready for you now," she whispered.

Sansi excused himself to Joyce and left the room. Eric seemed not to notice. He stood, legs apart, glass in hand, tweed jacket thrust behind him, watching the television. There was a news item about the French protesting British meat exports to the continent. "Bloody French," Eric grumbled. "Should have let the Germans have them."

Sansi followed Mrs. Chappel along the west-wing corridor until they came to a set of double doors. One of the doors was open and Sansi saw his father in a big, wing-backed armchair beside the French windows. The old man saw Sansi at the same time.

"George, dear boy," he called out, impatient with excitement. "Come in this instant. My Lord, but you do look well. Sorry I can't get up. Legs are buggered. But you just come and sit down beside me now. I want you to tell me everything that's happened since I last saw you."

Sansi crossed the room and gently clasped his father's hands. They felt like bundled twigs. The old man seemed to have shriveled with age. His sandy hair had turned a sparse, flossy white, there were dark, ugly liver spots on his scalp and his skin hung slackly from his jaw. He wore a thickly quilted dressing gown with a blue cravat. Beneath the dressing gown he seemed to be wearing warm-up pants and fur-lined leather slippers. He was dressed like a man who always felt the cold, no matter how much he loved the open air. It worried Sansi.

"Sit down, sit down." The General waved to an armchair on the other side of a small round table that held his spectacles and a couple of books with large print. Sansi hardly noticed as Mrs. Chappel left the room and closed the doors so father and son could be alone together.

"How are you feeling?" Sansi asked. "How are you feeling, really?"

"Oh, so-so." The General made a face. "You know you're getting old when a woman has to help you pee and you can't enjoy it anymore."

Sansi chuckled. The old man's body might be breaking down but his humor hadn't deserted him. He looked around the room. It smelled of medicine and old age and it was filled with the heartaching poignancy of a once-vibrant life coming to an end. It reminded Sansi of the Maharani's bedroom at Jaigapur Fort: big, comfortable and sunny, but somehow the sunlight was unable to breathe new life into the room's occupant. It served only to highlight the dust that hung in the air and to add to the mood of genteel decay. They were contemporaries, the Maharani and his father. They had witnessed the last days of the Raj.

One whole wall of the room had been filled with pictures. Pictures of India. Sansi recognized a photograph of the last British troops to march through the Gateway to India on the waterside at Bombay. There was a picture of Mountbatten during the Independence ceremony in New Delhi with General Spooner in the background among the massed ranks of army officers and dignitaries. And there was a color-tinted portrait of Pramila as a young woman. She was in a garden, touching a garland of hanging tree orchids and smiling at the camera. She was wearing Western clothes, smartly tailored slacks and a blouse. She was twenty years old. Her hair was as black as ink, her figure was striking and there was an unmistakable sensuality in her face. At the time the photo was taken, she and the General had been lovers for only six months. She had already decided to give up her family in exchange for a few years with him.

"How is your mother?" the General asked.

Sansi turned back to his father with a start. "Oh," he smiled awkwardly, "she is very, very well. She told me to give you her love, as always. She keeps herself busy. She lectures at the university, chairs a couple of committees. She has lots of friends. She's very respectable now: a society matron. The newspapers are always asking for her opinion on things."

The General snorted. "Your mother was always respectable," he said. "To those whose respect was worth having." He paused and looked at Sansi. "I doubt if she has ever told you all that she went through because of me. Because of our . . . relationship."

Sansi shook his head. Anxiety and fascination stirred deep inside him, resonating to the echoes of past deeds that could still be heard through the words of an old man.

"You can't imagine what India was like in the time leading up to Independence," the General continued. "There was no law, you know. We couldn't keep a lid on it. We were bloody glad to be gone, actually. And for a woman like your mother to stay behind and have a child out of wedlock to a British Army officer . . ." His words trailed into silence.

"And I left her to face it on her own," he went on. "All on her own. With a new baby. Many's the time I wanted to fly back to Bombay and take you both out of the country. Put you somewhere safe like Singapore or Penang. But your mother wouldn't have it. Wouldn't run away, she said. India was her home. And yours. Stubborn, stubborn woman."

He smiled at Sansi. "And now, none of it matters, does it? All the passion and the fury, every sin and hatred . . . It's history. Gone. Everybody's found new things to fight about. And people like me and your mother, we're so old . . . we've become respectable."

Sansi reached out and touched his father's arm. "You did everything you could have done," he said gently. "You gave us a home. You gave us security. And you gave us your love. We always felt it, you know. Over all those miles . . ."

The General looked at Sansi, his eyes moist with the guilt of half a lifetime. "I got your mother's letter, telling me you were on your way," he said. "She told me you had something important to ask me. Something to do with the past."

"It's nothing to do with . . . us," Sansi reassured him. "You mustn't worry about that. Everything about us is fine. It's about something else, something to do with my work, as a policeman."

The General nodded and breathed a deep, shaky sigh. "I'll try," he said. "I can remember things that happened a long time ago much better than I can remember what happened this morning."

Sansi smiled. "It goes back to the time you were first in

India. When you were in New Delhi in 1931. You were a colonel. . . ."

"Lieutenant-colonel," his father corrected him. "The youngest in the British Army at the time. Didn't get a full colonel's pips until thirty-three."

"Can you remember what your job was then?"

"That's easy," his father answered. "Paper shuffler, GHQ, New Delhi."

"GHQ?"

"General Headquarters . . . for the whole British Army in India."

Sansi nodded.

"Hated it. There was an awful lot of civil unrest at that time. Gandhi was making a particular nuisance of himself. I'd rather have been in the field, doing something useful. But I had to serve my time behind a desk. I remember there was a lot of toing and froing between the Viceroy and the Indian Congress about the distribution of powers. They were shaky times." Then he added, almost as an afterthought, "They were always shaky times in India."

"Do you remember a man called Cardus?" Sansi asked. "Antony Cardus? He was Collector of Jaigapur from 1930 to 1931 but was recalled under mysterious circumstances."

The General's watery blue eyes suddenly sparked with anger. "There was nothing mysterious about them as far as I was concerned," he growled. "And there was nothing mysterious about Cardus. . . . He was a squalid little man. He'd come from nowhere—town clerk at someplace in Berkshire, I think. Somehow he insinuated himself into the Foreign Office and was given the Collectorate of Jaigapur. God only knows how. But it was the sort of thing that went on. More than I care to say."

"Why was he recalled?"

"Cruelty to the native population is what I heard—unusual cruelty. There'd been a few deaths from floggings he'd ordered; it seems he liked to watch. Apparently there were a few occasions when he administered punishment personally. Absolutely barbaric. Inexcusable in a British ad-

ministrator of his rank. There was the suggestion of inde-
cent behavior with some of the boys he had punished.
There were some dreadful stories about Cardus. Even if
only half of them were true . . ."

"Why wasn't he ever charged?"

"You might well ask," the General grumbled. "Connec-
tions in all the right places, undoubtedly."

Sansi thought of the clandestine homosexual network at
Film City involving Coyarjee, Nayak and Kilachand. "Was
any reason given for his recall?"

The General pursed his lips. "Some administrative hum-
bug about being unfit for duty due to ill health or mental
stress or something. Easy to get from any army medical officer. A fast ticket home. Happened all the time."

"So there are no records, nothing official to say what really happened in Jaigapur?"

The old man shook his head. "Shouldn't think so. I
doubt if the truth was ever committed to paper."

Sansi frowned. "What happened to him?"

"Whistled through Delhi on his way back to England.
They couldn't wait to get rid of him. It would have been a
dreadful embarrassment for the government if anything had
got out. That's when I saw him. He called at GHQ a couple
of times to see some people."

"What was your impression of him?"

"He looked exactly how you'd expect a man like that to
look," the general said. "Like a worm, a human worm.
That's how I thought of him. A mean, insignificant, squalid
little man who'd been put in a position of power over people and had abused it without let or hindrance. That's what
I remember most about him. I looked him in the eye one
day and there wasn't an ounce of remorse there. He felt no
shame for what he'd done. No shame that he was being
sent home in disgrace. I felt ashamed for him—ashamed to
be an Englishman."

"That's what Mother said."

The General looked at him.

"She said you were the gentlest, most honorable man

she'd ever known. And this man had made you feel ashamed to be an Englishman."

The General sank lower into the folds of his dressing gown and slowly shook his head. "I loved India," he said. He had begun to sound weak, tired. "But it's a country that can break your heart. That seems to be the curse of the place. India affects people, changes them—some for the better, some for the worse. I'm sure it has something to do with the extremes of the place. People see things there. Things their minds cannot cope with—fantastic and terrible things. I knew men who lost all sense of reason once they got to India. Sane men who became drunks, despots or drug addicts. Some died for their sins. Some we sent home tied to stretchers because they had gone mad. Whatever you were inside, whatever kind of man you were, good or bad, India brought it out in you. To the extreme."

Sansi smiled mirthlessly. "Presumably, Antony Cardus lived an untroubled life and died peacefully in his sleep."

"Presumably," the General echoed. "I certainly never heard of him again." The old man looked curiously at his son. "What possible interest could he have for you?"

"He's come back."

A look of shock spread across the General's face and Sansi immediately regretted the way he'd said it.

"I didn't . . ." he said quickly. "I mean, someone like him. Someone with his name has come back to India . . . and taken part in the same kind of murders."

"Dear God," the old man muttered. He gazed distractedly around the room. "I can remember his eyes," the General said after a moment. "When I looked into his eyes I felt as though I was looking into the eyes of a man who had no soul."

20

ANTONY CARDUS LIKED to be on time. His day was structured carefully to keep him on time. He had always believed that an intelligent routine was the civilized man's only refuge in a world without order. The clock radio woke him every weekday morning at six-thirty. He got out of bed without disturbing his wife, Beryl. She never used the bathroom before him. Cardus liked to be the first to use it every day, when it was neat and clean. He hated seeing her long dark hairs in the sink or stuck to the side of the bathtub.

He brushed his teeth first—carefully, thoroughly. Then he shaved. He almost never cut himself. He hated going to work with a nick on his neck; it looked so untidy. Then he showered, blow-dried his thinning hair and brushed it gently so as not to damage it. If his mustache needed a trim he did it the night before, washed the hairs down the drain and wiped the sink fastidiously so that it would be clean for him in the morning.

Cardus always laid his clean underwear and socks on top of the dresser so they would be ready for him when he came out of the bathroom. A clean shirt and tie hung on the same hanger inside the dresser door. Beryl did the ironing every Sunday night to make sure he had five neatly ironed shirts to get him through the week. The rest of his clothes were in the walk-in closet, on hangers initialed with each day of the week. M was for Monday and that was his charcoal-gray suit. Tuesday was his gray herringbone jacket and black trousers. Wednesday, the blue suit. Thursday, the blazer and gray flannels. Friday, the gray pinstripe suit.

Whenever a jacket or a pair of trousers began to wear out they were replaced by others exactly the same.

Once he had dressed, Cardus liked to go downstairs and pick up the morning newspaper. The *Daily Telegraph*. He had been a *Times* man until it had been bought by Rupert Murdoch, years before. Cardus didn't like Australians. They were not an orderly people.

His weekday breakfast was always the same: a glass of orange juice, two slices of wheat toast with Chivers thick-cut marmalade and a cup of tea. He read the paper with breakfast until seven twenty-five. Then he got up, folded it neatly, put it in his briefcase, which had also been packed the night before, and left the house. Beryl got up when she heard the front door close.

It took Cardus about fifteen minutes to walk from his red-brick semi-detached house on Azalea Crescent to Dulwich Station. He almost always got there by seven forty-one or seven forty-two. Or at the latest, seven forty-three. Because he was a British Rail season-ticket holder he walked past the line of fools at the ticket office and carried on two-thirds of the way down the platform till he was in exactly the same spot where he always waited for the train, just in front of the second lamppost from the end. It irked him on mornings when the preceding train was late and the earlier commuters hadn't left yet, because it usually meant someone was standing in his place. But when he arrived with his usual fellow travelers who always caught the 7:55 to Blackfriars, it was generally understood that this was his spot. Everybody, or almost everybody, turned up at the same time and stood in the same spot and read the same newspaper. They were mostly *Times* and *Telegraph* people. A few *Mail*s and *Express*es. There were very few *Sun* readers on his train.

All the regulars knew each other by sight though they rarely, if ever, acknowledged each other. All had their favorite places where they liked to stand, exactly in line with their usual train compartment, or where the compartment would be when the train pulled in. Cardus hated it when there was a new driver who didn't stop the train exactly where it was supposed to stop and he had to walk up or down the platform and jostle with strangers to find his usual seat in his usual compartment.

His train began its run into town only two stops down the line and was still almost empty when it pulled in at Dulwich. Which was why Cardus was almost always able to get his usual corner seat beside the window, where he could put his briefcase on his knee and do the crossword in the half-hour it took to reach the city.

It was a precise, well-ordered routine with which Cardus had become comfortable over many years. If something ever happened to disturb his routine it had the potential to ruin his day. If someone was in his seat he would ask them to move, even though the seats were not reserved. Once he had encountered a man who refused, point-blank, to move and Cardus had found it hard to contain his rage. He took a vacant seat diagonally opposite and stared at the man all the way into London. The man had ignored him. He had even seemed amused. Cardus had wanted to kill him. He had followed the man for a short distance when he got off the train until he got hold of himself and hurried off to the Underground to catch the tube to Westminster. Antony Cardus was a man who liked everything in its proper place. And everyone in his or her proper place. It was the way the world was supposed to be. Everyone had to know their place. And keep to it.

That morning everything went like clockwork: the way he liked it. The Circle Line tube train delivered Cardus to Westminster Station by eight forty-two. It was a fresh spring morning and Cardus enjoyed the short walk along Parliament Street to the Foreign and Commonwealth Office. It was the most illustrious walk in the civilized world, Cardus believed, and he never grew tired of it. Big Ben and the Houses of Parliament behind him, Westminster Abbey, the Churchill memorial, County Hall on the south side of the Thames, Downing Street and the Cenotaph—all the symbols of Britain's greatness within a few square blocks. It made a man proud to be British. The Empire may have gone but Britain was still the greatest power the world had ever seen and was ever likely to see. The Americans didn't know how to run an empire, Cardus thought. Too neurotic. Too busy fiddling with democratic ideals all the time and trying to get everybody to like them. The British had no such qualms. They knew they were the best.

Cardus turned into King Charles Street, walked into the Foreign and Commonwealth Office and up two flights of stairs to his office in the Commercial Management and Export Department. It was ten to nine when he greeted Doreen, the secretary he shared with three other senior clerical officers. They were called officers in the British civil service. Cardus liked that. Ten minutes early. Time for another cup of tea before he settled down to the business of the day.

Cardus was in a good mood. He had been right to persuade them to let him go to India to help service a few key contacts in conjunction with the arms deal the department had been trying to push through with the Indian government. It looked as though the Indians might soon place a series of orders with British defense manufacturers to supply and install a new missile defense system for the Indian Navy. If it came off, it was a deal worth in excess of one billion pounds. And Cardus could join with everyone else in his department in taking some of the credit. Perhaps most of the credit. No wonder his boss was pleased. And so would be the Minister of Defense when the deal was confirmed in a week or two. Cardus had rarely felt better. Everything had gone exactly the way he had wanted it. His visit to India had been more satisfying than he had ever dreamed it would be.

Cardus was still in a good mood when he got home that evening, even though the train had been delayed twenty minutes because some idiot child had thrown a few bricks onto the tracks. Cardus knew how he would discourage that kind of thing.

Beryl was in the kitchen cooking his dinner. Two lamb

chops with mashed potatoes, peas, carrots and mint jelly: it was Thursday. He ate on a tray in front of the television set. His wife ate in the kitchen. Cardus and his wife shared the same house and the same routine but they hadn't shared the same life for eleven years. The only reason they shared the same bed was because sometimes they entertained guests because of his job and there was always an obligatory tour of the house. Cardus didn't want anyone to know that anything was wrong with their marriage. People still had funny ideas about what was normal, he said. Sometimes, when she asked him, he would hold her for a while. But he hadn't made love to her for a long time. He told her he couldn't bring himself to do it with her anymore.

She knew it was her fault. She had let him down early in their marriage. He had wanted children, but she had been infertile. It was as though she had shattered his dream of the perfect family and he had never been able to forgive her. But he loved her in his way: he kept her, provided for her. She knew he always would. She was his responsibility. All she had to do in return was to make certain that everything ran properly, that the house was kept clean and tidy, that his meals were ready on time. And to give him the space he needed to live his own life. Space was important to individuals, he said. People had to retain some independence. Everyone was allowed to have their secrets. But Beryl Cardus had no secrets left in her life.

A little after nine, Cardus went upstairs without saying anything to his wife. Like many semi-detached houses in south London, their house was small and narrow: two stories, with an attic that was reached through a trapdoor in the ceiling at the top of the stairs. Cardus pulled open the trapdoor and caught the sliding ladder as it folded out. This was another of his secrets. One or two evenings a week he would go up into the attic, where he could be alone for the rest of the night. His wife had never been up there. She wasn't allowed. It was his own special place, he had told her. And Beryl knew better than to upset her husband.

He climbed the stairs, pulled the ladder up after him and

locked the trapdoor with a bolt. Only then did he feel completely safe. He switched on the main light, looked around and smiled. His own special place. A tiny, precious corner of India in dingy south London. His own little corner of empire.

There were two small Indian rugs on the floor and two more on the walls along with a couple of tourist posters, one showing the ghats at Benares, another showing the Red Fort at New Delhi. There was an old wooden desk, one half empty, the other half cluttered with model boats and airplanes that he had kept from childhood. There were a few more on the floor under the desk. They looked out of place, forgotten. In front of the desk was an old red armchair that rested on blocks of wood. The rest of the attic was occupied by half a dozen tea chests, a couple of broken suitcases overflowing with discarded clothing that Cardus wouldn't throw out and a few more unopened boxes containing model airplane kits. Considering his usual fastidiousness it was not as tidy as his wife would have expected. But it suited her husband's purpose.

Carefully he moved the suitcases and pulled away some of the old clothing until he came to a green metal box about the size of a standard toolbox. The box had a lid and was padlocked shut. He lifted it onto the desk. Then he walked over to one of the rugs on the wall, pushed it back and plucked a small key from a crevice between the bricks. He used the key to open the padlock. Next, he opened the attic's one small window a fraction. Then he sat down in the armchair, facing the desk, where he could reach easily into the box. He opened the desk drawer and took out a small, amber-colored bottle. There were also a few slender wooden sticks coated with a gummy brown substance.

Cardus put one of the sticks into an empty jar on his desk and lit it. In a moment the sweet, pungent aroma of incense drifted through the attic and curled lazily toward the open window where it dissipated quickly in the night air.

Cardus smiled. It was the only smell he knew that could recapture the mood, the feel of India, so quickly, so completely.

Then he opened the lid of the green metal box. Inside was a stack of letters and other assorted papers tied loosely with a piece of dirty white ribbon. Beside them were two bundles, one a thickly bound red book, faded and dog-eared with age. The other was a small box of some kind wrapped tightly with a piece of green oilcloth.

Cardus picked up the book first. It was a diary. The diary of the grandfather who had passed on his name. Among other things. Cardus had never really known his grandfather. What he had seen of the old man he didn't particularly like. All he remembered was a harsh, white-haired figure with a thin, white mustache who hated children. Cardus's mother and father hadn't got along with the old man either, and family visits were always strained and difficult. His grandfather had died when Cardus was in his early teens, although his grandmother had survived her late husband by many years. She had died eleven years before and it was then that all the old man's possessions had passed on to Cardus. His mother was already dead and his father was in a nursing home gloomily awaiting his own death. Cardus had been intensely curious when he had taken possession of his grandfather's things. Some of them, like the green metal box, had not been opened for half a century. He had gone through everything carefully, hoping to find something of value.

Nothing had prepared him for the diary. Or the contents of the oilskin package.

He sat back in the armchair now, turned to March 17, 1931, and read down the page:

Disciplined she-boy of 13 years. Offense: theft. Sentence: six strokes of the birch. Personally attended punishment. Handsome boy when stripped. Took punishment well.

Cardus remembered when he had first absorbed the message hidden in those neatly penned words written with such a precise and elegant hand. His grandfather's hand.

He turned the pages forward to May 9:

Disciplined youth of 15 years for disturbing the King's peace. Sentence: 12 strokes of the birch. Attended personally. Youth appeared most handsome when stripped. His member grew quite large and erect during punishment. Much excitement from R.S.

Then another on June 17:

Special discipline for youth of 17 years. Offenses: pandering and public nuisance. Attended personally. Handsome youth disfigured by overmuch body hair. R.S. elected to play the barber. Personally administered two punishments of 12 strokes of the birch. Did not survive punishment. Disposed without record.

Cardus recalled the dawning of understanding that had accompanied his first reading of those words; the thrill, the pleasure he derived from them had not diminished since. The first awakening of desires buried deep inside that he had once been too afraid to acknowledge. And then the relief of recognition, the reckless joy of acceptance ... and the delicious heat of surrender.

Cardus had read those pages many times since. He had known instinctively that "she-boy" could mean only one thing. It was the perfect description for those boys who teetered on the cusp of adolescence: whose smooth, hairless skin was still as soft as a girl's, but who had already embarked on the path toward manhood. Those beautiful, precocious boys, luminous with incipient sexuality, who had not yet lost the charm and grace of childhood.

It was then that Cardus had understood what he was—what he had always been. Revealed to him in a diary by a man he had never known. A man whose blood he shared.

A man who had harbored the same secret lusts as he did. When he understood that much, he had understood everything.

Until then he had despised his weakness. He had despised his secret desires and the torment they imposed upon him. And most of all he despised the boys he watched and wanted every day but whom he could never possess. He despised the power they had over him, the pain they caused him without even knowing. He despised them because they reminded him of his own ordinariness. He yearned constantly to put them under his control, to strip them of the only power they had over him—the terrible power of physical beauty.

Until he had discovered his grandfather's hidden message, buried in a secret diary in a locked box to be opened only when he was alone, to rekindle his most precious memories. Then he knew there was a place where men could satisfy their deepest desires. A place where anything was possible. Others had already gone before him. His grandfather had included the initials of someone else in his diary, someone who could only have been an accomplice. So he was not alone. There were others like him. Then and now. In India a man might do things he would not dare to dream about in England. In India there was an inexhaustible supply of boys to satisfy the needs of any white man with money and power.

Cardus visited India for the first time in 1983. It was an exploratory visit, a four-week vacation on his own to see if it were all true. If it were all still possible. It was better than he had dreamed. In Bombay, New Delhi, Goa and Madras he found people who would give him anything he wanted. Pimps who would bring boys to his room for a few rupees, who would approach boys on the street on his behalf. No appetite was so perverse that it had not been served a thousand times in India.

The first time he had whipped a boy was an experience he would savor for the rest of his life. Every detail, every shadow in the room, every sob, was engraved on his mem-

ory. Cardus had never known such excitement. After that it
was as though whipping was the only thing that could bring
him back to the same pitch of arousal.

In 1988 he returned, this time to visit Bombay, New
Delhi, Agra and Jaigapur. With him he had brought five
years of accumulated desire. Five years of need. And afterward nothing would ever be the same again. Cardus had
come to know the greatest power and the greatest pleasure
that any man had ever known. He had joined the greatest
princes in history. He had known the power of life and
death. The pleasure of intimate murder.

Cardus closed the diary and put it down on the desk. He
reached once more into the green metal box and pulled out
the oilskin package. He unwrapped it slowly. Inside was a
black, leatherbound case fastened with a zipper and a small
brass buckle. He opened it and surveyed the contents, his
eyes glittering. A set of tortoiseshell combs backed with
sterling silver and brass. A silver-handled shaving brush
with brass screws, a silver and brass–bound mirror, scis-
sors . . . and a brass-handled straight razor.

He took the razor out of the bag, opened it, balanced it
in his hand. It felt heavy. He held it up so the electric light
would shine against the blade. It was an instrument of terrifying beauty. Carefully he folded it and put it back in the
bag.

Then he unzipped a pocket in the cover of the barber's
bag, pulled out a small drawstring bag made from black
silk and put it on the desk.

Slowly, he inserted his fingers into the bag and felt the
tiny fragments of material inside. They felt like the softest,
most sensual things that Cardus had ever touched, like doe-
skin or vellum. Gently, one by one he teased them out onto
the desk where he could look at them. There were twenty-
four pieces in all, in irregular shapes and sizes.

He picked up one of the fragments and studied it with
loving fascination. It was tanned darkest brown and embellished with soft parallel ridges. It fitted neatly into the palm
of his hand. A sudden giddiness overcame him. The frag-

ment slipped from his fingers and twirled gently to the floor like a falling autumn leaf. He stayed still and stared at it for a long time.

It was a human scrotal sac.

The moment passed and he reached down and returned it to his collection of cured and oiled pieces of human flesh, a grotesque museum of scrotal tissue and male nipples.

Cardus reached back into the box, took an envelope from the middle of the pile and gently shook the contents onto the desk. There were six pictures. Snapshots of his she-boys. He arranged the pictures in sequence beside the pieces of skin so he could see them all.

Then he stood up, loosened his belt and pushed his trousers and underwear down to his ankles. He sat down again in the armchair. He could feel himself getting hard. He took the small amber bottle off the desk, opened it and poured a few drops of patchouli oil into the palm of his hand. The strong, sweet aroma drifted up to his nostrils and combined with the incense to bring back an intense rush of memories. He rubbed the oil into the palms of both hands then began to smooth it gently into his crotch until his cock and his balls were slick and shiny. Then he leaned back in the chair, his eyes on the memorabilia he had laid out so carefully on his desk, and he began to stroke himself.

In a moment the memory he treasured most surged back, stronger than all the others. First he could see Sanjay smiling, then laughing as he leaned down to suck Cardus. They were in his apartment at Juhu Beach. It was their first time. Pratap Coyarjee had arranged it. Cardus had met the studio manager at Film City in 1988; Coyarjee had offered other services if he needed them. It was strange how men like them had a way of recognizing each other, Cardus had thought. Once you gave in to your real desires, your strongest desires, the rest was easy.

It hadn't been difficult to persuade Sanjay to go that one step farther. To try something more. To experience the thrill of real danger, real excitement. Coyarjee had been only too happy to arrange it. All it had taken was a little money.

They had driven up to Film City in the early hours of Monday morning in Coyarjee's car. He had taken them past the main gate and down the road for another mile where they had stopped and hidden the car in a thicket of bamboo. There was a hole in the security fence that Coyarjee knew about and he had made sure the guards had been given enough whiskey to keep them entertained at the guardhouse until morning.

It had taken half an hour for the three of them to walk up the hill to the temple, Sanjay carrying the wine and ganja, Cardus carrying his small shoulder bag. He had been very pleased with Coyarjee's choice of the temple. That had been worth a few rupees extra.

When they got there they were hot and thirsty and Sanjay was getting irritable. They sat for a while on the floor of the temple and drank some wine, watching the moonlight over Lake Vihar. Coyarjee lit a joint and shared it with Sanjay. Cardus didn't smoke dope or drink alcohol—didn't like anything that might blur the pleasure of the senses. Sanjay's mischievous good humor had soon returned and he had got up and begun to dance. A funny, stumbling parody of a Hindu dance with eccentric hand movements, staring eyes and grotesque faces. Every now and again Sanjay would burst out laughing at his own silliness. It had been charming to watch.

The ganja began to take effect and Sanjay became increasingly uninhibited. He took off his clothes and kicked them against the wall. His own nakedness seemed to excite him and his movements became lewd and exaggerated. He was enjoying himself, dancing the dance of a narcissus. His cock became partially erect and slapped against his thighs. Cardus and Coyarjee exchanged glances. They were both becoming aroused.

Cardus got up first and approached Sanjay. He kissed him on the mouth and gently stroked his cock. Then he led him deeper into the temple toward the altar and the statue of Kali.

"No bad hurting now," Sanjay raised his finger in warning to Cardus.

"No bad hurting," Cardus repeated. "Only good hurting."

Sanjay giggled and lay facedown on the altar. He shivered at the touch of the cold stone against his skin. Cardus pulled a length of blue nylon cord from his shoulder bag and began to tie Sanjay's hands and feet together. There were crevices around the bottom corners of the altar and Cardus looped the ropes tightly under them so Sanjay couldn't escape. He could still move but he couldn't get away. He was powerless. This was the moment when Cardus began to feel the first burning tendrils of real excitement.

Coyarjee went around to the front of the altar, knelt in front of Sanjay and put a fresh joint to his lips. Sanjay inhaled deeply. When he exhaled it must have burned his throat because he coughed and choked a little. Coyarjee waited a moment while Sanjay recovered, then held the joint to his lips again. He took another deep hit. Then another. It was good ganja. Strong. It would help Sanjay focus on the pleasure.

Cardus pulled a length of shiny white plastic from his bag. A piece of electrical cord. He wrapped one end around his fist and whipped it through the air so that it made a thin hissing sound. Without warning, he whipped the cord across Sanjay's naked buttocks. Sanjay howled, turned his head, and screamed at Cardus to be more careful.

Cardus smiled. This time it was harder. Sanjay screamed again and unleashed a flood of curses at Cardus in English.

Cardus whipped him again. A few spots of blood spattered across the floor. Sanjay shouted at Coyarjee in Hindi but Coyarjee melted back into the shadows where he couldn't be seen, safe in the embrace of Kali, goddess of human sacrifice.

Cardus whipped Sanjay again and again. Harder and harder each time. Sanjay's screams reverberated around the temple and seemed to echo between the hills and far across the lake. But no one heard.

Blood ran freely from Sanjay's buttocks. The cord was stained red. Cardus loosened it from his fist and dropped it to the floor. Sanjay sobbed and began cursing him again in English. Cardus undressed quickly, stepped up to the altar behind Sanjay, his cock hard in his hand. He used one hand to prize Sanjay's buttocks apart then pushed the tip of his cock against the bloodied anal opening and began to push. Sanjay screamed and tried to writhe away but it was impossible. Cardus became more excited and gave a series of hard thrusts, penetrating deeper each time.

He came quickly, moaning with pleasure. When he withdrew, his crotch, his lower belly and thighs glistened, dark with Sanjay's blood. The temple looked like a scene from a nightmare. Sanjay pleaded to be set free.

Cardus padded quickly over to his bag and pulled out something metallic. Something that gleamed in the moonlight. Sanjay squirmed around, looked over his shoulder and saw what Cardus was holding. He screamed so hard that blood spattered from his mouth. He thrashed back and forth against his ropes with such force that his skin ripped like paper.

Cardus hurried back to him, eyes glazed, panting with an animal ferocity. He came up behind Sanjay and reached between his legs to grasp at his genitals. Sanjay tried to pull away but the stone surface of the altar was slippery with blood, sweat and urine and there was nothing with which to protect himself. Cardus's hand slid over the wet stone between Sanjay's thighs and he grabbed hard.

Sanjay screamed. A terrible scream of pain and terror and misery. The dying scream of a tortured beast.

Cardus pulled the genitals taut with one hand, brought the razor up with his right and sawed. Slowly. Deliberately. A torrent of blood gushed from the opening. Cardus stepped back, the razor in one hand, Sanjay's severed genitalia in the other.

He held it up against the moonlight, feeling the warm blood stream down his arm. He could feel it moving in his hand. See it twitching. The cock was still alive, the severed nerves jerking in spasms. Trying to become erect.

Cardus brought the bloodied cock down to his lips and kissed it. Then he set it down gently, beside his shoulder bag, to be hidden in the oilskin pouch and preserved as a memento. A treasured souvenir of ultimate pleasure.

Sanjay had moaned softly then, barely alive as the blood pulsed in torrents from the gaping wound in his groin. Cardus had hurried back to the altar, the razor dripping in his hand. He had shown Sanjay the pain. He had to move quickly now to show him the power. He took hold of Sanjay's hair and lifted his head. Sanjay's eyes flickered dully as he tried to look up. Cardus held the tip of the razor to Sanjay's neck, then pushed. The razor sliced clean and deep and Cardus heard the squeak of metal against bone as the blade grated across Sanjay's vertebrae.

Alone in his special place, in the attic of his suburban home, Antony Cardus gave a short, animalistic grunt of pleasure and climaxed.

21

SANSI HAD A problem. He had no idea what Antony Cardus looked like.

The day after he arrived at Goscombe Park he got up early. He dressed in light pants, pullover and windbreaker, hoping for anonymity. He missed breakfast, took a taxi into town and caught the 7:06 train from Oxford to Paddington. He took the tube to Waterloo Station and walked along York Road to County Hall. He was at the front doors five minutes before they opened at nine o'clock and by nine-fifteen he was seated at a small booth in the public records office with his eyes glued to a microfiche scanner while he picked his way through the electoral rolls for every borough council in the Greater London area.

Cardus was an unusual name. By eleven-thirty Sansi had found eight Carduses in the inner London area whose first names began with the letter A. He wrote down the address of each one. Then he took the tube to Trafalgar Square, walked into the main post office and locked himself into another booth with the white-page editions of the London telephone directory. By two o'clock he had begun calling the numbers. Each time someone answered, he represented himself as a card services clerk from American Express and said he wanted to confirm an unusually large charge entry for a hotel in New Delhi. Sansi had kept a copy of the American Express card number Cardus had used to pay for all his hotel accommodations in India. On his sixth try he reached a softly spoken woman who sounded nervous but confirmed that her husband had recently returned from a business visit to India. She said he could be reached at work if it was urgent and gave Sansi the number for the Foreign and Commonwealth Office in Whitehall. Sansi hung up, satisfied. He looked at his watch: two thirty-five. Not bad for a day of routine sleuthing.

The Antony Cardus who worked at the Foreign and Commonwealth Office lived at 24 Azalea Crescent, Dulwich, a dull but respectable suburb in south London. Sansi had time for a late lunch. He stopped at a pub called the Lamb and Flag and had a light beer and a greasy Scotch egg that gave him heartburn. At three-thirty he took a walk down Oxford Street and spent seventy pounds on a Canon Sure Shot with automatic focus, zoom lens and light meter. He also bought a couple of rolls of color film and a London A–Z street map, which he stuck in his back pocket. As he left the store, Sansi glanced at himself in a wall mirror, and decided that he would pass as just another foreign tourist.

He took the tube to Blackfriars and caught an early commuter train to Dulwich. It took him less than half an hour to find Azalea Crescent. It was a little after four-thirty. Sansi hoped Cardus wasn't an early finisher.

Sansi strolled slowly down the street, guidebook in hand, hoping he wouldn't attract too much attention. If anyone challenged him, he might be in trouble. This was London suburbia at its most bland. He knew there weren't any major tourist attractions within a mile. Sansi decided he would pretend he was looking for the house of a relative. A number of people were arriving home from work and a few glanced at him but no one seemed unduly curious.

He paused briefly in front of number twenty-four and pretended to study his guidebook. The house was fronted by a low brick wall with a green wooden gate. There was a scrap of lawn with a few budding flowers around the border. The house was built from blood-red brick in a style that had been popular in the early 1930s. Its front was small and narrow and was occupied almost entirely by a bay window and a single front door, also painted green. There were net curtains at the window, preventing anyone from seeing inside. Upstairs the curtains were drawn. A narrow footpath ran down the side of the house, which was relieved only by two small windows: one at the ground-floor level which might have been a toilet, the other, high up near the roof, possibly an attic window.

Sansi loitered up and down the street for a couple of hours before he became afraid of arousing suspicion. He had not seen anyone leave or enter number twenty-four. He left for the day, disappointed.

It was after ten when Sansi got back to Goscombe Park. He was exhausted. London was always hard on the feet. He ate a sandwich and had a glass of milk in the kitchen, then went straight to his room. He set the clock radio for three-thirty A.M.

It felt like he had been asleep for only five minutes before he was shouted awake by some unnaturally cheerful British disc jockey. He showered, dressed, collected his new camera and made it to Oxford Station in time to catch the early train into London. He was back in Dulwich a little after six and at Azalea Crescent by six-thirty. There was a small café and a news agent on the main road near the corner. Sansi bought himself a coffee in a Styrofoam cup, a copy of the *Daily Express* and positioned himself near the corner so he could pretend he was waiting for a lift. The coffee tasted like hot diesel oil. He poured it down the drain and pretended to read the paper.

The main road was thrumming with traffic and early-morning commuters pouring in from the red-brick and net curtain maze that surrounded him. No one seemed to notice Sansi. He discovered that if he strolled back and forth a few yards into Azalea Crescent he could see number twenty-four some of the time. It wasn't perfect but it would have to do.

At seven twenty-five he saw a thin, angular man in a dark suit walk briskly down the footpath beside number twenty-four. He opened the gate and walked up the street toward Sansi. He was carrying a black briefcase and he walked with a sense of purpose, his eyes fixed in front of him, as if daring anyone to get in his way. Sansi turned his back on Cardus, walked around the corner, slipped the newspaper in his pocket and began fiddling with the camera, as though he was trying to test the focus. He walked over to the curb, put the camera to his eye and pretended to be interested in the view down the traffic-clogged main street.

Cardus appeared around the corner, still walking quickly. Sansi watched him through the viewfinder, a thin black praying mantis bobbing toward him at the far left of the frame. His face was pale and gaunt, his lips almost bloodless. His fair hair was thinning and brushed back severely from his face. It was the eyes that held Sansi's gaze. Cardus's face was expressionless, but his eyes looked hostile and bright. Preternaturally bright.

Sansi took a series of photographs as Cardus walked past him and out of the frame. He paused for a moment, then put the camera down and turned to follow. It wasn't easy. Cardus walked quickly, crossing the street, threading his way down the busy footpath toward the station, passing people, forcing others to step aside for him.

Sansi had to stand in the corridor on the train ride into Blackfriars. Then he almost lost Cardus on the Circle Line. Not that it mattered—Sansi knew where he worked. But now that he had him, now that he'd seen him, Sansi wanted to keep Cardus in his sight as much as possible. To study him. To get to know his habits, his routine. To get close to him. To get a piece of him without his knowing.

Sansi followed him from Westminster Station along Parliament Street and veered idly away only when Cardus turned into King Charles Street and disappeared through a large black door watched by a security guard. Sansi carried on down Parliament Street for one block until he came to Downing Street, the official residence of the British Prime Minister. Sansi turned away, bitterly amused. Only one city block. If only the British Prime Minister knew what he had working so close to him. But Sansi knew that prime ministers were often shielded from their nation's worst secrets.

Sansi strolled on down to Charing Cross and risked his health on a cooked breakfast in the railway-station restaurant. Afterward he walked back through Whitehall to St. James's Park, rented a deck chair and slept for two hours. He spent the rest of the afternoon idling his way back and forth along the Victoria Embankment, occasionally taking a photograph of Parliament, Big Ben or the Thames.

Cardus was late leaving work. It was almost seven when he exited onto King Charles Street and set off once more for Westminster Underground station. Sansi followed him, trying not to lose him in the crowded labyrinth. Instead of taking the escalators to the Circle and District Line platforms, Cardus took the staircase to the Northern Line. When the train came, Sansi got into the carriage next to him and watched him through the glass. They changed to the eastbound fork of the Northern Line at Euston and two stops later Cardus got off at the Angel in Islington. Then, instead of heading directly for the street, Cardus detoured into the men's toilet. Sansi loitered a few feet away in the busy tunnel, feigning interest in a very sad street musician.

When Cardus reappeared a few minutes later, he had removed his tie and jacket and put on a crushproof black cotton bomber jacket. With it, he had assumed a whole new demeanor. Much of the tension appeared to have gone out of his body. Instead of the fixed grimace and the fast, purposeful stride, he looked more relaxed. His jaw didn't have the same aggressive thrust, his eyes took a more leisurely interest in his surroundings, even his walk had become more leisurely. Sansi would have to be careful. Cardus would be harder to follow now, more observant. Sansi hung back in the crowd as far as he dared, struggling to keep Cardus in sight as he walked up to street level. At the top of the steps Cardus paused and looked around, almost as if he were expecting to be followed. Then he turned left and strolled down Duncan Street as though he had all the time in the world, stopping occasionally to look in shop windows, browsing just like any other late shopper, his briefcase hanging loosely in his hand. Sansi crossed the street and watched from the other side.

Cardus walked for a couple of blocks, looking idly at the various shops that caught his interest. He came to a small shop that sold model boats and airplanes and spent a long time studying the contents of the window. Then he went inside. The shop was too small for Sansi to dare follow him. He waited across the street and fretted. Cardus was a long time. After twenty minutes he came out carrying a plastic bag with a small package inside. Again he continued his stroll along the street. The next shop he visited was a greengrocer. He bought some apples. Then, at the next corner, he turned off the main street and quickened his pace a little. Sansi followed, trying to keep to the shadows. After a couple of blocks Cardus came to a large, well-lit pub, The Marquess of Queensberry. He glanced around then opened the door and stepped inside.

There were half a dozen shops across the street from the pub, most of them shut for the night. Sansi found the darkest doorway and settled himself in for a long wait. It was dark, the last commuters had gone home and the street was changing, turning over to the nighttime trade. Everyone who entered and left the pub was male. All gay, Sansi realized. Obviously there were occasions when Cardus, tired of the strains imposed by his double life, needed to relax with friendly company in familiar surroundings. But not entirely familiar, Sansi knew. Cardus was different. He doubted that anyone but he knew how different.

Sansi shuffled from one foot to another and tried to ease some of the ache from his legs and lower back. It had been a long day: his feet were sore and there was a blister swelling on his left foot. And he had no idea how long Cardus would be in the pub. Nor could he know if his quarry intended going home afterward. He would simply have to wait and watch. For however long it took. Because The Marquess of Queensberry could be the key to getting what he wanted from Cardus.

It was a little after ten when Cardus re-emerged. He was

with two other men: one was in his forties and wore a suit and was drunk; the other was younger and casually dressed. He was helping to support the older man. Sansi lifted the camera and took a couple of pictures through the traffic from his hiding place across the street. The three men talked for a while then said good night, and Cardus peeled off on his own, back toward the Angel Underground station.

Sansi left Cardus at Blackfriars and went back to Oxford. The next day he slept in. In the early afternoon he took the train back to town and waited for Cardus on Parliament Street again. He followed the same pattern for the rest of the week. And then the next.

Three nights a week Cardus went straight home. On Wednesday and Friday nights he went to The Marquess of Queensberry in Islington, and stayed one or two hours, depending on the company. Then he went home. He did not go to a barbershop. He did not take his clothes to a dry cleaner. The visits to the gay pub were his only social excursions of his week—apart from those he was a solitary man.

Sansi went through four rolls of film. When he had them developed he found half a dozen clear shots of Cardus by himself. Another dozen photographs showed him in front of The Marquess of Queensberry on different nights with a variety of men, some of whom were identifiable, some of whom were not. Sansi knew the pictures would be enough to suggest to the British that Cardus might at least be a security risk. They were also enough to support his evidence of Cardus's double life when the case went to extradition. But it was only a beginning. Sansi still had to get one vital piece of forensic evidence before he could close the case. And he couldn't watch Cardus forever to get it. He would have to make things happen. For that, he knew, he would have to visit the pub himself.

Sansi had difficulty deciding what to wear. He didn't want anything too flamboyant because it would attract attention.

Besides, he knew, not all homosexuals were flamboyant. In the end he chose a pair of plain brown trousers and a sweater, something he hoped would help him fade into the background.

He arrived at the pub a little before six, at least an hour before Cardus usually arrived. He had noticed that Cardus used his pub nights to be a good employee and put in an extra couple of hours at work. He hoped it would give him time to blend into the crowd before Cardus showed up.

The pub was divided into two bars. The front bar catered to a quieter, older clientele. The back bar hosted a younger, louder crowd, and throbbed with music. The front bar was half full. It was a mixed crowd . . . but all male. Distinguished, gray-haired men in suits; mousy men who looked as though they should have been at home in front of the TV with pipe and slippers; younger, well-dressed men who looked like bank clerks; men in jeans and T-shirts who looked like laborers; short, bald, swarthy men with bellies; gym freaks with short cropped hair, mustaches and muscles. All different. All the same. All united by the same common need.

Sansi threaded his way to the bar, waited and looked around. The theme was mock Victorian plush with burgundy flock wallpaper, dim lights and prints on the walls that showed old-fashioned pugilists squaring up to one another, wearing tights and sashes. Sansi smiled to himself. He appreciated the humor. The Marquess of Queensberry was the inventor of modern boxing. He was also the father of Oscar Wilde's lover, Lord Alfred Douglas, and the man who subsequently hounded Oscar Wilde out of England.

There were two bartenders. One was young with long hair, neat beard, and an earring, wearing jeans and a T-shirt emblazoned with a picture of Margaret Thatcher dressed in a man's suit and wielding a whip. The other man was older, with peroxide-blond hair, dark roots and bad skin covered with makeup. He wore a pair of black stretch pants and a voluminous white blouse to hide his belly. His name was

Viv, and from what Sansi overheard, Viv was the licensee and the star of the show.

"All right, Bungit-In, what will you be having?"

There was a small chorus of laughter around the bar.

Sansi flinched. It wasn't the bad joke. The last thing he wanted was to have attention drawn to himself.

Viv waited.

"Lime and lemon, please," Sansi ordered. He felt like a fraud. He was sure they could all tell just by looking at him that he didn't belong. He wasn't one of them. There was something in the eyes, he had been told. Homosexuals could recognize each other just by looking into the eyes.

Viv didn't seem to see it. He brought Sansi's drink. "Just visiting?" he asked, handing Sansi his change.

"Yes," Sansi answered. He tried to emphasize the sing-song Indian accent. "A friend told me this was a nice place."

"Oh?" Viv arched a mascara-coated eyebrow. "And who would that be?"

"Narendra Jamal," Sansi answered. It was the first name that came into his head. "He is a friend of mine in . . . Manchester."

Viv nodded, his face impassive. "We don't get many Indians in here," he said. "Not East Indians. Quite a few West Indians, Jamaicans, that sort of thing. Not many of your sort."

Sansi nodded, unsure how to react. "My friend said the people were very friendly here. Manchester does not have many places like this."

Viv stared at him for a moment. "No," he said. "I don't suppose it does. They are still a bit primitive north of Watford, aren't they?"

The bar was getting busy and Viv left, apparently satisfied. Sansi sighed inwardly and sipped his drink. After a while he felt more comfortable. No one seemed to notice him anymore. He must have passed the first test: smile . . . be friendly . . . do not threaten . . . do not disturb.

He hadn't been sure what to expect from a gay pub. But

it was more subdued, more discreet than he had imagined. A few hopeful souls tried to catch his eye but when Sansi looked away they did not press their interest. A couple of the pub's resident predators approached him directly but when he failed to respond to their suggestive conversation, they moved on, apparently accepting his excuse that he was waiting for a friend.

A half-hour passed and Sansi began to feel anxious. He needed to go to the bathroom, but he had never been to the bathroom in a gay pub before. What were the protocols? he wondered. What if someone propositioned him? What if there were men engaged in sexual activity in the toilet? How would a gay man react? What should his reaction be? He tried not to think about going to the bathroom anymore.

His glass was empty and he couldn't stay in a pub without a drink. He could not have another long drink or the need to go to the toilet would become unbearable. He decided on a short drink, like Scotch. Then he caught himself again. Was Scotch a gay drink? It seemed to him that Scotch was profoundly heterosexual. Perhaps he would attract attention just by ordering it.

"Like another one, dear?" It was Viv.

"Gin and lime, please," Sansi decided. It was something his mother drank occasionally.

"Oh," Viv pouted, "whipping ourselves into a party frenzy, are we?"

Sansi smiled back and felt ridiculous. He could not remember a time when he had felt so uncomfortable, so uncertain of how to behave. The bar was becoming crowded. All the stools had been taken and men were standing two and three deep at the bar. There were a few more demonstrations of familiarity. Men holding hands, the odd pat on the behind. Sometimes a kiss. Sansi felt more bodies pressing in around him. The sound level had climbed and people were drinking faster. Music boomed in from the back bar.

Sansi checked his watch. It was a little after seven-thirty and there was still no sign of Cardus. He wondered if he would have to come back another night. The thought of it chilled him. He wasn't sure he could bluff his way through another performance with Viv.

Then he saw Cardus through the crowd, on the opposite side of the bar. He was wearing the black cotton jacket, his shirt had a couple of buttons undone and he was listening to a man Sansi had seen him with the previous week. Sansi stared past the blurred faces of the crowd. Suddenly he remembered where he had seen Cardus's face before. In pictures of Nazi war criminals on trial at Nuremburg: ordinary, shabby men made extraordinary only by the power they had been given.

Sansi watched the two men for a while. They were joined by a younger man, whom Sansi also recognized. They were the couple Sansi had seen Cardus with on the first night. The older man put his arm around the younger man's shoulders. Perhaps, Sansi thought, these two were the way to Cardus.

Sansi could stand it no longer. He had to go to the bathroom. There were two toilets in the corridor outside, one marked "Gents," the other "Ladies." Men were using both. Sansi opened the door to the Gents. There were half a dozen urinals inside and three cubicles. The floor was wet and smelled of sweat, piss and cheap disinfectant.

Three men were gathered around the open door of one cubicle, laughing and whispering. They looked briefly at Sansi, then went back to their furtive conversation. Sansi stepped up to the nearest empty urinal. He glanced over his shoulder to see one of the men pop a small foil capsule in his friend's face. The man inhaled sharply and reeled backward with a whoop of pleasure. His two friends laughed loudly. Amyl nitrate, Sansi realized. Its main effect was to shut off oxygen to the brain. Sansi didn't have to try it to know how they felt.

He finished at the urinal and hurried back outside to the front bar. His place had been taken and there was no sign of Cardus or his two companions. Sansi scanned the room but they had gone. Anxious, he hurried outside and looked up and down the street. The traffic had thinned out and the sidewalks were almost empty. A couple of groups of men stood on the path in front of the pub, talking. Cardus was not among them. Sansi put his hands in his pockets, hunched his shoulders in an effort to make himself inconspicuous and hurried up the street in the direction the two men had gone the last time he'd seen them.

The road forked into two narrower streets, and Sansi decided to take the quieter street on the left. It looked more residential and Sansi assumed the two men lived nearby. If they did and if Cardus had ever been to their home, there was a possibility that he could go back there again. All Sansi needed was to get his hands on Cardus's jacket, or one of the jackets in his briefcase. A few small hairs on the collar—that was all it would take.

Something hit him hard on the left side of the head and drove him into the wall. Sansi staggered, almost fell. He raised his arms to protect himself. He felt another blow, harder this time, across the back. A bolt of pain seared down his spine and he gasped.

Sansi turned to confront his assailant but saw only a threatening sliver of blackness silhouetted against the glare of a streetlight. The sliver was dancing, circling. Holding something in one hand, a club of some kind.

"Afraid, Inspector?" The words sounded like a hiss, alien and filled with malice. It was a man's voice. Urgent. Filled with harm.

Sansi felt something warm and wet on the side of his head. The shape darted in again and Sansi lashed out with his foot. He wasn't fast enough and his assailant contemptuously swatted the foot away with the club. Pain lanced up Sansi's leg. He staggered backward, limping, fighting to keep his balance. He knew that if he fell he was finished.

"Not very good when a man is on his feet, are you, Inspector?"

Suddenly Sansi realised. The voice wasn't speaking in English. It was Hindi. An Indian.

"Who are you?" Sansi shouted back, shocked at the fear in his own voice.

The man sniggered, lunged again. Sansi backed away and tried to run. He felt another blow on his left shoulder, harder. He cried out, loudly this time. It felt as though he was being beaten with an iron bar.

Sansi lost his balance and began to fall in a headlong, stumbling rush, his hands in front of him. He hit the pavement hard, hands and elbows raking across the cement. His right arm connected with something hard and it rolled away from him. A rock. A piece of pavement. He grabbed it, wrenched himself around and hurled it full in the face of the man lunging down at him, the club poised to strike. There was a soft thud as the stone hit its target and the man recoiled, swearing, his hand to his face. The stone bounced onto the road, rolled and stopped. Sansi scrambled awkwardly to his feet and threw himself after his assailant. He knew he was bigger. Big enough to make a difference. He knew that if he could close with his attacker, his extra weight would give him a chance. He threw his arms around the man's waist, hoisted him into the air then launched himself forward, back onto the road, his assailant underneath him.

They hit the ground with a jolt. The man screamed: pain mixed with fury and frustration. The battle had turned as suddenly as it had begun. Sansi fumbled for the club, wrenched it free. He was breathing hard. Sweat mingled with blood and ran down the side of his face, staining the shirt beneath his pullover. He could feel his strength ebbing. Sansi looked at the club under the streetlight; it was a short, thick length of rubber pipe filled with cement. Enough to break every bone in a man's body. Slowly.

Sansi seized his attacker by the throat with one hand and raised the pipe in the other. Then he yanked the man up off the ground so he could see his face in the light.

Sansi stared.

His assailant was almost completely bald, his head covered only by a mottled web of scars. Burn scars.

It was Ajit, the scar man from Dharavai. Paul Kapoor's

thug. The former Naxalite terrorist whom Sansi had burned in the desert, near Tamori, twenty years before.

Sansi struggled to his feet, pulling Ajit after him, astounded, unable to speak.

"You have great karma, blue eyes," the scar man grunted between breaths. "It is only your karma that protects you now."

Sansi was transfixed by the scar man's face. There was new blood seeping from the scar tissue on the left cheek where the rock had hit him. Suddenly, Sansi was aware of other voices, people hurrying toward them. He tried to shut them out, to focus only on Ajit's hideous face.

"What are you doing in London?" Sansi demanded.

The scar man spat in his face. A mixture of blood and spittle.

"Is Kapoor with you?"

The scar man stared back, eyes aglow with hate.

Then they heard sirens. Drawing closer. The scar man looked around, seeing other people for the first time. Suddenly he looked nervous.

"I want to see Kapoor," Sansi said. "Take me to him. Now. Or I'll turn you over to the English police."

The taxi driver hadn't wanted to take them at first. Then Sansi showed him some money and convinced him they weren't drunk. Ajit spoke just enough English to tell him they wanted to go to Shepherds Bush. It took almost an hour to drive southwest across the city, through some of London's bleakest inner-city ghettos, before they reached the racial melting pot of Shepherds Bush. They had only driven a few hundred yards down Goldhawk Road when Ajit told the driver to stop.

They got out in front of a late-night laundromat, an Indian grocery and a chicken takeout. A number of sullen youths loitered along the street, smoking, passing cans of beer back and forth, calling out to one another in Cockney accents. Almost all of them were Indian. Sansi paid the driver and followed Ajit back the way they had come. They walked for about a hundred yards until they came to a small, dingy curry house called The Star of India.

"Wait," Ajit said and opened the door.

Sansi shook his head and followed right behind.

The restaurant consisted of one small room in which a lot of small tables had been jammed together, the kind of place that probably appeared frequently in cheap-food guides. Sansi saw a few white faces among the black. He heard familiar accents: Hindi, Marathi, Urdu—the voices of India in the middle of London. There was a sudden lull in the babble of conversation as people looked up from their meals and stared at the two newcomers. Sansi wasn't surprised. The side of his head and his shirt collar were caked with blood. And people always stared at Ajit. Once.

They walked to the back of the restaurant to a corridor that led to the kitchen and the toilets. A couple of waiters stared as they went past but no one tried to stop them. There was a stairway at the back of the building.

Ajit started up first then looked over his shoulder and scowled at Sansi. "If he's here, he'll be upstairs. I'll tell him. Otherwise he won't like it. All right?"

Sansi shook his head. "I don't trust you," he said.

Ajit sneered. "If Jackie's up there you could be in a lot of trouble."

"I'll take my chances," Sansi said.

He followed the scar man up the stairs to a small landing. There were two doors. One was open and showed a small, dark kitchen with a fridge and a few cases of empty liquor bottles. The other was closed. They could hear men's voices on the other side. Indian voices.

Ajit hesitated, no longer sure of himself. Sansi reached past him and knocked loudly on the door. There was a pause, then the door opened. Sansi found himself looking into the ugly, squashed face of Jackie Patro. Behind Patro, Sansi could see a smoky room with a table, glasses, whiskey bottles and a half-dozen men playing cards. One of them was Paul Kapoor.

Patro's expression changed only once, when he looked

from Sansi back to Ajit and his eyes narrowed in what
Sansi took to be a look of disapproval. Then he stepped out
onto the landing and closed the door behind him. Patro was
shorter than either Sansi or Ajit but he took up all the available space on the landing. He wore a black and white windbreaker with "Honda" embroidered onto the breast pockets
and his bald head gleamed dully under the single electric
light that hung from the ceiling.

"I want to speak to your boss." Sansi spoke first.

Patro ignored him. Instead, he stared unnervingly at Ajit.
The scar man fidgeted, dabbed his sleeve at the cut on his
face.

"I saw him a few days ago, on the street," Ajit explained. "I went after him on my own. I didn't think you
would mind. It was old business—my business. Paul under-
stands."

Patro didn't look convinced. "Why did you bring him
here?"

"I want to see your boss," Sansi repeated. "I want to talk
to Kapoor."

He tried to sound firm, authoritative. It didn't work.
Patro continued to ignore him.

"You fucked up," Patro told Ajit. "You shouldn't have
brought him here."

Ajit shrugged. "Somebody called the cops. . . . He said
he would turn me over to the cops. I thought it was better
to bring him here. He's on his own."

Patro glanced back at Sansi then made up his mind.
"Wait downstairs," he ordered Ajit.

The scar man turned awkwardly on the crowded landing,
gave Sansi one more hate-filled stare, then trudged resent-
fully back down the stairs.

"Wait here," Patro told Sansi. Then he opened the door
and disappeared. The card game had fallen quiet. The only
sounds on the landing now were the mumble of people in
the restaurant downstairs, the clatter of dishes in the
kitchen. The whole building smelled of curry and burning
ghee.

Sansi stepped into the kitchen, switched on the light then ran the single cold-water tap over a small sink. He wet his handkerchief and wiped tenderly at the dried blood on the side of his head. He could feel a large swelling near the left temple and imagined it had already begun to discolor. His back and his leg still ached from where Ajit had hit him with the pipe. Sansi still had the pipe in his trouser pocket, but he had no illusion about the security it might give him. He had no security here, he knew.

The door opened and Patro appeared on the landing, followed by Kapoor. As usual he was dressed entirely in black. The gang lord of Dharavai had a curious smile on his face. Patro was unreadable.

"On vacation, Sansi?" Kapoor asked gently.

Sansi rinsed the blood out of his handkerchief, squeezed it and balled it in his hand. It gave him something to play with.

"Business," he answered. "You?"

Kapoor's smile broadened. "Business," he said.

"Been coming to London for a while?"

"There's a lot of business in London, Sansi."

"The restaurant business?"

Kapoor shrugged. "I own this place. And a few others. All legitimate businesses."

Sansi grinned. He wondered how much of Kapoor's heroin came into England hidden inside sacks of Basmati rice or boxes of pungent Indian spices. There was nothing like a few sacks of turmeric to stop sniffer dogs from detecting a cache of heroin.

Kapoor grinned back at him. "Ajit holds a grudge a long time, doesn't he? But I can understand it. You gave him a lot of pain."

"I have no more business with him," Sansi said, trying to sound as though he was conducting a reasonable conversation between business associates. "I could have turned him over to the London police if I'd wanted. It's finished if he wants it to be finished."

"I'll tell him," Kapoor said. The tone in his voice could

have meant anything. He folded his arms and leaned back against the wall. "You in London on police business, Sansi?"

"Yes."

"Anything I should know about?"

"I don't think so."

Kapoor smiled. "You wouldn't be thinking of telling anybody about this place, would you?"

"It's a little out of my jurisdiction," Sansi answered.

"Then why did you come here?"

"You and I still have some business to discuss."

Kapoor's eyebrows lifted a fraction.

Sansi squeezed the ball of wet cloth in his hand. A couple of drops trickled between his knuckles and dripped onto the greasy linoleum. "You owe me a favor."

Kapoor sniffed as though trying to suppress a small laugh. He looked at Patro, then back at Sansi. "I owe you?" he echoed.

"You used me to set up Bikaner," Sansi said. "You made a fool of me. Remember what you said in Dharavai? You said if I did it right, you owed me?"

Until now Kapoor had been friendly. Wary, but still friendly. Now the mood had changed. Everything had gone on hold. Now, Sansi realized, it could go either way. It could go the way he hoped it would go, the way he'd gambled it would. Or it could end up with him in a bloody and broken heap in an alley in another part of London. Or worse.

"My business in London is with somebody else." Sansi persevered, trying to keep his voice level. "But there is a way you could help."

Kapoor and Patro waited.

"You could take care of somebody for me."

The light in Kapoor's eyes flickered. "What do you mean, 'take care of somebody'?"

Sansi took a breath. His life as a policeman had given him many bizarre moments, but none more bizarre than this. Standing at the top of a staircase at the back of a dingy

London curry house, trying to make a deal with the most vicious gangster in Bombay. The same man who had double-crossed him only one month before.

Sansi hoped he didn't look anywhere near as desperate as he felt. "There is a man who lives here in London," he went on. "I want him beaten up. Not killed."

Kapoor shifted position against the wall. Almost imperceptibly the mood had changed back again. Lightened. Kapoor had begun to understand what Sansi wanted. They were back on territory he understood. He could make a deal with a crooked cop.

The gangster's smile returned. His Elvis smile. "You're not asking us to break the law, are you, Sansi?" he said.

Sansi shrugged. "I need . . . I'd appreciate a favor."

Kapoor looked at the floor, thinking. "What for?" he asked.

"I want you to get something from him and give it to me."

"Like what?"

"Like a piece of his scalp."

Kapoor's smile came back. "Hey, man," he glanced across at Patro, "we're not those kind of Indians, remember?"

Then he laughed softly. Sansi smiled too, ignoring the pain in his body. Even Patro's expression altered fractionally to accommodate something that might have been a smile.

"What do you want with a piece of his scalp, man?"

Sansi hesitated, unsure of how much he dared tell Kapoor. But he realized he had nothing to lose. He had already taken so many chances.

"I'm building a case against him. I need one more important piece of forensic evidence. If I get a piece of his hair it will give me his genetic pattern. If it matches the evidence we already have back in Bombay, we've got him."

Kapoor stared at Sansi. "You can do that now in Bombay?"

"Yes," Sansi nodded. "But you have to get the root of the hair."

"I'll remember that," Kapoor said. "Is this guy Indian?"

"English."

Kapoor nodded.

"I can give you photographs," Sansi added. "I'll drop them off tomorrow. I can tell you where he lives. Where he works, where he drinks."

Kapoor leaned away from the wall. "What did he do?"

Sansi paused. "He killed some people who did not deserve to be killed."

"What kind of people?"

"Nobodies. Prostitutes. Pimps. An actor. Most of them were young. People who never did anybody any real harm. There is no reason I could give you that would make any sense. We're talking about a crazy man. A psychopath. It's not business with him. It's not money. It's pleasure. He does it only because he enjoys it."

Kapoor nodded, his expression giving away nothing.

"If we do this," he said, "you owe me."

Sansi shook his head. "We're even."

Kapoor flashed his Elvis smile again. "There's no such thing as even."

22

CARDUS LEFT THE Marquess of Queensberry around ten
o'clock that Friday night, alone. He walked along Duncan
Street, then took his usual shortcut between two blocks of
council flats on the way back to Angel Station. The footpath
was narrow with high wooden fences on each side, though
the surrounding flats were well lit with open windows and he
could hear the noise of TV sets and people talking.

Cardus started when he saw two young, casually dressed
Indian youths enter the lane ahead of him, engrossed in
conversation. He tensed, tried not to stare. It disturbed him
when he saw Indian boys in London. When they got close
to him. It made him feel a certain loss of control, as though
he were out of his element. They walked toward him, still
talking. Cardus fixed his gaze stonily on the High Street,
twenty yards away. The youths had to get into single file to
pass him. They had almost passed him when he felt a sav-
age blow to the back of his head and was thrown forward
into the arms of the other youth, who was ready for him.

"Don't . . . please, I'll give you—" he shouted.

His words were cut off when the youth in front seized him
by the lapels and butted him twice in the face. Cardus swung
his briefcase wildly but there was no one there to connect
with. A flurry of heavy blows to his head and shoulders
drove him to his knees. He opened his mouth to shout for
help but no sound came. Instead he felt a sudden, crushing
weight against the side of his head, then an unbearable burning sensation followed by deep dissolving blackness.

It was the pain that brought him back. Pain that seared

up from his gut and flickered like flames through every nerve in his body. He opened his eyes, but something warm and sticky blotted out his vision. He tried to move and wipe his face. Pain lanced up from his groin again. He moaned and lay still. He heard voices around him and flinched. Then he realized they were friendly London voices. He heard the undulating clamor of an ambulance bell drawing closer and he lay back and surrendered to the pain. Too afraid to move.

Sansi called The Star of India at noon the following day, as arranged. A voice he had never heard before told him to be outside the Shepherds Bush Underground station at four.

He was there twenty minutes early. At ten past four he saw the bare brown skull of Jackie Patro bobbing through the crowd of early commuters. He was wearing the same black nylon Honda windbreaker he had worn a few nights earlier and he was carrying a folded newspaper.

Nothing showed on Patro's face as he drew closer. Sansi stepped forward, opened his mouth to say something then closed it again. There was nothing to say. Patro passed him the newspaper, said nothing and kept walking. Sansi took the paper, felt the extra thickness of an envelope inside. Then he heard something. Something strange. Patro was a couple of paces away and still walking. But he had one hand up to his mouth and he was making an odd, high-pitched warbling sound. Like a Red Indian.

Sansi hurried down the steps to the station toilet, found an empty cubicle and locked himself inside. He sat on the toilet, opened the newspaper and looked at the square brown envelope inside. He opened it and pulled out a small, clear plastic kitchen bag. Inside was a tuft of fair hair. The roots were clotted with blood and a few white crumbs of skin. Sansi tucked the bag back in the envelope and put it in his jacket pocket.

Two days later, Cardus was discharged from St. Stephen's Hospital with a large surgical dressing on the side of his

head. There were three stitches in the skin underneath the
dressing and a section of bare scalp about two inches in di-
ameter. His other injuries were superficial: a few cuts and
bruises, a swelling in the groin where he had been kicked
a few times. He had been lucky, the doctor said. There was
no evidence of concussion. A lot of mugging victims
weren't so fortunate. They'd had one young man in the previous week who had lost an eye.

The policeman who interviewed him at his bedside confirmed it was a random mugging: a couple of opportunists
who had the lane staked out for a while, no doubt waiting
for the right victim. An unfortunate but routine occurrence
in London these days. Cardus's watch and his wallet were
both gone. His briefcase had been broken open and the contents strewn across the footpath, although most of them appeared to have been recovered by the occupants of the
housing projects who had come to his aid.

Beryl brought him a change of clothes and helped him
down to the taxi. His boss had given him as much time off
as he needed. Cardus insisted he would be back at work in
a few days. He didn't want to miss the announcement.

It was seven o'clock in the evening at Goscombe Park
when Sansi put his call through to Bombay.

"Good evening, Inspector," Dr. Rohan greeted him.
"How are you enjoying London? I hope you're not spend-
ing all your time working. Have you had time to visit any
good restaurants yet? I do so enjoy the food in London—"

Sansi cut him short. "Doctor, this is important. Did you
get the sample?"

"Of course." Rohan sounded more amused than miffed
by Sansi's abruptness.

"Have you—?"

This time Rohan interrupted. "Yes. The enzyme pattern is
the same. Congratulations, Inspector. You have your man."

Sansi hung up and stared at the wall of his father's un-
used study, hardly able to believe that it was all coming to
an end. The next number he called was for Jamal. It took

him several tries and it was after nine—a little after two in
the afternoon in Bombay—when he finally got through to
the joint commissioner.

"I know." Jamal stole his pleasure. "Rohan told me.
Good work, Sansi. I've already spoken to the governor. I'm
arranging for the extradition papers to be drawn up now.
I'll contact the high commissioner in London myself. The
governor and I both agree that we won't make any announcement to the Cabinet until the arrest is about to take
place in London. The high commissioner will advise you
on how to proceed. Give him a couple of days before you
see him. That should be more than enough."

Sansi was to remember those words when he walked into
the high commissioner's office in India House, just off The
Strand, at ten o'clock on Thursday morning. He wore his
suit for the occasion and carried complete copies of the evidence in an attaché case.

The high commissioner welcomed Sansi courteously into
his office and gestured toward a chair. Jyoti Dandavate was
a small, neat man with graying hair, glasses and a decep-
tively gentle manner.

"I understand you have been quite active during your
time in London, Inspector," he said, making himself comfortable in a chair that seemed far too big for him.

Sansi nodded. "It has been a difficult, time-consuming
investigation," he confirmed. "But I am sure Joint Commissioner Jamal of Crime Branch in Bombay has brought you
up to date. We have proceeded cautiously." Sansi thought it
wise that only he knew the way in which he had obtained
the last scrap of forensic evidence. "It is an important
case," he went on. "We did not want to proceed until we
were ready—"

"Please, Inspector." Dandavate raised the palm of his
hand, cutting Sansi off in a way that he found peculiarly offensive. "I spoke with Joint Commissioner Jamal the day
before yesterday. I assume you haven't spoken with him
since then?"

"There was no need—"

"Inspector, we do not propose to proceed with Bombay's request for extradition in this case at this time."

Sansi looked at the high commissioner. He saw Dandavate in almost excruciating detail. The gold-rimmed glasses. The red-and-white-striped tie, white shirt and dark suit. The tiny beads of perspiration on his forehead. The large, open pores around the corners of his nostrils. And he heard every word that Dandavate had said.

But he didn't understand.

The silence in the room lengthened. Suddenly the image reversed and Sansi felt as though he were looking at the high commissioner from a very long way away. It was real, Sansi knew. But he didn't want to believe it. After all he had been through . . .

"To the best of my knowledge External Affairs in New Delhi has never been notified about this investigation," Dandavate went on. "I informed Jamal myself that he would have to make his approach through the proper channels. Federal regulations are really quite explicit on this, Inspector. They are there for a reason. The Minister himself will have to consider the proprieties of a case such as this. As you, yourself, would be aware, this is a highly unusual situation. There are . . ."

"Political implications . . ." Sansi said flatly.

Dandavate gave Sansi a look of mild annoyance. "Political implications at the highest level, Inspector," the high commissioner continued. "It is quite unprecedented for an investigation of this . . . sensitivity to go this far without any reference to federal authority. We have been given no warning. External Affairs has been kept in the dark about the entire investigation. Neither the department, nor myself, nor the Minister has had an opportunity to consider the evidence."

Sansi flicked open the lid of his attaché case, turned it around and threw it forward so that it landed on the high commissioner's desk with a loud slap and the papers inside spilled out and slewed across the empty, polished surface.

"Inspector—" Dandavate began.

"Antony Cardus is a mass murderer," Sansi cut him short, his voice thick with anger. "There is the proof. Between 1988 and 1991 he murdered six Indian nationals that we know of in Bombay, New Delhi, Agra and Jaigapur. Is that a federal crime or isn't it?"

"Inspector . . . Antony Cardus also happens to be an employee of the British government. . . ."

"What has that got to do with it?"

"The government of India will not proceed with a case like this until it has been fully considered at the highest level. Something like this . . . the Minister would almost certainly have to involve the prime minister in any decision. As you are aware, the government has only recently changed."

"Again."

"Be that as it may . . ."

"How long?"

"How long what, Inspector?" Dandavate seemed annoyed by Sansi's presumption.

Sansi wondered if the high commissioner fully understood the physical danger he was in right at that moment.

"How long would you estimate that New Delhi would need to consider the evidence before we could expect a decision on extradition?"

Dandavate shrugged. "Who knows? Six months? A year?"

"Or five, or ten or twenty," Sansi muttered, unable to hide his contempt. "It really doesn't matter, does it, Mr. High Commissioner, because the government has no intention of ever filing an extradition order in the case of Antony Cardus, does it?"

"There is no need for impertinence, Inspector," the high commissioner huffed. "It does not help your position to—"

Sansi stood up, stuffed the papers on Dandavate's desk back into the attaché case, snapped it shut, turned and walked out of the room.

He was still shaking half an hour later as he walked aimlessly along The Strand toward Blackfriars.

For the first time in his life George Sansi knew how it felt to want to kill a man in cold blood.

23

IT WAS ALMOST midnight when Sansi got back to Goscombe Park. He had spent most of the evening at a pub in Oxford getting drunk by himself. It hadn't worked—it had only served to make him more depressed. After a couple of hours he had gone to the washroom, thrown up, then taken a taxi back to his father's house. He washed his face, then went to his father's old study and called Bombay.

"I heard," Joint Commissioner Jamal answered. "We were still fighting to get it through yesterday. That is why I had not called you. It is no use, Sansi. External Affairs doesn't want to know. They have thrown up a brick wall against us."

"Have you any idea why?"

"There could be a reason," Jamal answered. "But there doesn't have to be. Perhaps they are just being bureaucratic."

"What does the governor think?"

"He thinks you should come home and we should forget that you were ever in London."

Sansi took a breath. "What do you think?"

"It is out of our hands, Sansi. Come home. This man has gone. If he comes back to Bombay one day, perhaps . . ." He let the sentence hang.

Sansi paused. If Jamal had run out of strategies, perhaps it was all over. "I need time to think," he said. "I'll come back in a few days."

"Sansi?" Jamal's voice sounded an ominous note. "Don't do anything on your own. I don't want you to do anything

that will embarrass the department or the government . . .
any government."

Sansi gave a short, humorless laugh and hung up.

He went to bed and lay awake in the dark for hours,
wondering what kind of government could be embarrassed
by the arrest of a serial killer. He fell asleep shortly before
dawn.

When he woke up, three restless hours later, he still felt
angry. He got up, opened the curtains and looked out the
window. It was a beautiful spring morning. The sky was a
pale pristine blue, the leaves on the trees looked freshly
minted and the air itself seemed to sparkle. And everywhere Sansi looked he saw only corruption and compromise.

It was close to lunchtime when he walked up the short
flight of steps that led into New Scotland Yard, his attaché
case under one arm. He waited his turn at the front desk
until he was approached by a pink-cheeked police constable
who looked sixteen years old.

"Can I help you, sir?" the officer asked.

"I would like to report a murder," Sansi said.

Ten minutes later he was looking across a desk at the
big, red face of Detective Sergeant Wally Reith. They were
in a small, windowless interview room that smelled much
cleaner than the interview rooms at police headquarters in
Bombay. Sansi opened his attaché case, selected half a
dozen case reports from the pile of papers inside and slid
them across the desk.

Reith looked at the official letterheads, the stamp of the
Crime Branch, Bombay, and the Bombay coroner's office,
then glanced warily at Sansi.

"Just take a moment to read through them, if you
wouldn't mind, Sergeant."

Reith took a breath but he did as he was asked. He read
for twenty minutes before Sansi heard the first whispered
"Jesus Christ." There were more. After forty-five minutes

Reith stopped reading and looked at Sansi. "You're a police officer?"

Sansi produced his warrant card.

Reith studied it carefully. "Wait here," he said. He got up and left the room. Another young policeman came and offered Sansi a cup of tea. He declined. Half an hour later Reith returned with a man in a good suit and an expensive tie.

"Inspector Sansi, this is Detective Superintendent Barrett, from Special Branch," Reith said.

Sansi got up and shook hands. Barrett was a slender man of medium height with graying hair trimmed to military neatness. The same young policeman returned with another chair for Superintendent Barrett. The senior policeman took his jacket off, hung it over the back of the chair and sat down.

"Make yourself comfortable, Inspector," he said pleasantly. "We're going to be here awhile."

It was four hours before Barrett seemed satisfied. The desk was covered with papers and empty teacups. Barrett returned Sansi's papers to some kind of order and leaned back in his chair.

"Does your government know you're here, Inspector?" he asked.

"In London?"

"Here, talking to us."

"No." Sansi shook his head. He was tired but his manner was calm to the point of resignation.

"So there has been no official contact between your government and ours in relation to this matter?"

"That is correct."

Barrett nodded. "What do you expect us to do with this material, Inspector?"

"Whatever you like," Sansi answered.

Barrett looked surprised for the first time. "Assuming everything that appears in these documents is correct," he said, "these offenses were committed in India. Not Britain. The fact that they were committed by a British national is interesting to us. But he may not have broken the laws of England. I can see the difficulties involved, but, presumably if your government wanted him they would have filed for extradition by now."

"My government doesn't want him," Sansi said.

Barrett hesitated. "Then what do you hope to gain by bringing this material to us today, Inspector Sansi?"

"If I can't take him back with me, perhaps you'd like him."

Barrett worked his jaw, thinking. "We'll follow it up," he said. "I can promise you that much."

"You just want him picked up, is that it?" Reith interjected.

"He is a government employee." Sansi nodded at the open attaché case, the photographs of Cardus with known homosexuals in front of The Marquess of Queensberry. "There is enough evidence in there to suggest he might be a security risk. I'd like to think that he won't be coming back to India for a while."

Barrett nodded, then stood up and put on his jacket. "Would you mind waiting just a little longer, Inspector?" he said. "I'll be back in a few minutes."

He left Sansi with Reith. The two policemen chatted amiably for almost another hour. Reith seemed sympathetic, Sansi thought, but he was no longer sure he could trust his own judgment about anyone or anything.

When Barrett returned it was with a set expression that Sansi knew instinctively meant bad news for him.

"We appreciate you bringing this material to our attention, Inspector Sansi," Barrett said, his voice flat, intended to discourage further argument. "If you'll just leave it with us, we'll be happy to take it from here."

He offered his hand. Sansi looked at both men for a moment but saw only blankness. Distance. Official distance measured in miles. He stood up wearily and shook hands.

"I didn't come here to ask a favor," Sansi said. "Antony Cardus is an evil man, Superintendent. Somebody has to put him away. If not me . . . somebody . . ." The words died hopelessly on his lips.

Barrett looked uncomfortable. "Inspector," he said, "from what I can gather, your government has no intention of filing for extradition in this case."

Sansi nodded. They had already spoken to Dandavate at the High Commission.

"Now as I understand it," Barrett went on, "you have no authority to operate here. There has been no request from your government to ours that would enable the metropolitan police to assist you in this case in any way. I hate to put it like this, Inspector, but you're on your own. The best advice I can give you at this time is to go home. There is nothing more you can accomplish here, Inspector."

"May I have my warrant card, please?" Sansi asked.

Barrett shook his head. "Your high commissioner asked us to hold it on his behalf. We'll send it over to India House. I think the message is pretty clear, Inspector. Your government wants you to stop what you're doing and go home."

Sansi began pushing papers back into his attaché case.

Barrett reached out and gently but firmly restrained Sansi's arm. "We'll hang on to these too, if you don't mind."

"And if I do mind?"

"We'll still hang on to them." A chill undercurrent was just discernible through the professional courtesy.

Sansi felt the system squeezing him from the inside to the outside: slowly, deliberately and with terrible efficiency. Telling him he had crossed the line. He no longer belonged. He had run out of protection.

"May I keep my attaché case?" Sansi asked, not bothering to mask his sarcasm. He wasn't worried about the papers. They were all copies and related mostly to the circumstantial evidence against Cardus. The forensic evidence was safe. Sansi had already made sure of that.

Barrett removed his hand. Sansi closed his empty attaché case and turned to leave.

"Follow my advice and go home, Inspector," Barrett called after him. "There's nothing more you can do here."

"Annie?"

"Yes, who is this?" She sounded drowsy, not yet awake.

"George Sansi. I'm sorry I had to wake you up. I know it's the middle of the night there, but listen, this is important."

"Shit . . . three-thirty in the morning. Just a minute. . . . Okay, what is it?"

"You know all those papers I gave you before I left?"

"Yes."

"Put them somewhere safe. Somewhere nobody but you can get at them. Not the police. Not the government."

"Christ, is it that bad?"

"Yes. You'll be getting something in the mail from me in a couple of days. I want you to hide it too."

"What is it?"

"I sent two packages. One contains a couple of strips of film negatives. The other contains a few pieces of hair."

"Hair?"

"Yes."

"What kind of hair?"

"Human hair. From the murderer. You should keep it in your fridge."

"No way."

"Annie?"

"I'll find a safe, cool place for it but I'm not putting pieces of a murderer in my goddamn fridge!"

"All right. Just make sure it's safe. It's vital to my case against this guy."

There was a pause.

"You didn't get him, did you?" she asked softly.

"No."

"What happened?"

"The government, the Indian government, won't extradite him."

"Why not, for Christsakes?"

"I don't know."

"You want me to break the story yet?"

"No."

"When?"

"I'll tell you."

"You promised me I could have it first."

"Annie ..." His voice escalated to a hoarse whisper. "I'm trying to do what's right at a time when it feels like the whole world is trying to stop me. Now just help me, will you? I'm not doing this for the glory."

The line went quiet. "All right, I'm sorry. When are you coming back?"

"I don't know. Perhaps in a few days. I can't give up yet. There still might be something I can do. But if anything happens to me, run the story."

"What could happen to you?"

"I don't know. Anything. If governments can protect mass murderers, anything can happen. I'll call you. Will you meet me at the airport?"

"You want me to?"

"I can't think of anyone else I would rather see waiting for me at Sahar."

"You mean that?"

"Yes."

There was another pause.

"I've missed you, Sansi. You want to come back to my place first when you get back?"

Sansi smiled. "See you in a few days," he said. He hung up and looked at the clock. It was coming up to nine at night. Sansi was exhausted. He went quietly upstairs to his room, showered and climbed into bed. Everything seemed to ache. Even his bones hurt. He lay in bed, feeling the pain ebb and flow through his body, too tired to move. But still he couldn't sleep.

He got up late, unable to face the thought of running into Eric or Joyce. Sansi had seen precious little of them since the day of his arrival. It was a cold, strangely British kind of hostility they shared. He hadn't seen his father for several days. He would have to put that right, he knew. The time was drawing close when he would have to say goodbye again.

He took a long, hot bath and felt slightly better when he went down to breakfast. Mrs. Chappel welcomed him brightly to the breakfast room but he wasn't hungry. He settled for tea and toast. There were some newspapers piled untidily on a side table, left by Eric. Sansi leafed through them until he found a copy of the *Times*. All he wanted was something to occupy him while he ate and considered his desperate, dwindling options.

Page one was devoted to a story about a fresh leadership challenge in the Labour Party. There was a piece about more economic woes in Russia, some scandal about financial waste at the BBC. There was no news of India. Until he reached page five. There, in a photograph at the top of the page, was Jyoti Dandavate, Indian High Commissioner, posing cheerfully with a group of smiling corporate executives. The headline said, INDIA SIGNS $1.1 BILLION DEFENSE PACT. There was an accompanying caption which outlined the broad details of a deal between the government of India and a consortium of British defense manufacturers to supply the Indian Navy with a new missile defense system.

Sansi looked back to the photograph. Antony Cardus was standing in the background. Sansi recognized him first because of the surgical dressing on the left side of his head.

Sansi stared. Cardus was smiling, a thin, smug, self-satisfied smile. He wasn't identified by name, only as one of a group of officials from the Commercial Management and Export Department of the Foreign and Commonwealth Office, which had been instrumental in putting the deal together.

Sansi put the paper down, his hands trembling.

It was a little after two in the afternoon when he left the Underground at Wapping and walked the short distance through the docklands to the Thames-side bunker that produced some of Britain's biggest newspapers: the *Times*, the *Sunday Times*, the *Sun* and the *News of the World*. He presented himself at the gatehouse and asked to see a reporter from the *Times*. He was shown into a small waiting room in a single-story red-brick building just inside the main gate.

A few minutes later an attractive female reporter appeared. Sansi thought she looked no more than nineteen. He spent half an hour explaining what information he had to offer, leaving out only a few key names. The young woman looked increasingly skeptical. Sansi was well aware how improbable it all must have sounded, especially to someone so young. He finished by promising that he had material proof hidden somewhere safe. She looked at him, unsure what to think.

"I think it might be a good idea if you checked with someone, perhaps, just a little higher up," Sansi said. He said it with a smile but she looked back at him, obviously insulted.

"I've been a news reporter for two years," she said. Then she got up. "Would you mind waiting a few minutes?" she asked.

"No." Sansi forced a smile. "Of course not."

Ten minutes later she reappeared to arrange a visitor's pass for him.

"My news editor would like you to come in for a chat," she said, no longer quite as certain of herself.

Sansi followed her down a narrow lane to a pair of heavy doors that led to an elevator. Minutes later, Sansi was in a small, glassed-in office in a corner of a busy newsroom with a red-haired man whose shirttail was hanging out of his trousers. He said his name was Pat Smythe and he stared at Sansi with undiluted curiosity.

"You say you've got stuff to back all this up?" he asked in a strong Cockney accent.

"It's in a safe place," Sansi answered. "Official interviews, coroner's reports, forensic evidence, everything. I could have it here in a few days."

"And you'd give us a sworn deposition to go with it."

"If that's what it took."

"Jesus." Smythe shook his head.

"I'm sorry?"

"If what you say is true, this is one of the biggest stories to walk in here all year . . . and I can't touch it."

Sansi breathed deeply. "Why not?"

"Because we just got D-noticed this morning."

Sansi flinched as though he'd been hit. "I thought a D-notice applied only in matters of national security," he said.

"It does," Smythe confirmed. "Unfortunately for you this one relates directly to your Mr. Antony Cardus. It landed on my editor's desk three hours ago. Anything and everything that might identify Mr. Cardus, or anything pertaining to his work, is banned from publication. Prohibited. Censored."

Sansi lowered his head. He was beaten.

"We had no idea what it was all about until you lobbed in," Smythe went on. "We did a name search but we couldn't turn up anything on Mr. Antony bleeding Cardus. Then you front up with this incredible story. Who is he?"

Sansi sighed and glanced around the office. "Have you got a copy of this morning's paper?"

"As a matter of fact . . ." Smythe reached behind him, pulled the top copy from a pile of newspapers and slid it across the desk.

Sansi opened the paper to page five and pointed out Cardus in the defense deal photograph.

"Bloody hell," Smythe breathed. "That's why they're classifying it as national security."

"How long can this D-notice stay in effect?" Sansi asked.

"They can renew it indefinitely." Smythe shrugged.

"And it applies to all newspapers, all radio stations, all television programs?"

"Everything. Covers the country like a blanket, mate. Anybody breaks it, they go to jail. Automatic."

"I thought this was a free country . . . with a free press."

"Oh, it is," Smythe sniffed. "As free as the government wants it to be. And they can make up their own minds about what is and what isn't a threat to national security. This bloke Cardus might not be important on his own but obviously he's connected to something that is. The Foreign Office would have to be behind this. They must have moved as soon as they got wind of what was going on. Somebody had to tip 'em off. You take this to anybody else before you came to us?"

"I went to New Scotland Yard yesterday."

"And what did they tell you?"

"They told me to go away. A superintendent from Special Branch—"

"Special Branch?" Smythe interrupted. "Well, that's it, isn't it? The gaff was up as soon as you went to them. They moved fast, though, got to give 'em credit for that. They knew there'd be publicity over this defense deal so they D-noticed everybody this morning. Not in time to stop this one picture in our paper, but he isn't identified, so it doesn't matter. He's protected now. Nobody can touch him. Nobody can say boo about this bloke anymore, without going to jail."

Smythe shrugged his shoulders to indicate how helpless he was. "Believe me," he went on, "if you could produce the hard evidence to back this up, like you say, I'd splash it right across page one. A bloke who kills people in a foreign country but the government won't let anybody touch him here? Story of the year, mate. Story of the year. But you're twenty-four hours too late, Inspector. If you'd come to us first, yesterday, instead of the police. Well . . ." He threw up his hands to indicate how Sansi had blundered.

Sansi smiled. "I thought I could trust the British police," he said.

"Yeah, well." Smythe shrugged. "We all used to think that, didn't we?"

Sansi nodded and got up to go.

Smythe stopped him. "There is one alternative," he said.

Sansi turned, waited.

"You could try breaking this story through a newspaper in another country, like the United States. Like *Spycatcher.* You remember that?"

Sansi nodded. He knew of the book that had been banned in Britain but published successfully in the United States instead, to the humiliation of the British government.

Smythe continued, "If we can break this story in the U.S.—and I just might be able to help you there, old son—if we can get a paper over there to run with it, we could stick this D-notice right up the government. We'd have to be bloody careful not to tip our hand in advance, mind you. We'd have to make sure nobody knew it was coming out, so the government couldn't pull the old-pals act with Uncle Sam or start slapping court injunctions all over the place. Then, *wham!* It's right there on the front page for the whole world to see. And there's nothing they can do about it except say, 'Whoops, frightfully sorry, chaps, slight error in judgment.' Then they have to put this bastard Cardus through the courts, which is what they should have done in the first place."

Sansi listened carefully. "You think the Americans would be interested in a story like this?"

Smythe threw his hands in the air. "Serial killer, international intrigue, governments of two countries conspiring to pervert the course of justice . . . I think they'd be shitting themselves to get their hands on it."

Sansi nodded. "I'll give it some thought," he said.

Smythe looked disappointed. He fumbled in his wallet and handed Sansi his business card. "Don't think about it too long," he warned. "You saw what happened when you waited twenty-four hours. Call me. There could be a few quid in this if we act smartly. For both of us. Okay?"

24

CARDUS HAD BEEN expecting the call from his boss all afternoon. Ever since the visit to Plymouth for the official signing of contracts and the picture in the *Times* the following day. There had been unspoken tensions that had nothing to do with the ceremony and Cardus sensed that something was coming. He was ready. The call came a little after five.

"Thank you for coming, Antony." John Gore, chief executive officer of the Commercial Management and Export Department welcomed Cardus into his office. Cardus smiled. A thin, ironic smile. As though he had any choice.

"This is Detective Superintendent Barrett." Gore introduced a second man. "From Special Branch," he added, almost as an afterthought.

Cardus shook hands and took Barrett in at a glance. Shrewd eyes. Good taste in clothes. Strong handshake—a little too strong. An executive cop. The kind who always thought they were smarter than they really were. Cardus sat down, watching Barrett watching him.

Gore wandered back behind his desk and sat down. He was a tall man with thick gray hair and an academic stoop. He wore navy-blue suspenders over his shirt. Striped shirt, white collar, old school tie. Marlborough. He came quickly to the point.

"We had to D-notice the entire bloody country on your behalf this morning, Antony. Any idea why?"

"Couldn't imagine, sir," Cardus answered. His voice sounded surprisingly deep and resonant. Barrett had expected a weedy man to have a weedy voice. Certainly

335

Cardus had a weedy handshake. But his voice sounded strong, controlled. It suggested hidden reserves.

"Perhaps you'd like to explain, Superintendent?"

Barrett nodded. He had been looking at the dressing on the left side of Cardus's head. "Spot of bother?" he asked.

"I was mugged last week," Cardus answered.

Barrett waited but Cardus didn't go into it any further. "Have you ever been to India, Mr. Cardus?"

"Yes."

"Often?"

"Three times: 1983, 1988 and last year."

"And what was the purpose of those visits?"

"The first was pleasure. I've always been interested in India. My grandfather was an administrator there when it was a colony. The last two occasions were mostly for business, for the department."

"Did your wife accompany you on any of these visits?" Barrett asked.

"No."

"Any particular reason why not?"

"She wouldn't go to India if you paid her."

Gore smiled slightly. "Antony put in a great deal of work on his own time during those visits," Gore interjected. "He really has been a big help to the branch in servicing our government contacts over there."

Barrett nodded. "Where did you go when you were in India, sir?"

Cardus thought for a moment. "Bombay, Goa, Hyderabad, New Delhi, Simla, Jaigapur, Agra . . . that's where the Taj Mahal is. The last two were purely for pleasure. That's it, I think."

"When you were there, did you ever engage in any activity that might have brought you to the attention of the local police authorities?"

"No." It was flat. Unequivocal.

"Are you sure, sir? You might like to take a moment to think about it."

Cardus smiled inwardly. He knew Barrett was bluffing.

The policeman might suspect something but proving it was a different matter. "There's nothing," he said, his voice almost toneless.

"You're quite sure about that, sir?"

"Yes."

"Mr. Cardus, have you ever engaged in any form of homosexual activity?"

"Certainly not." His voice showed just the right pitch of resentment. He was very good, Barrett had to concede.

"Are you familiar with a man called Coyarjee? Pratap Coyarjee?"

"It depends what you mean by familiar."

Barrett smiled. "Are you acquainted with him?"

"Yes. He is an executive at the State Film Center in Bombay."

"Are you also aware that he is an active homosexual?"

"I formed that impression, yes."

"What do you mean, formed?"

"He didn't try to hide it."

"You said formed?"

"Yes."

"In the past tense?"

"It's the impression he gave me when I met him."

"And how often was that, sir?"

"Twice."

"Do you recall which occasions they were?"

"The first time was in 1988. He arranged for me to tour the studios. It was actually arranged through the tourist office. It's something they do for all visiting government officials. The second time was last April. I was invited to a cocktail party on the set of a film they were making out there. Again, it's something they do for a lot of foreign visitors."

"Yes, sir." Barrett paused. "Did you meet someone by the name of Sanjay Nayak in Bombay?"

"I don't recognize the name."

"He was an actor at the Film City studios, I believe."

"Sorry."

"You didn't meet him at this party on the film set by any chance?"

"I might have, but I wouldn't necessarily have known. Superintendent, there were at least two hundred people at that party."

"So you don't remember this young man at all?"

"No."

"And you weren't aware that both he and Pratap Coyarjee were murdered at the time you were in Bombay?"

Cardus stared blankly at Barrett. "I'm sorry," he said, "did I hear you say . . . ?" His voice faltered disbelievingly.

Barrett waited.

"Superintendent," Gore interrupted. "When I agreed—"

"Please, sir." Barrett cut him off abruptly.

Cardus shook his head. "I had no idea. . . ."

"You didn't see anything in the newspapers at the time you were there?"

Cardus's pallid complexion seemed to have grown even paler. He fiddled nervously with his wedding ring. "That's . . . so shocking," he said. "I saw him only two months ago. . . ."

"And you didn't know anything about either murder until this moment?"

"I told you," Cardus answered, his voice less certain, "I flew to and from the major cities all the time. I must have missed it."

"Mr. Cardus, are you aware that there was a murder in every major city you visited in India, at exactly the same times you were there?"

A short, sharp breath of air escaped Cardus's lips. "You can't seriously be suggesting . . ."

"It is a remarkable series of coincidences."

"Superintendent . . ." Cardus paused—a man under intolerable pressure—struggled to compose himself, to regain the dignity of innocence. When he spoke again his voice sounded calmer, stronger. "The death rate in India is astronomical. I imagine the murder rate isn't far behind. You can't possibly hold me responsible for all the sorrows of India. I've visited at least twenty cities in the U.K. during the past two years. I imagine there have been a few bank robberies in all of them. Perhaps a few of them when I was there. Do you intend to hold me responsible for those too?"

Barrett looked unimpressed.

"This is absurd," Cardus sniffed. "This whole conversation . . ."

Barrett opened a briefcase between his feet, pulled out six enlarged color photographs and laid them on Gore's desk in front of Cardus. "Do you recognize the people in those photographs, Mr. Cardus?"

Cardus leaned forward, examined the pictures of himself talking to a number of different men outside The Marquess of Queensberry. In one of the photographs, two of the men had their arms around each other.

"Yes, of course I recognize myself."

"Do you know the other people in the pictures?"

"Some of them. I don't know any of them very well."

"Are they homosexual friends of yours, Mr. Cardus?"

Cardus looked away for a moment, his bony white face set, annoyed. "They very well could be homosexuals. I wouldn't call them friends of mine."

"How well do you know them, sir?"

"Not very well at all. I see them occasionally at one of the pubs where I call in for a drink."

"The Marquess of Queensberry?"

"Yes, that's it in the picture, behind."

"A known haunt of homosexuals?"

"I suppose so."

"You suppose so, Mr. Cardus?"

"I don't discriminate against homosexuals, Superintendent. I never have. If I want a drink at a pub that happens to be frequented by homosexuals I will drink there. I also drink at a pub called The Greyhound in Dulwich and another called The Lamb and Flag in Streatham. To the best of my knowledge both of them are known haunts of heterosexuals. I don't see any pictures of me there." He looked across at his boss. "May I ask why and where—"

"Do you often go to Islington for a drink, Mr. Cardus?" Barrett pressed him.

"No."

"Then how do you explain your regular weekly visits to The Marquess of Queensberry, sir? It's hardly on your way home, is it?"

Cardus shook his head as though irritated at having to explain the obvious to a simpleton. "I don't go to Islington for the purpose of drinking at The Marquess of Queensberry," he explained, enunciating every word carefully. "I go to browse along Islington High Street. There's a model shop I've been visiting there for years. . . ." He looked to Gore for help.

"A model shop?"

"Model airplanes, warships, that sort of thing. It's a hobby I've had since I was a boy. It might seem a little eccentric to you, Superintendent, but I doubt if it's illegal. You can check with the owner if you like. You can see very clearly in the pictures that I'm holding two shopping bags. One has a new kit that I had on order and bought last week, the other is fruit and vegetables. One shop is a known haunt of model builders, the other is a known haunt of vegetarians. To the best of my knowledge, Islington High Street is a known haunt of housewives. Really, Superintendent . . ."

He threw another beleaguered look at John Gore. "Sir, I'd like to know where these pictures came from. If someone is trying to blackmail me . . . The whole thing is patently absurd. . . ." He let the words hang in the air.

Barrett looked at him silently. Cardus looked back. He knew he might not have convinced the policeman. But he didn't have to. Barrett couldn't prove anything. None of them could. And as long as John Gore was still on his side . . .

"Antony." Gore leaned forward on his desk and regained control of the conversation. "Have you ever spoken to an Indian police inspector called Sansi?"

"No."

"He walked into New Scotland Yard two days ago. His credentials were genuine. Apparently he has been conducting an investigation into a series of murders of young homosexual men in India. He seemed quite convinced that you were involved somehow."

Cardus looked from one man to the other. "Sir . . ." he seemed lost for words. "I don't know how to begin to defend myself against such bizarre allegations. . . ." He slumped back in his chair, the portrait of a man defeated by absurdity. A man for whom mere words would never be enough to proclaim his innocence.

"It's all right, Antony," Gore calmed his bewildered employee. "We don't understand it either. And neither does the Indian government. They've disowned him and his investigation. The Indian High Commissioner asked Superintendent Barrett to take away the man's credentials. We thought that would be the end of it. But apparently he decided to stick around and make a bit of a nuisance of himself. He'd been following you around for a couple of weeks. He took these pictures. He's put together a case that he believes, even if no one else does. He probably even means well, poor beggar. Sounds a bit obsessive to me. Probably got some grudge against the British for God knows what reason. So many lunatics running around the world today. Who knows?"

Cardus sat silently, a nerve working in his jaw.

Gore continued, "The purpose of this discussion wasn't to accuse you or humiliate you in any way, Antony. We have to make sure you understand the importance of what we've done on your behalf and why. We have to be sure you hadn't got yourself involved, albeit indirectly, in something that might compromise the reputation of this department. This branch cannot risk even the appearance of impropriety, Antony. Especially at the moment. The contract with the Indian government means a lot of jobs in marginal constituencies. We couldn't risk any kind of a scandal at this time. We have no idea why this policeman from Bombay was seeking to discredit someone in this department exactly at this time—that's a matter for Special Branch to pursue—but we can't afford to take any chances. I hope you understand."

"Yes," Cardus nodded. "Of course, sir."

"Don't worry about it, Antony," Gore reassured him. "We're taking steps to make sure this Inspector Sansi doesn't cause us or his own government any further embarrassment. Consider it finished, there's a good chap. Oh, and if I were you I wouldn't be planning any more trips to India for a while. Not until this business has blown over, at any rate."

"No, sir. Thank you, sir."

Cardus nodded briefly at the superintendent, then got up and left the room. A small, tight smile had already begun to form on his lips before he had closed the office door. A delicious thrill of excitement coursed through his body as he walked back to his office. Even when they knew, there was nothing they could do. He had won. He was smarter than all of them.

General Spooner seemed to have aged in the few weeks Sansi had been at Goscombe Park. He slept longer during the daytime, and never left his room. Mrs. Chappel said he was eating less and he complained of the cold more, even though it was almost June and the weather had warmed considerably.

"I can't give him the kind of care he needs," she told Sansi after breakfast one morning. "He needs a nurse, a real nurse. But he won't go into a nursing home. Not that anyone can blame him for that. Mrs. Spooner does what she can to help. She reads the newspapers to him in the morning, that sort of thing. But Mr. Spooner is ... busy. He's always busy."

Sansi knew that Mrs. Chappel was being charitable to his half brother. The sooner the General died, the sooner Eric would control the estate and all its finances, and the happier he would be. Even though that would inevitably hasten the decline of Goscombe Park. The only reason the estate was still profitable at all, Sansi had learned, was because the General had hired an experienced manager. Eric was nominally in charge but in reality he was a part-time assistant who preferred to spend most of his time watching horses race at Epsom and Newmarket. According to Mrs. Chappel, Eric's dream was to turn Goscombe Park into a racing stud.

"It'll be the end of the place," she predicted. "And I don't think Brian and me will be staying on after the General's gone."

Sansi wondered if Mrs. Chappel was making a naive attempt to involve him in the domestic politics of Goscombe Park. To thwart Eric's ambition. But there was little Sansi could do to influence events there, he knew. Eric had the law on his side too. It only reinforced Sansi's feeling of powerlessness in the face of even the most banal kind of evil.

"Mrs. Chappel tells me you're a difficult patient," Sansi said, sitting down in the chair opposite his father.

"It's one of the few pleasures I have left," the General acknowledged.

"You've earned the right," Sansi added gently.

He studied his father carefully. The old man seemed withered and spent. His skin was the color and texture of old parchment and looked dead against the rich gloss of his blue silk dressing gown.

"You look dreadful," the General said. "Are you all right?"

Sansi smiled. He knew he looked wretched. He hadn't slept well in almost two weeks. There were thick pouches under his eyes and the bruise the scar man had given him near his left temple had turned a sickly, yellowish color.

"English weather," Sansi answered lamely.

"Your business here hasn't gone exactly as you had hoped?"

Sansi shook his head. "Governments never learn . . . and so history repeats itself. He's going to get away with it . . . again."

The General looked at his son, his once-blue eyes veined and glassy. "You can't . . . get around it somehow?"

"I've tried," Sansi said. "It's difficult to explain, but it's almost as if there is something wrong with the tapestry of reality itself. As if I've discovered a thread of evil that has been allowed to wind its way from one generation to the next . . . and there is nothing I nor anyone else can do to break it. And so it will go on. . . ."

The General tried to moisten his lips to talk. Sansi handed him a glass of water but the old man almost dropped it and Sansi had to hold it to his lips while he drank.

"My years in the army, my years in India, taught me a great deal about power," he began. "But nothing more important than how ephemeral all power is. We ruled India for two hundred years. We had an empire. Then we blinked and it was gone. One day I was a general in the British Army—a man with the power to order other men to their deaths. The day I retired, I became a nobody. Yesterday's man. No one had to pay me a moment's heed ever again. Do you know . . ." He brightened for a moment and tried to sit up in his chair. "A couple of years after I left the army I was in London, walking along Shaftsbury Avenue. Going to get measured for a new suit, I think. Two young officers passed me, lieutenants in the Scots Greys. I stopped them and started bawling them out. Do you know why?" he asked, chuckling at the memory. "Because they forgot to salute me. Because they didn't know who I was. I completely forgot I was in civvies. Forgot that I wasn't a general anymore. Made a complete bloody fool of myself."

He paused for a moment to catch his breath. "I think about things like that all the time now. I should never have come back to England, George. I should never have left your mother and come back to Audrey. There was nothing for me here. What has been the point of it all, George? Things like duty and honor which seemed to mean so much at the time? What have I gained from any of it? I have a daughter who can't be bothered visiting me. I have a son who can't wait for me to die. My grandchildren are at boarding school so I never see them. And the only son I can be proud of lives halfway around the world."

Sansi leaned forward and touched his father gently on the arm.

"The world is full of injustice, George, large and small. Don't waste your life trying to correct it all. You can't. Look at you: worn out, beaten . . . and still a young man. You've given twenty years of your life to a profession that would disown you in an instant. Wouldn't even give you a second thought. The world can be a cruel and unjust place, George. That is the way it has always been. Don't waste your life trying to change it. If there is only one piece of advice I can give you, it is to urge you not to do what I did. To hell with duty, George. Find what will make you happy."

The old man's voice faded. He closed his eyes and shrank farther into the chair, exhausted. Sansi squeezed his father's arm, unable to speak.

They stayed like that for a long time. It was only when his father's wheeze had settled into a soft, rhythmic snore that Sansi got up to leave. When he reached the door, he hesitated. He turned to look back at the old man, alone in the gloom. Suddenly he was filled with foreboding. He was afraid to leave. Something told Sansi that he was never going to see his father again.

Sansi hadn't intended to go back to Azalea Crescent. There was nothing more he could do to Cardus, except perhaps . . .

The idea of taking matters into his own hands had occurred to him many times over the past few days and he had rejected it each time. Now it was getting harder to discount. And somehow, as though pulled by an irresistible magnetic force, he felt himself drawn back to Cardus's nondescript red-brick house in south London.

This time he didn't try to hide. He walked slowly up Azalea Crescent, past the postage-stamp-sized gardens, the severely barbered privet hedges, the Toyota family wagons, the occasional ten-year-old on a skateboard. The houses all looked the same. The paintwork on the doors and fences and the floral pattern of the curtains in the windows might be different. But they were all the same.

The first time, Sansi walked along the footpath on the opposite side of the street to Cardus's house. He walked slowly, hands in pockets, as though he were out for an early-evening stroll. Cooking smells gusted from open kitchen windows. They all smelled the same. On his second pass he was walking more quickly. He had made up his mind.

He kept number twenty-four firmly fixed in his sight as he walked back down the street. He took his hands out of his pockets. His palms were sweaty and he wiped them against his trousers. He was almost there. He started across the street, his fingers opening and closing at his sides.

Sansi had one single thought in his mind. He wanted Cardus to know that he knew. He wanted to see fear in Cardus's face, even if he had to put it there himself. Even if he had to squeeze it into him with his own hands. He reached out to open the front gate.

Car doors opened behind him. He heard the sound of running feet pounding on the pavement. An immense weight descended on him and Sansi felt himself crushed against the footpath. Several pairs of hands held on to him, pulled at his clothes, tore open his pockets.

"Put his hands behind him," a man said. A slight Scots accent, Sansi thought. He was helpless. All he could see was pavement. And there was nothing he could do to resist. His arms were wrenched behind his back and he felt a pair of cold metal bracelets snap around his wrists.

"Put him in the car."

Sansi felt himself lifted off the ground as though he weighed nothing. He was half carried, half thrown into the back of a black Ford Granada with the rear passenger door open. It had been there all the time, Sansi realized, but he hadn't noticed anybody in it. Then again, he hadn't really been looking. Big dark shapes bobbed all around him, men grunting, swearing. Sansi let himself be carried along.

He seemed to float into the back of the car. A man jumped in on either side of him, jammed him down into the seat.

"Who are you?" Sansi asked, surprised by his own calmness. "Where are you taking me?"

"You're going home, son," said the man sitting next to him. The man with the Scots accent. "Now sit still, shut up and behave yourself."

Two more men climbed into the front. The engine started and the car sped down the street, carrying Sansi away from 24 Azalea Crescent forever.

"Special Branch?" Sansi asked.

No one answered. Sansi shifted position, trying to ease the discomfort in his arms. An hour later he recognized the approach to Heathrow Airport. Still no one spoke. The car turned down a service road before the main terminal and stopped at a small door in the side of a large building. Sansi was taken out and half carried up a flight of stairs to a brilliantly lit room where a number of men and women in immigration department uniforms stared at him. He was taken into a small room and left alone in a chair, his hands still cuffed behind him, the door locked. He lost track of time. After what felt like a couple of hours the door opened and the two men who had sat with him in the back of the car appeared with an immigration officer.

"George Louis Sansi," the immigration officer said, "I have a deportation order in your name. We can get you on a British Airways flight leaving in two hours. If you give me your word that you'll behave yourself, we'll remove the handcuffs and you can complete your journey under your own steam. Otherwise you'll be escorted to Bombay by a police officer and the handcuffs will stay on until you're handed over to the immigration authorities there. Do you understand?"

"Gentlemen," Sansi began, trying to inject a note of reason into the situation. "I don't believe I have broken any of the laws of Great Britain."

"You must have broken something, sunshine," the immigration officer replied amiably. "Your government is quite happy for us to send you home, any way we choose. So, what's it to be? The easy way or the hard way?"

Sansi smiled. "I've always preferred the cabin service on British Airways."

Joint Commissioner Jamal was waiting at Sahar. Not Annie. She wouldn't know he was back until later. Jamal smoothed the way through immigration, then walked Sansi out to the front of the terminal where a car and driver were waiting.

"You can't do it on your own," Jamal had lightly admonished him. "You cannot go outside the system. You have to know how to get what you want from the inside. And sometimes you have to know when to let go. That is your only mistake, Sansi. Tenacity is all very well in a policeman, but there are times when tenacity becomes blind stupidity, and you have to know when to stop. . . ."

Sansi smiled. Jamal had to make sure he had Sansi's silence now, so there could be no possibility of political embarrassment later.

"Did they send my warrant card back?" Sansi asked, his voice pleasant.

Jamal shrugged. "It will come back in a few days. It is not important. I will authorize a new card for you."

"You're going to take care of me?" Sansi looked at his boss.

"Of course." Jamal's handsome face creased into a reassuring smile. "You're one of the best officers I have. I always look after my men. Losing one case is not the end of the world, Sansi. I know it feels bad now, but wait, you'll feel better in time."

Sansi suppressed a small laugh.

"What?" Jamal asked, his eyes warily curious.

"Corruption," Sansi said.

"What corruption?"

Sansi looked at his boss. "It doesn't have to be a plot or a conspiracy at all, does it? It doesn't have to be an orchestrated thing. Sometimes it can just . . . happen."

He paused. Jamal waited. The driver held the door of Jamal's car open.

"Sometimes," Sansi added, "a number of corrupt forces can come together, almost by accident, and create a great injustice like . . . a spontaneous combustion. Corruption doesn't have to be orchestrated. When the institutions are weak, it just . . . happens, doesn't it? All on its own. And if you know that—you can get away with anything."

"Inspector," Jamal said, his tone not unkind, "you're tired. Get in the car."

Sansi took a deep breath, put his hands in his pockets and shook his head. "I don't belong in that car," he said.

Jamal looked at him. "I'll drop you home, you'll take a couple of days off, I'll speak to a few people, I'll get you a new warrant card . . ."

"Keep it," Sansi interrupted. "Keep all of it."

He turned and began to walk away, toward a nearby line of taxis.

"Inspector . . ." Jamal called after him.

Sansi glanced back over his shoulder. "It's Mr. Sansi to you," he said.

25

THE LETTER ARRIVED almost two years after Cardus had the
interview with his head of department and the superintendent from Special Branch. It came to the office, marked
special delivery and postmarked Bombay.

Cardus closed the door to his office, sat down and
opened it. There was a letter on notepaper bearing the title
and crest of the Bombay Chamber of Commerce.

Dear Mr. Cardus,

Greetings on behalf of the executive committee of
The Chamber of Commerce of Bombay.

It is with great pleasure that we extend a warm invitation to yourself and your spouse to please attend
the Chamber's 49th annual conference to be held at
the Oberoi Hotel, Bombay, April 14–17.

The theme of the conference this year is to be "India in the 21st Century." Speakers will come from a
wide segment of government and private enterprise in
many countries.

In recognition of your great contribution toward
trade relations between India and the United Kingdom
we are asking if you would be so kind as to prepare a
50-minute address to the conference on the aforemen-
tioned theme.

We would be most in gratitude if you could telephone or transmit by facsimile your confirmation of
acceptance before the date of March 31 so that we

may schedule you to be included among our list of esteemed speakers.

Cardus smirked at the mangled English. It was typical of his experience with Indian executives. He looked at the date of the conference again. It was five weeks away. He had only a few weeks to make arrangements if he wanted to go. The next paragraph made up his mind.

Once we are in receipt of your acceptance we shall forward to you, by return mail, two first-class air tickets, London to Bombay return, for the use of yourself and your spouse. The tickets will be open dated for your convenience. Accommodations will be provided by the Chamber at the Oberoi for five nights, from April 12 to 17.

Mr. Pritam Prakash,
Assistant Executive Officer.

Cardus sat back in his chair, an ironic smile on his face. Almost two years and there had been nothing. Not a single comeback, not a breath of scandal, not a whisper of reproach from anyone, anywhere. It was exactly as he had thought. No one cared. The victims were nobodies. Less than nobodies. They weren't worth the price of a trial, let alone the price of a defense contract. Even their own people didn't care about them. The two or three people who had known had been eager to put it behind them. Special Branch hadn't been able to drop it fast enough. His former boss, John Gore, had been promoted to another ministry and now worked in another building. Cardus had even managed to access the personnel records to check on his own file. The only mention of the D-notice referred to the need for the overall security of the missile contract he had helped negotiate. No one remembered anything else. And if they knew, if they suspected anything at all . . . they didn't care. It had made him feel invincible. It was the feeling of raw power. The power to do anything to anybody. The mere recollection prompted a thrill of satisfaction, the kind of thrill that evolved rapidly into something else. A kind of longing. Recognition of a need that had long been denied. Cardus savored it a while, tasted it. He had been highly conscientious these past two years. He was owed six weeks' vacation time. The new department head wouldn't have to know where he was going. He had heard nothing about the conference on the grapevine. That told him something. Despite the delusions of the Bombay Chamber of Commerce, their conference held a low priority on the world conference schedule. That suited Cardus perfectly. He wouldn't have to alert Delhi. He would travel on his private passport and leave his diplomatic passport at home. No one would have to know.

It was a little after three in the afternoon when Cardus picked up the phone and asked the operator to get him the number on the letterhead. A few minutes later he found himself speaking with Mr. Prakash's secretary. She proved unexpectedly efficient. Perhaps it had something to do with the slight American accent he detected. He asked her and she told him she had gone to college in the States. Cardus complimented her on her professionalism and said he would fax a copy of his acceptance within twenty-four hours.

A week later the tickets arrived, as promised. Cardus smiled. One for now. One for later.

The Air India 747 had to battle its way through thick rainclouds to reach Sahar International Airport. The monsoon had arrived early this year. He could see it coming down in drenching gray sheets outside the terminal as he went through the laborious process of clearing customs and immigration. As usual there was a riot under way in the terminal. Or what looked like a riot. It was only the usual melee of disembarking passengers, hordes of predatory money changers, taxi drivers, beggars and hustlers. It started the moment you set foot in the country. The only difference this time was that there was a gray, sodden look about everything and everyone looked damp, either from sweat or from the rain.

Cardus realized he should have worn something other than his white cotton suit. It already looked slept in. Not that it mattered. He would have it cleaned and pressed at the hotel. He always believed that it paid to arrive at airports looking well dressed. Especially in places like India. The more important you were, the more they bowed and scraped and the more quickly you passed through all the nonsense.

At last he received his final stamp, put his two leather bags on a trolley and pushed his way out into the riot. Immediately he was assailed by a clamoring crowd of pests and parasites. Cardus jabbed his trolley forward, pushing people out of the way, running over bare feet, cursing at them. It was the only way. He looked around, irritably scanning the faces of the pressing crowd. The secretary at the Chamber of Commerce had told him somebody would be there to meet him.

Then he saw someone. A man holding up a piece of cardboard with the name "A. Cardus" scrawled on it. Cardus raised his hand and snapped his fingers to attract the man's attention but it was useless in such a throng. He swiveled the trolley viciously and barged the rest of the way through the crowd. Suddenly he realized the man had seen him coming. The man smiled. A strange, cool sort of smile, Cardus thought. Then he was struck by the man's eyes. They were blue. How peculiar, he thought. He felt sure something like that must be impossible.

"You're looking for me, I believe," Cardus said, intensifying his deep baritone to cut through the shrill roar that washed over them.

"Yes. Welcome back to Bombay, Mr. Cardus," the man said. "Would you mind looking this way for the camera, please?"

Cardus hesitated, confused. A man with a camera lunged forward and a light bulb flashed in Cardus's face. It annoyed him. All he wanted was to get out of this mayhem

and into the air-conditioned sanctuary of his hotel room
where he could have a shower and a stiff drink.

"That's for the *Times of India*," said a red-haired woman
who wore a sari but spoke with an American accent. "This
one is for the *LA Times*."

The light bulb flashed again. Cardus blinked the neon
snowflakes out of his eyes. "Are you Mr. Prakash?" he
asked the blue-eyed man, annoyance breaking the surface
of his voice.

The man ignored his question. "This is Inspector
Chowdhary of the Bombay police," he answered instead.

A tall, somber-looking man in civilian clothes stepped
forward. Cardus paused, ran the name through his mental
index, but it meant nothing to him. Warning lights flashed
inside his head.

"Look here," Cardus said, no longer concealing his anger. "I'm a little tired, if you don't mind. I asked you if you
were Mr. Prakash."

Cardus felt himself jostled by the crowd. People were
gathering, attracted by the camera and the flashing lights,
wondering who Cardus was to merit such attention. Cardus
frowned. It was never hard to draw a crowd in India. He
hated crowds. He had the disturbing sensation that things
were slipping out of his control. "I asked . . ."

"No," the blue-eyed man cut him off. "My name is not
Prakash. My name is Sansi. George Sansi. I am an attorney
at law."

Cardus froze. Suddenly none of it made sense. He looked
from one face to another. A sea of staring brown faces was
crowding in on him.

The tall man who had been introduced as a police inspector gripped Cardus by the arm. "Antony Cardus," he
said loudly, "I am placing you under arrest for the murder
of Sanjay Nayak."

Cardus recoiled, tried to pull away. The sea of faces
closed in on him. Accusing, hostile, Indian faces.

"Take your hands off me," he protested, his voice rising.
Then he remembered. Sansi was the name of the policeman

who had followed him to London. He hadn't been able to arrest Cardus there. And now, after two years, he was here, at the airport, waiting, threatening . . .

Suddenly Cardus understood. It was a trap. All of it. The letter. The conference. The free air tickets. The red-haired bitch with the American accent. She was the woman he'd spoken to on the phone. They were all part of it. They had lured him back to Bombay after two long years to seek their retribution. The pictures were for the newspapers here and abroad, to make sure that the story of his arrest got out before anyone had time to save him. To tell the story of his crimes all around the world so that this time, no one in government would dare try to help him. It was a trap and he had flown into it with his eyes wide open, propelled by the urgency of his own dark needs.

Cardus looked around wildly. There had to be people who would help him. It was a major international airport. Airports were full of government people. All he had to do was attract the attention of someone important, someone who would notify the British authorities so they could put an end to this madness. Suddenly, through the jostling ranks of people all around him, he saw white faces. Friendly, familiar white faces, less than twenty yards away. A British Airways flight crew. They would help him.

"Help me, please!" he shouted in their direction. They didn't hear him. Chowdhary grabbed his arm harder and pulled him. Cardus saw a uniformed policeman with him. Then another. He wrenched his arm free and threw himself into the besieging crowd, trying to batter a way through to his fellow Britons.

"You there," he shouted, a note of fear entering his voice for the first time. "Help me, for God's sake! I'm British. Please, do something. Call someone."

They heard, turned to look at him. He tried to push his way toward them. A flurry of hands grabbed him, pulled him back. He felt himself being dragged toward the exit doors, toward the dark drenching grayness outside.

"Please . . . !" His voice rose above the roar of the mob,

forcing a sudden lull. The British flight crew hesitated. They saw Cardus and they saw the men in police uniforms closing in on him. They looked at each other, exchanged a few words. One of them shrugged, then they continued on their way. Leaving him.

Cardus screamed in fury and despair. The doors opened and he felt himself being dragged outside. He twisted and turned to shake the clutching hands off his body, then he threw himself to the ground, lashing out with his feet and his fists, snarling and spitting like a cornered animal at all those who closed in on him. The crowd recoiled in shock. It was all Cardus needed. He scrambled desperately back to his feet, bent low, and fought his way through the pressing bodies. He found himself on the road, sprinting through the pouring rain between crawling ranks of taxis and motor rickshaws.

All he had to do was find another entrance to the terminal. There had to be someone in there. Some isolated patch of civilization where he would be safe. He saw Sansi running along the footpath in front of the terminal, keeping pace with him. He swore to himself. Spittle ran down his chin, mixing with the streaming rain. If only he could get his hands on the razor in his luggage, he thought. If only he could have a few minutes alone with Sansi. He looked over his shoulder and saw the policeman, Chowdhary, gaining on him with long, loping strides. He was followed by two policemen and behind them a crowd: taxi drivers, rickshaw drivers, beggars—all joining in the chase.

The road veered sharply away from the terminal. Cardus hesitated. There was a high, chain-link fence topped by barbed wire separating the road from the tarmac and the administration buildings beyond. He couldn't make it. To the right was a sea of slum shanties. Brown, sodden hovels, cringing beneath the relentless tattoo of the monsoon. He ran between two slow-moving cars. A taxi swerved, skidded, collided with the car in front. Horns sounded, people yelled curses at him. He had to double back, he knew. Cut through the slum village, lose them in the maze of alleyways, get back into the terminal. He could see its lights, shining brightly through the rain. If only he could find a way back. Someone would help him. Someone always had.

He leapt over the curb and slid down a muddy, garbage-strewn embankment into the slum village. He slipped and skidded the last few feet on his back. When he hit the bottom he scrambled back to his feet and took the nearest alleyway. An open drain poured down the middle. His feet sank deeply into the ooze. Cardus sobbed. The black, stinking mud sucked at his feet, slowing him, trapping him. He looked behind. Scores of people scrambled down the embankment after him, screaming, waving their fists.

He slipped, fell forward into the filth, struggled back to his feet and kept running. A bony mongrel appeared suddenly in front of him, bared its fangs, snapped at him. He struggled on, running, falling, stumbling. The thick mud sucked a shoe from his foot. He saw small, curious faces watching him from the darkened hovels that surrounded him. He cursed helplessly at them. Hating them. Hating their uselessness, their inability to help him. He felt himself losing strength. He came to a narrow intersection and staggered to the right. Something bit deep into his unshod foot. Glass or metal. He screamed with the pain, fought it down, kept running. A pathetic, shambling limp.

Cardus looked down at himself. His white suit had vanished beneath a thick coating of slum filth. He was covered in it, from head to toe, no longer recognizable as a white man. A crowd of angry faces spilled into the alley ahead of him, cutting him off. He was trapped. He hesitated, looked around wildly, plunged through a narrow slit between two shanties. The ground dived suddenly beneath him. He felt himself sliding, losing his footing, scrabbling for a handhold at the ramshackle huts around him. Lumps of sodden palm thatch came away in his hands. Suddenly he saw the flooded creek beneath him. A deep, narrow torrent filled with frothing brown water and dark, swirling shapes. Logs, tires, pieces of plastic, garbage. Rats.

He screamed and plummeted in. He felt himself go

under. Something hit him hard in the ribs and then the current grabbed him. He fought his way to the surface, gasping for air, flailing desperately in an attempt to grab on to something. But the sides of the creek were slick and muddy. He felt himself rolling, went under again. He struggled back to the surface, opened his mouth too soon. Thick brown sludge rushed down his throat. He broke surface again, gagging. He tasted excrement.

He fought hopelessly to keep his head above water. Swallowed more filth. The creek turned, widened, narrowed, and turned again. The momentum of the floodwater picked up. Cardus felt his strength melt away. It was over, he knew—in a few tortured moments his life would come to an end . . . in the gutters of a squalid Bombay slum.

The water spun him around again and he saw himself being carried toward a kind of dam. A fat metal pipe straddled the creek, supported by spindly metal legs set in concrete posts. The posts had trapped some of the larger pieces of debris and formed a kind of sluice, squeezing the water into foamy jets in the remaining open spaces. Logs, branches, plastic bottles and empty oil cans jostled crazily in a tangled web of wire and nylon rope snagged around the concrete posts, fighting to get through the narrow open spaces. Cardus felt himself being sucked down into the makeshift sluice and then he slammed into something solid. He scrabbled desperately for a handhold with broken, bleeding fingers. He caught something. It held and he wrapped both his arms tightly around one of the posts supporting the pipe. The rest of his body twirled in the current like a windsock. Broken shards of wood and metal battered him in the maelstrom, tearing at his clothes, stripping him naked. Something scrabbled across the top of his head and bit him. A rat. Cardus sobbed, tried to pull himself up to grab hold of the pipe. The pipe was too wide, too slippery. The rushing water sucked him back down again.

He heard people shouting nearby and he looked up. There were shapes moving on both sides of the creek. He could just make out their faces through the downpour.

"Hold on," a voice called to him. "We'll throw you a rope."

It was Sansi.

Cardus sagged, his head drooped to his chest. The current sucked hard at him again and he grabbed on tighter, more by reflex than desire.

They were offering him a choice of deaths. Death by hanging. Death in an Indian jail. Or death now.

Sansi called to him again from the creek bank. Cardus looked up. Sansi's hand moved and a length of blue nylon rope snaked across the creek toward Cardus. Cardus turned away. He felt the rope snap across his shoulders, then it was plucked away by the water. He could have grabbed it if he had tried.

Sansi pulled the rope back in and let it hang loosely in his hand by his side.

"What is he doing?" Annie Ginnaro shouted above the roar of the rushing creek.

"He's decided to die," Sansi said. Then he was aware of a small, thin man tugging at his elbow. Sansi looked down.

"I could get to him, sahib," the man said. "The water does not frighten me."

Sansi looked at the man. He seemed familiar.

"I am Mollaji, sahib," he said.

Sansi remembered. The *kuli* who had recovered Sanjay Nayak's mutilated body from Lake Vihar two years earlier.

Mollaji had seen the commotion in the airport terminal, where he had worked for the past two years with his new motor rickshaw. Like everyone else he had wandered over to see what the fuss was about. He had recognized the blue-eyed police inspector first; then the beautiful red-haired American reporter. Somehow they were both connected to the Englishman in the white suit. But then the Englishman had run away and Mollaji had allowed himself to be carried along by the pursuing crowd.

Sansi put his hand on Mollaji's shoulder and shook his head. "Your life is worth more than his," he said.

There was a sudden shout from the crowd. Sansi looked

up. Cardus could hold on no more. He was slipping. Slowly
his arms uncoiled from the rusty metal post and then he
was gone, snatched by the current. He disappeared beneath
the water but reappeared a moment later, snagged like another piece of debris in the web of tangled rope and wire
that stretched across the creek, bulging like a fishing net
between the legs of the metal pipe.

"Oh God," Annie Ginnaro mumbled and turned away.

Sansi stared numbly, unable to take his eyes away from
the dreadful spectacle of Cardus dying. A length of nylon
rope had looped around his head, forming a kind of noose.
As the current tried to pull him downstream, the noose
tightened, slowly strangling him. Sansi, Chowdhary, Mollaji
and all the others watched in silence, unable to help.

Cardus arched his back, struggled feebly to free his en-
snared arms and pull the tightening rope from his neck, but
he had nothing left. The rope tightened. Cardus's eyes
started to bulge, his mouth opened, his tongue protruded
and his face turned a dark bluish gray. Then he went limp
and the last breath of life seemed to drain visibly from his
tortured body.

Sansi turned, put his arm around Annie and guided her
away from the side of the creek. She went willingly, her
face buried in Sansi's shoulder, eager to put the torment of
the past few years behind them at last.

In the distance Sansi thought he heard the rumble of the
surf. The sound of the ocean embracing the land as the city
yielded to the power of the monsoon and cleansed itself of
all its sins.

Available now in bookstores
everywhere.
Published in hardcover
by Fawcett Books.

THE GANJA COAST

by Paul Mann

Read on for a sneak preview of
THE GANJA COAST . . .

PREM GUPTA'S SMOKE-BLUE CONTESSA nudged its way through the heavy traffic on Heliodoro Salgado Road until Gupta grew impatient with their slow progress and told his driver to pull over. He and Drew got out of the car and continued on foot, with Gupta's two goons following a few paces behind.

It was a little after eleven and the streets of Panjim were raucous with vice and commerce. The stores were all open, their brightly lit windows full of cheap jewelry, electronic junk, and trashy souvenirs. The *tavernas* and restaurants were crowded, spilling laughter, loud music, and clouds of marijuana smoke into the fumey night air. All along the street hustlers, beggars, and pimps harried the passing parade of tourists the way wild dogs would harry a herd of cattle.

Gupta led the way to the end of the block, then turned down a gloomy backstreet. In Bombay it would have been jammed with slum shanties, but because Panjim was small and prosperous, it was almost empty except for a few scavenging dogs and the odd group of men engaged in something illicit. There were houses on both sides of the street, most of them converted into offices and small businesses with apartments over the top, where the occupants could be seen through open windows eating, drinking, laughing, arguing—acting out the intimacies of their lives in public. Occasionally the back door of a taverna would open and a kitchen wallah would step outside to smoke a *bidi* or decant a bucket of swill into an overflowing garbage bin.

The houses were all two or three stories high, old town villas painted brown and blue or rusty red and linked together in a haphazard way, so that their rooftops lurched and swooped into each other at all different heights and angles. With their painted exteriors and brilliantly lit interiors, they looked like a chain of paper lanterns. It could have been the waterfront in Lisbon rather than India.

Drew tried to project an aura of calm, but inwardly he was afraid. If Gupta wanted to kill him, it would happen something like this—lured to some squalid backstreet under the guise of business as usual, then a sudden and unpleasant death. His fingers wandered nervously over the heavy brass buckle on his belt, which could be twisted and jerked loose to reveal a short knife blade. Its complete inadequacy under the circumstances only added to his fear. He shouldn't have come. He had miscalculated badly. His early-warning system, usually reliable, had let him down this time. His relationship with Gupta had always been fractious, and now Gupta had grown tired of him and elected to teach him a lesson. Drew thought about making a run for it. It would be better to risk making a fool of himself than to tough it out and wind up dead.

A raw-ribbed dog darted in front of them and lunged at something in the shadows. There was a scuttling sound, a high-pitched squeal, then the dog reappeared with a rat twitching in its jaws. Gupta gave Drew an amused glance. Drew looked straight ahead, his muscles tense, ready to run.

At last they came to a small print shop with a solid-looking door at the side. The shop was closed, but Gupta banged on the door hard. There was a moment's delay, then the door opened a crack and a man's face appeared—thin, dissipated, and wearing a ragged turban. He knew Gupta and opened the door wide, pressing his hands together and murmuring the words *"Namaste sahib"* over and over. Gupta told the two goons to wait outside and stepped into the shop. Drew hesitated, peered through the open doorway, and saw an empty hall lit by a single lightbulb. Then he looked at the goons. He was relieved that Gupta was leaving them outside. Maybe his instincts had been right after all. Maybe there was no danger. Maybe Gupta was only playing with him, the way he always did. Drew's instincts had always served him well in the past. He summoned up all his nerve and followed Gupta into the building.

The hall was dingy and bare and smelled of machine oil. There was a door to the right that seemed to lead into the print shop and a narrow staircase directly in front of them. The doorman shut the door behind them and pointed to the stairs. Gupta went first, with Drew a short distance behind. When they were out of sight, the doorman squatted back down on the bottom step, took a *bidi* out of his shirt pocket, and lit it.

At the top of the stairs was a high-ceilinged, poorly lit corridor that ran toward the front of the building with two or three doors on each side, all of them closed. Drew assumed they were in a private apartment over the print shop, but the shop only occupied the back half of the building. There was no indication of what was at the front. Gupta kept going toward a door at the end of the corridor. He turned the handle and the door opened onto a room that was in total darkness. He turned and beckoned impatiently for Drew to follow. Again Drew hesitated, his fingers clasped around the belt buckle.

"What's going on here, man? What is this place?" He tried to sound calm, but he could hear the fear in his voice.

"Shut up," Gupta whispered. "I want you to see something."

Drew moved slowly forward. His legs felt weak and wooden. Sweat poured down his back, soaking his T-shirt and the waistband of his jeans. He was within a few feet of the open door when he realized that the room was not completely dark. There was a pale yellow glow at floor level, a window of some kind with a light behind it. Drew looked quickly around the room and saw the outline of some furniture—junk piled in a corner, a sofa, and a few straight-backed metal chairs arranged in front of the window to form a kind of viewing gallery. The only figure visible seemed to be Gupta.

"Come in and close the door," Gupta said. "And don't make any noise."

It took every last bit of nerve that he possessed, but Drew did as he was told. With the door closed, the room became dark and threatening, and Drew felt vulnerable again.

"Sit down and watch," Gupta said. "And whatever happens, you don't say or do anything."

Gupta moved to a chair at the far side of the window and sat down with his back to Drew, telling him there was nothing to fear. The fear crested in Drew's throat, then subsided again. He felt his way numbly through the darkness and took the seat next to Gupta. Then he looked down at the window at his feet.

It wasn't a window at all, he realized, but a glass-paneled louver, one of many that would allow cool air to circulate from the downstairs of the house to the upstairs. The building had once been a commodious town house owned by some Portuguese grandee, though it had long since been bastardized and partitioned into numerous shops and apartments.

Drew tensed as Gupta leaned toward him in the darkness.

"If I wanted to have you killed," Gupta said, "I wouldn't go to this much trouble."

Despite his fear, Drew smiled. His instincts were right. Gupta had only been playing with him. But his nerve had held and Gupta still didn't know how close Drew had come to running.

He turned his attention to the window at his feet and found himself looking into a bare-walled room with a single door, no windows, and no furniture except a single mattress on the floor. The distant hum of the city told him the room was situated in the middle of the house, which made it virtually soundproof. There was a man in the room, sitting cross-legged on a thin black cushion with his back to the wall facing the door. Drew could not see his face because it was obscured by a large, grayish turban with a puggaree that hung down his back. He was dressed in a white *kurta dhoti*, the shirt and loincloth favored by traditional Hindus. His bony hands were folded comfortably in his lap, the fingernails a bright pink against skin the color of jute. At his side was a stick with a cushioned handle at one end. It looked like a crutch, though it was only a couple of feet long. In front of him, on the floor, was a crumpled burlap bag.

Drew stared at the bag. Something inside it stirred.

"Goddamn . . ." Drew said. "What is it?"

Gupta reached over to him and squeezed his arm hard. Then he jabbed a finger at the window, and suddenly Drew understood. The louvers were open slightly. Anything that was said in this darkened room could be heard downstairs. And everything that was said downstairs could be heard above.

If the man in the room below had heard, it didn't show. He remained quite still, like a guru or a swami, meditating. Drew settled down to wait. He would show them. He could wait, too. However long it took.

After a while the door downstairs opened and a man dressed like a house servant appeared. He padded across the tiled floor on bare feet, whispered something to the swami, then turned and went back out of the room. The swami gave no indication that he had seen or heard anything. A few more minutes passed and then the servant reappeared with two men in their twenties who looked like *kulis*. Their clothes were dirty and their hair was long and matted. Whatever money they made wasn't spent on their appearance. The servant spoke softly to them and they slipped off their sandals, pressed their hands together, and bobbed respectfully to the swami. He did not acknowledge them in any way.

"Who are they?" Drew whispered.

"Laborers," Gupta answered. "They have come down from Bombay to work on the railway."

Drew leaned forward so he could see better, his fear supplanted by the morbid fascination of the voyeur.

The servant set two more cushions on the floor in front of the swami, one in front of the other, then stood back against the door. One of the *kulis* took off his shirt, folded it, and put it on the mattress like a pillow. Then, barechested, he stepped across to the first cushion and sat down, cross-legged, so that he faced the swami, the burlap bag between them. The other *kuli* followed and squatted on the cushion behind his friend.

For a long time no one moved and no one made a sound. All three men remained perfectly still with their heads slightly bowed. Then the murmur of a chant began to emanate from the swami, a high-pitched nasal mantra that Drew had not heard before, either in the ashram at Pune or the temple at Madurai. He strained to hear the words, but the swami ran them together so rapidly they blurred into an unintelligible drone. Drew thought he heard the name Ananta. He listened closely and this time he was certain. The swami said the Ananta several times, but repeated it so quickly it was almost indistinguishable through the monotone.

Drew recognized the name. Ananta was the many-headed cobra in Hindu mythology, the force of eternal life.

The swami moved for the first time, precisely and fluidly. He gripped the bottom two corners of the burlap bag, shook it gently, and lifted it into the air. A tightly coiled cobra slid out onto the floor in front of him. The swami put the bag down at his side and picked up the stick with the padded handle. He held it by the shaft with the handle pointed away from him. The snake remained motionless. The swami reached forward with his free hand and prodded the cobra out of its defensive coil. The snake reacted sluggishly, reluctantly, and did not attempt to strike. Instead it rippled the length of its shiny black body and started to move across the floor, away from the swami, looking for a means of escape. The swami wielded the stick quickly and deftly. He aimed the handle at a point just behind the reptile's head and pinned it to the floor. This time the snake reacted angrily. Its thick body whipped and thrashed as it tried to get away. From his position overhead Drew heard the harsh scrape of the cobra's scales against the floor. Still, no one else had moved. Drew watched, transfixed. He knew what was about to happen and still he couldn't quite bring himself to believe it.

The swami kept the cobra's head pinned to the floor beneath the padded handle of the stick then reached forward with his other hand. He spanned the snake with his thumb and forefinger and ran his hand up the warm dry body until he came to the flat bulge of the head. He stopped for a moment. Slowly, carefully, he worked his hand the last few inches, feeling the tough, rubbery cartilage under the scales, until his fingers were right behind the jaw. Again he stopped. This was the most dangerous moment. The moment when everything had to be coordinated just right. He pinched his thumb and forefinger together fractionally until he could feel the hinge of the cobra's jaw. If he pinched too tightly, he would choke the snake and kill it. If he pinched too loosely, it would break free and bite him.

The cobra writhed violently, coiling and uncoiling around his arm. The swami dropped the stick and lifted the enraged snake into the air. Its hood flared, its fangs glistened, and a loud, threatening hiss filled the room as it fought to escape its tormentor. The swami got up onto his knees and used both hands to try to hold the cobra still. The *kuli* on the first cushion leaned back to avoid the serpent's thrashing tail. His friend held him by the shoulders and patted him on the back. In the room above, Drew felt his flesh grow cold and clammy.

"Shit . . ."

At last the swami brought the snake under his control and settled back on his haunches. Then he turned to face the man in front of him. Slowly, he held out the serpent's head, offering it. The *kuli* paused, preparing himself. His chest rose and fell quickly. Sweat glistened on his thin body. Then he too leaned forward. Slowly and deliberately, he closed the gap between himself and the cobra's darting tongue. With only inches separating them, he extended his own tongue toward the snake. As if to taunt it. To taste it. To savor the moment of contact, the catalyst that would plunge him into the primal energy stream and carry him to that dark and dangerous place that lingered somewhere between life and death.

His companion edged up behind him, holding him, bracing him. The man leaned closer. The cobra's tongue flickered and brushed the extended human tongue. The man flinched and gave a slight gasp, but he didn't pull back. Instead, he leaned closer. The swami leaned closer, too, and closed the gap between them. The cobra extended its fangs, lunged, and bit deep into the offered flesh. The man uttered a choking cry of pain and tried to pull away. But his friend held him firm and the swami followed with his hand so that the cobra continued to pump its venom into the sensitive tissue. Once, twice, three times. Then the swami jerked the snake's head upward and back in a single swift motion so that the fangs came out quickly and cleanly, without tearing the tongue.

The *kuli* fell backward into his friend's lap and gave a series of short, breathless cries. His eyes stared wildly, his face was an agonized grimace, and his arms and legs spasmed uncontrollably. His companion held him and whispered to him, but he seemed unable to hear. Inside his body, behind the staring eyes, the neurotoxins in the cobra venom burned through his bloodstream like napalm, searing the nervous system, shutting down the respiratory system, assailing the muscles of the heart, and igniting an hallucinatory firestorm in the synapses of the brain.

He slipped deeper and deeper into coma. His breathing became shallower and he mumbled in Marathi. Then his voice weakened and faded to nothing. The fibrillations in his heart stopped and his pulse started to fall. His chest stopped moving and his limbs stopped twitching as paralysis became complete. Finally, his head lolled to one side, his eyes half-closed, his mouth open and slack. Blood from his punctured tongue trickled thickly down his chin and dripped onto his chest. Then that, too, stopped.

For a moment nobody moved or spoke. Then the swami picked up the burlap bag and dropped the writhing cobra inside. Returned to its dark nest, relieved of its venom and its fury, the cobra became still and docile again. The swami pushed the sack against the wall and settled back to wait. The servant beside the door stepped forward and helped the other *kuli* lift his companion onto the mattress. They wiped the blood from his face and chest and arranged him so that he was on his side, his head cradled on one arm. The man's companion sat down to wait. The servant opened the door and disappeared. The swami sat on his cushion, silent and indifferent.

Drew felt something brush against his arm and he gasped and pulled away. Gupta took him by the elbow and prodded him toward the door. It was only when they were outside again in the jaundiced light of the corridor that Drew realized how fiercely his heart was pounding. How afraid he was—and how excited. He pushed his hair back from his face. It was soaked with sweat. His body was slick with it. He wiped the palms of his hands nervously against his pants. Gupta watched him with an amused half smile.

"That guy's not dead, is he?" Drew asked. "He can't be dead?"

"No," Gupta answered. "There wasn't enough venom for that. He will be in a coma for about twenty-four hours. When he comes out of it, he will feel as if he has been born again."

"Okay," Drew said, though he still did not understand. "What happens to him now, for the next twenty-four hours?"

"He has already experienced many fantastic things," Gupta said. "In his mind he has been killed. He has experienced terror and tranquillity. Now he knows nothing. That is how it will be for the rest of the night. Tomorrow he will see more things in his mind. He will fly through the universe like Garuda and he will speak with the gods. He will

371

look down on his own life as if he was a god and it will give him strength. When he comes back he will feel a great hunger for life."

Gupta paused and then added, "When his senses are re-awakened, they will be very great. Food and drink will taste better than they did before. Everything will feel better . . . and his appetites will be great. For a while he will be able to go with a woman many times. Maybe more than one woman, maybe many women."

Drew paced agitatedly along the corridor, innumerable questions swirling through his mind. "How do you know he won't die?" he said. "People die of snakebite in this country all the time. It's not like you use a measuring cup or anything?"

"Sometimes they do die." Gupta shrugged. "Sometimes the handler makes a mistake. He milks the cobra in the morning, but he doesn't take out enough venom. Or maybe he gets the cobra confused with another that has not been milked."

"There are more?"

"Of course," Gupta replied. "Or there would be no money in it. The handler has twenty or thirty cobras. He will have many customers tonight. Tomorrow we make more money from the whores they need. That is the beauty of it. One need feeds upon another . . . and so it goes."

Drew looked at the closed doors along the corridor. That was what the rooms were for, he realized. They were for the johns to use while they tripped out on the cobra venom and then tested their prowess with Gupta's whores.

"And now you tell me something," Gupta added quietly. "You think this is something foreigners would like? This is something we can sell to the tourists?"

"Jesus . . ." Drew's mind swarmed with the possibilities. It was the most bizarre ritual he had ever seen—and it had the potential to earn him a fortune. "To do it or to watch it?" he said.

This time it was Gupta who looked surprised. "You think people would pay to watch that?"

"That's where you'd make most of your money," Drew said. "You'd need the right kind of place, but they'd pay. That's why they come to places like India. This is exactly the kind of shit they want to see."

Gupta nodded, his expression thoughtful. Clearly, it had never occurred to him that foreigners would pay to watch others take a snakebite.

"Americans . . ." he said. "There is nothing you won't sell." Then he turned and walked back along the corridor, down the stairs, and out onto the street. Drew hurried to catch up to him, his head still full of unanswered questions. Gupta's bodyguards were waiting outside and they obediently fell into step a few yards behind Gupta and Drew.

"Why do they do it like that?" Drew asked. "How come they can't drink it or shoot it? Why do they have to let the fucking thing bite them on the tongue?"

"You know about drugs," Gupta said. "The tongue is very sensitive. Plenty of blood. When you inject directly into the tongue, the effect is immediate."

"Sure." Drew nodded. "But do they have to let the snake do it?"

"It has always been done this way," Gupta said. "The venom is pure. No refrigeration, no syringe, no AIDS. It works as well today as it did five thousand years ago."

They came to a streetlight and Gupta stopped and looked at Drew.

"I don't expect you to understand," he said. "All you care about is the thrill, the pleasure. But this is the Indian way. You taste the pain before you taste the pleasure. And the pleasure is like the pleasure you had the first time you had a woman, a feeling no man can have twice in one lifetime—unless he is prepared to die and be reborn."

Drew looked at him. "How come you know so much about it?"

Gupta paused. "Every Indian should do it once," he said. "You've done it?"

Slowly Gupta extended his tongue. Halfway along, at the

373

fleshiest part of the pad, were two tiny pink buds. Scar tissue. And the moment Drew saw them he knew he would have to do it, too. Just once.